The Shadows Rule All

ALSO BY ABIGAIL OWEN

DOMINIONS SERIES

The Liar's Crown
The Stolen Throne
The Shadows Rule All

The Shadows Rule All

AWARD-WINNING AUTHOR

ABIGAIL OWEN

Entangled Publishing, LLC
644 Shrewsbury Commons Ave., STE 181
Shrewsbury, PA 17361
rights@entangledpublishing.com

Entangled Teen is an imprint of Entangled Publishing, LLC.
Visit our website at www.entangledpublishing.com.

Edited by Heather Howland
Cover design by Elizabeth Turner Stokes
Stock art by Matrioshka/Shutterstock
Map created by Kellerica Maps
Interior design by Britt Marczak

Trade Paperback ISBN 978-1-64937-999-3
Hardcover ISBN 978-1-64937-307-6
Ebook ISBN 978-1-64937-540-7

Manufactured in the United States of America

First Edition February 2026

10 9 8 7 6 5 4 3 2 1

To Kait Ballenger—my fellow AuDHD, romantasy-loving, writing soul sister—thank you for the chats and brainstorms, the tea and sympathy, and lots and lots of laughs.

N
ARYD
Obsidian Desert
Crimson Desert
Crystaline Desert
Enera
Land of Eternal Death
Oaesys
Singing Dune Sea
Desert of Asp
Lazuli Desert
Salt Flats
SAWANAH
Protectorate
Remirel
The Temple

Nova
Rimba Crater
Pantrea
TROPIKIS
ILDERNYS
The Queen's Tower
MARIANA
Caerror Island
Sentium
Pontine Marshes
Mt. Tyrh
The Twin Temples
Mt. Ynferno
TYNDRA

The Shadows Rule All is an addictive, action-packed upper YA/NA fantasy romance; however, this story includes elements that might not be suitable for all readers, including but not limited to: violence, gore, death, illness, grief, amnesia, and sexual content. I trust you to know your own triggers and limits, so please take note and take care.

The instruments of light deceive.
Darkness is not evil, fiendish, false, or foul.
Shadow simply fills the holes the light forgets,
And the light would not endure without it.

Prologue

In the Beginning

Eidolon

A thousand years ago

There is nothing more breathtaking than watching the woman I love taking her power as she's crowned queen.

This day feels like the start of something new. A turning point in the turbulence of these past few decades. Even the Celestial Alignment, which happens only once every hundred years, has arrived on this day to mark the occasion, blessing and sanctifying the new queens.

Gauzy light glints through the stained-glass windows of the Arydian throne room. At the beginning of the coronation, radiant sunlight poured rainbow-colored beams over the dais, but the eclipse is almost upon us now.

Through the moonhole above the gathered guests, our three moons hover like dark discs in front of the sun, inching ever closer together.

Even in the growing darkness, the two women standing on the dais in front of me glow in the lights of the braziers and lanterns all over the chamber, sending the jewels adorning their matching coronation gowns glittering in dazzling sparkles. Twin sisters, Esha and Lillnya, only twenty summer solstices of age, identical in beauty and grace, kneel before the masses of authoritates and rulers.

But I only care about one.

Esha.

She is my everything. My heartmate. My bondmate. Never to be separated. Even in all our afterlives to come, we will find each other.

Always.

And now that she is queen, together, we will be unstoppable.

I let my gaze trace the curve of her cheek, the line of her jaw, the shell of her ear, the sweep of her neck. I want to put my mouth to that spot that I know makes her quiver when I suck there. Maybe after the coronation is over. I have a fantasy of what we will do together on her throne. Forbidden in such a sacred place, but it belongs to her now, and we do what we want. After the celebrations are over and the palace is asleep, I will bring her here for our own very private celebration.

At the peal of the bells in the tower overhead announcing the new rulers of Aryd, a shout of jubilation echoes around me, filling the throne room to the vaulted ceilings. Pride swells within me along with every expectation I have for the future.

Our future.

Mine and Esha's.

Ruling together for the rest of our lives—me on the throne of the icy dominion of Tyndra, and her sharing the throne of the desert dominion of Aryd. United, we will become the strongest dominions in all of Nova. We will bring a desperately needed peace and prosperity to the world after a century of fear and upheaval.

Thanks be to the goddesses.

The bells continue to toll, and a new roar of sound joins the musical clanging—approval from the masses of people gathered around the palace and throughout the capital city of Oaesys.

Across the room, I catch Esha's glance, and I send her a brief smile. Nothing overly demonstrative. I am a king after all.

My queen does not return the smile. She is not allowed. This occasion, the responsibilities she is taking on, are solemn. To anyone else, I am sure she looks serene, but I do not need our bond to be able to see she is tense as a desert mouse holding still to avoid being pounced on by a nearby cat.

As her bondmate, I can help her, send her reassurance and all my love and support down our connection, but I am not allowed to keep that open to her during her coronation ceremony. The high priestess does not want to risk the wrong soul being ordained to rule here. Maybe I should risk it, now that the crowning is complete. The twitchy way Esha has moved throughout, the tightness of her face, the way she keeps seeking me out, have gotten worse with each passing moment. Her tension makes me want to break protocol and stride to her side, wrap her in my arms, and soothe away her worries.

Placed on my own throne at the age of ten, at twenty-five now, I am a veteran king. I can show her how to rule, how to govern her people to the best of her ability with whatever blessings and torments the goddesses deign to grant her during her reign—be that famine or feast.

I pray for feast. A bounty.

Surely that will come to us at least, given that my own mother is the Goddess Tyndra herself. We all deserve a break.

A herald bangs a bronze staff against the marble floor three times, and throughout the throne room, all take a slow inhale of anticipation, even as the celebrations outside continue. The priestess who performed the ceremony holds her hands over the new queens' heads. She says a quick blessing, then bids them to rise.

The priestess smiles widely, and in a raised voice, proclaims, "I present to you Queen Lillnya Tabranelle I and Queen Esha Mereneith I of Aryd. May they reign in wisdom, grace, and peace all their summers."

"All their summers!" I shout along with the others.

The members of the court drop to their knees before the new queens, fists held over their hearts. All except for the rulers of the other five dominions of Nova—the queens and kings of Mariana, Tropikis, Savanah, Wildernyss, and me, Eidolon Calix I. We bow our heads in a sign of mutual respect.

Ceremony complete, all but the sovereigns file out of the room to the ringing of bells and excited chatter. We remain behind for the final private blessing.

Once they have gone, the priestess steps aside and a sand nymph enters from an alcove behind them. In Aryd, sand nymphs are known to honor events like births and even deaths, the same as ice nymphs in Tyndra, especially for royalty.

Esha does not meet my gaze.

Standing between the sisters, the sand nymph's lips move in silent words. A blessing. Someday soon, one will do the same over our children on their name days. Perhaps tonight, I will put a baby in Esha's belly, and we will start our legacy together.

I know she is not able to hear my thoughts right now, but I catch a tiny glance in my direction from my lover's amber-hued eyes.

Eyes I have watched widen, then go slumberous with pleasure. Eyes that appear to glow with an inner fire when she is angry or when she laughs. Ebony hair that spreads out on my pillow and over my chest when she curls into me at night. And a mind and heart that are my truest match.

How have I been so blessed to find her? To have her choose me?

I am tempted to run a finger over the winding, invisible lines of our bond that mark my arm the same way they mark hers, to awaken that connection, but it will have to wait.

The nymph finishes her rite with a kiss on first Lillnya's forehead, then Esha's, and then faces us once again. "New sovereigns," the nymph announces. "To join you in the goddess-anointed ruling of our lands."

I sneak a look at Esha and wink.

I expect her lips to twitch in the shared moment, but she does not even blink.

Esha and Lillnya bow their heads silently, then lift their gazes to the moonroof. The sun is now a bright halo circling a black center. Once again, I am struck by the rare blessing they have received on their coronation. It is as if Nova herself has anointed them this day.

After the Alignment wanes, we will make our way into the gardens and palace proper to begin a reception where we will celebrate for the next three nights, in honor of the three full moons, of which the Goddess Aryd is the patroness.

Esha nods to someone at the back, and the guards open the massive double doors.

With my own goddess-given power to control and sense darkness, I feel a familiar tug on the shadows that fill the corners and crevices of the room—spaces the light has left behind. A tug that I have felt all my life.

The Goddess Tyndra is here.

Why?

I turn and find she is not alone.

Her five sisters stand beside her, adorned so splendidly they are almost blinding in their beauty.

I frown. They should not be here.

The people will not want them here.

Not after these last decades.

First, the Devourers appeared in the oceans, raining terror down upon any who dared to breach those waters, creating a forced separation between the people of the dominions. Followed by years of…less. Famines, plagues, droughts, and death. Not created by the goddesses, but not stopped by them, either.

Their people blame them. So have some of the rulers of their dominions.

But I know why the goddesses changed. Why they seem cruel

and unfeeling. Why they have retreated to the Allusian heavens and hardly speak to their creations anymore. I have told Esha those reasons. Did she feel pity for them? Compassion? Is that why she invited them here today? To start a new relationship between the goddesses and us mortals?

The six goddesses start down the long, velvet-carpeted aisle.

I glance back at Esha to find her staring not at the goddesses approaching the dais, but at me. Rather than the hope I would expect, her gaze is filled with something…darker. I try to open the connection between us, to ask her through our minds what this is about.

She keeps me out.

Beside her, Lillnya claps her hands. "We wondered if you would hear our prayers and come, goddesses of Nova!"

Esha drags her gaze from mine, a tight smile pinned to her lips. "Be welcomed here!"

But I know her, and her voice is strange around those words. There is a ring of something insincere. Wrong.

"*Now*." The word comes from Lillnya. A whisper directed only at Esha, but I am seated close enough to catch it.

Both the sisters' hands alight, a sign they are using their powers. Esha's palms glow a yellow that is sunny like her, and her sister's a luxurious hue of deep purple.

Bile surges up my throat. They cannot mean to fight the goddesses? They will lose. They will be obliterated.

"No!" I try to jump to my feet, only I do not make it.

The moon and stars must align in that instant, because the room goes eerily dark. At the same time, everything about me just stops. My body feels paralyzed. Immovable. I cannot even access my powers, the shadows refusing to do my bidding.

How?

But I already know the answer. Only one person in this room has that ability. Chetan, King of Mariana—a Hylorae Imperium with the ability to freeze objects in place. People, too?

Another Imperium's powers?

What happens next comes so fast, I see it as flashes of moments as time seems to both crawl and escape its bounds.

The sand nymph screams as sand is dragged from her body—six colors from the different deserts of Aryd that sand nymphs are made of. As fast as it comes off the nymph, floating through the air, the grains start to glow as my Esha—a Hylorae Imperium who wields power over sand—manipulates it.

Mother goddess, *she* is doing this to that poor creature. She is stripping her of the element that makes up her very flesh.

At the same time, a shriek of fury rises from the goddesses.

"Faster!" Lillnya cries out. She is visibly shaking, sweat beading on her face.

What are they doing?

"Esha!" I try to reach my bondmate the only way left to me, through our minds. Through the bond that she participated in with me, went through the ritual and the vows with me. Because she *loves* me.

I know it works when she glances back again with a look that is all things desperation and apology. *"I'm sorry,"* she mouths. *"You know I have to."*

"No!"

Agony rips through me, rips through all of me, leaving behind shreds of my heart and soul until there is only the darkness left.

It is all true. She did this. She planned this.

Then I see them. The goddesses have moved down the aisle, but not of their own will. They look like I feel, frozen while wide awake.

Chetan again.

In less time than it takes a flying ice fox to beat its wings, Esha forms the different colors of sand she took from the nymph, like six small colored piles in the air, heating and molding each into a small molten mass I know will eventually cool to glass.

She works so fast that rather than taking a smooth shape, they remind me of lightning glass from the desert, roughly shaped, still glowing with heat, each about the size of a scarab beetle.

In that same beat of time, Lillnya—who is starting to look like death warmed over, eyes sinking into a face hollowing out—does the unimaginable.

Before my frozen gaze, the goddesses' corporeal bodies… disintegrate.

Mouths already painfully, grotesquely open, their screeches splinter the air like broken glass scraping my skin. Their solid forms continue to dissolve and fade. The last thing I see is the shock and fury in my mother's eyes—my eyes—before her body is…gone.

She is gone.

All that remains is a glittering haze of what must be the essence of their souls.

Lillnya keens, the sound like a tear in the fabric of the world, but she does not stop as she forces the goddesses' souls floating in the air like stardust into Esha's glass.

Amulets, I can see now.

One amulet for each goddess.

An amber light sparks inside the green glass amulet as Wildernyss disappears inside it. Then Aryd into the white glass, Mariana into the black glass, Savanah into the red, Tropikis into the purple, and Tyndra into the blue.

Except my goddess…my *mother*…makes a last desperate attempt to fight, her stardust soul crawling out, reaching toward me.

"Eidolon!" her voice calls my name, though I think I am the only one who can hear it. *"Save me, my child!"*

"Mother!" I try to reach for her but am not able. I am helpless to stop this.

Then silence as the amulet closes around her. Their souls, like lights inside each amulet, spark one last time as Esha seals them closed. Then those lights sputter out, leaving just the glass.

But it is not over.

Indoua, Queen of Wildernyss, uses her power to create fine metal filigrees which she binds around each piece of glass, then links them to matching metal chains.

Were all the other rulers part of this horror? This treasonous act? Was only I duped?

Maybe not. I can hear the Queen of Savanah crying about how she can feel the goddesses' fear and fury. As an empath, she would.

Lillnya gives one last whimpering cry, then collapses to the floor, eyes glassy and face lifeless. I am fairly certain she is dead.

"Lilly!" Esha lets go of her own power to drop to her knees beside her sister. The amulets fall to the floor with a tinkling clatter, but they do not break.

In the next breath, the moons complete their path out of line, lifting the darkness in increments. The Alignment is over.

The King of Tropikis falls to the ground in a limp heap.

The hold over me abruptly disappears, and I stumble out of my seat. Immediately, I drag my power forward, my own palms igniting in a lavender glow as, at my command, a new darkness descends over the room. A total darkness through which only I can see.

I do not wait to ask questions and I do not go to Esha.

Goddess, how could she?

What she has done to me. To my mother. To our people. She has doomed us all.

My bondmate. It is unfathomable.

I run straight for the amulet that holds my mother. I pick her new prison up off the marbled floor, the blue glass dangling from the fine metal chain attached to the filagree aground the glass. I try to sense her, feel her, but there is nothing. Twisting my other hand in the air, I try to break the glass with my shadows—crush it, stab it, disintegrate it, infiltrate it.

Seven hells, I have no ability to reverse this.

The sand nymph appears before me and drops to her knees,

staring in agonized horror at the terrible monstrosities made from her own body. If it is possible for a creature made of sand to lose color in her face, she does.

She shakes her head once. Twice. Then looks at me. "I had no willing part in this, domine. You must believe me. I *want* no part of this. My people will kill me for it."

Esha's voice is a whisper in my mind. One trembling word full of sorrow and regret. *"Eidolon."*

My name is spoken in her beautiful, lying, betraying voice. The same voice that just last night called my name so sweetly as our bodies joined together. That sound ricochets through me, and my insides shrivel, darkness trying to consume me. To protect what is left.

As I lift my gaze, I send the shadows away and allow my building rage to shut my connection with Esha down so hard, she flinches. Then she reaches a hand toward me. "Listen to me. We had to—"

My darkness whips out at her, making her duck. I do not hurt her, though. That is not possible for me.

"*No.*" The word comes out as a snarl.

Though I have cut Esha off from our bond, I still feel the slice of agony that skewers her.

I take a step back. "Never speak to me again. Never come to me. This is my only warning. If I see you in any of our afterlives to come, you had damn well better run."

Esha sobs as she holds her sister in her lap. I stare back at her. At her beautiful, perfect, deceitful face.

I take the sand nymph by the elbow and do not even have to will my power to do my bidding, because getting away from this place, from Esha and the pain building inside me under the rage, is a burning instinct. Shadow swirls, coming up and over us, darkness obliterating my vision.

When the shadows dissipate, I am standing in the throne room in the palace of Tyndra. In *my* palace. My mother is in her amulet that swings from my fingertips. The sand nymph shivers in shock silently beside me.

And my precious bondmate, still in Aryd, is now my most hated enemy.

Pain wrapped in rage shreds through my body. My soul had torn with Esha's betrayal, but it was nothing like this. Now it shatters and splinters within me, agony hitting in wave after wave as I feel my very being ripped apart. As if looking through a kaleidoscope, my vision fractures, loosing a thousand voices, all my own and yet not.

Then, as fast as it started, the pain is gone. My vision returns to find the sand nymph's horror-filled eyes on me, and I am whole again.

But not.

All the pieces I have become, all the shards of my soul, are trapped inside me, a cacophony in my head.

Esha.

Esha did this to me. To my mother.

A cry rips from my throat and I drop to my knees as the future lays itself out before me.

One without Esha in it.

Worse…a future that pits us against each other.

Curling my hands into fists at my sides, I make a vow then and there. I will undo everything Esha and Lillnya did this day. I will release the goddesses from their prisons.

And may they curse anyone who gets in my way.

PART 1

OPENING MOVE

1
BURIED ALIVE

REVEN

I yank myself out of the memory.

Seven hells. I can't believe I found that.

I've been looking for any memory of where the book might be, Eidolon's book where each iteration of him has written down the details of their reign and instructions to the next.

I haven't found it, but what I just saw…that was information we didn't have before.

Specifically, the event that shattered Eidolon into all his Shadows and set him on an unwavering, ruthless path of destruction in an attempt to reverse what Esha had done. One thousand unsuccessful years of festering vengeance and a thwarted need to free his mother, started by a single terrible act.

An act I just witnessed as though I was in it, living it. As though it was *my* memory.

I guess in some twisted way it *is* mine. Was mine.

I have to tell Meren.

Getting myself out from the depths of Eidolon's mind where I wriggled is like clawing my way out of a grave. It took me ages to get down here, the pressure of being so deep building with every creeping ooze inward, but now I force myself to back out just as slowly.

He can't know what I've seen, what I've discovered.

I may be trapped inside of him, but damned if I've been sitting on my existential ass.

No, I've been searching. First, for a way to kill the bastard from the inside. But in trying that, I stumbled onto a memory locked deep inside the king. One from his first life. It had been simple—his first taste of chocolate—but it made me wonder if there were more. Since then, I've been digging for memories… and it just paid off in pure gold.

Now I know what we're up against.

"Meren." I send the thought out to her as soon as I think I safely can and brace in case Eidolon heard.

I can still feel her sometimes. Eidolon didn't count on *that*. She's faint. It comes and goes, this sense of her. When it comes, every so often we can talk through our connection, and those moments feed me the strength I need to keep going. And every time she disappears again, the terror that she'll never return threatens to consume me.

"Meren."

Nothing.

"Princess, talk to me." She both hates and loves when I call her that. I'm counting on it. Stronger emotions seem to make the connection clearer.

Still nothing.

What feels like eons later, I try again. *"Meren?"*

I *need* to hear her voice. Know she's all right.

Instead, all I get in return is silence.

The nothingness is so total here, I don't think I'll ever get used to it. Not after centuries of existing with the other Shadows, first trapped with me inside Eidolon like terrible siblings, then after I was shed to become a younger version of the king, the years I spent caging those same Shadows inside myself.

They never shut up.

But they aren't with me or the king anymore. Meren is their

vessel now. I gave them to her, forced them on her, cursed my own bondmate to be tortured with the Shadows' voices, their filth inside her like poison.

Goddesses forgive me.

Terror rises like a blizzard of ice and fire inside me every time she goes quiet. I fear that my giving her the Shadows will eventually kill her.

But she's strong. She can take it.

"Meren." Please let her hear me.

Out of nowhere, her soul barrels into mine down the bond we forged between us through magic and ritual and love.

"Reven. Thank the mother goddess." Her voice comes through in patches, fading in and out, but I catch the words. I catch the sound—a gorgeous raspy slide over my senses. Relief at hearing her again is like clear water after wandering the desert parched.

There's an echo of her own relief underneath her near-frantic tone. *"Where have you been?"* she asks. Demands more like, which is so her. *"Why couldn't I—"*

"I found something important."

Silence. Did she hear? She knows what I'm trying to do. She's fighting him out there. I'm fighting him in here. I wish I could see her face. Touch her.

"What...find?"

Only a few words are getting through now. *"I saw why he's doing all this."*

His bondmate's betrayal, his shattering, his mother...

The last thing I need is to understand Eidolon, to sympathize with him. But if Meren had done that to me, had betrayed me in that way, I don't know what I would have done.

"Reven—" I catch the single, thready word. My name on her lips.

Did she not hear me? *"Meren—"*

"I love you."

My entire being expands with those three clear, ringing

words. Words she sends me often, pouring her love for me down our bond, feeding me her strength.

"Meren?"

She doesn't answer. I can still feel her, though. She is all things warmth and light, and also abrasive like the sand she wields—just like the woman herself. She's still here with me.

"Princess...did you hear me?"

"You just had to go digging into our past." Eidolon's voice, a harsher version of my own, echoes around me in the void.

Fury, as raw and hot as a branding iron, blisters my heart. *"It's a good thing I did. You actually believe everything you've done through the centuries was justified."*

"To return the goddesses to the world? Worth every sacrifice."

Holy hells, he's so far gone, rage and a singular goal blinding him to all else in a way that is chilling. *This* is why I took his remaining Shadows the first time I escaped him. To stop him.

"And now you've gone and bonded with Esha's reincarnation," he accuses now.

If nothingness could go cold, it does. He knows Meren is Esha's reincarnation? Did he follow me? Watch that memory with me? Impossible to ignore how the twins of old looked exactly like Meren and her sister Tabra.

The fates really messed up with us.

Or rather, Eidolon and Esha did.

Everyone knows how bonding is supposed to work. Once the ritual is complete, bondmates will find each other in every life they are born into—be it the Allusian heavens, one of the seven hells, or another life in Nova.

But Eidolon never died entirely. Only pieces of him did, his Shadows scattered across time like petals slowly plucked off a flower.

Esha died while he remained partially immortal.

The cold starts to burn as Eidolon's anger grows. *"You are determined to fight me when you should be standing with me.*

Especially after seeing what she did to us in her previous life."

"Meren is no more Esha than I am you. Not anymore." I may have begun my existence as a piece of my maker's soul, but now I am myself. After being shed, I became my own man, with my own life, soul, mind, experiences, and goals. And I became Eidolon's enemy.

"If you believe that, you're even more of a danger to me than I realized," he muses. Then his voice goes razor sharp. *"Which means you leave me no choice."*

The bottom drops out from under me.

Followed by pain.

2

THE VOICES IN MY HEAD

MEREN

The sneering voices of Eidolon's Shadows inside me are nothing new, but they get louder the rare times I can hear Reven. The only reason they haven't killed me is because of a sand nymph's curse.

"Reven?" I call out to him again.

He was just here with me. His voice was muted, muffled, coming in fits and spurts, but he was *here*, stealing my breath and filling the hole where my heart is supposed to be.

"Did he go away again?" one of the Shadows taunts.

Reven used to say that the Shadows craved me. I can't say I've felt much of that now that I carry them, but I think that curse might be why, that link between me and the king. Maybe they felt it, too. That, or the bond made long ago between Eidolon and the ancestress I am a reincarnation of.

It doesn't stop them from being assholes, though.

"Is he still looking for that book?" Yet another snorts a derisive laugh. *"He'll never find it."*

Another slides through my mind. *"You can't hear him, can you, love?"*

Their voices and my own guilt grate like sand against my insides, because the Shadows sound like him. Like Reven. They make it hard to listen for the only voice I want to hear. He's alone, trapped inside a monster. I promised I'd free him, only I haven't figured out how.

Yet, damn it. I'm not giving up.

I swallow back the bubble of panic threatening to expand inside me and try to sift through the noise in my head, to feel him.

Tabra slips her hand into mine and I flinch at the physical contact that yanks me out of my head and back into the real world where I'm standing in front of a glass portal I just made, getting ready to go to yet another place that's off-limits.

No longer bony and frail, Tabra has fully recovered from being possessed by a ghost of Eidolon faster than anyone thought possible. "The Shadows again?" she asks quietly.

"I'm fine."

No use telling her things she can't do anything about. I don't tell any of my friends about hearing Reven sometimes, thanks to our bond I think, only to keep losing him again. It would only make them worry for too many reasons to count.

Tabra's lips tug down slightly as she glances behind her at the others—my best friend Cain and his sister Pella, Hakan who never leaves Pella's side, my bodyguard Horus, Reven's second-in-command Vos, Tziah who is essentially Vos's little sister, and Bene, one of the Devourers, shrunk to the size of a raven and perched on Tziah's shoulder.

Our friends. Family, really, even if not by blood. They are all waiting to follow me from the beaches of Mariana's abandoned Isle of Caerror—our most recent hiding place—through a portal I made into the dominion of Savanah.

They share a look among themselves. They share a lot of looks they think I don't notice these days.

"What about you?" I ask my sister. "Are *you* okay?" I inspect her face, then her hands, but there is no purple glow. Tabra may have regained her strength, but her power has been giving her problems. Turning on without her meaning to, getting out of control.

She smiles. "I'm fine."

We're both using that phrase a lot lately. Neither of us points that out.

I scan the group. "Everyone ready?"

My friends' postures change, weapons at the ready. It's the way we go through every portal these days.

Before, when they came to Savanah to ask Queen Wynega about the amulet here, she was already waiting for them at the portal. Hopefully that's true this time. It would make our passage easier. But just in case, we're prepared for anything.

"You sure about this?" I ask Hakan one last time.

He refused to join the others on the previous trip to this dominion, though he's never said why.

"I'm sure," he says.

I place my palm against the glass, still slightly warm against my skin from having just forged it before Reven interrupted. Picturing the destination in my mind, I will my power into my creation, and after only a moment of nothing, the opaque glass changes, goes clear, and then, like throwing open a window, shows us the temple of Savanah.

No one is waiting on the other side to greet us…or kill us. That we can see.

I let loose a silent breath.

Hakan is through first. Since he's from this dominion, we're hoping that helps us if we encounter anyone on the way out. Quietly, the rest of us follow him into the temple.

As Cain passes me to go through, he squeezes my shoulder. A silent reminder that he's here if I need him. That he'll always be here. A small swell of affection leaves behind the only warmth I feel these days.

I'm the last to enter. Rather than simply close the portals, I shatter the one I made without affecting the one on this side. After all, we can't be leaving portals around for anyone who comes across them to use willy-nilly. The last time I did, Omma used it to find me, and I can't guarantee only allies would come through.

"You're getting better at that," Pella says from behind me.

"I should be by now." I've been portalling us all over the goddess-damned world, from dominion to dominion, keeping us just out of reach of those hunting us.

"No guards," Vos comments, his lavender eyes dead serious in the dark of his face, no spark of his usual irreverence in them. He's in warrior mode today.

"Your people are too trusting," Cain tells Hakan as he checks carefully around a corner.

"Maybe," Hakan says. "This way."

He leads us through chamber after winding chamber. This temple is made up of a series of halls and rooms. The carvings and glyphs here are more intricate than the ones in the obsidian-and-gold temple in Aryd. The doorways are formed into swirls and lacy lattices. Even the floors are etched. And all of it, every single speck, has been carved out of one single, massive stone.

Rather than build their temple up, Savanahans chose to build down. Hakan told us it's because they wanted to keep their cities and temples hidden from those who would harm them, and in the flat, grassy plains of this dominion, a tall structure would stand out like a beacon. Here, hiding means going underground, so they tunneled into the rock buried deep under the fertile soil.

What I don't like is that it's empty. We should see someone. An acolyte. A priestess. Someone come to give an offering to their goddess.

This can't be simple luck. I don't have luck like that.

It takes a while until finally I spot a doorway up ahead, squared off and showing what I think is the dark sky, but the closer we get I can see it's actually more rock. A chilly wind blows through the passage and over my skin and I shiver, but not because of the cold. Every instinct is telling me something is wrong.

This place feels like a tomb.

We're not ten steps out of the temple before, with no warning, a stark, jagged burning splinters through my mind. I pitch forward as darkness steals my vision, every part of me focused inward, although I'm still lucid.

This isn't coming from me. It's coming from…

"Meren! Please—"

Reven.

Panic rises with the pain. What's happening? Is he hurt? The stabbing heat spreads from my head, lower to my chest, then to my heart, and from there outward until every part of me is in agony. I bite my lip to keep from screaming.

Then, as fast as it started, it's gone. No pain. No heat.

No Reven.

Heart slamming into my ribs, I blink rapidly, coming back to myself, to Tziah kneeling in front of me, her frosted black eyes wide with concern. I'm breathing like I sprinted twenty leagues, the harshness of it loud in my ears. Then the cold breeze blows over me and my entire body shudders. Or maybe that's shock.

"Meren?" Tabra's hand is on my back, I think.

The panic grows. What in the seventh hell just happened? Before now, when Reven came to me, it was softly, gently. And when he's disappeared on me, he just goes. But this…this was like he was cleaved away. Did Eidolon discover our connection?

"Meren?" Cain's voice now, more urgent. His hand brackets my face, trying to make me look at him. "Talk to me."

"I'm—" I suck in sharply. "Give me a minute."

I squeeze my eyes shut. *"Talk to me. Please."* I will Reven to come back, return to me, to feel him—the solid presence of him, his strength, his unwavering love.

One of the assholes in my head pipes up. *"Such a shame."*

"I wonder what Eidolon did to him," another Shadow says, cruel laughter curling through his voice. *"Maybe you'll never hear him again."*

"Never," the rest all take up the chant with glee. I'm pretty sure one cackles.

By now the panic is flaying my insides. Something is wrong. Really wrong. The Shadows are pleased. What do they know that I don't? Or are they just trying to make me think they know something?

I try to filter through the noise in my head. *"Reven?"*

Please answer me. Please be there.

"We can't just sit here, Mer," Vos warns.

"I told you not to call her that," Cain bites out. He claims that nickname is his alone to use. "Mer, c'mon," he says more quietly. "You have to give us something. You're scaring me."

I press my palms to my eyes, fighting with myself. Vos is right. We don't have time for me to lose it or wait around while I try to reach Reven. We're too vulnerable, and what we're about to do needs my full attention.

Forcing myself upright, my eyes still closed, I rock a little on my feet. *"I'm sorry,"* I whisper into the void between me and my bondmate, praying he hears me. *"I love you."*

Then, deliberately, I burrow into the numb inside me that has been my only refuge the way a child might hide under blankets. It's the only way I've found that can shut the Shadows up. It makes it harder to feel or hear Reven. But they seem to feed off my emotions…so I try my best to give them none.

It helps to picture a little scenario in my head. An image of a rope dangling over a deep, dark well, and the Shadows climb up it to get to me. Until I use one of the knives I always have hidden on me and cut it.

I sever that metaphorical rope now, ruthlessly severing my own emotions.

"Don't—" the Shadows collectively protest. But the sound of it fades as they drop back down the well, disappearing into the same numbness where I bury my feelings. No more heart-pounding hope. No more stomach-twisting fear. Definitely no more ache of indescribable loss.

All that's left is me…without him.

3

SAVANAH

I take one more calming breath before I open my eyes to find my friends staring at me warily. Cain's teeth are so tightly clenched he's probably giving himself a headache.

"I'm okay," I tell him, pulling his hands away from my face.

A muscle ticks in his jaw. "What was that?"

"The Shadows," I say. The easiest explanation. If I told him that I'm terrified Eidolon just did something terrible to Reven, I'd have to undo the numb state I'm in, and it's the only thing holding me together.

"But now you've got them?" Cain demands.

So tempting to laugh in his face. As an Imperium himself, you'd think he'd know better.

All of us who wield a power have to learn it and grow in it gradually over time. With sand, I came into my ability too young, long before Tabra, and was told by Grandmother—ordered by queenly edict, more like—to never use it. Ever. A ruling that Omma, who raised me, enforced by pretending I had no power to speak of. I had to figure out how to control and use it on my own and in secret.

That was before the curse kicked in.

I can also now wield shadows and darkness because the sand nymph connected me to Eidolon's massive power, allowing me to siphon it into myself.

I suck at it.

Turns out power means absolutely nothing without control. It took me years…*years*…to learn my own power to control and manipulate sand.

I don't have years.

"They're locked down," I tell Cain.

He stares at me. They all stare at me.

I need to get better at lying if we're going to survive what's to come.

Bene flaps his wings from his perch on Tabra's shoulder and I imagine he's offering me support. If anyone would know what being separated from their bondmate feels like, it's Bene. Communication with him has been limited since I gave Aryd's amulet to Eidolon. I need it to be able to hear Bene in my mind.

I pat a hand over my heart, hoping he'll see it as gratitude or a show that I'll be fine.

"Arms in the air and face us slowly!" a voice suddenly yells out from above.

Damn it all.

The blast of purple that lights us up is a problem. Tabra makes a small sound in her throat. I grab her hand, giving it a squeeze, and the light goes out.

Hakan looks up. I follow his eyeline to find the deep pit in which the temple sits now surrounded by at least fifty Savanahan warriors, spears, bows, and other weapons trained on us.

"What was that about Savanahans being too trusting?" Vos murmurs at Cain.

Cain, meanwhile, sidles closer to stand in front of me. "I take it back."

"What business do you have here?" that same guttural voice, not unlike Hakan's, demands from above.

Time to play the royalty move.

I touch Cain's shoulder and he moves—reluctantly. Tabra and I step forward to stand beside Hakan, then throw the hoods of our cloaks back. "We are the Queens of Aryd," Tabra says, her voice calm and melodious. "And we request passage."

That's all we need. Passage. Not even safe passage. We just need to know the Savanahans won't stop us.

"To where?" comes the immediate response.

Bloody hells. We'd hoped they wouldn't ask.

"The Snarl," I answer.

A low murmur rises from the soldiers above us, and several shift on their feet. I don't need to be close enough to see their faces to recognize apprehension.

"Denied," their leader says flatly. "Go back to where you came from."

The blanket of stars in the clear sky dims in a way that reminds me of Reven pulling a veil over the world. I tense. Except the darkness lifts as fast as it came on. Was that me? Did one of the Shadows get out? Or was it just a cloud passing in front of the moons? I shoot a furtive look around to see if anyone else noticed.

"Crone's eyes," Hakan mutters, then tugs back his own hood, exposing his face and tattoos. "I am Hakan, son of Queen Wynega."

He's *what*? The shock that ripples through our group is practically a physical presence. This is the first we've heard about his being the queen's anything, let alone her son.

"If that is true, then you have been banished from these lands," the leader answers. "Leave now. Don't make us warn you again."

"I will speak with my mother," Hakan demands.

"Denied."

Hakan holds up his hands and bands of lightning dance along his fingers, sparking and snapping with each move. The air around us sizzles, filling the space with an odd smell of burning, along with a palpable tension and a strangely metallic taste on the tongue.

"You wouldn't dare!" that voice cracks over the sound of Hakan's lightning. "We are your people."

"You *were* my people," Hakan answers, deadly calm. "I have new people now."

Yes, he does. But antagonizing them is not how I want to start this. Our fight isn't with these people. I need to stop him before he torches the place. "Hakan."

He glances at me, and for the first time, I see past his passive expression to the pain underneath. These people feared his power so much they forced him out. His own mother—the queen, apparently—let it happen.

Is that my future? One where my friends and family fear me to the point of abandonment and exile?

I give him a small, encouraging nod.

Reluctantly he lowers his hands, the power dissipating, and we're plunged back into the calm of early dawn.

"We don't wish to make enemies of you," I say to the guards. "Aryd and Savanah have long been friends. But it's important we get to the Snarl. Don't make us fight you to do that."

There is a pause, and I can hear the low murmur of voices but not what's being said.

"Fine," the guard calls back finally. "It's your funeral pyre."

That was fast. I glance at Tabra, who shrugs.

"We will allow you to pass," he continues. "But on two conditions."

Of course there are conditions.

"The banished son of Savanah may pass no farther. He remains here."

Hells. We could really use his power for what's coming next. "Hakan?" I ask him.

"Agreed," he says through clenched teeth and with a glance toward Pella.

"And the other condition?" I ask.

"Queen Tabra—the *rightful* queen of Aryd—remains here

with us as well. Under our protection."

But for me, the false queen—nothing. They don't say it, but I hear it anyway.

I share another look with Tabra, this one full of a thousand questions and worries. She tilts her head ever so slightly. Her answer.

Relief that at least she'll be safely tucked away here tries to bubble up with a side of leftover resignation, but I smother both with the numbness inside me.

It's better this way.

After all, I was always meant to be the sacrifice.

4

THE CURSED LOVERS

A guard appears at the bottom of the stairs that lead out of the temple, so quiet and out of nowhere he reminds me of the ghost who sent me here. "Follow me," he says.

His serious gaze sweeps over the lot of us but pauses on Tabra before moving on to me, which is when his eyes narrow slightly.

"Stay with Tabra," I tell Bene, not looking away from the guard.

Tabra goes taut beside me. "Meren, no—"

"I'm not debating this." The Devourer is my best way to keep her safe when I'm not with her, even if it makes my own task much harder.

"Who are you talking to?" the guard asks.

"The raven."

His frown clearly calls into question my power of thought.

Bene, meanwhile, doesn't argue, and Tabra closes her mouth around any more protests.

"Careful," I tell the guard. "He bites."

The guy eyes Bene, both curious and wary. Good. No need to have them complacent.

Our goodbyes are brief after that, and we follow the guard away from the temple. As soon as we are out of Hakan's hearing range, Pella pushes me aside to pull up by Horus, who is ahead of me. "Did you know?" she demands.

"Know what?"

I can't see Horus's face, but I can hear the amusement tinting his voice, eyes no doubt crinkling around the corners. He's fully aware what she's asking.

Pella tosses a glare first at him, then over her shoulder at me. "Did you know," she all but growls, "that Hakan is *royal*?" Her voice spikes as she flings her arm out. "Did *anyone* know that?"

She's asking the others more than me. Horus, Vos, and Tziah are all part of the Vanished, the people Reven saved and who lived together in the Shadowood he created before Eidolon's soldiers destroyed it. Hakan was also one of them.

I frown. "Didn't he go with you to Savanah when you spoke with Queen Wynega before?"

"No. And now we know why he didn't," Pella mutters darkly.

Vos pats her shoulder. "He didn't tell us either, if it makes you feel better."

Pella's scowl deepens as she shrugs off his hand. "I don't feel any which way."

The guard ignores all this and starts us up a steep path that scales the sides of the pit walls. Horus and Cain, ahead of and behind me, are no doubt positioned to keep me from running away screaming. Heights and I don't get along, but I have it locked down this time.

A fall to my death, I've learned, is not the worst thing that can happen to me.

Their leader—a captain I see by the markings on his uniform—meets us near the top. The tattoos marking the dark skin of his shaved scalp differ from Hakan's. One side is a bull, which is known to be a stubborn creature. Is that a warning of who we're dealing with? Maybe, given the way he's regarding us with distrustful curiosity.

"There's a bounty on your heads issued by the King of Tropikis," is the first thing he says to us.

All five of us reach for our weapons, but he holds up a hand.

"Queen Wynega has given orders not to honor it." His gaze slowly roams me from the top of my head to the tips of my toes. "So there *are* two," he murmurs to himself. "I see why you inspire such…violence."

My mouth drops open. "What is *that* supposed to mean?"

His eyebrows shoot up almost to his hairline. "Just that you're beautiful, domina."

If I wasn't wrapped in a cocoon of numbness, his words would probably have thrown me into a swirl of confusion. People don't just…say stuff like that. I pull myself up to my most regal stance, giving him my best imitation of Grandmother's haughty disdain. "I'm well aware but watch it. I'm still royalty."

A spark of respect ignites in hazel eyes. "Now I see why you're the decoy."

I guess word of the hidden princess in Aryd has spread.

"This is getting us nowhere fast," Cain grumbles.

The guard's gaze shifts between me and Cain, a light of speculative amusement glinting in his eyes before he returns to the serious soldier he's supposed to be. "No one goes to the Snarl for a good reason."

Cain glares at him. "We already know."

The captain's gaze doesn't so much as flicker away from me. "I doubt that."

I sigh. Having to stand here and prove myself is a delay. I hate delays. "Hakan told us the legend."

While we waited for nightfall in Mariana, Hakan briefed us on who—and what—we'd be up against.

A long time ago, a man named Aesthetus saw his reflection in a still pond and couldn't look away from his own beauty to the point he began wasting away, dying of starvation. Finally, a woman named Mimick came along, a Hylorae who could shapeshift. She entered the water on the other side, then swam up under his reflection and took on his features in female form so that he'd fall in love with her and come out of his trance.

During their bonding ritual, Aesthetus claimed that, together, they were the most beautiful creations alive, even more beautiful than the goddesses.

Savanah punished their vanity by turning Aesthetus into a beast who can only see his reflection from underwater and turned Mimick into a monster of unknown form who can only repeat other's words.

The Snarl is the maze the cursed lovers built to keep out prying eyes.

The captain glances behind me, off to the east, then slings his bow over his shoulder. "They kill anyone who tries to enter. Why in the name of the goddesses would you want to go there?"

I could tell him the truth—that the only thing that matters to us is getting Savanah's amulet—but that would mean telling him that a ghost in the Land of Eternal Death told me it was here and how to get it.

I'm sure that would go over well.

This is the last amulet containing the six missing goddesses, and our biggest bargaining chip in our fight against Eidolon. Thanks to my foolish ass, the king holds two—Tyndra's and Aryd's. We have three—Mariana's, Tropikis's, and Wildernyss's—sort of. They're hidden away in a secret shadowy pocket Reven made that only he can access. I haven't figured out how to get into it yet or if I even can.

If Eidolon gets this one before us, that gives both of us three, and we need the upper hand before we confront him again.

"We have no choice," I say simply. The fewer people who know, the better. For them and for us.

A frown flickers over his features, and he glances down into the temple as if deciding if he should just send us back the way we came or let us go off to die.

He doesn't have to voice his thoughts aloud. I've already thought them myself.

A smarter queen would have found another way to do this.

A braver one would have come here on her own. An honest queen would admit that Eidolon's ghost said only Tziah and one other person needed to come. He said nothing about me.

The captain finally gives a single nod. "Then I hope you are successful. Goddess speed to you."

"Thank you." I pause. "Any tips?"

"Yeah. Don't go."

Everyone's a jester. "Except that."

"I voted for the not going," Vos tells him. "But I was overruled."

The captain looks off to the east again. "When we hear something that sounds like a flute, the grasses past the Sacred Tree move, and screaming usually follows. Even though we're leagues from there, we can see it and hear it."

Eidolon's ghost told me about the flute, but not that it may be what triggers the monster. And what's this about the grasses moving?

Maybe we *don't* know everything.

I look at Cain and he shrugs. He's the only one who's supported this idea from the beginning. As long as he's still with me, we're doing this.

"Thank you," I say to the captain.

He nods again, then executes a sharp about-face and leads us the rest of the way up. Before I follow, I glance back down into the temple where the others are standing, peering up at me.

Looking down at Tabra now, in a hole in the ground, is like looking down into a grave.

Not that a queen would ever be buried. Tabra has a tomb waiting for her, adorned and glittering. So maybe I'm seeing my own death as the copy of myself—down to every freckle and scar, except for the more recent ones—staring back at me. I should shiver with fear while worry vaguely gnaws at my stomach.

But I've got a handle on the Shadows, the numb spreads through me and over me like I've been buried under a sand dune. The marks of my bond with Reven are silent and so is he.

So is my heart.

"She'll be okay," Horus murmurs from behind me. My sworn bodyguard lost a sister himself.

"I know." The words come out cold. As cold as I feel inside.

Please let Reven be okay.

Tziah gives my arm a squeeze, and I force my legs to work, walking away from the people I love. Not the first time I've had to, and I'm sure not the last.

I pause when we reach the top of the pit as I get my first real look at the grasslands of Savanah. I can see leagues and leagues across the fields—all brown if what's closest to us is any indication, not spring green the way they should be this time of year. Tyndra's winter has her hooks in this dominion even more than in Mariana. Each blade is individually sheathed in a layer of thin ice. A tinkling crackle of sound follows the wind as it plays gently across the fields.

A slow-moving river flows nearby, its usually fertile, black banks covered in drifts of snow.

The temple pit is out in the open and solitary, no structures anywhere in sight. Savanah is the only dominion with the temple not located directly in or close to the capital city. In fact, it's at the opposite end of the long, narrow dominion, as far from civilization as it can get. I turn slowly, taking in the vastness of it, and spot our destination in the distance.

"What do you think?" the guard asks.

Is he expecting me to wax poetic or something? *Ooh* and *ahh* in wonder? The me before all this would have. "It's beautiful."

I hear Cain sigh behind me. Tziah, standing at the guard's back now, gives me a pointed look. I guess that wasn't gushing enough. She then makes a sign with her hands that the captain can see, and Vos translates. "Peaceful."

The Savanahan soldier looks out over the fields, and I study his expression, which is somewhere between sad and angry. "You should see it when there's no ice and snow. Lush and green, bountiful. But Tyndra's freeze…"

He trails off.

Many of the dominions, Savanah included, won't survive Tyndra's winter. It's too cold here, while the glass walls, made by the goddess Aryd herself along our borders to protect her people from the Devourers, are making it too hot, drying up our oases and shortening the periods of rain we get. Wildernyss rises higher into the skies every day, and the void it's leaving on the ocean floor is sucking Tyndra deeper into the waters. Mariana has been taken over by winter, decimating the temperate dominion. Even Tropikis's southern borders have been breached by the cold.

The dominions are breaking because the goddesses aren't here to fix them.

I want to set them right, but that means releasing the goddesses. We still don't know why my ancestress trapped them in those amulets in the first place. Instead of helping, I could very well unleash the hells on all of Nova.

That's assuming I can do what Eidolon failed to and figure out how to release them at all.

The captain points off to the east. "Two leagues that way to the Sacred Tree, then turn south and go another league."

At least three hours of walking, in other words.

I turn to where he's pointing, and a pinprick of wonder penetrates my blanket of numbness.

The Sacred Tree.

It's fully visible on the horizon. Impossible to miss. A massive watchtower standing tall against the slowly pinking skies, covered in glittering bluish-white ice, different from the frozen land around us. Their tree has always been frozen, never melting. Savanah and Tyndra are twin goddesses, and each gifted their tree to the other.

Do they miss each other? Separated in their different amulets and scattered to the dominions' rulers, Savanah's even lost to memory. I know what not seeing my twin for extended periods of time feels like, and that was only weeks and months, not centuries.

Cain bumps me with his shoulder. "At least we can see this one together."

I elbow Cain back to hide my smile. As kids, before either of us had ever left our dominion, we always said that someday we'd see every Sacred Tree for the first time together. It was a promise we both ended up breaking.

"How long do we wait for you?" the captain asks.

I don't pretend to misunderstand. People don't come back from the Snarl. He's assuming we won't, either. "Let my sister decide."

5

THE SNARL

It takes us hours to get there.

The sun is high in the sky by the time we reach the entrance to the Snarl. We're cold, tired, and hungry and taking on a deadly maze is the last thing any of us want to do, but here we are.

We peer through a vined archway into a hallway of sorts formed by thick, tall grass. Everything is green, not a single glint of frozen anything, and the alluring scent that wafts to me is of fertile soil and spring. I was warned this place is deadly all by itself, full of bottlenecks, blind alleys, dead ends, and vortexes… and the sense that death watches from behind the walls.

"At least we're not trying this at night," Pella says in a hushed voice.

Vos claps a hand on Cain's shoulder, pushing him forward. "Go ahead."

Cain waves him on. "Feel free to go first if you're in such a hurry."

"It will be fine," I say. "We'll all be fine."

Two fines in as many sentences. My friends aren't the only ones reluctant to do this. The ghost told me the way through—the grasses inside the Snarl form walls that map out a maze so thick there's no way we could forge a different path even if we wanted to—but I'm starting to worry the ghost left out important information.

Tziah rolls her eyes and steps forward, ignoring the way

Cain reaches out to stop her. Vos, caught on the hop, runs to get ahead of her, which makes her roll her eyes again at his back.

When the grasses don't immediately eat them, we follow.

Left. Right. Then left again. After we get that far without incident—beyond the odd sense that we're not alone—I focus on navigating the maze.

A gleam of something bright white flashes between the grasses. I catch another glimpse, along with a whisper of trepidation. "Does anyone else see that?"

"See what?" Horus asks in a hushed voice.

"White— Oomph." I stumble over a root. Scowling, I hop on one foot, nursing a now throbbing toe. "Watch where…"

Looking down, I forget my toe.

It isn't a root sticking up from the ground. It's a bone bleached white in the sun and woven into the grass walls down low around the roots.

"It's just a bone." Pella nudges a different one with her shoe and frowns at it. "The captain said people die in here."

"Not exactly helping, Pell," Cain grumbles.

"Didn't the ghost say not to stop?" She prods me in the back, and we keep going.

More bones greet each cautious step, scattered around and piled up at the bases of the grasses. Stalks sprout up through hipbones and out of empty eye sockets.

"Not a single ounce of flesh on them." Vos points this out, reaper grim. "This was a jewel of an idea, Meren."

If we were anywhere but this place, I'd assume these bones were picked over by animals as they lay out in the open, but that doesn't feel right. Instead, these seem to have been stripped bare in an instant. It doesn't even smell of death in here. No rotting.

What could do that?

"Maybe they're old." The bright side is not usually the side I walk with ease, but neither is borrowing trouble.

Horus, with his bow out and an arrow already nocked, scans

the narrow passage we're walking down with wary eyes. "I don't think having come here in daylight is going to help us much."

Too late now. We only have another two turns to reach the center of the maze.

I could stop them here. Send them all back the way we came, reversing the directions we have. They don't have to risk their lives because of me.

What kind of horrible queen lets her closest friends—people who are more like family to me—do this? I have authority. I should have ordered them to stay back. Stay out. No matter how much they insisted.

Vos stops up ahead before the maze takes a sharp right. He holds a finger to his lips and points to himself and Tziah. We agreed on this next step. They insisted on this part, ganged up on me even while we planned this, making sure I don't try to protect them…because I'm their queen. Vos and Tziah move forward without us, and all we can do is wait. Every stir of the breeze has me tensing, so brittle with worry that I might snap at any second.

I check the sun in the skies. They've been gone too long.

I shift on my feet, craning my neck and trying to see any sign of them, any hint.

A strong hand steals around mine, giving me a squeeze, and I look up into the deep brown eyes of the man who's been my friend since I was a little girl lost in the desert and he found me. Cain got me through my painful childhood and adolescence. He was the only one who came for me when I was kidnapped. He gave his people—no, *sacrificed* his people—to protect me and mine, and now, even against the wishes of his father, he came here with me today. He could have just sent Pella. She would have looked out for their zariphate's interests.

But he didn't.

Reven would have told me to bring them all, I'm sure. I can picture sitting with him around the fire when we were discussing this plan. He would have been grim faced, and he'd hate risking the others as much as I do, but he'd have insisted…to protect me.

Which is why I should have done the opposite. Maybe if he hadn't been so hell-bent on protecting me, he'd still be here.

"You shouldn't have come," I say quietly.

The look Cain bends on me is familiar from our years of friendship, a blend of frustrated amusement. He lifts my hand and spreads it over his heart, which beats strong and steady against my palm.

I know what he's saying with that gesture. The unspoken words between us chip away at my own heart, which is already like a broken mirror pieced back together after being dropped.

The Shadows stir.

"You're going to get them all killed," they whisper. *"That'll hurt. Especially losing him."*

Him. They mean Cain.

I wrap the numbness tighter around me like a wall, and they quiet again. Which is when Vos appears around the corner of the maze with Tziah right behind him. I let out a silent breath of relief. Her gaze tracks to my hand on Cain's chest, but she doesn't react. Tziah notices everything.

I tug my hand away, which makes Cain stiffen.

After this day is over, I should leave him. I should take Tabra and the Vanished and leave Cain and his people behind. I know we've been building alliances with other zariphates throughout Aryd, but I can let that go. If I kill Eidolon, we won't need allies. Being tangled up with us isn't fair to Cain. I have a bondmate who I love beyond all measure, even if I may never see him again in this life. I try not to allow Cain any hope where I'm concerned, but our friendship is familiar and comforting. This feels like I'm using him.

I catch Pella's gaze on me. Not accusing. More…sad.

"The pond is where the ghost said it would be," Vos tells us in a low voice.

Good. "Only Tziah and I can go from here." Not exactly true, but I'm not risking anyone else. "You need to be ready in case this doesn't work."

"Ready for what?" Cain demands.

"Whatever that flute does, if the captain was right. The ghost only said not to let one monster wake the other. Hopefully Tziah is all we need to keep that from happening."

Horus jerks a step closer. "I'm not leaving you, domina."

I knew he'd say that. I put a hand over his, staying him. "Remain with the others. That's an order."

A muscle in his jaw ticks, his throat corded so tight, I'm surprised he can swallow. But he nods. I really hate playing the queen card.

"Trust me," I say to them all. "This is what I was told to do."

Cain stares at me long and hard before looking away, jaw working.

It takes Vos, who's been gesturing back and forth with Tziah, saying, "Go," for the others to back down.

Tziah shoots Vos a closed-mouth smile, which earns her a flat-lipped stare in return. He isn't any happier than the others about this, but they trust each other.

I usher Tziah to lead the way. "If you see the flute, do your thing."

She reaches a hand back for me, and I take it and follow her down the maze. After turning at the first right we come to, our isolation presses in on me. All I can see are long, slender green leaves, patches of sky overhead, the back of Tziah's bright white hair, and the deep blue skin of her neck. And the bones at our feet, of course.

One more turn and she stops, then waves me closer. I peer around her, catching the way the maze opens up into a broader space and a shimmer of bright sunlight on water. Inching forward, carefully I search the small clearing around the pond. Sure enough, no one is there. But I expected that.

I hold up a hand, asking Tziah to stay put while I move closer to the pond. When nothing happens, I get down on my knees beside the glass-still waters that reflect the blues of the sky with little puffs of white clouds floating lazily by, then lean out over the water.

Please don't let anyone die today.

My reflection stares back at me from the surface—wide, cat-like amber eyes, lips that tip up at the corners, the dimple in my chin, thick, dark hair pulled up into a braid that coils over one shoulder.

This better work.

I call out, high and clear, "Aesthetus?"

6

WAKING UP MONSTERS

My reflection in the water wavers, changing shape and color, and I think I see the outline of another head—horns, a large snout, dark brown fur, and beady black eyes. Before he emerges, I duck back quickly, hiding my face.

Nothing happens.

Huh. That was supposed to lure him out.

Then again, Eidolon's spirit's instructions were specific. To call Aesthetus, a woman must imbue her voice with longing. My stomach knots just a little, despite the numb. Hells.

I look over my shoulder at Tziah, who waves at me to try again. I face the water, knowing I'm actively trying to stir a hornets' nest without getting swarmed, let alone stung.

Longing. I can put that in my voice without actually letting myself feel it, right?

I clear my throat, then lean out over the water and call him. And still nothing happens.

Hells and damnation.

I'm going to have to feel something. Let myself. It's a risk. I sign at Tziah. I tell her to be careful. She knows, they all know, that if the Shadows take me over, they have to try to stop me. I made them promise.

This is going to…hurt.

Closing my eyes, I take a deep breath. I think of every time I've called out to Reven since Eidolon took him, waiting to hear his voice answer me. Praying. I lean into that hope now, dangling over the deep well the Shadows dwell in, hanging onto my own rope.

Despite feeling for it, my connection with Reven remains so…cold. So empty.

Resentment bubbles up, along with a dollop of guilt. But I hate that he left me, that he gave me the Shadows, that he decided to sacrifice himself at all. I want to hit him for that. Hit him hard.

Don't think about that.

I center myself on the emptiness instead. At first, the need to hear Reven's voice just one more time is a fluttering in my belly, one that blooms and spreads until everything I am yearns…but something darker lies beneath. A razor's edge of hopelessness slices at me over and over, because instinct is telling me he won't answer.

"What are you doing?" one of the Shadows crawls out of the hole I stuck them in.

Not cackling this time, though.

Good. I let myself feel *more*. Everything. All of it. Including the poisoned, pitiful faith that is as likely to kill me as it is to keep me going. The resentment, too. And the guilt. The fear of failure and not being able to do this without him. The loneliness. The bone deep fear.

And I'm tired. Really tired.

I fill myself up with everything I've been burying with the Shadows until I ache. Until tears leak out from under my closed lids. Until my throat closes in on itself. Until my heart cries out at me to stop.

Has Aesthetus been feeling this same desperation for all these centuries? Goddess, how has he endured it?

I open my eyes and lean over the water to see my image and call out. Not Reven's name, but it might as well be. "Aesthetus?"

My voice catches on the sounds of his name.

And it works.

My image in the water wavers, and I gasp and duck back quickly.

"Are you a fool?" More Shadows slink out of my well.

The part of the pond I can see from my new vantage point remains glassy, but I hear it. A man's voice, rife with the same bleeding hope, comes from under the water. Though it sounds as clear as if he was standing right beside me. "Mimick?"

Aesthetus is calling his lover. I glance, wide-eyed, around me, waiting for the other monster to appear. But nothing happens.

I wait again. I give him time to look and see nothing and no one. I need to lure him out of the water. The ghost didn't say, but it seems like this is going to take several tries. When I think I've waited long enough, I force myself do it again. To let the emotions through, to let more Shadows slither out of the well. They fill me up. I lean out over the water and call for Aesthetus. Then duck back.

"Mimick?" he answers. Louder this time. "Don't hide from me."

His despair is growing. I don't have to see him to know, because I've heard that tone in my own voice. I hold up a hand, signaling Tziah to be ready. We'll have a split second to do this when he comes out of the water.

My heart thumps against my ribs, because I don't know if I can open myself to my own pain one more time.

"Don't do it," Reven's voice, but not Reven, whispers. Hushed.

Are the Shadows afraid?

I reach down my connection to Reven, wishing and wishing and wishing, but not feeling him as I count down with my fingers where Tziah can see—Three. Two. One.

I stick my head over the water. "Aesthe—"

Water explodes in my face, and a creature—half-man and half-beast—bursts forth from the depths, hoisting me by the throat with one hand. He stands on the banks of the pond, at least eight feet tall, dangling me over the water.

Once rumored to be the most beautiful man alive, his torso

and face are now that of a bull. Even so, I can still see the beauty in the lines of his shoulders, the ridge of his stomach that dips below the waist of his pants.

Rage rolls his eyes back as he bellows. Dark spots dance before my vision. I claw at his hand, trying to get away. To breathe. To fight.

"You are not Mimick," he says in a voice that is somewhere between human and animal, the low thunder of it like a stampede of hooves over hardened ground. Then he squeezes harder. "For that, you'll pay."

He lifts his other hand, and I see it.

The flute.

Made from the bones of his lover. Mimick's bones.

It is not shaped out of fingers or maybe a whittled, hollowed arm bone like I pictured. It's a skull with the jaw hinged open like she is forever screaming, another bone full of holes protruding from her gaping maw.

"Maybe *your* lovely bones will finally make her whole." Aesthetus lifts the abomination to his lips…and blows through a hole in the back of the skull, the sound coming out of its mouth like a scream.

Summoning the monster.

"No!" the Shadows shout as one inside my head.

7

DEATH HAS MANY SOUNDS

I don't know if a single note emits from the grotesque instrument at Aesthetus's lips, because a different noise rises around us, fast and furious.

Hissing at first, like a riled den of snakes. It grows louder, building pressure inside my head. I grit my teeth against the familiar sensation.

Tziah's power.

Sound as a weapon. If she keeps her mouth open long enough it becomes paralyzing. Debilitating. Even deadly.

The way Aesthetus is holding me, I can't let go of him to put my hands over my ears. The beast looks around manically, snorting and snuffling as he does, then blows harder into his bone flute, but the sound isn't audible. Not over the noise. Tziah steps out into the open and spreads her mouth wider, and the sound turns unbearable. Wetness leaks out of my nose and over his hand at my neck. Blood drips from his own snout.

Aesthetus drops me. Shock follows me down, and I flail as I hit the water with a splash, half the pond going up my nose or down my throat. Thank the goddess. From the soothing safety for my ears under the surface, I can see the creature as he uses both his hands on his flute, blowing until his bull-eyes bulge and start to bleed from the corners.

"Get away!" The Shadows are pounding at me now. Clamoring. *"Save yourself."*

"No." I have to get that flute.

Aesthetus turns on Tziah, charging straight for her with a bellow of rage that rattles me even in the water.

There's a flash of blue and white that I can tell is Tziah spinning as she darts out of the bull's path. She knicks him with the wicked curved blade in her hand, but he doesn't bellow again in pain. Instead, he smiles.

Because to defend herself and fight him, she's closed her mouth.

I break the surface and scramble out of the pond, weighed down by soaked clothes and the slippery bottom. But not fast enough.

The flute is at his lips in a blink, except a whip of leather lashes out from the opening of the Snarl we came through and wraps around his wrist.

Pella. It has to be.

Aesthetus rolls his big body over, which yanks the whip out of the wielder's hand. He comes back up to his feet with the flute to his lips, and a single note, clear and true, sounds through the air.

It's not a blast. Not a whine. Not a scream, either.

It's music all by itself. As sweet as a birdsong, and more haunting than an empty grave.

The Shadows' fear could be mine. *"She's going to kill us all."*

She? The blasted ghost didn't tell me what happens if the flute is blown, just that if it is, running isn't an option and dying is likely.

With a self-satisfied smile, Aesthetus backs up. "*You* made me waken her."

With a leap, he jumps back into the pond. I lunge for the flute clutched in his hand, but miss, bellyflopping hard on the ground at the bank. Grunting at the impact, I stare at the water where he disappeared. It's already turned glassy again. Not a single ripple. As if he never emerged in the first place.

"Stay hidden!" I call out to the others.

"Too late," Vos says.

I climb to my feet to find all of my friends are here, weapons drawn or glowing hands at the ready. Goddess damn it. I walked them all into certain death.

I'm not fit to be queen of anything.

I'm at their side in seconds. We position ourselves back-to-back and wait for whatever is supposed to come next. If we go down, it won't be with a whimper—it'll be bloody and broken.

A breeze stirs the grasses that make up the Snarl, which *shooshes* at us, the sound not restful but ominous, dread growing heavier inside me.

"You've killed us all, you stupid bitch!" a Shadow barks.

"See anything?" Vos asks, low voiced.

Cain pulls Tziah closer, putting himself between her and the walls that form the Snarl.

"Noth—" Pella's answer ends on a yelp as her legs jerk out from under her.

She shoots across the ground, dragged by something that's got her feet. Shocked horror freezes her face but quickly turns to fury as she lashes out with her whip, trying to stop herself. Vos slams down an axe made of ice that he creates so fast I don't even see him do it. He severs whatever rope had hold of Pella and she skids to an abrupt stop.

"Seven hells," she grumbles as she pushes to her feet with a wince. Blood leaks from a long gash in her leg, dribbling over her boots to pool in the dirt.

We hardly have a chance to take a breath before the ground beneath our feet undulates, like the swell of a wave passing through it, only to settle firmly again. Except the swell must keep moving outward, because the grasses of the Snarl all around us shake and hiss angrily, and the tops rise and fall against the sky.

"Well, *that's* bad," Cain says.

But he isn't facing the ripple. I track his gaze and the bottom drops out of my stomach.

The doorway into the Snarl, into the maze we came through to get here, is gone.

The blood drains from my face.

That ghost of Eidolon's told me how to get in and get the flute. Until this moment, I failed to realize that I only asked him how to get the amulets, not how to survive.

The bastard didn't give me a way out.

Intentionally?

From the burning lands, Eidolon's ghosts can see everything. Was this a ploy? Did he send us to the Snarl hoping to eliminate the threat I pose to the current Eidolon? By not telling us how to get out, he's handed down a death sentence.

A laugh—possibly with an edge of hysteria—bursts from me, earning me a few concerned glances. The ghost didn't know I'd drag all of Eidolon's Shadows into the Snarl with me. I didn't have them yet when I visited him. They'll die with me if it comes to that.

Poetic. Fucking. Justice.

Bet he's kicking himself now.

The Snarl rustles again, and suddenly six doorways open in the circle of grass surrounding the pond. Six ways out? But they close just as fast, only to reopen somewhere else, and beyond the openings, I can see the passageways of the maze…changing direction?

Yes. The maze is moving. Reconfiguring.

This time, the ground doesn't just undulate; it pops under our feet, knocking us all down. I scramble up onto my hands and knees, but it doesn't stop, like something is bucking and punching, trying to break through from underneath and tossing us all around like we're debris.

Forget the flute. The world feels like it's turning upside down in a chaos of movement.

"Run!" the Shadows yell.

"Run!" my own yell echoes.

Too late.

The ground splits apart all around us, between us, scattering us. As I'm rolling ass over head down a hill that wasn't there a second ago, I'm vaguely aware of Cain flying through the air in the opposite direction.

An earsplitting roar thunders around me. I manage to stop rolling just in time to see teeth. Razor-sharp teeth made of what looks to be rocks in the wide-open jaws of—

What in Nova *is* it?

The bottom of this new monster is the black soil, its head and back are covered in grasses, eyes and teeth of rocks, and yet alive. It's shaped somewhere between a dog and a toad. And it's massive.

Sticking out from all parts of it are the bones. The dead it's killed before, I assume.

Wonderful. The ground has come alive and is going to eat us.

I frown. Wait. Is *this* Mimick?

We're dead. We're all so very dead.

The monster—Mimick, it has to be—roars again and then lunges with a clattering snap of those rock teeth. Not coming for me. For someone else.

"Everyone run!" Vos yells from somewhere on the other side of the grassy expanse. "Get yourselves out."

In the same moment, the grasses nearest me open a doorway to the maze. I jump to my feet and take off into the Snarl, running down a never-ending passageway, the sounds of the fight fading as I go, until, with a snapping fizz, the grass moves to open a different passage. It seems to aim away from the pandemonium, so I run through it, but a rattle sounds at my back, and I glance over my shoulder to see the part I came from closing behind me.

Are the grasses aware of me and…herding me?

A sharp shout comes from somewhere in front of me, followed by a boom.

And all I can do is keep running.

8

IT'S HER... OR ME

I skid to a halt at the familiar sound of crackling a heartbeat before a fountain of ice sprays up into the sky over the tops of the maze. It explodes in a shower of ice chips.

Vos. Mimick is definitely after Vos.

A chunk falls at my feet, narrowly missing me.

"Get your ass moving," one of the Shadows commands.

But even as close as they all are to the surface, they aren't in charge of me yet. And if the grasses are determining my direction, then damned if I'm following where they lead.

So I stay here, listening and watching the skies.

I need to find the others, gather us together. We're strongest together.

Another shout—Horus, I think—sounds close to my right, like he's running on the other side of a thin wall parallel to me. An arrow flies out of the grasses and directly across my path, close enough to my chest that I yelp in surprise.

A shadow overhead is my only warning. Dirt and grass and rock block out the sun as Mimick lands fifty yards in front of me. The Snarl magically clears out of the monster's path, like it's giving us an arena in which to face off.

Mimick stares me down with creepy-as-sin stone eyes that don't blink. Can she see me if I don't move? Some predators are like that.

What other options do I have?

Sand isn't readily available in this soil, I can feel that much. Running is out—she's too fast and the Snarl is helping her. My knives would be an annoying spike in her paw at most, only likely to piss her off more. And the darkness doesn't listen to me like it does Reven. I can't create weapons, or walls, or even a puff of smoke to hide within. Beyond containing the shards of Eidolon like a vessel, I'm useless.

Mimick rears back, then runs straight at me. The ground shakes with every pounding lope.

When I was ten, Cain taught me to mount a running horse. And that's all I can think of in the seconds I have.

I wait, staring her down, not running, counting the rolling lope of her feet. I have to time this perfect. Just as she gets close, I jump to the side and spin to run parallel to her. I don't think she expected that because she doesn't immediately change course, giving me time to take several running steps as she pulls up beside me.

Mimick tosses her grassy head, spraying dirt everywhere, swinging to the side like she's trying to pulverize me or knock me to the ground, but I leap at her and grab a tuft full of the grasses that make up her back and sides, the way I would a horse's mane, allowing her speed to pull me.

Using her momentum, I swing and toss my body up and over her back.

What I don't account for is the fact that this creature is much taller than a horse and so I really just end up clinging to her side, like a burr to a tail, my body straining not to be shaken loose.

Thank the goddesses there aren't any trees or structures out here for her to slam me against. Mimick skids to a halt, her dragon-like talons leaving deep gouge marks in the ground, and a terrible noise like the roar of a storm surrounds me. She whips her head around, mouth open, trying to pluck me off her side, but her neck is too thick and shoulders too broad to reach me.

That's right, bitch. Sometimes being small and smart is better than being huge and not smart.

The thing gives a full-body shake, but I manage to hang on even as a wet stickiness starts to trickle down my arms, making it harder to grip. Out of nowhere, something long and slender snakes around my ankle and jerks me into the sky just like Pella earlier. This time I see what it is.

Long tendrils of grass sprout directly from Mimick's body like a tail.

I'm high up enough in the air that I can see across the maze and all the pathways the Snarl has reconfigured itself into. *Keeps* reconfiguring itself into. It moves like it's alive. Jerking around desperately in the air, I search, but I can't see or hear any of my friends.

Where'd they go?

"They're dead!" a Shadow shouts.

"Shut up!"

Fear ratchets through me like a lever cranking through gears. The monster opens her jaws wide and dangles me overhead, and I swear the thing gives me a big, rocky-toothed grin.

I'm looking down into a pit of my own death.

"You've killed us all," the Shadows wail. *"Let us free."* Their voices are so close to the surface, it's as if they're standing beside me rather than trapped within me.

"Never!"

I'll die before that happens and take them with me. One less evil in the world.

Reven didn't give them to me just to let them loose on the unsuspecting world. He didn't sacrifice himself for that.

I swing my body back and forth, flailing and kicking and trying to get loose. With a grunt, I reach for the knife tucked into my boot. I'll bloody well cut myself free.

But another tail of grass snares around my wrists, binding them together and pinning them to my stomach. I don't stop fighting, though, wriggling like a worm on a hook. Maybe if I can hold off death until Cain or Vos can get to me…

Even though I'm braced for it, I'm so focused on getting away that when Mimick lets go, the drop sends my stomach into my throat. In that instant, it's as if the sands in the hourglass of time slow just for me and I can count the jagged teeth I'm falling toward.

The Shadows all punch outward in a desperate bid to escape, and agony is everywhere.

I've known fear. Battled through it. Conquered it. Sometimes given in to it. But not like this. *This* fear clears my thoughts like rain knocks dust from the air, and in those seconds that feel so stretched out, I realize the most important part.

I *want* to live.

When I was a child and would take my sister's place sleeping in her bed in the palace, when the servants would draw back the heavy curtains in the morning, flooding the bedchamber with sunlight, the brightness of the sun always made my eyes water.

This is like that. Like I'm blinking at the truth which was there all the time. I've been walking around numb since Reven left me, half-dead already. I had to do that to keep the Shadows at bay.

But I was doing all this, putting one unsteady foot in front of the other, without really believing I could win in the end.

Now, I want to live. For him. For me. For Tabra. For my friends. For my people. For the possibilities of a future that will die a slow death if I don't at least try to stop Eidolon.

So, it's Mimick…or me.

Rage sizzles through me like Hakan's lightning bolts, except this is bitterly cold, unstoppable, physical fury so frigid it burns, purifying me from the inside out.

Time suddenly speeds back up. Faster than my mind can track, a purple glow lights up the monster's mouth. One instant I'm falling to my death, and the next, the monster beneath me disappears without a trace. Not a sound. Not a puff of smoke.

Existing and then just…not.

9

BLAME

Instead of being eaten alive, I hit the ground hard enough to rattle my bones and knock the wind from me. It knocks the rage out of me, too. I lay there, stunned, hoping I didn't break anything. It only takes two or three wheezing breaths before what I just did hits me.

Or what I think Eidolon's Shadows did through me.

I'm honestly not sure who wielded that power. Me or them.

"Oh goddess." The words punch from me with what little air I've managed to drag into my body as I lumber to my feet. "No, no, no, *no*."

Mimick's soul is trapped here now in the same way Reven trapped Eidolon's soldiers' souls in the Shadowood, leaving that place scarred and poisoned. I wanted to kill her, not curse her.

Oh goddess.

The guilt threatens to crush me. Is this what Reven carried with him afterward? How could he endure it?

"Meren!"

Cain's voice, coming from far off, breaks through my stupor.

I look at my hands. I'm bleeding badly. So much blood everywhere. My palms, which were sliced to ribbons by Mimick's grassy mane, and my ankles show similar razor-smooth gashes. Those must be from Mimick's tails.

I didn't even feel the cuts. Still don't. Maybe there's something in her that dulls the pain?

Like the Snarl was waiting for me to realize the danger the grasses still pose, the maze rushes closed, boxing me in, then opening up a single narrow pathway pointing in a new direction.

The Snarl is still herding me.

Mimick is no longer a threat, though, and I need that flute, so I follow the path. It doesn't take me long. In seconds, I'm back at the pond at the center.

I step out of the Snarl cautiously, expecting to have to go in after Aesthetus or coax him out again. But I don't have to do either of those things because Cain is dangling Aesthetus over the pond using water. Tendrils of it wrap around the beast's ankles and wrists and around his neck. Not that he's fighting.

The creature looks...broken.

His shoulders heave in silent sobs and his head is turned at an awkward angle around Cain's water noose, so he can look at the bone flute still clutched in his hand.

"She's gone," he's saying in choked whispers. "My bondmate is gone and no bones can make her whole again."

Make her whole?

Is that what they were trying to do by killing anything they got in here? Was their love so tortured and yet so strong for each other that they would sacrifice anything and anyone in an attempt to save her?

I stare at the pathetic creature in front of me.

Is this what Reven and I will become? Is loving each other going to warp us until we're monsters? I glance back to where Mimick had been.

Has it already?

An expression whispers across Aesthetus's face. One I know. I've seen it on Reven, on the battlefield, in the palace.

Resolution.

"I am coming to you in the afterlife, my love." Aesthetus loosens the fingers of the hand holding the flute, almost as though he has to force them to pry open, and the bone flute falls from his grasp.

What feels like a thousand reactions happen all at once.

The labyrinth of snarling grasses all around us screams. That's the only way I can describe the horrendous, unnatural sound—like a shriek of pain and a death rattle blended. The blades of the Snarl shake and shiver and reconfigure the parts of the maze I can see from here over and over and over, faster than I can track.

Keeping hold of the flute made of Mimick's bones must've kept Aesthetus alive, because starting from his toes, Aesthetus turns into water, as if he's melting but morphing at the same time, drip-drip-dripping back into the pond below, slowly at first and then in a *whoosh*.

Cain uses his power to bat the falling flute out of the air, tossing it to Tziah.

She catches it just as the last remnants of Aesthetus splash into the water, his impact rippling outward, and the Snarl goes dead still. More than that, the walls and paths they formed vanish. The grasses around us now appear the same as those we walked through to get to the Snarl—including the thin layer of ice coating the stalks.

I drop to my knees and sort of fall sideways to sit on the ground in a heap, breathing hard and trying to reach for the numbness that protects me.

But I can't. Not anymore. Almost like deciding I want to live and fight won't let me burrow into it anymore.

Vaguely, I'm aware of Vos going to Tziah, then Cain and Horus both kneeling in front of me, their mouths moving. But I'm busy.

Without the numb, the Shadows are running rampant inside me. So loud I can't hear, pressing outward, testing the strength of my body and my will. And taunting. Taunting me in Reven's voice.

"You did that to Mimick when you know what it means."

But I don't think I poofed Mimick. It had to be them. They're just toying with me, trying to screw with my head.

"It was you," I tell them weakly.

"Are you so sure?"

My stomach hollows out. If I did this, if it was me, then not only did I send Mimick into limbo, but I also separated bondmates. Murderous, bloodthirsty, twisted bondmates, but still.

Aesthetus's life was clearly tied to the Snarl and to his lover, and as soon as he thought she was dead, he gave up. Only, he did so believing she had gone to the afterlife ahead of him, and he would meet her there.

But he won't.

He won't because she's not in the hells or the heavens, and she won't have an afterlife. Because I trapped her here.

"You see, now. It wasn't us, princess."

They don't stop there, saying things I've secretly started to worry about, sending urges through me to hurt, to take revenge. Trying to convince me that I'm something I'm not.

I put a hand to my forehead, giving it a shake, trying to loosen their grip on my mind. I know better than to believe those evil things. I'll never be the monster they want me to be.

"Meren."

Cain's harsh scrape of a voice finally penetrates, and I look up into his wide eyes.

"What did you do?"

He's not accusing me, but my body takes the hit like he is. As soon as his words are fully uttered, the air above us shimmers like a mirage in the desert. But this mirage blinks into existence so fast, there's no time to scramble to my feet.

I gasp at the creature now towering over me. I've only met one like her before.

A centimane.

She is one of the massive creatures of legend from before even the time of the goddesses. A hundred feet tall at least, her face and body are etched from layers of obsidian. She doesn't have two arms…she has a hundred.

And she looks *furious*.

A rock fist lands on the ground beside me, sinking into the soft dirt as she leans over me, terrifyingly close. She ignores Cain who flings himself over me like a human shield, tipping her head to the side to stare at me over his shoulder with a single narrowed eye.

"Yes, little human." Her voice is like silk, in contrast with her appearance, but the silk is frayed and snagged with anger and blame. "What *did* you do?"

PART 2

COUNTER GAMBIT

10

SCORIA

"Get off me, Cain."

He grits his teeth. "No."

I push ineffectually at his shoulders. "She can flick you off with a finger, and that would be worse. I need you whole." Goddess knows I couldn't stop her. She's made of the black rock from the Obsidian desert in Aryd, not sand.

I can feel the way he tenses against my hands. "Damn it, Meren."

"*Please*."

His chest moves with a silent breath, then he crawls back but not entirely away, sitting on the ground at my side with a mutinous expression aimed at the giantess.

She's only focused on me, though. "You just instantaneously ripped a soul from its body, discarded it as a Shadow of itself, and destroyed the body so it can't return." The giantess leans closer, and I try not to shrink in on myself. "I *felt* it."

I shake my head hard enough that any hair that didn't escape my braid earlier does now and flops into my face. I open my mouth to deny it. "I—"

"*Lie,*" the Shadows warn.

Doing the opposite of anything those voices suggest has become my new measurement for doing the right or wrong thing in any situation. I assume they want me to do the wrong thing. Always.

Maybe they aren't always wrong.

"What was that?"

My eyes widen. Did I say that out loud? I don't think I did, but I'm coming undone.

The giantess leans in more. She'll start to crush me soon. "Don't try to lie to me, Imperium. You're the one who's been stealing the souls from the burning lands. I've been hunting you."

"No!" I raise both hands. That, at least, isn't a lie. "That's not me. I can prove it."

"How could you prove such a thing?" she demands.

"Better talk fast."

She makes a sound like a grunt. "That's not your voice. What am I hearing?"

"Holy hells," Pella whispers off to the side. "Can she hear them?"

"Hear *them*?" With the rough rasp of rock on rock, or more of a screeching slide since obsidian is closer to glass, the eye turned my way narrows on me until it's just a slit. "Are you swallowing the souls you steal?"

I'm so screwed. The Shadows were right. *Talk fast.* "Your name is Scoria, right?"

"How do you know that?" she asks. "I have not met you before."

"No, but I have met your mate, Basalt."

Scoria doesn't so much as twitch. "Someone else could have told you his name."

"True. But he also told me about the disappearing souls when I visited the burning lands."

It's difficult to tell among the cracks and crevices that make up the features of Scoria's face, but I think maybe her lips press together. *Please don't be thinking of the most expedient way to squish me.*

"She's never going to believe you," the Shadows say.

Scoria rears back slightly. "I heard that. I *hear* the voices inside you. You are the soul thief."

"Meren…" Cain warns.

I need to shut them up now or she'll never believe me. I try to close down my emotions again. Draw the numb over me and shove the Shadows back down into the well.

But it doesn't work.

What now? I frantically cast about for an answer, but all I have is the truth.

"Those aren't stolen souls," I rush to tell her. "They are Shadows. Like Mimick, only…not."

"Shadows?" she scoffs. "I know what I felt, and I can smell the power on you. You ripped that soul out and swallowed it."

She pokes me in the belly with her rock finger, like she could squish the souls out of me. She's not gentle and I grunt at the impact. In a flash, Cain jabs at her with a dagger he wasn't holding a moment ago. It just bounces off her rock body.

I grab his wrist to keep him from doing it again. "No!"

Despair and fear take hold, twisting my insides. Reven shouldn't have given me the Shadows. I can't handle this power.

"It's not her!" Cain shouts. "She's telling the truth."

"We've all seen it." Vos joins him, edging closer, hands up.

Horus, too, Pella at his side, and Tziah tucked in behind Vos.

"Listen to her story first," Pella urges.

Without moving her head, Scoria rolls her eyeball to look first at them, then at me. "Speak."

The words start tumbling out. "As a baby I was cursed by a sand nymph and bound to the current King Eidolon. The nymph was supposed to bind him to my twin sister, since she was the firstborn who would eventually become Queen of Aryd."

"Why did the nymph curse you then?"

"I don't know."

"I see." Scoria still sounds doubtful. "And the curse?"

At least she's listening. "The nymph betrayed Eidolon. In addition to cursing the wrong princess, she also changed the curse. He doesn't control my power. I— "

"Control his power?" The centimane's voice takes that edge back on. "That's not possible. More than one power is unheard of."

"The power isn't inside me. I just sort of…tap into it, like drawing water from a well."

Scoria stares at me unblinking. "Then you used Eidolon's power on the creature here. Stole her soul," Scoria says. "*You* did that."

"Fool," the Shadows rail. *"She's going to kill us."*

"I won't kill the souls in you, just you," she says.

Lovely. "That's the Shadows talking," I tell her. "Not me."

"Explain."

I close my eyes. I'm so tired. Exhausted from fighting, from constantly holding the Shadows back, from everyone watching me.

"You have to know, after so many versions of him have appeared in the afterlife, that Eidolon sheds pieces of his soul—his Shadows—to maintain a sort of immortality."

Is it possible for obsidian to go pale? "How did you know that?" the giantess whispers.

"I carry the king's remaining Shadows inside me. That's what you're hearing."

Because Reven gave them to me, but that complicated mess would take too long to explain right now and would probably only add to her suspicion.

She's shaking her head. "Not possible."

What she said a moment ago finally sinks in. That she'd kill me but not the things inside me. "Can you take them?"

Her brows snap down and dust rains over my face. "What?"

Cain whips his head around and gapes at me. "Meren!"

I know what he's saying. Tabra and the Shadows are the only bargaining chips we have against Eidolon. But even the smallest possibility of one less evil to deal with coats my throat with relief so thick it's hard to swallow. "Can you take them out of me? Take them to the burning lands?"

This is the answer. Let the giantess pull them from me and contain them in the hells. Maybe this was the answer to this particular problem all along.

"It could kill you," the giantess says.

Cain braces. "No—"

I hold up a hand. "Do it."

"You can't," he says. "We need you to fight Eidolon."

I turn my head and meet his eyes, which are wild. He's shaking his head so hard, it's like all of him is rejecting this option.

"I can't keep doing this," I whisper and will him to understand. "Not if I can't control these things. I've tried—" My voice breaks. I look at Scoria. "Please."

The Shadows have nothing to say now. That silence is its own sweet kind of relief.

She stares at me for the longest time, probably deciding what to believe. What if I'm tricking her? That's what I'd be thinking now. And just when I think she's going to say no, she closes her eyes. "Prepare yourself. This is going to hurt."

Cain grabs my hand, lacing our fingers together. He barely finishes before a storm of pain blasts through my body. I bow off the ground, my mouth open in a silent scream. It's like she's trying to rip the blood out of my veins through my skin, pull my entrails out through my navel, shear the flesh from my bones, and turn me inside out all at the same time.

The Shadows unleash a sound of such fury that it drowns out everything else around me.

And then, as if my body can't handle this level of horror, oblivion claims me.

My last thought, in that blink of darkness before I die, is to Reven. *"I'll find you in the next life."*

11

FOLLOW HER

I come to still on the ground surrounded by trampled grasses, my body so cold I'm shaking and my teeth are chattering. I frown.

Wait. I'm not dead?

"Maybe this is the hells," a Shadow whispers.

Beside me, Cain sucks in a breath so sharp, it sounds like it hurts. The way he's gripping my hand definitely does, but I don't protest. I need the way he's grounding me.

Scoria stands over us.

"It didn't work," I croak.

She sort of shakes her head. Why not, though? I can't tell anything from her expression. I look to Cain, who has gone a shade of pale that should be impossible with skin the shade of bronze his is.

I struggle to sit up just enough to see our friends. Pella is looking away. Horus's bow is trained on me. Slowly, warily, Cain pulls gently on my hand to help me. He doesn't let go once I'm upright, searching my face.

"You're back," he says.

I frown. Back? "Was I gone?"

"Not exactly," Vos says slowly, not taking his gaze off me.

"What?"

Cain tugs me closer and wraps his arms around me, taking a deep breath. "The Shadows took over."

His words hit like he took a sledgehammer to my sternum. I go very still against him and take a closer look at my friends. I know we just dealt with Aesthetus and Mimick, but they look… worse.

Cain has a bloody gash in his thigh that's seeping through his pants. Pella's shirt is torn, and Horus is listing to one side like he can't quite put all his weight on one foot. Vos is standing a few yards away, wrapping what looks like wide blades of grass around his forearm. All four of them are bleeding from their noses and ears. The metallic taste in my mouth finally penetrates through the haze I'm in and I lift a hand to my face to find I'm in the same shape.

"Tziah stopped y—" Cain pulls back to look at me with a pained face. "Stopped them."

"Bitch," one of the voices snarls.

Cain grimaces. "They tried to shadow you away from Scoria, but she was able to stop them. When we pinned you down, they came after us."

I attacked my friends? I know I didn't personally, but they had to fight my body while the Shadows used it to—

"No." The word is a mere wisp of sound.

Goddess, my nightmares just came true. All my worries.

"I couldn't get them out of you," Scoria whispers, and her voice is raw.

Despair washes over me. I've been changing since Reven put Eidolon's Shadows inside me. I've buried the growing realization with the rest of my fears. Refused to accept it. It's only been in small ways so far. Random thoughts. Bursts of anger that are unlike me. Will it only get worse the longer I contain them?

Bile sears up my throat like even my fear is trying to escape the evil inside me. I swallow it down. I can't do this. I'm not strong like Reven thought. I can't…

"Kill me," I say in a voice stronger than I expect.

Cain's arms tighten around me reflexively.

"Meren." Horus's voice is raw.

"Kill me." I'm begging now. Scoria is the only one who can. "It's the only way to stop them."

She turns away from me. "They won't let me."

Which means she tried.

I never thought I was someone who gave up easily. Turns out I was wrong. I pull away from Cain and wrap my arms around my knees. No tears. No more begging. Just defeat.

A soft hand smooths over my hair and I don't have to look to know Tziah is beside me. I drop my forehead to my knees. I can't bear to have her see me unravel like this. Have any of them see.

"*Pathetic little princess*," the Shadows sneers.

"Enough," Scoria snaps.

Then…silence. More than silence. Peace.

I frown.

"I can't feel them." I look up at Scoria. "They're quiet. They're gone. I thought you said—"

"I trapped them inside you."

"Trapped?" I thought they were already trapped. "What does that mean?"

"Maybe locked down is a better description. As Shadow, I may not be able to pull them out, but they are still souls, even in pieces the way they are. I have…some control."

"Can you keep me from being taken over again?"

She pauses, then slowly shakes her head. "They'll be quiet and still as long as I'm near you."

"That's something at least," Cain says. But his voice is too cheerful. Too bright. He doesn't believe it any more than I do.

"That's like stopping a sand storm with a single shield," I mutter. "It might keep the sand out of my eyes for a little bit, but I'll still be buried when it's over." Scoria can't stay with me forever.

"I can teach you more of this power that is not yours," she says.

Exhaustion drags at me again, and various aches and pains are making themselves felt. I don't know if they're from fighting Mimick or my friends. Maybe that's why I'm having trouble latching on to what she's saying. "Teach?"

"I believe what you've told me. The truth is, I don't handle souls in such large numbers." Her lips twist in a rocky grimace. "And never souls that are made of shadow. But you clearly need help until we can remove them from you."

A bitter laugh escapes me. "I guess it's better than nothing."

The rock giantess sighs. "I may not be able to get the Shadows out of you, but the ability to control darkness versus souls seems to have some similarities. Let me try to teach you."

I lay my cheek on my arm, thinking about that. "We don't have time." The Celestial Alignment is soon. The way the sun and all three moons sit in our sky a certain way that day has something to do with this. One of Eidolon's escaped ghosts told me in the desert that it meant something. We just don't know what yet. "Eidolon is coming for me. He wants the amulets and his Shadows back."

She tips her head, giving a slow blink, and I realize she doesn't know what I'm saying.

I don't have it in me to explain this. Not right now. Not after everything that's just happened. "Cain?"

With a nod, he tells her. Everything.

When he's done, she sighs again. "I see. In that case, you have no choice. Accept my help."

"I told you—"

"You don't have time. I understand." She leans down. "I *can* help you. Would it not be better to face that with more control?"

It's a sign of how little I believe her when anticipation

doesn't even so much as spark inside me. "Maybe a day or two." I straighten, wincing at the pull of bruises all over my body. "One other thing…"

"Yes?"

"Can you teach my sister, too?" I've only been able to help her so much.

"Yes." She glances at the sun, high in the skies and bright with it. "If I only have days, we had better get started."

12

THE UNLEARNABLE

"It's not working, is it?" I ask with my eyes screwed closed. Scoria's not letting me use the numb, not that I seem to be able to find my way back to it. Instead, it's like my emotions are all over the place, pushed this way and that by any little thing, even a breeze. She explained that numbness was like smothering fire with oil. It might put it out for a second, but it will only reignite and burn hotter.

With her close by, at least the Shadows are silent. I'm not fighting them and trying to use two powers at the same time.

Vos went to get Tabra, only to return and be told that that wasn't the deal—Tabra stays in the temple—so we set up camp outside the temple pit. While the others hunt, cook, and wait, Scoria drills me, and drills me, and drills me in increasingly difficult exercises. Tabra she spends time with separately, down inside the temple, usually when I'm passed out asleep from the exhaustion of both healing from my wounds and using power as much as I have been.

We've gone back to the basics, as she puts it.

For each new task, she starts me off doing something similar with my power over sand until I get decent enough at the specific technique.

Which makes sense. If I get it wrong or get overwhelmed, sand doesn't have the ability to bury my soul alive inside my body like a tomb or disappear the corporeal bodies of every person in my vicinity.

So there is that.

Once I can do what she wants with sand, she then moves me over to trying it with shadow, the benign darkness tucked into cracks and crevices during the day, and all around us at night.

Right now, she just wants me to make a shape with it.

I picture the darkness I'm trying to manipulate like my sand, as if there are individual little grains that can be melded together to form a bigger entity. I think about what I've seen Reven do with shadow. Eidolon, too. They can manifest physical elements from the darkness, including razor-sharp blades that can cleave a person in two.

"Good," Scoria says.

"About time," Vos drawls.

Really? I open my eyes.

Ha!

Darkness that appears almost solid, like smoke that has been captured in a glass bowl, actually looks like what Scoria asked me to form it into—a rabbit.

I saw a real one hopping through the grasses before. It didn't stop to bow to me like other animals used to—a kirin in Wildernyss and an old she-wolf in the Shadowood, among others. I think maybe because I'm not wearing Aryd's amulet. Creatures only did that when I had her with me.

The tiny little body of my shadow bunny is seated, puffed tail at the back, long ears pricked. I did it. It's not just a blob.

I did it!

Off to the side but still in my line of sight, Tziah gives me an encouraging thumbs-up and I smile back.

A flare of pride is followed by an immediate fall because the first thing I think about is Reven. Would he be proud, too?

I'm not numb anymore. Damned erratic emotions. Reven should be able to reach me more easily, at least, but he hasn't. He's still gone from me, cold and unresponsive. Like a void out there in the world.

Without the numb, I can feel the piece of my own soul that's missing with him gone, a hole at my center that aches unbearably all the time.

I haven't told the others that yet, blaming the fear for them that rolls through me regularly on other things. They haven't questioned it so far, probably because they're getting used to my mood swings.

Vos breaks into my thoughts. "It's not enough."

Up till now, he's been leaning against a rock, legs indolently crossed, offering a plethora of unhelpful comments. Unless he thinks provoking me is helpful.

Knowing Vos, he probably does.

Tziah raises a hand to smack him in the arm, but his sharpened gaze gives away how serious he's become. She must see it, too, because she lowers her hand.

I try not to flinch.

"We're running out of time," he says.

We've been running out of time since the day Reven stole Eidolon's Shadows, but Vos is right. It's been three days. A shadow rabbit is all I have to show for it, and even that was pushing it.

"I know," I say.

"I'd like to see you learn it that fast." Cain points at my work.

"We have the rest of the day," Scoria insists. "Close your eyes again."

I blink at her. "But I—"

"Do as you're told," she says in a voice that reminds me a lot of Omma, grounding me unexpectedly.

I close my eyes and breathe, fighting through the exhaustion and the roiling emotions that make me feel like a bird in the air being tossed about by rough winds.

"Now," Scoria says, "I want you to make an exact replica of the rabbit."

"You've got to be joking," I grumble.

"I do not joke."

That much I've figured out by now.

I furrow my brows. It took me all day just to make *one* rabbit. But after three days, I'm well aware the giantess won't stop pushing me until I at least try. So I cling to my wavering focus and picture again the darkness that forms my individual grains, like sand.

Rather than trying to make another rabbit from scratch, an idea tickles my mind. I create a hole in the bottom of my rabbit and another smaller one in the top and let the shadows that make up the insides of it drain out, leaving only a hollow shell.

"What is it you're trying to do, exactly?" Vos wonders somewhere off to my right.

I keep my eyes closed. "A blacksmith had a shop not too far from the hovel where Omma and I lived in Enora when we weren't at the palace. I used to go and watch her work."

"Uh-huh."

My eyes may be closed but I recognize the thump of sound that tells me Tziah didn't stop herself from smacking Vos this time.

"Hey!" Cain's voice wobbles on a laugh. "I thought I was the only entertainment you had growing up."

If he's teasing… Is my effort that bad?

I'm tempted to take a peek. Except in the last three days I've learned that if I check on my progress, my disappointment at the results weighs me down, makes me second guess myself, and eventually stops me from succeeding. Now I just don't look. Vos or no Vos. "Let me work."

"Yes, boss."

Ugh. He knows I hate it when he calls me that. Goddess, I hope that shadow bunny isn't just melting in on itself or something equally frustrating.

I keep going despite my own doubts. When I think I've got

it right, I split the hollowed rabbit in two and in my mind set each half on the ground.

Why don't you open your eyes? an insidious voice whispers. Not the Shadows, though. These are my own thoughts replacing the sound of them in my head. I think.

"Keep working," Scoria says.

Right.

Now that I have the hollowed-out form, in my mind's eye, the darkness is like sand when I heat it into a malleable thick liquid, and I imagine pouring it into both of the rabbit-shaped molds. I press the halves together, picturing the shadow inside melding and hardening together. Then I peel away my molds and do it again.

I don't stop there, though, keeping my eyes closed as I picture each completed shadow bunny together as if they're sitting side by side and facing me. Sometimes it takes time for what I'm actually doing to catch up with what I'm picturing. I breathe and wait through what I hope is enough time.

I don't crack an eye. "Am I close?"

A huff of laughter sounds from behind me, followed by Pella's mumbled, "Only if you consider a child's first sentence to be close to the poetry of the Unknown Bard."

Cain sighs. "Not helping, Pell-mell."

I'm guessing it didn't work.

Vos sniggers, and I hear another *thump*, followed by, "Ouch, Tzi."

When I open my eyes, all it takes is one look before I flop back on the frozen ground and fling a hand over my eyes. Pella was right. My previously recognizable bunny is now more like two blobs of darkness connected by strings of shadow that remind me of drool. "I need more time to get this."

"Maybe an eon," Pella agrees.

I sit up, barely noting that my drooly bunny blobs have dissipated like mist burning off under the heat of the sun. A lump of porridge sits in a bowl made of woven grass blades on the ground in front of me. I scoop it up with one hand and fling it at her. Only Pella ducks, and it smacks Horus in the face, right on his gray-and-black stubble-covered chin, probably getting some in his mouth. Then the lump drips down to land in his lap.

At his grimace of disgust and the almost prissy way he picks the smear of oatmeal off his clothes, I have to press my lips together to keep from laughing. Laughter feels like pain to me now. *Every* emotion is too much. "Sorry, Horus. That obviously wasn't meant for *you*."

"I should have moved faster, domina," Horus murmurs, still plucking at his clothes.

Pella doesn't even bother to hide her wide grin. "If your control of shadows is as bad as your aim, we're screwed."

I narrow my eyes, glaring. "I dare you to find out what I'm feeling right now."

She tips her head, expression clearly indicating that my attempt at a comeback is weak at best. "I don't need my empathic abilities to know that," she says, nectar sweet. "Your emotions are like a simple glyph on a wall. Easy to read."

Gritting my teeth will only make her keep going. I may understand Pella now, even respect her, and maybe a tiny bit like her, but that doesn't mean I have to like her *all* the time.

Cain elbows his sister. "Give it a rest, Pell."

She rolls her eyes, then settles into a position that says she's done, but I know better. Pella is like a cat that grows weary of toying with a mouse it intends to eat and takes a nap right beside its mousy hole. She's just saving it up for the next time she thinks I need a good whack to the ego.

"One more time," Scoria demands.

I drop my head into my hands and groan. "I'm exhausted."

"You are not ready to be without me yet."

Ouch.

Fair, but ouch.

"Fine." I pull my shoulders back, keeping my eyes closed.

With the Shadows no longer nattering in my head or fighting me, it's easier to focus when I draw on Eidolon's power. I've discovered his power feels different from mine. Mine is easy, right there, and warm. But his…it's more like reaching down a long, chilly tunnel and pulling it to me and through my body. Instead of the pins and needles of my power, his coldness seeps into my blood and bones.

But I've used so much today, I'm drained and starting to shake just to siphon him, but I dig deep, down, down, down, to draw it in and in and in. I'm sitting in the quiet of the effort, tuning out everything else.

"Found you," a voice growls in my head.

The shock of it has me flailing with a gasp, like someone jerking awake in sleep. I open my eyes, but I don't see Savanah or my friends around me. I'm in a dark room lit by the purple glow of my hands, and in front of me stands Eidolon.

He looks so much like Reven except for the slight silvering at the temples and more lines around the eyes that it hurts to look at him.

I jerk back a step, looking around me frantically. I don't think he shadowed me here. Wherever *here* is.

"I can feel when you use my power, Meren."

I jerk my gaze to him to find him smiling at me, face eerie in the violet light. Ghostly. That smile grows, showing me his teeth like a predator.

He can feel it? I spin around. "Reven!"

The king's dark chuckle echoes around me. "I buried him," he says. "Cut him away from you like cutting out rotting flesh."

"No more Reven," a Shadow whispers from within me.

Scoria's influence must not work wherever this is.

Ignoring it, I tip my chin up. "I don't believe you."

Eidolon scoffs. "Have you heard him lately? Felt him?"

The fear that's been pounding at me changes, turning to fear for Reven. I try to hide my reaction. Give him nothing. Show him nothing.

He sees straight through me, though. A smug smile tugs at his lips. "You'll never find him in any afterlife to come."

Cold fear burns away to fury. It takes up a spot in my chest, right at the center, swirling and burning like a storm of fire inside me that is just sitting for now, gathering power and speed.

I swear it to the six goddesses, to the mother Nova, to my ancestresses who died at that monster's hands, and to myself. If I get the chance, I will rend the flesh from Eidolon's bones and leave it all under the desert sun to rot away, bleach white, then crumble to dust where no one will find him again. Where, in time, no one will even remember he lived.

"You better hope that's not true," I snarl at him, my voice wild and unrecognizable. "Because I have all the other amulets now. I have your Shadows. I have Tabra. And I have your power."

His smile drops away to leave only burning hatred in his eyes.

"You want them?" I taunt. Listening to the Shadows has taught me how to do that well. "You'd better ask nicely."

I do the only thing I can think of, the only thing I've learned to do well with Scoria's help so far. I picture the darkness around us like sand. Piles of it. Dunes of it. Then I blast Eidolon with it. Bury him in it. Pile it on so fast and hard, he's gone from view in seconds.

That's when Scoria yanks me out of my own head. The sensation is like the first time I was thrown from a bucking horse as a child when Cain taught me to ride. Like being tossed around like a rag doll, then launched through the air to hit the ground hard.

I scramble to my feet like a feral thing. "Where did he take me?" I croak.

Part of me expects the Shadows to answer, but they don't, contained again.

"Take you?" Cain is in front of me in an instant, searching my gaze. "Nowhere."

"You never left," Horus says from behind him.

That was all in my mind?

Was it even real? Or was I having a waking nightmare? Given what he told me about Reven, I'd almost it rather be that.

But deep down I know it's not.

Despite shaking hard with the effort all that cost me, I start to pace. "Eidolon got to me. I talked to him. He knows I have the amulets." And he did something to Reven. I don't know what, but I believe him. Time is up. I'm out of options.

I stop in front of Cain and Pella. "I need to speak with your father."

13

FLOWERS & PORTALS

"Tziah, I need the pouch," I say.

She riffles through our packs and produces a leather pouch. She undoes the drawstring and tips it over to dump a small pile of sand from the salt flats into my palm. Beneath the sand, pure white to the point of opalescence, the glow of my power ignites, making the pile appear to shine and shimmer yellow from within.

At my silent will, a small amount lifts into the air, heats, and melts. With a flick of my fingers, I shape the small bubble into a petal. Quickly I add more petals, layering them one on top of the other in a circular pattern, forming a glass rose. I've made so many of these lately, I've gotten fast and pretty good.

I used to only make my flowers for Tabra, for our secret garden off our rooms in the palace. But now they're for something more helpful.

As soon as I finish and clasp the already air-cooled glass in my hands, I don't turn off my power, but instead push my light into the glass. As I do, I picture Zariph Cainis's face and where he would likely be this time of night, which is in his tents. Possibly with his zaripha, Magda, beside him. I picture that, too.

The Zariph Cainis, the leader of their zariphate of Wanderers in Aryd's deserts, is an ally, albeit a reluctant one, pushed by his children and his desire for power into helping me and Reven and the Vanished. I am, after all, a queen. Of sorts. His people bowed to me, named me their ruler, making me a strong ally for him, too.

The glass changes and tiny versions of the space I pictured reflects in my flower. Cainis keeps the flower I gave him on him at all times, but at night, he sets it beside where he sleeps. I can see the lump of his form outlined in the dark that is illuminated by a single lantern.

I hold my flower out to Cain.

"Father," he calls.

No answer.

"*Father*." Cain's voice is sharper this time.

To give the Zariph credit, at that second call, he's on his feet, a wickedly curved knife in his hand, sharp-eyed gaze scanning every inch of where he sleeps for the threat that woke him.

"Down here," Cain says.

Behind him Tziah passes a hand over her mouth, hiding her grin.

"Your son is calling you, tesara," Magda mumbles sleepily from somewhere far enough away I can't see her.

Cainis swoops the glass flower up, holding it to his face so we see his features in each petal. "Cain?"

Who would think to use a flower as a portal directly to us? I've made them for all the spies I've sent off into the dominions to gather information. It turns out the Vanished blend into their original home dominions Reven rescued them from in ways we've found incredibly useful.

"It's me, Father," Cain says.

The zariph is immediately all business. "Did you get it?"

"Yes." Cain shoots me a wink. "We have the last amulet."

Sort of. We have the flute. We just haven't figured out how to pry it open. Smashing hasn't worked. Neither has any of our powers.

"Excellent." The tiny reflections of his face look satisfied. "We have heard from the last of the zariphates. All is prepared."

Prepared? I frown, catching similar expressions in the look Tziah and Vos exchange. I know Cainis has been reaching out to the other zariphs and zariphas around Aryd, hoping to gather more allies, but beyond that, we haven't agreed to a specific plan. The next step isn't so clear cut.

"When should we expect your return?" he asks.

Cain starts to answer, but I cut him off. "What is prepared?"

Cain and Pella share a glance, and I don't have to hear the next part to know I'm not going to like it. "What have you been holding back?" I snap at them, the burn of anger rising.

The zariph answers for them. "We will take back our capital city of Oaesys and return you and your sister to the throne."

I glare at Cain, who stares unrepentantly right back.

"Our queens did *not* agree to that," Horus reminds him.

We've had this argument way too frequently. All of us.

"You weren't there. Physically, yes. Mentally, no," Cain says to me. "Not really."

"But Tabra was." Horus is quieter, angrier now. "And they are *both* our queens."

I'm still snagged on Cain's words. Maybe I didn't do as well hiding my struggle with the Shadows as I thought. "I may have been…distracted. But I was here, Cain."

"I'm sorry, love," Vos crosses his arms, giving me a pointed look. "You weren't."

I glance from face to face around me. Was I really that bad?

"It's the right move, Meren," Cain says quietly. He sounds… tired. Of fighting with me? Of helping me? "You know it is."

Ever since the fight on Tropikis, they've been after me to make a decisive military strike and reclaim Aryd. They're not wrong that it would put us in a better position, not having to run and hide, and it would make it more difficult for Eidolon to attack. But what I keep pointing out, and what they don't seem to understand, is that he's so determined to free his mother from the amulet he wears that Eidolon won't hesitate to wipe out an entire city of innocent people to get to me and what I have—his Shadows and the rest of the amulets. Not to mention Tabra. He may not have made her power work to free his mother before, but I'm sure he still thinks he needs her.

I shake my head. "It's risking our people."

"The Celestial Alignment is in a little over two weeks. The stargazers are sure," Cain points out. "Even more reason to take Oaesys now. To be ready and operating from a position of strength when it does happen. It's time to make our move."

Hands on my hips, I drop my head forward. *Hellfires.*

"The Celestial Alignment?" Scoria's lilting voice interrupts the desperate thoughts swirling through my head.

"Who is that?" the zariph's small portal voice demands.

No one answers him.

"That's the second time you've mentioned it. Why is the Alignment important to you?" the giantess asks.

I sigh. "One of Eidolon's escaped ghosts told me that it has some significance." He did this while informing me of exactly what was trapped inside the amulets. "But the ghost told me I had to discern for myself why it was important."

If he knows what the Alignment has to do with it, so does Eidolon. And yet, many Alignments have passed since my ancestresses did what they did, and the goddesses remain in their amulets.

"I do not know about the connection to the amulets," Scoria says slowly. "What I do know is that all Imperium are at their strongest during that event. The Alignment opens a direct path to the Allusian heavens, from which they draw their powers—you included, young Queen of Aryd."

A few of the puzzle pieces snap into place. Is that how my ancestresses trapped the goddesses? They used the Alignment to bolster their powers? That would explain why Tabra couldn't free them before.

The question is, could she handle the extra power? My

sister's not ready. Her control is still limited, even after Scoria's tutoring.

Plus, if it was that easy, Eidolon would have released his mother by now. There has to be more to this.

"Eidolon has two of the amulets—Tyndra and Aryd," Cain reminds me. "All he has to do is release his mother, and the decision will be taken out of our hands. She'll come for the rest."

I know. My mind has been spinning with all of it like the vortex of the whirlpool of Mariana.

Hells. Eidolon is running out of time, too. That makes him even more dangerous. Threatening me like he just did was a risk on his part—he knows that. So why did he do it? Is he trying to make me come after him to get to Reven? Counting on my overwhelming need to save my bondmate to draw me in?

Curse the fates.

I look at Horus, then Pella, before finally landing on Cain. "Let's take back Oaesys."

14

MAKE HER MORTAL

There's no reason I should have woken up, except for maybe Vos's snoring behind me. The man sounds like a desert sandstorm when he sleeps. A glance around the camp shows him out cold, Tziah snuggled up against his back. The others don't stir, either.

It wasn't the Shadows that woke me. Not with Scoria here.

A small part of me—a very small part—almost wishes it was. Just for a second. So I could hear Reven's voice.

Stop. I think it to myself. Goddess, I can't believe I even considered it. *It was probably Vos.*

I'm lying on my side. The icy grasses crackle around us as the breeze rustles through them and a shiver racks through me. Vos makes a windbreak out of ice at night, but it only helps a little.

At least this is the last night like this. Tomorrow, we start gathering with our allies.

I pull my legs up to my chest and burrow into the animal pelt covering me. Closing my eyes on a sigh, I reach for sleep. At the low growl that rumbles directly above my head, my eyes snap back open.

Actually, just for a second, I debate keeping them shut and pretending I didn't hear it. But I've come across too many monsters lately to believe that method still works. Not like it did when I was little and afraid of all the things Omma warned would come for me, and I would hide under my bed at night.

I force my head to turn very slowly to look up...directly into the gaping open maw of the grass monster Mimick had become.

Except she's not the same.

This cursed woman is no longer made of grass, but of darkness, and her new form has finally awakened.

Just like in the Shadowood, this darkness is something else, slick and oily like tar. Similar to my attempt at making two bunnies, strings of drool-like shadow drip out of her mouth, connecting the teeth inside.

My heart decides it wants nothing to do with this situation, lodging itself halfway up my throat. The Shadows are locked down, thanks to Scoria. How am I supposed to stop Mimick again? I barely survived the first encounter.

I try to call out. But the only sound that comes out of me is a hoarse squeak.

Where is Scoria? Why doesn't she feel this thing's presence if she feels souls? Oily shadow drips onto my face and runs down my cheek.

"Help!" I'm yelling inside my head, but the cry won't come out.

"We can help you, love." The voices of Eidolon's Shadows knock around inside my skull, all of them speaking as one, in unison.

I should be shocked at hearing them again after days of silence. I should be asking myself where Scoria is. Instead, their offer slides through me, tempting. Maybe I can use them...

"But you have to ask us nicely."

Forget that. I'd rather be eaten by the monster above me.

"I die, you die, assholes."

One of the Shadows *tsks*. *"Someone got her fire back. The mouth on Reven's princess,"* he says, almost like he's speaking to the others, and I can picture them all there, hazy versions of Reven and Eidolon, nodding to themselves and agreeing they should do something about that. About me.

*"Maybe we can make Mimick a deal. Trade being trapped inside you for being inside her now that she's made of shadow. She might help us. After all…*you *did this to her."*

A drop of the drool lands on my neck, rolling under my top, between my breasts, and then down one side of my ribs. Gross. I can't even squirm.

"Go ahead." I'm calling their bluff. *"Show me what you can do."*

Except, instead of the words sounding in my head, they come tumbling out, over loud and gibing.

Oh shit.

Mimick doesn't even hesitate. She lunges at me, jaws snapping. I roll, but don't make it far, tensing as I wait for the violent pain coming my way. Except nothing happens beyond an arrow flying overhead with a telltale whistle. It doesn't strike anything, that's for sure.

I roll back to find her still above me, still trying to bite me, but it's like something has a hold of her body and only those snapping jaws can move. The rest of her is arrested above me.

"I've got her," Scoria calls out in the dark, her voice coming from somewhere above the monster trying to eat me. "Move."

She doesn't have to tell me twice. Using my elbows and my feet, I scramble backward, out from under Mimick until I'm far enough away to be able to safely get to my feet.

The others are all close, Horus with his bow dangling at his side. I'm guessing he's the one who shot at her.

"Kill it," Eidolon's Shadows snarl in unison. And that rage, the same as the last time I faced Mimick, bubbles up from within me, spewing hatred through me with the force of an avalanche. *"You know you want to. Save yourself."*

"Quiet," Scoria snaps. Not at me, not at Mimick, but at the Shadows.

Inside me the Shadows cringe away from her, the sensation

like bugs moving through my gut as they crawl deeper inside me where they hope she can't get to them.

She lost control of them? How? When?

"Meren, we must try to help her."

What? "How?"

"Prepare to follow my instructions." Scoria's voice is as calm as I've heard it in three days.

Me, on the other hand? I would really love the luxury of losing it. She wants me to use Eidolon's powers on Mimick? I'm not ready for this. Then again, when have I had a chance to be ready for anything I've done since Reven kidnapped me from our palace?

I know I'm risking Eidolon getting to me again, but I have no choice. I tap into his power, yanking on the cold inside me. A gentle purple light illuminates the darkness and reflects off the oil-slicked monstrosity in front of me in hideous ways.

"What do I do?" I ask Scoria.

"Draw on the darkness around you." Scoria's voice gentles even more, like she's afraid I'm going to run away screaming or something. "You know the difference now."

I do. She's shown me how to *feel* the darkness, to recognize a simple shadow that merely fills the holes the light forgets to touch. Those kinds of shadows are my safe haven, a source of camouflage, protection, and even comfort, and always have been.

Meanwhile, any Shadows that have a soul attached—like the ones inside me, like the monster trying to kill me now, and like I imagine even the ghosts of Eidolon's past—have a different feel. Colder, emptier, and angrier.

Scarier.

I feel for the darkness that is warm, safe, gentle.

"Now," Scoria continues. "Gather that darkness and feed it into her. Think of the way you tried to do with the bunnies. What you're giving Mimick is something of *this* world to latch on to, to fill her up. The darkness she's made of right now, that's not from this realm. That comes from the hells."

I ignore the shiver of fear that slithers down my spine, allowing it to pass through me and out through my extremities. I let myself feel it and then let it fade.

Then I focus.

Closing my eyes, shutting out the monster that Scoria can at least hold still, I picture the way I put holes in the top and bottom of my bunny to drain it and make a mold. Only this time, instead of draining it, while the oily shadows drain out the bottom, through the top I fill her with the kindness of the shadows of my mortal world.

She lets out a whine that turns into squealing, a terrible, piteous sound of inflicted agony. My hands shake, but I don't stop.

Please let this work.

Given the results with the bunnies, I'm pretty sure it won't.

"There you are," Scoria says. Not to me, I don't think. She sounds…pleased.

Pleased is good. Right?

"Seven hells, Meren." I hear Cain's whispered words close by.

"Should I stop?" I ask without opening my eyes.

"Stop." Only that voice is not the giantess, or any of my friends.

I allow my eyes to flicker open and gasp.

What I've made is not a monster filled with a new kind of darkness. She's still all things darkness, but smaller, with a womanly body and the delicate features of a beautiful face, including lips tipped into a small smile. I can't tell if it's tinged with gratefulness, or sorrow.

My chest swells with a confidence I haven't had for so long that I started to forget what it felt like. *I* did that. I fixed her, helped her. I controlled Eidolon's power the way I wanted, and it felt…good.

"Mimick?" I ask.

"Mimick," she repeats her name, the lilt giving it a different meaning. Not a question like mine, but a statement. I glance behind her at the faces of my friends who stare at her, awe in their eyes.

"I'm sorry," I say to her. I hope she knows that it's more than those two words.

I'm sorry that she was cursed the way she was. I'm sorry that she was controlled by her own bones, carved by her lover into a horrendous instrument. I'm sorry Mimick and Aesthetus were willing to cause others' deaths just to keep each other, just to survive. I'm sorry I brought the Shadows down on her.

She tips her head to the side. "I'm sorry." Again, her tone gives the words a different meaning, and I know what she's saying in return. She's sorry she attacked me. She's sorry she attacked all the other people who happened upon them. She's sorry she forced me and the Shadows to defend ourselves the way we did.

I nod my own forgiveness.

Mimick holds out her hand and a rustling across the camp draws my gaze. One of our packs shifts and moves until it tips over, the flap opening, and the flute bursts out of it. Too fast for us to stop, it flies into her hand.

I jerk toward her. "Wait! We need that—"

The bones change before my eyes, becoming shadow like her, almost like a fine dust, to be absorbed into her own body. She's taking back herself.

When it's gone, something shiny drops to the ground.

Savanah's amulet.

Holy hells, she did it. She got it out for us.

"Need that," she says.

It's more than I would have expected from her, honestly. She could just as easily have taken it to one of Eidolon's souls, given where she's probably headed now that she's sort of whole again.

I look at Scoria. "What happens now?"

Scoria is difficult to make out in the dark, her rocky black body blending into the sky. But I think her lips form into a kind smile, and I can imagine how it must feel as a recently deceased soul to come across a creature that is so strong and confident to lead you to the next phase. I'd think it would be comforting. Especially after the disorienting task of dying.

"Now I can take you to your bondmate, who has already moved on to the afterlife," Scoria tells Mimick. "Do you want that?"

It's a question I never would have imagined asking bondmates. That bond was formed for a reason—to find each other in their afterlives. Of course she would want that. Except, after what they became, what they did together that left them worse monsters in their souls than on the outside...maybe she wouldn't.

"Want that," Mimick says.

Scoria shifts to standing, towering above us. "Then I shall take you."

Take her to the burning lands, the land of souls...

Souls.

I frown.

Souls. I turn the word over in my mind. There's something there.

Then what just happened hits me from a different angle.

"Don't leave!" I call out.

I think Scoria raises her eyebrows.

I swallow, but I need to ask this. "Can you come find me after you take her?"

She considers me for a moment. "More souls?"

I nod. It will take a day or two to get in touch with our allies before we can even gather. In that time, I could do what I'm thinking. I could leave this world knowing I'd done one thing good. "Many more souls."

"We don't have time," Cain reminds me.

Only if what I'm thinking works, it's worth taking a little extra.

Another pause. "Don't leave here until I return," she says. "This will take me a few hours at most."

Then in a mirage-like haze, she and Mimick fade away together.

The second she's gone, I face Cain and the others all lined up behind him. "If we're going to take Aryd back and hold it, we need as many allies as we can get. And I know how to add to our numbers."

And right a wrong.

15

MAYBE

"I don't like this," Tabra says. She hasn't stopped saying it all the way from Savanah, through the portal to the Arydian city of Poileh, and deeper into the desert between the city and where Cain and Pella's zariphate is camped. "I know you have to go. I get it. But I'm not useless anymore. I can—"

Her hands suddenly light up, the purple glow not as obvious in the sunlight, but there all the same.

"Easy," Scoria murmurs.

Tabra closes her eyes and the glow disappears. Same as me, emotions are still setting her off, even after Scoria's tutoring.

She opens her eyes, then wrinkles her nose in frustration.

"Aryd needs at least one queen." I say it softer than I would have for anyone else. I don't point out that this is what I was born to do. To handle the dangerous tasks in her place. She hates those reminders.

"I do not like this, either," Bene grumbles.

I don't have Reven's shadow pocket to hide Savanah's amulet in, and damned if I was going to let anyone else risk themselves wearing it. But now that I have it around my neck, at least I can hear Bene again.

I don't translate for the others, ignoring his glare.

Unaware, Tabra huffs out her own frustration through her nose. "If we need to negotiate for allies, it should be me. I've been trained for that."

Fair point. "We won't be able to negotiate until I clear the Wildernyss temple of what Reven did." Of the souls he trapped there in shadow.

Assuming I can even get into that temple.

An eager spark lights Tabra's eyes in a way that reminds me of…me. "Okay, so you go first, but don't destroy the portal you make here. I'll wait. When it's safe, bring me through to talk to Trysolde and Istrella."

She isn't going to let this go. I can see she isn't. "I think my stubborn is wearing off on you," I grumble.

She perks up. "Really?"

I roll my eyes.

"That's not a good thing, T," Vos tells her.

She laughs, still eyeing me. "But you're going to let me."

I sigh. Really, I shouldn't be the one granting permission here. I've been wondering when Tabra will figure that out. That no matter who bows before me, *she* is still the Queen of Aryd. Firstborn and, as she said, better prepared and trained to rule. I was only trained to pretend.

Someday soon, I know she'll realize it, too. She'll stop asking and start commanding. Part of me dreads that day, because how can I protect her then? But part of me is waiting, because that's when I'll know she doesn't need me anymore. Not really. She'll be ready.

"Fine," I say.

"Are you certain?" a Shadow slithers into my mind. I stuff him back down. Scoria's tutelage has helped me contain them better. But shut them up? Nope.

Unaware of that too, my sister shoots me a triumphant smile.

I rush to add, "But until we come get you, hide out of sight behind that dune." I point.

"I can do that." She immediately starts plodding through the sand.

Pella follows, tossing an, "I'll keep her safe," over her shoulder.

Hakan watches her go, not that she sees.

Pella is more than capable of protecting my sister, but I look at Bene anyway.

He gives a growl that raises the hairs on my arms. In Savanah, he stayed in his raven form to keep from alarming the guards. Here, he can't be full-sized, or he'd be spotted on the horizon. Instead, he's taken on the form of a massive wolf made of sand but more vicious than any real wolf could ever be. *"You left me behind before and unfortunate events transpired."*

"Please?" I ask him.

After giving me a hard look, he snorts his displeasure, blowing up sand, but prowls after her all the same.

Hakan stays with us. I know it's killing him not to follow Pella, but for now I need him more.

I immediately get to work making yet another portal. It doesn't take me too long until the workable wall of glass stands firm and tall in the sands. I place my hand on the smooth surface, but don't press my power into it. Not yet.

I look over my shoulder. The trapped shadow souls should be sleeping, like the ones in the Shadowood did, but just in case, Cain, Hakan, and Vos already have their glowing hands up. Horus has an arrow nocked. I glance at Scoria, who nods. The plan is to get me in and set before she comes and forces the shadows to wake up and come out to play.

Goddess, please let this work.

The glass goes opaque, then it clears and I'm looking into a room I've been in only twice before—the Wildernyss temple, with its simple gray granite stones, arched doorways, and scrolling carvings across the mantle of the door. There are other adornments, but I can't see them clearly—or any of it clearly—because the glass on the other side is cracked, distorting the view.

"At least you didn't shatter it completely, Mer," Cain says

with forced cheer.

"Though you may be torn to ribbons getting through," a Shadow offers.

I grit my teeth, reminded of a Wanderer proverb. *In the moments of your successes are sown the seeds of your own destruction.*

I'm pretty sure I'm looking at a seed right now.

Eidolon was coming at us through the Wildernyss temple portal the last time we were here and I shattered the side we were standing on, apparently cracking this one in the process. No one can pass through it in this state. They'd come out the other side ground up bits of flesh and bone.

"Can you fix it?" Vos asks.

"We'll see." Leaving one hand in place, holding the portal open, I use my other to call sand to me, heating and molding it the way I did earlier. Then, I carefully press the molten liquid into the cracks. It's a painstaking process, moving little by little. When I'm done, I sit back on my heels, having worked on the bottom portion last, and stare at my patches.

"Good job," Cain says behind me.

I hum vaguely. "The question is will it work without maiming or killing anyone who passes through."

A flash of movement out of the corner of my eye is my only warning before Horus jumps through. He does it so fast, I gasp, certain I'm about to see him sliced all to the hells.

"It works fine, domina. You did well."

He's still whole. Unharmed. I could shake him. "Goddess help me, Horus."

His gaze softens, the lines around his eyes easing. It's not the first time I've caught myself pretending he could be my father who died before I was born, and this is a moment between father and daughter.

He reaches out a hand to beckon me through. "I'm your bodyguard. It's my job and my honor." Throwing my arguments to Tabra in my face.

"If you die for me, let it be doing something less foolish and more honorable than that."

"If I did not like him, I would question his methods," Bene comments from back in the dunes where he's tucked.

"I knew you'd try it on your own." He smirks, the lines bracketing his mouth crinkling. "Sometimes you have to be saved from yourself—"

"Never mind," Bene says. *"His methods are sound—"*

Darkness, slick like tar, curls around his stomach and yanks Horus off his feet.

"Shit!" Vos yells as he runs through the portal, Cain and Hakan right behind him.

I thought the shadow souls here wouldn't have awakened yet, that we'd have time to get us all in place on the Wildernyss side first. It took Reven's presence to stir them to life in the Shadowood. Or...maybe it was Eidolon's Shadows' presence? After all, Mimick woke. But none of those have been here. Why are they awake?

"They're alive—"

The voices of the Shadows inside me cut off abruptly. Then Scoria's voice sounds from on the Wildernyss side beyond the portal room. "Here!"

Wait, what? She was supposed to give us time to get set before meeting us in the temple.

I jump through, shutting the portal down behind me before I sprint into the darkness toward her voice. The hairs on the back of my neck, my arms—hells, all over me—stand at attention like I'm too close to Hakan when he's using his lightning, and I swear I can feel the breath of a trapped soul breathing down my neck.

Any second, I expect a tar tentacle to knock me off my feet or drag me away. But none do, and I burst into the massive sanctuary with buttressed ceilings soaring overhead. Enough room for Scoria to stand within, though she's flattened several wooden pews. The others are with her, including Horus, though I have no idea how he got free.

"I have them frozen," she assures me. She doesn't look away from whatever she's focused on behind me. "Your turn, Meren."

That's the first time I've ever heard strain in the giantess's voice. Is she shaking a little?

I spin around and feel the blood drain from my face at the sight of a wall of darkness. Within it, at least twenty different faces writhe and press outward, trying to get free of Scoria's grip.

Reven did this.

To protect us—to protect *me*—Reven did something he despised himself for. He did the same thing that happened to Mimick.

I fixed her. Can I fix twenty?

"Hurry," Scoria urges, even more strained.

I close my eyes and picture everything the way I did when I helped Mimick, then I move from soul to soul, like they're in a queue. I know one is healed when Scoria says, "Good," from behind me, and I move on. Not once do I open my eyes. It's not worth the risk that I mess this up in my usual royal fashion.

The cold of Eidolon's powers coursing through me turns more intense with each passing moment until it feels like I'm sitting in the middle of Tyndra, allowing the miserable cold to turn me into an ice princess, except I'm freezing from the inside out, until I'm shaking with it so hard, my teeth are chattering.

But I don't stop. Not until Scoria grunts. "That is all."

I manage to stay standing as I open my eyes to the sight of twenty shadowy individuals, now shaped like humans.

Great mother goddess Nova, I did it.

I honestly didn't think I could. Or that it would work.

Did Reven feel when I released these souls? Will he know what it means? That he can let go of the guilt he carries for what he did to those people?

Faith flickers inside me like the flame of a dying candle. If I can do this here, I can do it in the Shadowood, too.

That's right. Release those souls and build yourself an army. One that can't be killed. One loyal to you.

I still. Was that the Shadows? Did one get past Scoria? Only, it didn't sound like them. I look up at the giantess whose obsidian eyes glint back at me in the lantern light, but she's not acting like she noticed anything.

Which means it wasn't Shadows.

I think over the words, the idea. *My* idea. Building an army isn't the worst thing I can think of. Scoria will come if it means saving more souls.

The question is, will the others let me go? If Reven were here, he'd support me. Though probably not if I told him the part about the army being immortal…and loyal to me.

I'll just keep that to myself.

16

ALLIES

I stand up straight, head held high, as the King and Queen of Wildernyss cross the sanctuary toward where Tabra and I stand together, the rest of our friends positioned behind us in a line of solidarity.

"There really are two of you," Istrella says in her soft voice as they stop before us.

"I truly worry for Wildernyss with leaders of such... observation," Bene murmurs in my head.

I shoot him a warning look before Tabra and I share a quick smile. Istrella searches first my sister's face and then mine, before shaking her head. "Fascinating. I've spent time with Meren, but I honestly can't say which of you is she."

Should I raise my hand? Curtsy? Do a dance so they know it's me?

It probably doesn't help that Tabra and I are both dressed similarly. While we've been waiting for this royal reunion, Vos managed to find us warmer clothes. Wildernyssian clothes, which will be fine for Tabra here, and hopefully warm enough for me where I'm going.

Bene leaves Tziah's side to prowl to mine, nudging my hand.

"The Devourer," Istrella murmurs, eyeing my sandy friend still shapeshifted to a massive wolf—jagged teeth and all.

Trysolde gives me a sharp look. "You must be Meren."

"He is merely speculating," Bene says to me, unimpressed.

I lay a hand on his withers, rough against my flesh. "Bene protects both of us now, but yes, I am Meren."

"Of course you are." With a smile Istrella approaches to give me a kiss on each cheek, then turns to Tabra. "I am glad to see you are healed. Meren told me of you."

"Thank you for your concern." Tabra is everything sovereign that I struggle to be—posture perfect, gaze clear and steady, hands folded neatly before her, expression both welcoming and unreadable. "Meren also told me of *your* help, and I thank you for that as well."

Trysolde, silent and watchful, glances beyond us into the chamber we came through. I don't have to turn to know what he's looking at. No doubt Trysolde is studying the blue glass of the portal just visible through the doorway, originally made from Aryd's Lazuli Desert, though now shot through with white thanks to me.

I clear my throat. "I'm sorry about…"

I trail off. How exactly do I apologize for the list of transgressions? In the end, I wave behind me at the room. "All of that."

Istrella shakes her head. "You gave me Trysolde back, and now you've fixed our portal to the other dominions."

Aryd may have many, one in each of the major cities, but the other dominions were only given one each. Istrella somehow managed to get her hands on a second, secret one that we also smashed in the same moment of self-defense, but a single point of entry to each dominion was the original idea.

Trysolde puts a hand to the small of his queen's back. "After helping to free me from the spirit that possessed me and reuniting us, all the thanks should be ours. We can never hope to repay you."

I let out a silent breath of relief. Just the opening we need.

I look to Tabra, who was already in perfect princess mode, but for the first time, I see our grandmother, the previous queen, in her, as her eyes take on a more calculating light. "We need allies," she says, before I can. "I am here to negotiate terms."

Neither king nor queen seems too surprised by that, except Istrella shoots me a questioning look. "Not you?"

I shake my head. "Tabra is the true Queen of Aryd, and I have to be somewhere else."

"Anything we should be aware of?" Trysolde asks.

"Tabra will fill you in. I hope to return before nightfall."

"You're leaving now?"

I glance at the snowy skies outside the wide-open windows of the cathedral. "We're running out of time."

All of us.

"Then I hope you return successful." Trysolde gives me a formal little bow, which Istrella echoes with a regal nod.

"Me, too," I murmur, then shoot a glance at Horus and Bene.

Ignoring Cain's scowling face—because we already all argued who should go and he wasn't picked—the three of us walk through the portal, right into the chamber in the temple of Tyndra, a place possessed by more shadow souls Reven ripped from their bodies.

And these ones we already know are very much awake.

But we also know what to do with them now.

17

AND ENEMIES

I stand at the edge of the Shadowood, the air around me dead calm, and wait for Scoria to arrive. Apparently carting souls around means it takes longer for her to teleport.

Sun sparkles off the white snow- and ice-covered lands, the blinding light giving me a headache that's stirring my stomach in bad ways. Hours spent flying here on Bene's back is not the most comfortable of rides.

Just when I think the discomfort will become unbearable, Scoria arrives. Not wanting to waste time we don't have, I forget the pain in my head and the rolling in my gut and get to work. Scoria has control of the Shadows, and now I'm together we face the murky wall that hovers in the trees.

The now-familiar oil-slicked, tar-like darkness of the hells, of trapped shadow souls, is a solid barrier around the southern tip of the forest where we stand. I can no longer make out the details of the towering, red-barked trees that form the woodland that I hope still lies behind this veil of… wrath.

Eidolon's Shadows stir within me. They feel it, too.

"Mother Goddess," Horus whispers at my side, horror in the words.

"Do you still wish to do this?" Bene's voice rumbles through me.

I reach behind me to pat his nose with gloved hands. Scoria

and I can do this.

For just a second, I wish Reven was here, doing this with me.

You can't let him be a distraction. Not now.

If not now, though, then when? When do I get to make saving him the priority? I can practically hear his voice telling me that my people come first, stopping Eidolon comes first.

I know that. It still doesn't make it easy.

"Scoria, will you be able to hold them all?" I ask her, forcing myself into the here and now. She struggled with the number in the Wildernyssian temple. This is more.

Her rocky eyes scan the wall of shadow before us, as if she's counting each of the souls within. "I do not know."

I go to take a step, but Horus jumps between me and the trees, arms wide like he's corralling a herd of horses, expression daring me to try to dash around him anyway. "We should wait for nightfall, domina." He glances over his shoulder. "You'll need to harness more darkness to deal with this. Won't you?"

"The Wanderer is of the right mind," Bene says. *"And you should rest more."*

More waiting. In the freezing cold. Sure, that will be restful.

Without a word, I crawl back on top of Bene, who lifts a sandy wing so that I can sit beneath it protected from the wind, like a chick under a mother hen. After a second, Horus climbs up and joins me. "Tabra will need time to settle everything with Wildernyss anyway. She'll forgive the delay."

I snort. "Tabra will. Cain…not so much."

He was pissed enough at being left behind, but as the son of Zariph Cainis, he holds a position worthy of negotiation. He also knows the plan for taking back the city of Oaesys better than I do. He needed to stay behind to talk with our new allies. Pella and Hakan had already returned to the zariphate, or I'm sure Cain would have insisted on her doing the talking and him coming with me.

Horus chuckles. “I was worried he was going to follow us anyway.”

Me, too, actually. It’s exactly something I would do, and Cain and I are a lot alike that way. Plus, he’s followed me to this very forest before.

A gust of wind sneaks under Bene’s wing and I shiver, which makes the Devourer adjust to block it better. *“It is, perhaps, advantageous that Tziah was there.”*

“Tziah?” I ask.

Horus makes a sound that might be a laugh and I turn a questioning frown on him. The creases around his eyes deepen, dark-brown depths twinkling with humor. “They’ve been close since Tropikis.”

I guess so. “Well, if anyone can talk Cain down, it’s Tziah.” Even without the ability to speak.

“She does have a knack for that,” he agrees.

Have Cain’s affections moved on? I don’t think so, but maybe I’m too close to see it clearly.

Cain was mine—my best friend since childhood, my own personal hero, the person I have always trusted most. And he confessed his love for me, asked me to marry him. But Reven and I…we were always supposed to find each other in this life.

I think I’d be thrilled for Cain to find happiness elsewhere. But am I just telling myself that to ease my own guilt for hurting him?

I’m not sure yet.

I don’t realize I sigh until Horus pats my hand. “My sister used to sneak off into the desert most days for, as she called it, ‘a little peace and quiet,’ which I never understood, because she did this when the zariphate was camped during the heat of the day, and at its quietest with most everyone asleep.”

That he can talk about the sister he lost like this, with a smile hovering around his lips… I wonder if he realizes. “Did you ask her?"

"Yes. She said she'd sit by the wells or oases. That clear waters made for clear thoughts." He chuckles. "Never did figure out what that means."

"It makes sense to me," I tease.

Horus lifts his eyes heavenward. "Of course it would. You're just like her."

He's never said that to me before. "I'm honored you think so."

"Without knowing her?"

I grin. "I assume you mean I remind you of all her best parts, of course."

Horus chuckles, and my heart warms despite the freezing cold seeping through my layers of clothes.

I'm starting to recognize those rare moments of pure happiness life gifts us. I've learned these past months to never turn away from even a smidgen of happiness. To absorb it and carry it with me into the dark days that I know are ahead, like a small flame that can never be extinguished inside my heart and soul.

Scoria shifts, the snow and ice crunching under her rocky feet from outside Bene's wing, followed by the sound of her muffled voice. "Someone else is..." Bene lifts his wing, and I can see her searching around us, obsidian eyes sharp. "I sense a presence—"

A flash of cold hits my blood a second before a swirl of smoky shadow spirals up from the ground. When it dissipates, a man stands close to the walled-off forest. I jump off Bene and run for him before I know what I'm doing.

"Domina!" Horus yells after me.

I don't stop.

Neither does Eidolon.

Even when Bene takes off behind me with a roar, the bloody king makes no acknowledgement of our presence, focused on what he's doing. The night all around us sucks through him and into the forest. Faces and arms and legs punch from the wall, thrashing as though in pain. Hundreds of them.

Faster than I could ever have believed possible, he feeds the warmth of shadows from this world into those trapped in the hells' limbo. More than that, though. I stumble to a stop, watching as a misty form lifts off the king himself, different in color. Is he…is he feeding parts of his own flesh to the shadow souls?

"Meren!" Horus shouts behind me.

Eidolon's blazing turquoise gaze collides with mine. Before I can do anything, he offers me a sly smile and disappears behind the thick swirl of night churning around him.

It blasts outward, consuming us. I plow through the fog of darkness, trying to get out, unable to see and feeling my way through as his Shadows inside me scream out for their maker. Not even Scoria can keep them silent when he's this close. I'm about to ignite my own access to his power when the night suddenly turns crystal clear, and I'm standing not even ten feet away from the evil bastard who has wrecked my life since long before my birth.

And behind him stands an army.

My army.

Except, they look…different. Not like the souls I've freed. These are more human, more alive, as though their bodies exist just beneath a layer of darkness.

What did he do to them?

And why are they all focused on me, furor written across their creepy-as-hells features?

Whatever the reason can't be good.

"Scoria?" I toss back over my shoulder.

"I cannot. They are something else now."

Bene plows through them from above, snapping them up in his maw only to have them disappear.

"Thank you for showing me the way," Eidolon says with so much self-satisfaction that my hands fist at my sides, impotent rage pumping inside me, making my ears pound.

Anger rips through me. "The hells I did—"

With a flick of Eidolon's hand, the army vanishes.

18

ONE SHOT AT THIS

Eidolon offers me a smug smile. "You think I haven't been watching?"

The rage I'm clinging to stumbles. He's been watching me? How?

"Thanks to you, I can make even more use of the souls I took from the burning lands." He tips his head. "And the ones I'll drag out of your body."

Before I can reply, Scoria roars. Now she knows. He just confessed he's the one who has been breaking the natural laws of death and stealing souls. The giantess disappears only to reappear before us and scoops Eidolon up in her rocky hands.

I wait for him to shadow himself away, but he doesn't. His eyes bulge and he shouts, pounding ineffectually at her fist.

He can't disappear. He can't shadow. Her magic holds his soul *here*.

But I can't let her kill him. Reven is still in there.

Darkness lashes out at her in a bone-smashing strike to her side. Razor-thin shards of obsidian rain down over me and Scoria howls a sound that is both anger and agony. But she doesn't let Eidolon go.

"Meren!" she shouts for me.

"Help her, for goddess sake!" Horus yells.

I'm pulling Eidolon's own power through me in an icy rush, which is when it hits me. Scoria can't defeat Eidolon, not even with my help. The most I can do is try to protect her, stop him from hurting her, until she and I exhaust our powers and he breaks free and kills us both.

I could free Reven, though.

I'm not ready. I know that. But when has this world ever waited for me to be ready?

"Story of my life," I snarl under my breath, even as the cold of Eidolon's power builds within me. "Bene, help her while I work!"

I hate closing my eyes, but I have to. I need to hold onto my control, and I can't do that if I'm panicking.

A thundering crash sounds overhead, followed by a new roar of pain. Bene, I think. I can't look.

Instead, I picture my own band of darkness, pulling from the warmth of the shadows now left behind in the Shadowood. The forest has been freed from that army of trapped souls, and the darkness that remains isn't the cold kind. The place was Reven's safe haven. Mine, too. In my mind's eye, my band of shadow is not hard and rigid, it is soft and flowing, like a ribbon of silk. But I don't use it to bind Eidolon.

Instead, I shove that ribbon right down the bastard's throat.

I know it worked when I hear his yell cut off on a gurgle. I reach into his hollow, frozen form and I search for Reven, for the only spark within a soul so evil it's like light can't exist within him anymore.

Another series of crashes sounds from overhead, followed by more roars—goddess, I hope Scoria is weathering this beating with Bene's help. Horus grabs me, whirling me out of the path of something that is falling around us.

For just a hair's breadth of a second, I lose focus, but that's when I see it. The spark in the darkness.

Got you.

I try not to choke on my own relief as a sob wells up my throat. I focus on wrapping my ribbon around Reven's shadowy shard of soul and yanking him out of the king.

Another blast booms overhead. Only this time, rock doesn't hit me. A terrible *thud* followed by a roar directly over me tells me Bene is protecting me now instead of Scoria. Standing over me and Horus.

"Work with speed!" he yells into my mind.

My hold on Reven slips a little and he falls deeper into the king. "I'm not letting go," I grit out through clenched teeth and wrap my own shadow around him tighter.

Then I pull as hard as I can, a shout punching out of me with the effort that feels the same as pulling on a rope. Until, finally, he comes up and out of Eidolon in a violent slide. Whatever force was dragging against me suddenly releases and I fly backward, landing on the icy ground, my head hitting so hard it leaves me dizzy.

I push myself to sitting as another boom of sound is followed by a terrible silence that descends all around us. Even the winds stop blowing.

"Eidolon's…gone," Scoria says, her voice thready. "I couldn't…hold him any…longer."

Vaguely, I'm aware that the giantess is struggling, weakened by that encounter alone. But I can't focus on her because I'm staring at the form laying not five feet from me.

It's Reven…but not.

With limbs shaking from the effort, I crawl across to him. A mere shadow of the man I love lays on the ground, his vague features etched from darkness, eyes closed, thick brows drawn in a frown as if he's in pain.

I don't know how the king makes his shadows real when he sheds them or…

I vaguely remember something about how over time Reven became more real until he was a fully formed man.

Bene, who is shaking from whatever Eidolon did to him, moves from standing over me to reach for Reven with a single talon, but his claw goes right through the shadowy form that is my bondmate, coming away with nothing.

Holy hells on fire.

I don't know what being yanked out instead of deliberately shed did to him. Maybe he's just a shadowy ghost, one Scoria will have to take to the afterlife. We'd find each other again someday, but that's better than giving him back to the king. I don't think I can make myself do that.

We can't move him unless I can make him real. We don't have time for that, though. Eidolon could return for him at any second.

"Reven," I whisper. He doesn't so much as twitch.

I take a breath. *I can do this. I have to do this.*

I close my eyes again, hands hovering over him. Combining what Scoria taught me with what I think Eidolon did to his army, I create that band of warm shadow again and picture it connected to him, my heart to his. I feed myself into the rope of shadow, into Reven. The part of me I give him is the part of me that *is* him. It's a piece of the scars made of shadow in my side, the darkness that he used to heal me after I accidentally skewered myself with my own glass spear.

I remember every word of the healing ceremony he performed on me that night. I don't have the elements to sacrifice, but I say those words anyway.

"I invoke Tyndra, goddess of strategy and the stars." My voice shakes with the effort of what I'm doing. I don't care. I keep going. "With no sacrifice but the fire in which all others will be made, I ask for your blessing of knowledge as we carry out the rite of shadow healing."

Behind my eyes a flicker of fire ignites orange in the dark. I crack open my eyes to find Horus there with one of the lanterns we brought.

"Keep going," he says.

I don't dare look at the form laid out on the ground before

me. I swallow. "I invoke Tropikis, the goddess of healing and life-giving plants. To you I offer a sacrifice of water."

Horus digs a canteen from his pack and the drip sizzles as it hits the fire inside that lantern.

"Darkness is about compromise, filling the voids left by light. I ask that you let it lead to blessings." I pause. Trying to remember what came next. "I invoke Wildernyss, the goddess of the arts and storm. To you I offer a sacrifice of wood."

Horus looks around almost frantically, then pulls one of his arrows from the quiver on his back and holds it over the flame.

"I ask that you let this man's loyalty to the shadows that bind be a blessing in your eyes."

The next one is easier. "I invoke Aryd, the goddess of magic and the moons. To you I offer a sacrifice of land."

Holding the shadows steady with one hand, the sparking heat of my own power flows through the other and with a flick of a finger, sand chips off Bene and floats through the air to the flame. "Patience is the truest form of blessing, as is a life tied to shadow. I ask that you bless him with this gift."

A life tied to shadow is already his. Mine now, too, but I'd give everything for him. For my Shadowraith.

"I invoke Mariana, goddess of music and the sun. To you I offer the sacrifice of metal."

Horus flips the arrow and puts the arrowhead over the fire.

"Passion is the beating heart of life. We ask that it be a blessing to all who dare let it in."

Now I move. I lean over the form on the ground but only dare to lower my gaze to him once I'm close. He's still a mere shadow. Nothing has changed. This isn't working. Stomach clenching, I lean over and brush my lips to his in a chaste kiss, then gasp.

Because he's warm, as if I'm touching flesh.

I whimper with the desperate longing I haven't let myself indulge in.

"Finish it," Bene urges in a thready voice.

I take a shuddering breath. "I invoke Savanah, goddess of fertility and animals. To you we offer the sacrifice of air."

I gesture around us, and Horus waves the lantern in the air. After the seventh time, I signal him to stop. "And I ask you to bless our sacrifices with our vow of honesty."

Honesty. Last time Reven and I both had secrets, but this time…

"With these sacrifices and rites," I say, "I bind this man with shadow and flesh."

Pain rips through my side and I pitch forward. Blood splutters out of my mouth onto the snow-covered ground, a red stain in the white. But I force myself to keep going. Even hunched over, I let the darkness be taken from me as parts of him start to turn more real.

"Damn you all to the hells," Eidolon's voice booms out.

The whispers of his Shadows turn into a ruckus inside my head. I look up from under Bene's belly just in time for the king's first volley as Eidolon wields a scythe made of shadow, slicing through the air at Scoria and Bene both.

Fear has me reaching out like I could stop it from happening. "No!"

With the last of what I have left, I shadow us all away from here. Not far away. We disappear and then reappear a second later on the other side of where that swinging scythe was headed.

I flop to the ground as unconsciousness tries to drag me under. Vaguely, I register that Eidolon has disappeared again. Maybe he didn't expect me to have learned this much about his power yet.

He's gone, but not for long.

"Have to get…" My mouth won't work, and goddess forgive me, my eyes won't stay open. "Get us away."

That's the last I remember.

PART 3

BLOCKADE

19

THE ONLY WAY TO CONTAIN HIM

I blink my eyes open, the fuzzy haze of sleep still clinging to me, making me sluggish. The air on my skin is the first thing I notice—dry and hot. I frown. Last I remember I was in Tyndra. It takes a second to realize I'm in a tent in the desert. The space surrounding me is lit by fire in a single brazier, and the sound is crackling at me in pops and hisses.

How did I get here?

"Back in the doomed desert," a Shadow's voice mutters.

That familiar sound is all the trigger I need.

Reven.

His name, my memories, finally penetrates the fog of confusion weighing me down.

The Shadows are murmuring unintelligibly as I force myself to sit up, wincing at the pull to the reopened wound in my side, which I ignore. Vos, Cain, Pella, and Tziah are here with me, watching me carefully. "Where is—"

Reven.

He's lying on a blanket not far from me, eyes closed.

Reven.

Alive. Whole. Breathing. Here with me.

He's here with me. *Mother goddess.* I go lightheaded and breathless, and my ribs can hardly contain my heart, which wants to fly to him.

Before I consciously decide to, I'm on my hands and knees

crawling to his side. "Reven?" I wrap my arms around him, pressing a kiss to the corner of his mouth. "Reven?"

Only his arms don't come up around me. He doesn't turn his head to capture my kiss. I sit back slightly. The turquoise of his eyes is still hidden from me.

I toss questions over my shoulder. "What happened? Has he been out this entire time? Is he hurt?"

Before anyone can answer, I'm shaking his shoulders. "Reven. Wake up."

He doesn't move. I grab his hand in both of mine, holding it to my cheek, rocking a little. Out of control, I know, but I've been so horribly desperate for this moment and I never quite believed it was possible. "Reven, I got you out. You're safe now. The king doesn't have you anymore."

"Looks like you don't have him, either," the Shadows taunt.

One offers a satisfied murmur. *"Maybe he's dead."*

"Maybe you broke him," another slides in.

Scoria's not here to silence them, so I drop them back into that deep well inside me, mentally bricking over the top. In the subsequent silence, I look at the others and lock gazes with Cain, who is standing at the back of the tent in wary silence. "Is he hurt?"

Vos is the one to shake his head. "As far as we can tell, he's sleeping."

Sleeping. The part of me that loves him fiercely wants to let him sleep as long as he needs to recover from whatever happened to him when he was trapped in there. But the part of me that is a princess commanding too many to count tells me we need him with us now.

I give him another shake, with no effect.

I try to find him through our bond, search in darkness, but it's still quiet and empty at the other end.

Oh hells. What if I didn't get all of him out? Or he's trapped in his own mind by Eidolon somehow?

"Where is Scoria?" I ask. "Has she tried to help him?"

The gaping silence that seems to fill the tent tells me all I need to know. "What happened?"

Vos is the one to answer again. "The fight with Eidolon hurt her. She's returned to the Land of Eternal Death to recover."

"For how long?" I need her here for Reven.

Goddess, when did I become so selfish? The others must be thinking the same thing because no one answers.

"Are Bene and Horus..."

"Right as rubies," Vos says.

At least there's that.

Not sure what else to do, I put my hands on Reven's face and draw on the king's power, eyes closed, and search for any sign of darkness within him.

Nothing.

I don't know if I should be relieved or more worried. I sit back, feeling helpless, and look at the others. "What do we do?"

Vos and Cain both shake their heads. Pella looks away. Tziah's expression is all sympathy.

I lean down and press my lips to his again, fully this time. *I'm here,* I think at him. Maybe he'll feel our connection. *I'm here.*

He stirs slightly.

Finally. A small sob of relief wells up as I wrap my arms tight around his neck.

Only he forces his hands between us and pushes me off him.

We stare at each other for a silent, stunned beat.

"Reven?" I whisper. "Thank the goddesses."

Going up on his elbows, he swivels around, looking for something.

I frown. "What—"

He snaps his gaze back to me. Not relieved. Not happy. Not elated to have been freed from his prison.

His eyes narrow, glittering in anger and growing suspicion.

I reach for him, and he lurches back. I pause, hands in the air, not touching him. "What's happening? Talk to me. Are you okay?"

He stares at me for forever, and then his gaze shifts a beat before a purple light penetrates the dim of the room, and I know it's coming from him.

"No. Wait—"

Reven disappears. I squeak my shock only to yelp again when he reappears.

My shadowraith looms over me.

"Give them back!" Reven growls in a voice that he's never used with me before, not even when he kidnapped me. This is pure Eidolon.

Cain is at my side in an instant. "Something's wrong." He grabs me by the arm, tugging me to my feet and behind him.

Reven doesn't even acknowledge him, jaw clenched, glowing hands raised, eyes hard. "You stole the Shadows. Give them back."

Wait. I *stole* the Shadows?

I stare at his face. At the face of my bondmate who is supposed to know me above all others, love me above all others. My giving him myself worked, making him whole again, but in those turquoise eyes all I see is...

Suspicion.

Blame.

And not one single ounce of recognition.

I lick my dry lips. "Reven, it's me. Meren."

His brows snap lower over his eyes with a wrath that storms at me. "Is that supposed to mean something?"

My heart cracks open like a precious porcelain vase hit with a hammer, and I gasp.

"This is bad," Vos mutters.

Reven doesn't even pause. "If you don't know the evil you're dealing with, you're in grave danger. If you do…"

The implication hangs in the air. If I do, he'll think I'm just as evil, taking the power for myself. What in the seven hells happened to him?

Reven clenches his teeth. "Give. Them. Back."

A rope of darkness lashes out and around my waist, jerking me from behind Cain and across the large tent space to his side. He wraps one arm around my ribs in a bruising grip and grabs me by the jaw with his other hand, not gently. I wince as tears spring to my eyes.

He's my bondmate. Even if he doesn't remember, shouldn't he feel that?

Cain starts toward us. "Let her go—"

"Don't!" I call to him, then say to Reven, "You can have the Shadows." He's going to take them anyway. Maybe if I give them to him, offer them up, it'll help?

"Are you sure?" Thanks to my own riot of emotions, I'm losing my grip on them already.

"You're better at controlling Shadows than he ever was," they say.

I know something is off about their words, but I have more dire things to deal with.

"Shut up," I mutter.

Reven's face hardens, eyes going flinty with determination. "This is nothing personal," he says, then presses his mouth to mine.

His body is rigid against me, every sinew tight with anger as his lips force my mouth open wider. Then something pours down my throat and I can't breathe.

I cling to him, trying not to panic, even as my heart withers and dies. This will be over in a second. I know what he's doing. He's dragging the Shadows out of me and into himself, the same way I dragged him out of Eidolon.

I squeeze my eyes shut and try to help him, try to shove the Shadows up to him. Except they aren't moving. More than that, it's like they've grown claws and are digging into my insides to hold on. To not let him take them.

Agony lances through me. I'd scream, except the darkness shoved down my throat won't let me. The lack of air kicks in hard, my body cramping with the need to breathe, and I thrash in his arms.

I'm hitting him. Battling against him. He's going to kill me, but the Shadows won't come out.

A wall of water slams into us, between us, and the force of it throws Reven off me. I land in the sand on my hands and knees, dripping and sucking in air, trying not to pass out again.

"No!" Vos's yell has me jerking my head up in time to see Reven wielding another rope of darkness, fury-filled gaze still trained on me. He whips it forward, only ice hits him in the chest hard enough to knock him to the ground.

I shove up to my feet, but in a blink, Reven shadows away from where he landed to appear directly in front of me. Darkness reaches for me, but I jerk Eidolon's power through me so fast the ache of the cold spears through my head like an ice pick. Hand glowing, I knock back Reven's darkness.

A gurgle of water nearby, reminding me of a slowly rolling river, tells me Cain is going to drown Reven if he keeps this up. "Stop!"

My yell is for both men. But I stay focused on Reven, trying to quiet my voice. "We're your friends—"

"Lies!" he snarls, and tries again with the shadow, and again I knock it back.

I can't believe it works. Based on the shock that widens his eyes before his face pinches with anger, I think he can't, either. His time inside Eidolon must have weakened him or… I think the Shadows are helping me. I can feel them. They don't want to go back to him. Probably because they think I'm easier to control.

Reven tries again, but ice and water come at him from either side.

He slams up a wall of shadow around the two of us, cutting the others off, and for the first time it sinks in…

I might have to hurt him.

I *definitely* have to stop him before he does something he'll regret.

I let go of Eidolon's power and my own surges through me, hot and tingling, and I wrap a bubble of sand around him, trapping him inside. His darkness falls away instantly, but I don't stop. My power is painful, I'm forcing this so fast, but I have to, or it won't work. I flash-heat the sand and it turns molten red.

Something punches at the barrier I've created from the inside, but the malleable bubble only bulges with the impact. I need to cool it fast.

"Cain!" I yell.

Vos's ice will be too much and crack it. I need water. Cain must figure out that's what I want, because instantly, a gush of liquid douses the bubble, which hisses and steams so hard that, for a second, it's obscured from sight.

Goddess don't let me have hurt him.

I tried to make the bubble big enough that it wouldn't touch him, even anchoring the bottom of it under the sand in such a way that his feet wouldn't be near the actual glass.

The steam clears and a warped monstrosity of glass remains—one filled with shadow like billowing smoke. As I watch, the darkness rears back and pounds at the inside, and a telltale *snick* tells me it's cracking already.

There needs to be more to hold him.

I swallow.

He's going to hate me for this.

Dropping my own power, I draw on Eidolon's once again and close my eyes, breathing in through my nose and out through my mouth. Centering myself, I picture the veil Reven used to protect the Shadowood. I imagine the walls of shadow that Eidolon used to trap me in the palace when I was there with him for months, so thin they were invisible. I remember those and surround the bubble of glass with them. An added layer of protection. If the glass fails, the shadows will hold.

The Shadows feed me more of their power. Suspiciously obliging bastards, but I'll take the needed boost for now.

Hopefully just long enough to get through to Reven.

"Merciful hells, Meren," Cain whispers from somewhere to my right.

I open my eyes, and I know it worked. I know because the smokey shadow from inside my glass cage isn't gone, but has settled around Reven's feet, swirling like a brew in a cauldron.

Reven prowls back and forth inside the glass like a caged predator, face all things wild violence, sparking eyes promising terrible retribution.

I swallow, trying to hold the disintegrating pieces of my heart together. I got him out. We were supposed to be together again. Nothing about this is right.

Taking a shaky breath, I approach the glass. He stops prowling to stand before me, glaring.

"I will let you go when I have your promise to stop fighting us," I tell him. "We don't want to hurt you."

His gaze narrows. "Then give me the Shadows, and I'll be on my way."

"I tried."

"You fought me."

I shake my head. "*They* fought you. I don't want them." Is that true, though? Was a part of me holding onto them? Why would I do that?

"More lies." He slices a hand through the air in agitation.

"Reven—"

"*Stop* calling me that. My name is…" He trails off, then puts a hand to his temple, wincing hard. "My name is…"

Wanting to soothe him, help him, I place my hand against the glass, but he lances me with a look laced with warning, so I drop it back to my side.

"I won't take my maker's name," he says. "I don't have a name yet."

Goddess, he truly remembers nothing. "His name is Eidolon. Yours is Reven."

He cocks his head, that intense searching thing he does so familiar I have to brace against the impact of it. "How do you know I come from Eidolon? Did you see me escape him just now when he shed us?"

I barely contain my gasp. He thinks he was only just shed?

"Where is the mortal husk of the king?" Reven finally looks away, searching all around us only to scowl, thick brows practically meeting over his eyes. "This isn't Tyndra. Where the hells did you take me?" He whips his gaze back to me. "And how did you interrupt the shedding to steal his Shadows?"

Oh my goddess, I can't. How do I explain everything that…? I just can't. I glance at Vos, then at Cain, and neither will meet my gaze.

Cowards.

Tziah stands, hand over her heart, tears turning her black eyes glassy.

Swallowing, I open my mouth, only I don't even know

where to start. I close it and think, then try again. "You were shed from Eidolon over twenty years ago. At that time, you successfully took his Shadows and ran from him. Hid. You called yourself Reven, became the Shadowraith."

I can see from the stubborn set of his jaw and the skepticism searing his eyes that he's not believing a word I say.

"You saved my life using a shadow rite." I lift my shirt to show him the now-seeping wound in my side. Seeping because I gave him some of those scars back, enough to reopen the wound partially. "My scars are like the ones on your wrists—"

He glances down. His expression goes blank, then lifts his hands to show me. No scars. "Try again."

Goddess damn it. "They must have healed when Eidolon took you back."

His lip lifts in a sneer. "If Eidolon managed to take me back, he'd have all his Shadows, too. Instead, *you* have them. I can feel them inside you."

"*You* gave them to me," I insist. My voice is rising, desperation turning it high-pitched.

"I wouldn't. I have to destroy them. I saw the king's book, the way his soul has become more and more evil over time—" He stops, then leans closer, forehead almost to the glass. "I do remember you."

I scoot closer, too, hope a pinpoint bright in the darkness of despair inside me. We are separated only by glass and shadow, eye to eye.

Except his gaze turns predatory. "I saw a memory of Eidolon's, only it's..." He gives his head a shake, though his gaze never leaves me. "It's hazy. Your name is Esha. I can see you on the day of your coronation with your twin sister, Lillnya. *You* did this to him, to us. Both of you together. You took something from us that wounded Eidolon so badly it shattered his soul. He's evil...*we* are evil...because of you."

"No! That wasn't me. Or not..." How do I explain any of this? He already doesn't believe me. "It was my ancestress. That was centuries ago."

"More lies." Reven pounds a fist against the glass, which *snicks* again, weakening more.

The Shadows inside me cackle in delight. *"He doesn't remember you,"* one crows. *"How delightful."*

20

GAMBLE WITH HAPPINESS

"I need those Shadows back." Reven snarls the demand with a look that flays me.

"So you can kill them." Defeat lays heavy in my voice as I take a measured, heavy step back. "I know. It didn't work before, so you tried to end your life—"

"Stop! Just stop."

I blow out a breath, trying to keep my heart from shriveling up and dying. "We are—"

"I don't want to hear another word. Give me the Shadows and I'll go."

"Go ahead, Meren," Shadows say. *"Try to give us away."*

I happen to glance down, which is when I see it. The slight tremble to his hands. My heart shrivels even more. He's afraid. As much as Reven lets himself be afraid. I'm pretty sure if I tell him we're bondmates now, he'll lose his shit completely.

What do I do? What do I… "I'll make you a deal."

"I don't make deals with liars."

Frustration cuts through some of the heartache, followed by a flash of familiarity. I'm dealing with the stubborn, suspicious, secretive, inclined-to-be-an-asshole version of the man I first fell in love with all over again. The version of him that kidnapped me and dragged me through the Wildernyssian forests all the way to Tyndra. A sense of calm drops over me.

I know *exactly* how to deal with him when he's like this.

In control of my emotions and my power again, I shove the darkness inside me back down into silence, then cross my arms and raise my eyebrows at Reven, unimpressed. "Call me a liar again, and the deal is off."

"I told you. No deal—"

He cuts himself off as I shoot him a smirky, extra-sweet, know-it-all smile that I know gets under his thick skin.

"You think this is funny?" he snaps.

If I wasn't desperate, I'd laugh. I guess it still works. "I have your Shadows, and I've shown I can defend myself against you." I let that sink in a moment as he glares at me. "So, of the two of us, I'm in the greater position to negotiate."

A long bout of silence greets that statement.

"Tell me I'm wrong."

More silence. I don't look away, waiting for him to give up and acknowledge I'm right.

"What do you want?" he asks, grudging and resentful now.

Easy question. "I want you to stay with us. Either until your memory returns, or until you realize that I'm not lying to you."

"Give me the Shadows back, and—"

I shake my head. "Uh-uh. If I do that, then you'll just take them and run."

Reven lifts a single, disdainful eyebrow. "I guess we're stuck then."

I roll my eyes. How did I fall in love with this version of Reven the first time? He is so…maddening.

"I guess *you* are." I spin around, my back to him. I take a step, then another, and keep going.

"Stop," Reven calls out, voice loaded with resentment.

I pause, then slowly turn to face him, eyebrows raised in extra-patient inquiry. "Yes?"

He sets his feet, arms crossed. "What's your offer?"

"Stay with us for…a month…" A month should get us well past the Celestial Alignment. "Give us a chance to prove we're not lying. That you are our…friend. After that, if you still want to go, we won't stop you."

I'll follow him wherever he goes, but he doesn't need to hear that now.

"With the Shadows."

I hesitate. Should I cross my fingers behind my back while I semi-lie to my bondmate's untrusting face? I know my Shadowraith. He's going to try to take his Shadows and escape every chance he gets. I'll just have to trust that we'll both figure things out by then. "With the Shadows."

"I'm here as your prisoner?" he asks.

"As our guest." I wave at his glass prison. "I'll let you out of there if you promise not to hurt anyone."

"If I'm attacked, I will defend myself."

As if anyone here would try that for so many reasons. "Fair enough. You won't be."

He stares at me. Goddess, I've missed that look so much. Missed *him* so much. All I want to do is wrap my arms around him, lay my head on his shoulder, and let go. Breathe again.

But I can't.

I could howl at the unfairness of it all. Cry for days and not run out of tears. They're burning the backs of my eyes, threatening to fall. But weakness is something I can't show right now, can't *be* right now. Not when he needs me to be strong.

Pella rushes up, Hakan and Horus hard on her heels. They must've heard the ruckus. All three skid to a halt when they see Reven.

"Mother goddess," Pella whispers.

Curse the fates and the goddesses and everything else that has brought us here.

Reven's stare turns harder, if that's possible. "I don't know what game you are playing, and I don't trust you."

"You wanted to kill me. So we're on equal footing there."

"Two weeks," he says. "I'll give you two weeks."

Less time. Damn. I should've asked for two months. Tabra would have negotiated better. I can see in his face that he's already thinking he won't really give me that long.

"I have your word you'll stay?" I ask.

His entire being goes still.

Ha! Got you.

Even without his memory, I *know* Reven. I know that honor is big with him, and he won't give his word unless he means to keep it.

"Two weeks."

"Two weeks while you give us a true chance." I nod. "Your word."

He glances away. "Fuck," he mutters. And I almost smile, because that's so *him*. Then his focus is back to me. "Agreed. You have my word."

If he wasn't watching my every move, I'd pitch forward and take a long breath of relief. Two weeks isn't much—we have a king to fight, my kingdom to win back, and goddesses to release… or not. At the very least, a decision to make about them.

But I have the truth on my side.

Reven will either remember, or he'll see the truth for himself. He has to.

"I've given my word," he says, voice all-things-commanding king that he came from. "Release me."

It takes only a few seconds of effort before the glass and shadows containing him fall at his feet at my command.

He stares at me, and I stare at him.

What I want to do, so despairingly it's like a sandstorm inside me, is wrap my arms around him and hold on tight until he remembers. Obviously that's out.

But I know Reven. He's part of me, mind and soul. I need to trust in that.

In him.

In who he is at his core.

In who *we* are.

Even if it means going against every wish in my heart crying out that he's back, he's not really. If I was the one in his place, I'd want to feel safe first. Build trust second.

Hells, that's how I learned to love him in the first place.

I force my feet to take me away from him, give him space. "Get Reven set up with his own tent," I say to the others.

Cain clears his throat. "I'll assign guards—"

"No guards." A glance over my shoulder shows me Reven tensed at those words, but eases slightly, watching me with wary distrust. Trust is going to have to be entirely on my side. "We are not going to treat him any differently. He's one of us. He just… needs to remember that."

His features twitch with the tiniest hint of emotion. Too fast for me to catch the nuance. I pray to Nova that it's the first glimmering of second guessing what he thinks he knows. But probably it was just suspicion.

"Follow me," Cain says in a voice full of his own doubts.

Vos and Pella go with them.

Reven's gaze doesn't leave me until he's through the door. The second he leaves my sight, I sink to the ground, my shaky legs unable to hold me up any longer.

Drawing my knees up to my chest, I wrap my arms around them and squeeze my eyes tight, trying to hold another wave of feelings, knowing if I don't, the Shadows will ooze back up. Reven is safely back with us, I try to tell myself. The rest we can figure out, but he's here. He's here with me.

Only he's not. Not really.

The reality of that settles deep.

Tziah sits down quietly beside me and wraps her arms around me. I lay my cheek on her shoulder…and cry.

And ignore the voices.

21

TIME IS NOT ON MY SIDE

"We should delay this," Vos grumbles as we make our way through the camp.

"It's a seriously bad idea," Cain says at the same time that I say, "We can't."

We really can't. But by taking Reven back from Eidolon, I've stirred up a scorpions' nest. There's no way the king won't retaliate. We take back Oaesys now, or never.

"Never" loses us allies and a strong position of power from which to fight.

We've already taken more time than I like. Once Reven agreed to my deal, we immediately moved the entire zariphate to the Crimson Desert, hiding within a deep canyon as guests of the largest of the zariphates that normally roam these lands. From here, we'll stage our attack.

All sense of scale is lost in this place as the canyon walls climb and climb and climb above us from where we stand beside the wide Aramithra River that carves through the land. We're camped along the waters, nestled among red-rocked columns, arches, balanced boulders, and cathedral-like spires that should look huge, but are dwarfed by the canyon itself. Our tents, dotted over a wider, flat area, are meant to blend into the tans and whites of the Singing Dunes to the south, so here they pop against the background like maggots on a log.

To say I'm a nervous wreck would be an understatement.

We haven't seen Reven since we moved here. He's been holed up for two straight days in the smaller tent we gave him. The idea was to offer him privacy and space, but now it feels more like he's planning to avoid all of us until this is over.

Yet another thing Tabra would have negotiated better.

Every second of those two days, I've had to fight my own longing just to see his face. Even a glimpse. But I get the sense that he's testing us, and I won't force him. If there's one thing my odd family setup taught me, it's that sometimes loving from a distance is just as powerful.

"He's not ready," Vos insists.

No kidding. "I know he's not."

"*You're* not ready," Vos says more quietly.

Horus walks silently beside me. He's *always* beside me, now. A shadow I can't shake. I shoot him a sideways glance, but his expression reveals nothing.

I roll my shoulders. "I'm fine."

Vos slides an assessing gaze over me that I don't have to see to feel. "You sure about that?"

"Is making me say I'm not fine going to help anything?"

"Fair enough." But then, like a dog with meat still on the bone, he keeps gnawing away. "You need to make him fall back in love with you before we go attack the capital," he insists.

Has *been* insisting.

The last two days have really sucked.

"Does she really?" Cain grumbles behind us.

Vos shoots him a look over his shoulder. "Yes. She does. We need Reven on our side—"

"Vos!" I jerk to a halt hard enough that my shoes scuff the packed, red sand. Fast enough that Vos trips over himself a bit to stop with me.

"How?" I ask him.

He gives me a confused frown. "How what?"

I take a breath and lower my voice. "How am I supposed to

make him love me?"

All he does is look more confused. "You did it before. You're bondmates."

"I'm pretty sure if I tried to tell him that right now, he'd kill me, take the Shadows, and disappear."

Cain crosses his arms. "Maybe we should let him. I mean, not the killing part."

"Not helping," Vos snaps at Cain, then takes me by the shoulders. "Those feelings have to still be there, Meren. The bond makes sure."

A truth I've been holding onto with what little hope I have left in me that the fates can only be so cruel.

"The bond makes sure we find each other in our afterlives. That's not what this is." I tilt my head back and stare up at the crystal-clear blue sky. Is crawling into a hole and hiding until this is over an option? "I don't know how to *make* him fall in love with me."

There. I said it. Admitted my deepest, darkest fear. The one that's made it impossible to sleep, impossible to eat or breathe or think. That makes me a failure as a bondmate, right?

Vos drops his hands to his sides. "Meren..."

Behind him, Cain's expression is unreadable. I've always been able to read him. That I can't makes my already piss-poor mood even worse.

"I'm not saying I'm giving up on him." I could *never* give up on him. Not even after I take my last breath in this life. "But we've got to let him figure this out. And until he does, we're his friends."

I'm going to just let myself love him—even if that means giving him space and time I don't have—and let him figure out his half of the equation. I don't care if the others don't agree.

I take off walking, catching both Vos and Horus on the hop again. Twice is a lot for Vos to be surprised in a row.

Cain is slower to follow, and that only adds its own layer of turmoil that I can't deal with right now. We get to Reven's tent, and I draw back the flap, stepping inside. "Reven, we need to—"

The words cut off abruptly at the sight of an empty tent. "Shit."

"He's gone!" a Shadow crows, the sound tiny from deep inside me.

"What?" Cain sticks his head inside and his immediate scowl is so harsh he reminds me of the gargoyles that are carved into high spots on our palace rooftops. "I *knew* it. I'll get guards—"

I grab his arm. "Don't. He's not a prisoner."

"He shouldn't be loose—"

I give him an exasperated little shake even as I'm trying not to panic. "Just…make sure he's okay."

Cain's lips flatten so much they disappear, but he nods and ducks back out to go search.

Which is when Reven appears in front of me in a swirl of smokey shadow. "I'm here."

Horus immediately puts himself bodily between us. Vos steps in front of him, right in Reven's face. I don't miss the assessing look in Reven's narrowed eyes.

They definitely aren't understanding the "he's still our friend" concept. It probably wouldn't help the whole lack-of-trust situation if I threw something at…well, all of them. At least Cain is still outside.

I maneuver around Horus. Vos is more stubborn, but after aiming a chilling look full of don't-mess-with-us at Reven, he shifts out of the way.

"Where were you?" I ask Reven, trying to project calmness that's far from the pounding of blood and worry in my veins. Only, I can't help but tack on, "You gave me your word."

"He's not your Reven," the Shadows whisper, barely audible. *"His word means nothing."*

His shoulders pull back, suddenly military smart in stance. "I wanted to see if you'd let me go."

I think about that. "And?"

"You're a woman of your word."

I narrow my eyes. "You were listening?"

He shrugs.

I should be treating him gently, wooing him, something. But irritation is what strikes first. I don't have time for games. "Well, at least we know *one* of us keeps our word."

The filter of self-satisfaction on his features disappears. "I didn't go, and I didn't hurt anyone."

There is no point to this argument. "We're gathering our allies to attack the capital city of Oaesys and reclaim our dominion."

He scowls, inflexible and immediate.

"Way to ease into it," Vos grumbles.

It's not like I can take it back now. "I would like you to be part of it."

"Why? For my power?"

I cross my arms, lifting a single eyebrow. "I'm pretty sure at the moment I can do a lot more with shadows than you can."

He grunts. Reven for irritated, the sound so familiar it makes me want to smile.

I soften. Slightly. "It's your choice. If you wish to be part of this, or even just observe, follow us."

Hoping like hells he joins us, without another word, I'm out into the sun, only to pull up short.

Tabra is waiting outside the tent with Cain. She's dressed beautifully in a simple garment fashioned after the Wanderers' clothing but made of something soft and silky and pale pink, her long dark hair swept up in an intricate braid, looking like a true queen should look.

I sigh. "I told you not yet."

"There are two of her?" Reven mutters behind me.

I glance over my shoulder. "One of me is already a lot. I know."

His glower is unimpressed and unamused. "Are you a shape shifter? Or just a liar?"

Heavens help us both at this rate.

"I—"

"She is neither of those things," Tabra says. "We are twin sisters."

He gives a jerking shake of his head. "There are no twins among the queens of Aryd."

My eyes just sort of roll themselves. "Eidolon keeps a lot of secrets from his Shadows. Get ready to find out just how much."

At the sound of the king's name, the Shadows flicker. Not as bad as they have been. I'm getting better at containing them, I think.

His jaw goes glass hard, a muscle ticking at the corner of his mouth. "Sarcasm is the strategy of...weaker minds."

I snort a laugh. "Says the man using sarcasm to knock me down a peg." I search his eyes for any hint that this back and forth between us feels familiar. It does to me. I sigh. "I missed you, even when you're like this."

Confusion flashes through his eyes. Confusion and...goddess help me, was that a hint of curiosity?

Cain's father and his closest advisors as well as the zariph hosting us here in the red desert are waiting. With a wave, I let Tabra lead the way and follow closely behind.

The looks the Wanderers give us as we pass by are all directed behind me. To say that everyone watches Reven like he's a wild thing that might attack at any second wouldn't be doing justice to wild things. Even the Vanished among our numbers eye him.

Eventually, Reven makes his way up to walk at my side, leaving the others to trail behind. He stalks along, hands clasped behind his back like he's trying to make sure he doesn't accidentally touch me, eyes straight ahead. He moves with the prowling gait of a predator, and my mind conjures up a swirl of shadow dusting up in his wake.

I'm used to being watched myself these days, anywhere I

go—with distrust, with curiosity, with criticism, with an eye to aligning with power. Particularly from Ledenon, Cainis's second-in-command. He used to watch Reven the way he watches me now. But even *I'm* getting twitchy under their gazes. The Wanderers were always wary of Reven, but now it feels worse than before Eidolon took him.

Or maybe it's me.

Or the combination of us.

Reven acknowledges none of it. Meanwhile *I* have to restrain myself from snapping at every single one of them as we go.

We make our way out of the camp and around two bends in the river, then down a small side canyon to the place I was told would be best for creating a portal. With every step I scour my mind for something, anything, to say to my bondmate who has no clue who I am.

I mean, what can I say?

Time. Just give him time.

I don't have time. I have two measly weeks, minus the two days already passed.

"Where did you go?" It's the first lame thing I can come up with.

He glances at me out of the corner of his eye.

"Just now," I clarify.

"As far as I could."

His voice sounds odd. Off. "How far was that?"

"Not as far as I would have liked."

Now I remember why I was constantly frustrated with him in Wildernyss. Cryptic is his style when he's not on your side. "What does that mean?"

"It means I should have just kept going on foot." He shakes his head, more at himself.

A Shadow crawls higher. *"He wants to leave you."*

I try to breathe around the pain of absorbing that hit.

I mean, I knew logically that's where he was. What's the

point of a bond if it does nothing to help him now? Help us both?

Our bond has failed me twice now. In my previous life, because one of us died and the other didn't. Because the bondmates clearly had some sort of falling out or they'd be together. Because Eidolon's soul should have recognized mine in this life, and yet the king is cruel. But is it failing me in this second life, too? With Reven?

Part of me wants to fight. Not let us fail again. But I can't deny there's also a small part of me that's terrified that our bond might keep breaking because it was never meant to be.

I try to listen to the first part and shake off the weight of those thoughts.

He couldn't shadow far. Please let it be because of the bond. Because of me. That deep down, he doesn't want to leave me.

He's not going to want to hear that, though.

I clear my throat. "It takes a while when your powers first manifest to learn the skills." I could barely move a single grain of sand when I first got mine. I'm not sure how it works for Reven, though. "It will come back to you."

"Not fast enough."

"Why'd you return? Why not keep going?"

"Because." He shakes his head again, lips pressing closed, and I know he's not going to answer anything he doesn't want to.

"Last time, you told me—"

"I don't want to hear about last time," Reven snaps.

Cain glares around me at Reven. "Watch it."

I wave Cain off. "This isn't about the past, it's about right now. The faster you relearn your powers, the better."

"That's my problem."

I swallow down a frustrated sigh.

"You could just give me what I want and just let me go, princess."

The Shadows chuckle in my head, delighted that he's being

this way. But it's his use of the nickname "princess" that has my shoulder blades grinding together in the center as a gasp drops from my lips.

"What?" he gibes softly. "Did I find a sore spot?"

Would he still learn to love me after I bury him to his knees in sand? I clear my throat. "You called me princess."

There. Rational, reasonable, the truth...maybe I've grown.

"So?" His slashing brows draw together slightly. "Aren't you a princess?"

"Actually..." Tabra, that most wonderful of sisters, says from ahead of us. "We are not sure exactly which of us is queen, and which of us is princess at this point." She offers him a smile that is pure Tabra—open, pleasant, and naively assuming the best in all people, actions, and outcomes.

Until her expression shifts subtly into something new. Fortitude. "But we really don't care about technicalities like that. As long as we put an end to Eidolon and reclaim our throne. Our people are what's most important."

"We agree on that at least," Reven says. His voice is gentler with her than with me, and a stab of jealousy earns me another chuckle from the Shadows.

My sister shoots me a smile, then turns away to talk to Tziah.

I lean toward Reven. "I reacted like that because you used to call me princess," I murmur in a soft aside. "First to bother me, like now. Later as a kind of tease, a joke just between us."

Our gazes connect and hold, and I search the depths of his eyes for any hint of what he's feeling. "I'm sorry. That you're going through this."

He doesn't respond, but he doesn't scowl, either.

"I don't think anyone has said that to you, but you should know we're all worried."

He huffs a bitter laugh. "That I'm a danger."

I shake my head. "We're not naive. Of course we know you have that potential. But we also trust who we know you are, and you gave us your word. Mostly, we're just hurting for our friend."

"Friend." He sounds the word out as if testing it on his tongue.

"Yes, friend. Maybe it would help to have time with each of us where you just get to know us again."

No reaction.

"After the evening meal, I could come to your tent—"

"No."

"Just to talk, I mean."

He slashes a hand through the air. "Let me figure it out on my own."

You love him. You love him. He sacrificed everything *for you. You bloody well love him, so you can't maim him.* I take a deep, fortifying—in theory, at least—breath.

Vos, behind us, clears his throat. "Maybe give us a chance, old friend."

"You're Eidolon's general. We *aren't* friends."

Reven is so sure. How can he be so sure when he knows we're part of his past?

Vos sighs. "Keep this up and you'll be right."

"It's fine," I say to all of them. "Think about how disoriented and wary you would be if you lost all your memories."

Cain stuffs his hands in his pockets. "He needs to not be an asshole, at least."

I glance from him to Reven, who, if possible, looks even more intimidating now, like he's contemplating shadowing Cain somewhere unpleasant.

"Maybe you can try for respectful asshole," I suggest.

Now *I'm* calling him an asshole. *Way to woo, Meren.* What did I ever do to make him love me the first time?

Reven flicks me a glance that is a thousand different things, none of which are amused or loving, then grunts.

I'm not sure if that's a yes or a no.

Bene chooses that moment to fly down, having apparently

shifted again into his smaller raven form, and lands on my shoulder. Not quite a raven, I guess, since he didn't use sand from the obsidian desert like he does when he wants to hide what he is.

Immediately Reven jerks back, the purple glow of his hands unmistakable in the candlelight. No one else bothers to try to stop him, though. Because it's Bene.

"Your timing could have been better," I say to him.

He plucks at Savanah's amulet chain around my neck. *"He might as well learn all the hardest to swallow things now."*

I glance at Reven, who is no longer glowing and is now leaning forward, confusion written all over his face. "What is that?"

Even the Wanderers around us, still resentful of the way they met Bene the night he trampled the camp and scared everyone half to the hells trying to find the amulet I was wearing, grin.

"That"—Cain leans around me to tell Reven with visible glee—"is the Devourer known as the Elimination."

22

GATHERING OUR ALLIES

"He's staring at you again," Pella leans over to whisper, not so softly, in my ear.

I don't need to look to see what she means. She's talking about Reven.

I can feel his gaze on me like a physical touch. What my heart wants to believe is that he's remembering, or intrigued, or feeling something. Anything. It's been three days, and at least he's stopped glowering at everyone, keeping it to only a frown here or there. And he *does* watch me. I take that as progress. So maybe…

But it's more likely that he's studying me. All of us.

The days have been taken up with preparations for taking back Oaesys. That's why we're standing here, still hidden in the Crimson Desert, today. Gathering *all* our allies together for one final run through of the plans.

Every single night, I've offered to spend time alone with Reven, just to talk, answer questions, or, honestly, so I could simply be with him. He's said no each time, and walking away from him has been so damn hard.

"He's just making sure I don't run off with his Shadows," I say to Pella.

Out of the corner of my eye I see Tziah lift her gaze to the sky as if seeking patience there.

Even Horus, positioned off to the side but close enough to

put himself between me and the portal, gives the tiniest shake of his head.

"Uh-uh," Pella says. "I accidentally brushed against him when I walked past to get to you, and suspicious is not what that man was feeling."

The sand I've been playing with while we wait for the next appointed time to bring the last group through drops to the ground in a hiss that draws eyes.

Pella snickers into her hand and Tziah has to button her lips shut so she doesn't let sound out with her own laugh. A small movement has me glancing to my right to find Reven frowning at me. He lifts a single eyebrow in question.

I'm not sure if he's asking if there's something wrong with my power, if he caught what Pella said and is taunting me, or if he's wondering why I looked his way. All three are equally viable.

A spark of mischief left over from the days when I was his ignites. "She said you're staring at me again," I call across to him.

He stills, then twitches a shoulder. "Given what you carry, someone should be keeping an eye on you."

Ouch.

"You are really bad at flirting," Pella murmurs.

"And you're a pain in my ass."

She pokes at my pile of sand with the toe of her booted foot. "At least I'm not trying to drown you anymore."

Like she did when we were kids, she means.

"Lucky, lucky me."

A shadow passes overhead, and several Wanderers around us sort of duck. On a cloudless day like this I don't blame them, but it's just Bene. Or maybe that's even more reason for their caution. He's full-size at the moment, watching over everything from up above.

Meanwhile, Cain and his father aren't far away, already escorting the group that came through before this to a different side canyon where we're all gathering. He and Cainis look like they're in a stand-off with the way their shoulders are pulled back and the glares passing between them.

I catch Pella's eye and hitch my chin in that direction. "Anything I should be worried about?"

She studies them long enough that I have to deliberately keep from tensing. "Cain would tell you if there was," she says. But her softly muttered, "I would, too," takes away some of the reassurance.

The brush of a hand against my arm tells me Tabra has come over. She was standing with Cainis earlier.

A bead of sweat is tracking its way down my left temple from lingering in the sun and having just built yet another portal. No doubt the special dress they trussed me up in—layers of black gossamer material with embroidered black silk flowers following the scalloped edges—is unattractively damp.

Meanwhile, Tabra, dressed the same but in blue with a diadem of copper and lapis lazuli in her braided hair, looks princess perfect. Did Grandmother teach her how to not sweat? Why didn't I get *that* lesson?

"Oh my goodness, Meren," Tabra murmurs. "The way he looks at you."

"*See*," Pella hisses. She is the least subtle person I've ever met. "Tabra sees it, too."

"If Achlys stared at me like that, I'm pretty sure I'd soak my underclothes."

Goddess give me strength.

"If Achlys stared at you like that, *you* could do something about it."

Tabra moves around to where she's facing me. "It's still *him*, Meren," she insists, keeping her tone soft.

Other than Tziah, Pella, and maybe Horus, no one else should hear. "I know that."

She's not finished. "He loves you, he just doesn't remember."

I'm trying very hard to hold onto that. "I can't force him."

She nods slowly. "It's obvious he wants you—"

"Even if he doesn't want to want you," Pella fills in.

I twist my lips together. "You'd know something about that."

Meaning Hakan, of course. I can't quite figure the two of them out.

"Low blow," she grumbles in a much less amused voice.

"The man hardly leaves your side. Please tell me you've at least—"

She shoots a quick glance over her shoulder to where the man in question stands off by himself, arms crossed. "None of your business."

All three of us swing our startled gazes her way. "You *have*!" I say.

"Shhhh…" She gives my shoulder a shove. "People are looking."

I'm not through with her yet. "How did you… I mean, without getting zapped?"

No one can touch Hakan without warning him. I saw a sand rat brush up against him once and the thing screamed like a mountain banshee, fur standing straight up on end, then keeled over, dead at his feet.

"Let's just say he can control it when he knows he has to," Pella says in a low voice, shifting on her feet as she glances over her shoulder, probably making sure he's not within hearing range.

"Control it?" I ask, teasing now, because thank the goddess we're not talking about me. "Or *control* it. If you know what I mean."

Tziah's shoulders shake, and Tabra at least manages to keep her laugh quiet.

"I think everyone in earshot knows what you mean," Pella grumbles, red seeping into her cheeks.

I have *never* seen Pella blush.

I laugh, and as I do, I glance up and my heart flips over.

Because Reven is watching me, but this time I finally see what the others must have.

Interest.

Not wanting exactly, but the curiosity I thought I maybe saw a flicker of yesterday. That's something.

Tabra tugs on my sleeve and points to a small sundial on the ground at my feet. "It's almost time!"

This is the last group we're bringing, and where they're coming from is the most dangerous location. "Maybe you should go with Cain—"

"It's Achlys," she says.

At least her hands don't light up. With Scoria, who was helping her maintain control, gone, she's been struggling. Not as much as before, but still. "What does it matter if you have your reunion here or safely not here?"

Tabra puts on her patient face. The one that gets every other sucker to do exactly what she wants. "Meren…even if things get perilous, you are not going to get in the way of me doing my part. Right? And I mean not just today."

Nope. "This isn't how it's supposed to work. I'm supposed to be the one at risk—"

"That's our family's *old* ways," she insists, stepping in closer, voice tight. "Ways that didn't work. Time for new ways."

I shake my head. Protecting Tabra has been ingrained in me from the second I was born.

"Sissy…" She's insistent, not letting this go.

Damn. "I will try."

"Not just try—"

I grit my teeth. "Fine."

"Good." She grins. "You won't be anywhere near me during the invasion, so it should be easy."

I roll my eyes. "Brat."

She perks up, giving a little bounce. "Me? Really? That's fun."

"Fun?"

"I never got to be the brat before. I might give it a whirl." Then she leans closer. "And he's still staring like he can't make himself stop."

Pella and Tziah both turn to look. Blatantly.

My skin tightens, prickling with awareness, heat flushing up my neck. I don't want Reven to stop. I want his hands on my skin, his lips claiming mine. I want to feel him *everywhere*. He's right here, with me, and so far away I want to scream.

I can do this without Reven. That's not the problem. I've been doing this without him since Eidolon took him away. But that doesn't mean I like to.

That's a problem for later. I'll try again tonight.

For now, I check the Shadows, but they're minding their manners. Or, more particularly, given who is about to come through my portal, I have them locked down tighter than the coffers under the Arydian palace.

I send my power into the glass and picture the sister portal all the way across Aryd. Not one of the known portals in the Arydian temples, though.

This one is mine. One I made and set there.

The portal flashes like lightning strikes, coming in and out in rapid blinks in a way I've never seen a portal do before. Ever. Then, for a split second, it settles and the glass shows me a different place. Somewhere on a high peak looking out over lush, flower-blanketed mountains. And a woman. She stands right in front of the glass, staring at me with wide cobalt blue eyes and deep red hair twisted up on top of her head. Except she's pale, her eyes sunk into her skull, cheek bones prominent because of her emaciated form.

Nothing about this—the lands, the woman, her style of clothing—is familiar. I've never seen this place. Given how portals work, how is this possible?

Immediately, Horus draws his bow, arrow trained on her.

She takes a jerking step toward me. "Wait—"

Reven grabs me around the waist and yanks me away from the portal. Immediately, it changes back to blood-red glass.

I don't know what to respond to first—what we just saw or the way he's still holding onto me. My body definitely wants to lean into his touch. The first he's initiated since we got him back.

Wait.

Protective.

He's being *protective*.

Of me.

That's how it started the first time—his caring for me. At least I think it did. He'd wanted to keep me safe.

A memory rushes at me. I see us caged on icy ground in Tyndra, me straddling his lap as we pretended for Eidolon's soldiers—who had no idea who they'd actually caught—that we were bondmates and couldn't keep our hands off each other. And that's when Reven had confessed that keeping me safe, protecting me, made the Shadows worse for him.

I can feel the bone-deep cold held off by his warmth below and around me, can picture the way Reven went still as stone when a soldier approached, eyes closed, not even breathing.

Before a Shadow had rippled across his face.

"I'm okay."

He doesn't let go. "You take too many chances with those blasted things inside you."

My heart dips. But no, that doesn't fit, either. That was reflex. Maybe his heart remembers, or his body, even if his mind doesn't. "The Shadows are all you care about?"

"Of course."

I snort. "Liar."

He gives a tiny growl, maybe warning, maybe irritation.

"Where *was* that?" Tabra asks in a shaken voice, jerking me out of the small moment where it was just him and me. "I don't remember anywhere that looks like that."

Get it together and focus, Meren.

"She saw *both* of you," Reven points out.

She did. She saw us and might have recognized us. Although…where in Nova was she? Nowhere I recognized. But that doesn't matter. What does is she saw.

Damn the stars. We have to move our timeline up. Otherwise, we risk whoever that was running off to tell someone what she saw.

We can't do nothing. I go to slip out of Reven's hold. He resists almost reflexively, and just for a second, before he lets me go, I remember what it feels like to be hauled up against him when he wanted me.

"He's never going to love you again."

Seven hells. Emotions always make my control slip a bit. I haven't had time to master as much control as I need.

Trying not keep my mind on the task, I slap my hand to the glass and try again, picturing the flowers and the mountains. Maybe we can stop her. Instead, I get the original location—my portal in Aryd. A solitary man with a short gray beard and a shiny bald head is waiting.

A man whose jaw drops as he takes in me and Tabra standing together. His gaze moves on to Reven behind me, and the man visibly swallows before taking in the rest of the people with us.

Our head vizier, Ishaf Andore, was a young man when our grandmother took the throne, with no idea that Omma, who was Grandmother's twin, even existed. He knew our parents before their deaths. He's known Tabra—and sort of me—since we were babies.

This is the first time he's seen us side by side, and he's only been informed of there being two of us for a short time. I can imagine it's a bit of a mind bender.

"Remarkable," he says, more to himself.

Tabra and I exchange a smile.

He shakes his head. "I was told you were twins, and that you've been switching places on us all your lives, but…" Another shake. "Which is which?" His gaze lands on the signet ring I wear on my pinkie before moving to Tabra's empty hand, and he beams at her. "You must be Mereneith."

Tabra shakes her head and pulls a long, thin chain from around her neck to show him her matching signet ring. Ever since our fight in Tropikis when the Wanderers and Vanished alike all bowed to me, she's refused to wear it.

I'm working on changing her mind.

Tabra tucks it away and then, if anything, her posture turns more regal, though I don't see how she adjusts specifically to achieve that effect. Omma definitely never got me to do that.

Ishaf's face creases with a smile, making it difficult to see his dark eyes under the droop of his lids. "Queen Tabra."

She gives a nod of her head.

Ishaf turns to me and his smile fades to something more like regret. He steps through the portal onto the rough, burnt-red ground and crosses slowly to stand in front of me, studying my face. "I wish I had known," he says quietly, just to me. "I could have helped you, domina."

To be called that word by him when it's actually meant for me…

I don't know why that, combined with his soft admonishment, sets off a longing in me for something that could never have been, thickening my throat. I shake my head. "No one but the princesses and queens who are twins, not even the generations in between, have known for a thousand years. It was just our way."

Understanding seems to ease the regret still tugging his lips down into his jowls. "Well," he says. "I guess I'll just have to get to know you as you now, won't I?"

I have always liked and respected Ishaf. "I would like that."

I glance past him into the empty room that is hidden just off the catacombs of tombs in the palace-temple. Not where Tabra will be buried—she has a special place waiting for her in the Tomb of the Sovereigns out in the desert near Poileh—but minor ancestors, cousins, aunts, and uncles who never ruled are in urns tucked into alcoves lining the walls I can see. "The others?" I ask.

"We didn't want to risk being caught meeting together." Ishaf walks through to stand before us. "But many are waiting for our queens' orders."

A niggling thought, like a worm burrowing through my head, is impossible to ignore. "How is that possible? Many? Achlys hasn't been with you long."

How Tabra's long-time personal servant hasn't been recognized in the palace is still amazing to me.

"Don't trust him," a Shadow hisses and slithers around inside me.

Ishaf, meanwhile, smiles. "We have been waiting for our queen to return to us since the day Eidolon informed us you were taken."

Beside me, Tabra gives a small, telling twitch. The most I've seen her break from her persona as queen since I first opened the portal to our allies. "Achlys?" she asks Ishaf. "Where—"

Ishaf pats her hand. "She is coming. She said she had one last thing to check." He looks at me. "Is it possible to keep the portal here open for her?"

"No," Reven says in a voice that brooks no argument. "That's a risk too far."

Ishaf, who knows all about Reven and Eidolon because Achlys told him, glances from him to me to Tabra, who has lost color in her face.

"You don't really get a say right now," I say to him under my breath.

Which, of course, makes him stiffen.

"I'll stay on the capital side and wait for her." Pella, who ignores a few spluttered protests from members of her zariphate, steps forward. "I've seen this side. I can bring her through."

After a second, I nod, then wave a hand to indicate Ishaf should follow. "The rest of the gathering is this way."

Tabra reluctantly follows me, glancing over her shoulder as we head toward that direction. Tziah takes her hand and that seems to help soothe her, the two of them moving ahead of me with Tabra less reluctant, though she keeps glancing back toward the portal.

The fine hairs on the back of my neck raise like I'm standing near Hakan, and I know Reven is following me.

"The way you acted when I first woke up, and the way the others are around us..." He says slowly as he comes alongside. "Were we in some kind of relationship?"

My feet just stop walking and I look directly at him.

I don't know what I was expecting him to say, something about the woman in the strange lands that I opened a portal to, maybe. Definitely not that.

Suddenly all the watching takes on a different meaning. Not intrigue. He's trying to solve a puzzle.

That's all.

Disappointment drags at my feet as I make myself keep walking.

For a few steps I debate what exactly to tell him, especially about being bondmates. But we don't have time and he's holding himself so stiffly, I know our peace is still fragile. "We were," is all I say.

He doesn't say anything for a long minute as he keeps pace, and neither of us looks at the other. Then suddenly he takes a deep breath. "That was another person," he says. "Even if it was me... I'm not that man anymore."

"Told you," the Shadows' tiny voices call out in unison, hardly audible from where I have them held.

I drop my gaze to my feet. That hurts.

"Maybe," I say. "But even if that's true, that doesn't mean we couldn't be...friends...again. Don't you think?"

"Maybe," he says. "You have the Shadows under tight control."

I have to blink at the sudden change in topic. "I try to."

"But they slip out."

I swing wide eyes up to his face. "You could tell?"

He gives a sharp nod.

I'm not sure if that's a good or a bad thing. "Could you… hear them?"

Reven stops walking so abruptly that I have to pull up sharply. "What?" I ask.

"They speak to you?" he demands.

He didn't know? "Sometimes."

He stares at me with an expression that is a wall of blankness to me, but I suspect he's fighting a bit of a mental battle. Probably wondering if he could take the Shadows now.

"Do they do more than that?"

Yes…and no. "Not if I can help it."

He frowns like he doesn't like that answer.

"If they get out," I tell him, "kill them. And if I turn dangerous…" I slide my gaze away from him, tracing a crack in the canyon wall. Would asking this of him be too much? Would it build trust? The thing is, without Scoria here, he's the only one who might be able to help.

"Yes?" he demands.

No good choices, but the thing is, even without his memories, I trust Reven to make the right choice, and he might be the only one who can. I look him straight in the eyes. "Kill me."

23

THE CRUX

"You want Meren to do *what*?" The snarled question, coming from the Shadowraith with no memory that he should trust anyone here, drops into a silence that stretches across the rest of us. I almost expect to see the red sands ripple in the wake of his voice.

There wasn't a tent big enough to hold all the leaders of our allies. Not just the zariphs and zariphas of multiple zariphates—the five biggest from each desert in Aryd—but Istrella and Trysolde are here, too, along with their most trusted advisor and general. So instead, we've gathered away from the camp in a side canyon, sitting, spread out on and among the rocks. We provided food, figuring we'd be here a while.

We were right about that. Night has claimed the skies.

Above us in the cliffs is a perimeter of guards provided by the zariphate that lives here. Their only job is to make sure no outsiders come anywhere near the canyon where we are, let alone overhears.

Especially overhears.

With this many, the possibility of a traitor walking among us is increased. Whoever that woman was in the portal doesn't help. And taking back Aryd is already complicated enough, involving a coordinated attack from multiple points. If a single group fails…

Omma taught me about warfare, strategy, and working

together with my advisors and military leaders, but only as much as a queen would need to know. Not enough to make me an expert. Still, I can see from the faces of the warriors here who *are* experts that I'm right to worry.

In order to be sure that no one group is stopped or sacrificed, our timing must be flawless. And that depends entirely on me.

"I think this *Reven does not listen so well,"* Bene comments.

I glance up to the top of the canyon where I know he's watching but can only make out the shadow of his full-sized form against the starry night sky.

"I don't like it," Reven says.

Vos, surprisingly, speaks up from my right where he's leaning back against a time-smoothed rock with one elbow. "None of us like it, my friend. But taking back the dominion is critical, and that will go best if we keep the elements of surprise and speed on our side."

Vos wasn't any more thrilled when I broached this idea than Reven is now, which is why I lift my eyebrows at him. He winks, acknowledging our earlier arguments.

Reven leans forward, only slightly, and at least half of the people watching him lean back. "You think the best way of accomplishing what you need is to send one of the two—or I guess three, if you count me—people who Eidolon is most interested in getting his hands on? More specifically, the one who carries evil inside her?"

Vos straightens off his rock.

Before he can lay into Reven, Tabra steps in spreading her hands wide. "There is no other way to get everybody where we need them, when we need them there. No one else does what she does."

Today she has taken the lead, Grandmother's training showing in how she's handled this group of powerful people and strong personalities.

Reven's jaw tightens, but he softens his voice. "It's too risky."

Tabra steeples her fingers before her, nodding with her eyes wide and serious. "We agree. Do you have a different solution?"

She says this so reasonably, as if she truly hopes he does, that Reven doesn't glower back but, after a second, shakes his head. He slides his gaze to Cain. "You also agreed to this?"

"Hey!" Without thinking, I hurl the hunk of bread I've been nibbling on at Reven's head. "I make my own decisions."

Shadow barely even twitches to knock the bread aside. It lands on a nearby rock.

"Feel better?" he asks.

"Not really," I mumble.

Then his brows lower in a dawning frown. "Did you throw a knife at me once before?"

Someone to my right covers a laugh.

A spark of hope has me curling my hands into fists at my side. "Do you remember?" I ask slowly. "Or do you just think that's something I'd do?"

"Both."

"Well, he's got that right," Vos murmurs.

I'm too busy trying to keep the spark inside me from blazing to a fire to glare at Vos. Does Reven really remember something? His remembering, even the tiniest bit, would change everything. I swallow. "The night you kidnapped me instead of Tabra, I chucked a knife at you." I shrug, trying for nonchalance I don't feel. "I was aiming that time."

"I see."

I frown. That's it? I can't help but push a little harder. "You deserved it. I promise."

Tabra gives a small groan, and I can practically hear her saying, *"You should be trying to win him over."*

Well, this is how I did it the first time. So…

Horus brings us back to the topic in his quiet way. "I will be with Meren in Oaesys."

Cain, meanwhile, says nothing. Not a single word.

"For once, I agree with the Shadowraith," Cainis speaks out. The man gets to his feet to turn in a circle, assessing reactions. "We should keep *both* our queens safe."

A small rumbling of agreement starts to stir among the people, and that uneasy sense I've been having about the zariph wriggles through me more insistently.

"That is a…kind thought," Tabra starts to say.

Unlike him, I do not get to my feet. "I know that city better than anyone here," I point out. "I've spent eighteen years of my life sneaking through the streets and in and out of that palace without being noticed or recognized, despite who I am. No one else here can say that."

Not even the others from Aryd. Not even Tabra. Maybe, just maybe, Achlys could, but she's not here yet.

"I'm also the only one who can make portals." That's my biggest point. If they don't let me go, our allies will have only two portals to get armies of fighters into the city with—the one in the temple and the one I made in the palace tombs. That means taking turns using them and funneling a lot of people through two locations.

It's too dangerous.

Reven's eyes glitter as he considers me in that intense way he does. Always has. And just like always, my belly turns squishy. Is he remembering anything else? Or maybe he's still thinking about me throwing that knife.

"But you're also one of only two people here who can say that they're the intended ruler of this dominion," he points out.

"Well…technically, I'm the—"

"If you say *expendable one* even one more time," Tabra snaps at me, "I swear to the goddesses, Meren, I don't know what I will do. But it will not be nice."

I blink at my sister, who never snaps, especially when in queen mode the way she has been all day. "But I am—"

"Tabra?" a faint call comes from the mouth of the canyon.

Achlys, with Pella on her heels, stops as soon as she's in sight of all of us and searches until she finds my sister's face in the crowd.

Forget keeping her queenly dignity—Tabra breaks rank entirely. With a small cry, she runs for Achlys, who doesn't wait, running, too. They collide into each other, and I think both whimper. Arms wrapped around waists and heads buried in each other's necks, they both stand there tightly entwined and breathing each other in.

The way I imagined Reven and I would be the day he returned to me.

I very deliberately keep from glancing his way.

Because Ishaf is near me, I catch the way his eyebrows slowly lift in what I consider a mild expression of shock. "I didn't know they were so…close." He glances at me. "How close—"

Before he can finish that thought, Tabra pulls back to frame Achlys's face with her hands—hands I can see now are trembling. "Thank the goddesses," she whispers, then crushes her lips to Achlys's in a kiss not just of reunion, but of visible relief, saying more with that one anxious touch than most communicate to a lover in a lifetime.

Everyone else looks away or lowers their gaze to give the two women privacy.

But I don't.

It's another one of those moments of joy to hold onto. For Achlys and Tabra. But it is for me, too, seeing my sister reunited with the woman that makes her happier than I've ever seen.

Finally, they break apart, murmuring soft assurances to each other. That's when I glance away, over my shoulder, because I can't help myself. The first person I see is Cain, who is looking away. Then my gaze snags on Reven, who is standing so still he could be a sphinx turned to stone.

He's watching me again.

The Shadows twitch restlessly in my belly…or maybe that's

my own restlessness.

Do something, Meren. Say fucking something.

I should flirt with him. I should beguile him, tell him that what I see between my sister and Achlys is how he and I love each other. Hells in a handbasket, anything.

But I don't know how, or what to say.

Flirting and beguiling aren't me. Not before and not now. I wasn't even trying then. I was just me, and he was just him… and together we were just us before I even had an inkling that I wanted or needed to be part of an us.

My gaze skitters away from his to land on my sandaled feet, my toes peeping out from under my black clothing.

Achlys abruptly steps back from my sister. "Where is he?"

We all glance around.

"Who?" Cain asks.

She's not listening as her gaze moves rapidly from face to face, from ally to ally.

"You." She points an accusing finger directly at Horus, and her face, trained over the years as a servant in the royal house of Aryd, curdles to something near hatred. Her next word is like throwing a match into a field of dried grasses.

"*Traitor.*"

24

WANDERER, FRIEND, FATHER, SPY

Horus goes still, as does every person in the canyon. Then, before any of us can take a breath, he moves. Runs. Straight at me.

Or maybe straight at Reven, who is suddenly in front of me, shadow wisping away from him like trails of dark mist. He reaches back, curling a hand around my wrist.

Horus pulls up short, and I think maybe for the first time since I've known him, fear freezes my friend's features. Before anyone can grab him—and many are trying by now—he falls to his knees, prostrate, hands on the ground, head lowered. "Forgive me, my queen!"

Forgive him? For what? What is Achlys talking about?

"Kill him," the Shadows whisper. *"He betrayed you."*

Heart plummeting, I slam a lid over the well inside me to silence them while I figure out what is happening. At the same time, I try to scoot past Reven, but he doesn't budge, his shoulders blocking my view. Can he feel the Shadows rising inside me?

Horus offers more choked apologies into the sand, but I can't *see* him. I can see Tziah, though. Her hands are clapped over her ears like she doesn't want to hear any more.

Beside her, Vos's reaction is worse.

He stares at Horus for a long, hard moment, then a muscle twitches in his jaw and he deliberately turns his gaze away, like he can't bear to look at his friend a second longer. He's already decided that Achlys's accusation is true. Just from a look.

Please don't be true, my heavy heart whispers. *Defend yourself. Tell us you're being set up. Tell us she's wrong. Tell us anything.*

Horus has been my protector. My confidante. My connection to Aryd when I needed it most. A father figure. I couldn't have accomplished any of what we've done without him.

"I have seen nothing to make me believe he is a traitor," Bene says from wherever he's watching overhead. *"But his actions are clear."*

The world shifts and a swirling sort of panic sets in. My hand finds Reven's arm. He flinches at my touch. How am I supposed to handle this? How should I react? The eyes of our allies are on me as one of their queens. As the queen who has had Horus by her side day and night, specifically.

Hakan, who'd been farther up the side of the canyon away from anyone who might accidentally brush up against him, strides our way. "Explain, Achlys."

Cainis, off to my right, looks between Horus and Achlys, thick brows meeting over his eyes. "What proof do you have?"

Achlys lifts her chin and stares the zariph directly in the eye, something I don't think she would have done before all this. "I've only just discovered it. He was in the palace last night, meeting with Eidolon's man, Pollux."

Mother goddess. For how long? When Horus was in the Shadowood with the other Vanished? Reven doesn't react—he wouldn't know how much that should hurt him—but Vos flinches and Tziah makes a tiny noise in her throat.

I maneuver around Reven, keeping my hand on his arm, and take in Horus, still on the ground and head bowed.

Defend yourself! I want to yell. Not that he isn't guilty. But surely, he had reasons…

"Reasons," a Shadow scoffs in my mind. *"Eidolon has reasons,*

too. Are we starting to consider reasons now?"

Shut up!

Beneath my fingertips, Reven's forearm flexes. "*This* is who you chose to guard Meren?" he snarls at Cain, who glares back at him.

Before Cain can respond, Tabra looks at me, worry darkening her eyes. "We should let him explain."

"No." Achlys slashes a hand through the air. "I also found the lever Eidolon pulls to keep Horus under his thumb. That's what took me a while."

She glances at Pella, who signals the guard, and immediately a woman is brought into sight, one maybe five or six summers younger than Horus. A tremor of whispers runs through our group, maybe due to the burn scars that mar the entire left side of her face, the skin puckered and angry red, her eye on that side barely visible under a lid of scar tissue that droops over it.

I study the woman. The resemblance is clear.

The woman stares at Horus, tears welling in her eyes. "Abren?"

Horus flinches at the ancient Wanderer word for "brother" but doesn't move. Doesn't speak.

Confusion swirls through me. Is this…

"Eidolon blackmailed the spy Vida with her family," Achlys says. "He did the same with Horus."

I've thought of Vida every single day since she died trying to kill me. The king had her family, threatened to kill them if she didn't spy for him. That's how he bought her betrayal of her friends. I think about how, if she'd come to me, I could have helped her. Of how alone she must have felt. Of how she could have chosen so many other paths to solve her problem.

Vida must have known Horus was a spy. That's why she had begged him to help her family. Because he was the only person who could.

"She was just desperate," Horus had said about Vida.

"Desperation is as close to depravity as a pure soul like hers can get. Trust me. I know."

Only he meant it differently than I took it then. He meant it as the other spy sent to share our secrets with Eidolon. And then he killed Vida before she could name him as the other traitor.

The images of that moment are all I can see as I look at him now. The way he had pulled her onto his lap with frantic hands and wrapped his arms around her, bowed his head, murmured prayers over her body. Cried.

Wanderers don't cry. That's not how they grieve. And I thought…stupidly…that his grief was in having to kill a friend he'd known for years. Years together in the Shadowood. Years with that cheerful smile and her insistent friendship that could win over even the most guarded person.

But it was all a show. A lie.

"I have found a new purpose here," he'd told me the day we met in the Shadowood. *"I am a hunter by trade, and I help to feed these people. In exchange, I have a home and acceptance."*

I remember fighting beside Horus in the Shadowood as Eidolon's soldiers attacked. His face the day I told him he was worthy of even a princess's sacrifice. That every soul is worthy. The thousands of times he put himself between me and harm's way.

Did he mean any of it?

The day he asked to be my personal guard. *"I couldn't protect my own sister, my only family, and I lost my honor and my place in my zariphate and in this world all the same. Let me serve you. Let me regain my honor at your side."*

Was he only asking to get closer to me for information? To kill me eventually?

Horus's sister jerks toward him, but Pella yanks her up short. She flinches, as if bracing for a strike.

"Horus," the woman says again, her voice breaking over his name.

"I am sorry, Lana," I hear the man I've wished was my father whisper.

He might as well have lit his own funeral pyre with those words, and I *know*.

How could he?

I want to scream. I want to beat my hands on his chest and sob and let him see my hurt.

But I can't. Because I'm a queen.

"Seize him," Tabra orders quietly.

Wanderers from all the zariphates here—a rainbow of clothing in tans and whites, blacks and blues, reds and various other shades—surround Horus, strip him of his curved blade, telescoping bow, and urumi belt, then stand over him, weapons drawn while he remains on the ground, bowing to Tabra.

"*Traitor*," someone growls.

And others take up the call, getting louder, gaining heat and anger until the word pounds through me, over and over and over.

Tabra shouldn't be the one to mete out his punishment. Not this time. He's *my* responsibility.

I draw one last bit of strength from Reven before letting go of his arm and stalking toward Horus. The Wanderers surrounding him tense. They probably don't know who the bigger threat is.

"*Meren*," Cain warns.

The chanting of "traitor" ceases, leaving only the stirring of the breeze.

I stare down at Horus. His betrayal flays so deeply, I feel it cut to my bones. I *trusted* him. With my life. With Tabra's life. With my affection. With secrets. With detailed plans. People have died. *Omma* died. Many of the Vanished died. Many Wanderers died.

Because of *him*. And everyone here knows it. They know he's been exiled before—his being among us at all should spell his death at the hands of any zariph here—but because he's under my protection, he lives. I need these people to follow me and trust me as we go into battle together, and he just shattered that.

He's left me with no choice. I have to punish him in the most brutal of ways. One the Wanderers, and even the Vanished, will respect.

I already hate myself for what I'm about to do.

Even if his actions are what brought us to this.

25

LIES AND LEARNING

"Get up," I command.

Is that my voice? Controlled and full of authority, not even a hint of a wobble.

There is hope in Horus's eyes as he lifts his head to look at me. That only breaks my heart and at the same time hardens my resolve as he slowly gets to his feet. "Domina—"

"Don't—" The word comes out too hard and I pause, barely, to lash my emotions and the Shadows down tight. "Don't call me that."

He called me that in the Shadowood when he thought I was Tabra. But he also was the first to call me that after he knew I was Meren.

"Be well, domina," he had said right before Reven performed the rites that saved my life by shadow.

For a Wanderer to call me that was an honor. Or so I thought.

Horus swallows and tries again. "My queen—"

"No."

He was also the first to call me *that*.

I take a breath. "You may not address me by any name. Never again."

I see the hope fade to shame and then a finality settles over his face. His familiar face, lined with time and care and worry, with the harsh elements of Aryd and later Tyndra.

"Is it true?" I ask.

I know the answer, but I want to hear it from him. I *deserve* to hear it from him.

"It is."

Even knowing the answer, I have to breathe through the instantaneous surge of voices. *"Give the order to smite him,"* they say.

Bene.

My lips actually form his name.

"Meren?" The Devourer's voice quiets the others, and I come back to myself.

I can't hold myself together in the face of this, so I definitely can't hold the Shadows at bay.

Unable to look at Horus a second longer, I force my gaze above his head to the top of the canyon where the rock meets the sky.

"Forgive me," he begs. "He had my sister."

"Forgive you?" My throat seizes around the words somewhere between anger and tears. "Was it your information that brought Eidolon's soldiers to the Shadowood and killed so many of the Vanished?"

"Yes."

I still can't look at him. "Was it your information that warned Eidolon to marry my sister before we arrived to stop them?"

Silence.

"Was it?"

"Yes."

"He deserves death."

Another breath. "Did he find us in Wildernyss when we went to Trysolde because of you?"

"Yes."

So many betrayals. So many—

"Did he come to Tropikis because of you?" I demand. I lost Omma in Tropikis. I lost Reven in Tropikis.

"No."

That gets me to look at him. "No?"

Horus draws back his shoulders. "The day I pledged myself as your bodyguard was the day I turned my back on my sister's pain to serve you faithfully."

A whimper of sound comes from the woman's direction and his gaze slides that way. "I couldn't save you both," he says to her, expression twisting with regrets.

"Lies and more lies," Vos spits the words like a viper. "We should cut your tongue out before we kill you slowly."

Words I know cost him, but this betrayal cuts him as deeply as it does me. Deeper, maybe even. They were friends all that time, long before I showed up. Worked together to build and protect the Shadowood and the Vanished. They were both voted in together as representatives of their dominions among those people.

And Horus *destroyed* all of that.

Their home, their safe haven, the second chance they were all given, including him, by Reven. The man who stands behind me with no idea what this means to him.

26

JUDGMENT

A purple glow unexpectedly lights up the night, the faces all around us, and the arch overhead spanning the narrow canyon where we are. Those standing closest to Tabra step away, watching her warily.

My sister isn't doing this on purpose. I know this for a fact, because her face takes on a mix of panic and apology. She's upset, and it's setting off her power.

Tabra gasps, then wobbles on her feet before sitting down hard.

I'm across to where she stands in a heartbeat, dropping to my knees in front of her. Cupping her hands between mine, I give her a squeeze. She's trembling so hard, trying to contain her power, that I'm surprised she's not causing the rock she's sitting on to crack.

"Look at me," I say.

She doesn't take her gaze off her hands, though, shaking her head over and over. I try to think of anything that might distract her. "Tell me one good thing and one bad thing."

It doesn't help. "I can't stop it," she says. "I can't stop it, Meren."

I thought her time with Scoria teaching her had helped this. But knowing how emotion sets me off now that I can tap Eidolon's power, maybe Enfernae struggle with this more than Hylorae.

"Look at me, Sissy." I'm harder with her now, harsher, trying to snap her out of it.

Slowly, almost as though she's having to pry her eyes from the glow of her hands, she drags her gaze up to mine.

"Don't fight it. Accept it," I tell her. "Accept the gift. It's a blessing. It's in your blood and part of you. Accept it, then it will listen to you."

Her brows snap together so hard they meet in the middle. "The Shadows don't—"

I grip her hands harder. "*They* aren't part of *my* power. Reven's either. They're a bastardization of what Eidolon has done to himself and something foisted on me against my will. That's different."

"Different," she whispers more to herself than me. "Accept the power. Accept the power." She repeats the words over and over like she's willing herself to believe them.

The glow starts to dim and the light in her eyes shifts from subdued panic to calm to hope until her power is absorbed back into her and under control once more.

After a second, Tabra nods. "I think I understand now."

I hope so. I had years to learn, but we need my sister to master her control faster.

She looks beyond me to where Horus waits for my judgment. "What will you do with him?" she asks me. Deliberately. She is letting everyone know that as queens we will always stand together. Even in judgment. Even if she hates my decision.

I lean closer and put my forehead to hers.

Cainis steps up. "We should discuss his punishment—"

He cuts off at the cold look I shoot him.

"His sister, Lana, will be given a home among the Cainis Zariphate, and treated with kindness," I announce.

Cainis's hand goes to the weapon at his side. "You dare to—"

"Daring has nothing to do with it," I snap. "I am your queen."

I ignore the murmuring that circles the gathering and

continue my pronouncement. "Horus will be bound and guarded until after we take back Oaesys. He will have no contact with anyone but his guards during that time. As far as we are concerned…" This is going to hurt. "…he is dead to us."

Tziah makes another tiny noise of distress, and I force myself not to look at her. I have to do this. He brought this on himself.

"Once we have Oaesys, his guards will take him to the Singing Dunes, strip him of all belongings, and exile him."

"Meren—"

I stare Cain down, unyielding.

After a second, he looks away. Pella, too. Tziah goes quiet, even as tears streak down her cheeks. But it's the way Vos snaps his gaze to me, eyes narrowed as if I'm the threat, that makes me pause.

"Let me take his life," Bene offers. *"He will not suffer. His death will be quick."*

No. This is the right punishment. I know it is, even if they can't see it.

I am doing to Horus what his zariph did to him when he was a younger man for trying to protect his sister, a situation that Reven once saved him from. It is considered the worst possible penance for a Wanderer. It's not just possible death, it's the total and utter loss of their community. His betrayal of the man who saved him—and the resulting consequences for so many others—demands that. The people here today will respect it.

Even in the middle of being so horribly angry and crushed that part of me wants to hurt him back, there's still a small part that…doesn't want this.

I mentally shake myself. I am giving him the only chance to live that I know how to—it's possible to survive the desert, though the chances are so slim as to be laughable. But he already did it once. I'm counting on that, actually. The only other option is the immediate death that Bene is offering.

I owe him my life on so many occasions. And he was a friend, even if a false friend. This is the sole shard of mercy I can offer him.

"I understand," Horus says.

Does he? I thought I knew his face, but the features are foreign to me now.

"I'll take him," Hakan says.

Horus's head lowers even more when Hakan stands beside him.

Knowing I will never see him again, I turn away, gritting back tears, as Hakan and two other Wanderers lead Horus away. He doesn't fight, doesn't protest. Not even when Lana calls his name and follows after.

Some pain goes too deep to feel right away. I know this is going to barrel through me any second. I need to be not here when that happens.

"Meren," Cain whispers. "Are you sure?"

Finally, I glance at Reven, but he's giving me nothing. No emotion in the blankness of his features, of his posture.

The words don't want to come, but I make them. "I'm sure."

27

NUMB WOULD BE NICE

Silence settles over the gathered allies, and I know every eye is on me.

Damn it. I'm second-guessing myself already. How could I not? Omma used to tell me every leader questioned their decisions, but the good ones decided and then stuck with it. At the time, I doubted that, because Grandmother so obviously never did, but Omma also told me that a leader should never let their people see that doubt. Visible doubt spells death for people in charge.

Way harder in action than in theory.

My chest is tightening. I need to get out of here.

Reven's expression is still blank. No emotion. Not even confusion. Horus means nothing to him…the same way I mean nothing now.

Even so, I want to chuck a knife at his head just to make him feel *something*. Or maybe it's me I want to chuck the knife at.

"The plan for taking Oaesys is a good one," I say. "I'm doing it."

Reven crosses his arms. "Then I will be the one to go with you, now that Horus is unavailable."

"No—"

Vos cuts himself off at the glance Reven cuts his way.

Reven is not asking. He's telling.

"If anyone can help her should the things inside her decide to come out, it's me," he says.

He has a point. I would probably have said the same thing if I were in his shoes right now, and he's stopped actively trying to kill me. It's the best we've got. "Fine. Just so long as you don't get in my way."

That signals the end of our talks. The plan is in place.

I manage to keep from losing it through every whisper in my direction, every searching look from allies, friends, and the zariphs as I send our guests home through their various portals. And then the canyon clears out as those staying here return to the camp and their tents to sleep, and I lag behind deliberately. My friends, what happened with Horus visibly weighing on them all in different ways, pair off ahead of me probably without even realizing that they are. Meanwhile, the thought of going to my bed alone, dealing with the choice I made alone, trying to sleep alone—actually not alone, with the things crammed into me—all when Reven should be with me…

I'll never sleep.

"Mer?" Cain has stopped at the turn to go down a narrower part of the canyon.

I remain where I am. Worry lines my friend's face, which just makes this worse for me. I glance away only to collide with turquoise eyes, but I don't think I see concern beyond curiosity from my bondmate.

Suddenly, I just can't anymore. I need to get away from this place.

"Bene?" I call to the top of the cliffs high above.

"I'm coming," he answers.

"Meren," Vos says. "You shouldn't be alone."

"I'm already alone," I say. "And Bene will protect me."

A shadow looms overhead, dimming the moonlight in the canyon. With a beat of wings that scatters the rocks and sand around, Bene drops down, but he doesn't land. And he doesn't ask questions, just offers me a talon.

A small part of me expects, or maybe even hopes, that Reven

will protest. After all, Bene is the Elimination—a Devourer—and is taking away the woman who holds Eidolon's Shadows.

But his expression remains blank as I step into Bene's talon, which curls around me, and then we fly away, wind tugging at my clothes.

Once we're out of view of the others, I drop my forehead against the sandy column of Bene's foot, rough against my skin, and close my eyes and try not to think about Horus, or Reven, or what happens tomorrow.

I try to burrow into the numbness I held onto before and let it all go. So much easier than feeling it. But Scoria said I need to feel it, and I can't seem to find the numb anyway.

"I need to be alone," I say.

Bene doesn't ask questions or give me reasons why that's a bad idea. *"I know a place."*

It's not long before he drops back down into a different side canyon, and the sound of running water tells me exactly where he's brought me.

The perfect spot to try to forget everything, just for a second.

Even at night with only the light of the three moons, the Usavah Waterfalls that spill over deep-orange and red travertine cliffs are a brilliant aqua-blue. I step out of Bene's talon and onto the ground, then look around. The stark contrast between the red, rocky arid desert landscape and the lush vegetation near the water is almost too much to believe it's real.

Here the rush and burble of the water as it cascades over the cliff to the pool below might be the most soothing sound in all of Nova, as if it's flowing through my limbs, loosening the tension there.

Horus's sister was right about clear water and clear thoughts.

Bile surges up my throat along with a slide of the darkness within.

Don't think about Horus.

I cut off the memory and focus instead on the oasis. The

water near where I am is bluer under the moonlight. Blue is such a calm color.

I make my way to the side of the pond where a slight widening of the canyon allows the water to pool, though not too deeply. Without hesitation I strip, dropping all my fancy-ish clothing to the ground in an untidy heap. Then I tuck my knives into the rocks nearest the edge of the water before I gingerly walk in, careful of my bare feet where it's slippery. The water at the tops of my thighs is cold, losing the heat of the day to the chill of desert nights. Cold is good. Cold is numbing.

I dive in, and the instant icy water is a shock that has me coming up, gasping for air. But it wears off quickly while I tread water, and gradually the chill turns into something more manageable, something luscious and lovely.

And quiet. Even the Shadows are giving me peace.

Tomorrow—

No. I'll deal with tomorrow when it gets here.

I undo my hair and dunk again. After having it up and braided all day, the release of tension in my scalp is heaven, and I groan a little. Seriously, no more ceremonial updos, just simple braids from now on. How Tabra, whose hairstyles have always been more elaborate than mine, doesn't end every day with a headache the size of the dominion, I don't know.

I duck under the water, swimming down to the bottom to trail my fingers across the rocks and sand there before resurfacing to brush my wet hair out of my face with one hand.

"How did you learn to swim?" The familiar deep voice reaches out through the night.

Reven.

28

MISSING HIM

I'm trying not to let my wildly beating heart escape into the night air. He came to find me. Even with the distance between us, I'm not entirely alone.

Goddess, I didn't realize how much I needed to know that.

I search along the banks in the shades of the trees on that side of the water, and finally spy a man-shaped form with one shoulder leaned up against the trunk of a lone willow tree, the graceful branches arching and falling in a canopy that grazes the ground gently. I think maybe his arms are crossed as he watches me.

"What do you want?" I ask, a little breathless.

I shouldn't be breathless. It's silly to be. He's probably here with a question, or he's worried I'll unleash the Shadows.

Reven doesn't answer, and he doesn't move.

Hells, Meren, don't be a fool.

I should be taking advantage of being alone with him. This is a chance. A chance for me to…I don't know…figure out how to flirt better really fast.

But I can't. Not right now. Not after Horus. Not with everything that happened tonight. The tangle of all the emotions I'm trying to not let get in my way is a problem.

I glance to the moon-bright skies above, wondering how much Reven can see of me below the water. "I am completely naked at the moment," I warn.

"I can't see anything indecent," Reven assures me, sounding almost bored.

Great. This man has touched and kissed, licked and nibbled, possessed and worshipped my body, and he sounds bored. Bored is the opposite of what I need right now. A spark of challenge rises up in me. "That's a shame."

He sort of stills even though he doesn't really move or change posture. "Horus— "

"Cain taught me."

There's a beat of silence long enough that I decide to elaborate. "To swim," I say. "You asked. He taught me when I was a child after I almost drowned in a well."

"I see."

Does he, though? Has he figured out who Cain truly is to me? I know for a fact Reven hasn't figured out who *he* truly is to me. He still has no idea we're bondmates. I try to feel him, feel that connection, but there's nothing there.

He clears his throat. "Horus— "

"I don't want to talk about Horus. Not with you." I swim toward the side of the pool where my clothes are.

"Why not me?"

"Because you don't remember him." I'm not accusing him. It's not his fault. "What he did means nothing to you, and it should."

How would Reven before he lost his memories have dealt with it? A more merciful killing? Or maybe he would have understood my reasons for exiling our friend when no one else seemed to?

I wish I knew.

"We should talk," Reven says each word slowly, carefully, rolling them around in his mouth as if he's not entirely sure that he should speak them because the second he puts the suggestion out there, he'll have to do something about it.

"Not the best timing, but all right. Turn around." I don't

wait for him to comply before I climb out of the pool and dress. There's no way to dry myself, so it takes a little while to get my clothes back on as they stick to my skin uncomfortably.

"Is there ever a good time?" Reven asks while I struggle to secure my knives under my clothes.

"These days, not really." I drop my skirts.

"Do you mind joining me over here?"

I plunk my hands onto my hips. Just once I'd like it if he was the one to bend a little. "Why do I have to come to you?"

A sound that is all things frustration still manages to reach my ears. "Does everything have to be an argument with you?"

The sudden, small smile that tugs at my lips surprises me. A fact I cover with sarcasm. "Only with shadowraiths who have trust issues. And quasi daddy issues, and— "

"I get your point." His voice is dust dry and coated in irritation. "Where I'm standing is more protected if anyone should happen by, even above in the cliffs. They would be less likely to see us or overhear. That's why."

Valid. I'm really starting to hate valid and logic.

I brush the small gravelly rocks off the bottoms of my feet and slip my shoes on, then pick my way around the pool into the denser foliage nearer the waterfall, eventually having to go farther out from the water before returning down a very narrow path. I find him standing in a pool of moonlight with his back to the water, waiting for me.

The way he's looking at me, with one eye kind of squinted, I wonder if he's trying to make up his mind about something that has to do with me.

"Shall we sit?" He waves a hand at the ground.

Together, we find a large, flat rock right at the edge, and sit facing the water. It's easier this way, with no eye contact.

It also reminds me of a long-ago night sitting beside a rushing river in Wildernyss. And another time in a water garden. More memories to etch into my mind with a chisel so they can't be erased. Or maybe I should be burying them with all the other distracting things like trust and friendship.

Maybe to rule is to be isolated so that emotion doesn't enter the picture.

We sit in silence longer than is comfortable. Long enough that I start rolling little gravel pieces around on my rock with my fingertips, lining them up like a little army under my command.

Not so long ago, when he shadowed me out of my own palace and away from Eidolon, we sat like this in the desert outside Oaesys, neither knowing what to say or do. Eventually, he groaned and lifted me onto his lap and kissed me within an inch of my life. We were both so desperate for each other.

I miss that. I miss him.

Tell him. I open my mouth—

"I have no idea what to think of you," he gets in first. The words drop between us, closer to an accusation than anything.

I swallow my first knee-jerk response of *you're not the only one.*

"It must be hard." I feel more than see him glance over. "I mean, not remembering. I imagine it feels like someone else stole your body and your life, then did and said and felt all these things, but now he's gone and you're back, trying to make sense of it. To live *your* life and not another man's."

"So you agree?" he asks. "That the Reven you fell in love with was another man?"

My heart pinches. Trying to ease the ache, I lean back on my hands and accidentally brush against his fingers. He scoots away, and my heart pinches more.

"In some ways, I agree," I admit. "I've also been around Eidolon. He looks and talks like you, but he is not you. That man is an entirely different person with thoughts you would never have, actions you'd never take. You, though… There are little things, like you'll give me a look, or walk a certain way, or use a turn of phrase. But more than that, the way you think and act are all...*you*. All Reven."

"Like what?" Doubt lines his voice.

"Like showing up here to talk when I don't want to. Like not trusting me as far as you can throw me but trying to protect me anyway." I miss that, too.

"Is it hard to be around me?"

"Yes."

His eyes slowly narrow as he searches my expression. "Because of Eidolon's Shadows?"

I shake my head. "It's because I lost you, and I was... terrified I'd never get you back. But now you're back but not, and..." I prop my chin on my shoulder, letting my gaze trail over the harsh planes of his face, to look into eyes that used to look back at me differently. "I guess in a way I'm still missing you, and that...makes me sad."

And I'm definitely still terrified that I've lost him.

"Is that why you let me stay alone in my tent for days? Because I make you sad?"

"No." Only, that's not quite true. "Maybe a little," I admit. "I... wanted to give you time, to see things and decide for yourself."

Choose me again. I want to say the words to him. But if I beg, what if he gives in out of pity? I won't beg.

Make him love you.

My heart shrinks a little. For the second time tonight, I'm not sure if that thought was me or the Shadows. Reven doesn't blink, though. Not a good sign since he seems to sense when my control slips. I almost wish that was the Shadows because the only kind of love I want from Reven is the kind that is freely given.

"Thank you for that." There's a heaviness to his voice. Is he... disappointed? His mouth sort of twists.

"And we didn't stop you, so we passed your test."

He shakes his head. "It wasn't a test. I was actually going to leave. But it...hurt."

Hurt? More bubbles in my stomach, insidious hope trying to float up again. "Hurt how?"

"An ache at first, here." He points to the center of his chest. "But the farther I got, it spread, everything too tight like my mind was leaving, but my body was trying to rip away and stay."

Hells. I think I know why—our bond—but I don't want him staying because of that, either. Love should be a choice every single time.

It's like there's this glass wall between us. I can see him, but he's still as far from me as when he was trapped inside Eidolon.

"And I don't like it when I can't see you," he admits, each word a grudging growl.

I can't help the way I straighten, because that sounds more like the stirrings of...something. "Why?"

"Damned if I can figure it out." His crooked lips hitch in a self-deprecating smile. "It's not pain. It's more like a sense of panic."

I deflate a little. Panic doesn't sound like love.

Tabra's voice rings in my memory. Only yesterday she was telling me all sorts of ways to, as she put it, open up to him. "Tabra says I should be more vulnerable with you."

His brows draw together, and a small part of me smiles. I love those thick, expressive brows. "What does that mean?" he asks.

A short, sharp laugh pops from me. "Hells if I can figure it out." I toss his phrasing back at him.

That crooked smile widens to a small grin, only a little reluctant. "Were you vulnerable before?"

My own amusement fades as I think about that. "Eventually, yes," I say slowly. "But it came from knowing each other, trusting each other. Until you can do that, it..." I shake my head. "It doesn't feel..." *Right* isn't the word. *Awkward,* either, although it is. "Fair to you."

He looks out over the water. "That makes a certain kind of sense."

"I'm glad you get it because mostly I'm confused." And frustrated with myself. Where did that girl who would fearlessly do anything for him go? Or maybe that's who's in charge? She's protecting him? I don't know. I've never been in a relationship, let alone bonded, let alone...whatever this is now. I'm only nineteen. I have so little experience in life to draw on for what I'm facing.

Has anybody in the history of Nova had to face this?

Probably not. It seems to be my lot in life to be the outlier.

I peek at Reven to find his focus still on the water, but... Is that a smile hovering around his mouth?

"You love your sister," he says.

Okay, I guess we're done talking about that. "Of course."

"No."

The stark, low word snags my attention. He's watching me again, different this time, and I try to ignore the shiver that feathers over my skin. "No?"

"I imagine most people in your position would have resented the sibling who wasn't...what do you call yourself?"

"Expendable."

Darkness flashes through his eyes. "I don't like that word any more than Tabra does."

That's something at least.

"I watched you with her today," he says. "When she was kissing that Achlys woman, you looked..."

"Pathetic, probably," I grumble.

"No. You looked heartbroken. Just for a second, but the pain looked...real. Deep."

Everything about me constricts, like he wrapped a corset around me and tied it up tight. "Oh."

"And then you looked at me. And your heart was in your eyes. I could *see* it." He swallows, the first show of vulnerability

I've seen from him. "I could feel it, like you'd reached out and punched me in the gut."

Oh goddess. What was my heart saying to him without my knowing it? All I remember is yelling at myself to say something.

He lets out a breath that sounds all kinds of frustrated. "That's the first time I realized just how much you care. How much pain I've caused you."

29

THE STORY OF US

I can't tell what Reven thinks about me caring for him, but a new knowing settles over me, inside me, as if the goddesses themselves are whispering that it wasn't the right time before, but it is now.

I pull my knees up and lie my cheek on them. "I care deeply," I whisper.

And for the first time since I discovered his memories were gone, I let him see it. In the way I let my gaze trace the angles of his face. In the way I try to memorize every part of him and absorb every nuance of this moment, despite the imaginary glass wall between us. The tightness in my chest that hasn't eased, the heavy thump of a heart that isn't whole yet making that impossible, but now I don't try to hide the way it's hard to breathe.

Reven stares back at me, aquamarine eyes even more brilliant than the waters, questioning and wondering while we sit together in the paradise that should be a lovers' hideaway.

But it can't be that for us.

The smile I offer him is tinged with the sting of sorrow weaving through every thought and feeling I have about my bondmate. "If I showed you how much I care, even now that you've seen a little…you'd run."

His gaze sharpens. "I don't run."

Did I offend him? "From this you would." I swallow and

don't let myself look away. "You don't trust it."

Not yet.

He doesn't deny it. He doesn't say anything.

"Also…" I hesitate. Do I admit this?

"What?"

I twist my lips, searching for the words to express this right. "When we met the first time, we didn't like each other to start with. Love wasn't really something either of us had been searching for."

"You think the circumstances led to our falling for each other?"

"I…not entirely. But the circumstances are how and why we got to know each other. I got to see the people you saved, see your determination to stop Eidolon, how protective you are of the people around you who need it. You got to see…" I wave a hand like I'm swatting something away. "Whatever you saw in me. But I didn't realize—"

I cut myself off. I almost said I didn't realize how hard it would be to trust the magic that binds us. I do still believe we will find each other again in another life, but it wasn't until this happened that it sank in how much I don't trust that he'll fall in love with me all over again, even then.

But I can't tell him that part. Not yet.

Telling him about being bondmates would only make it harder for him, maybe even make him trust us less. He could see it as a lie to trap him.

"Tell me about how it happened," Reven says.

I blink at him. "What?"

"How we met. Our story. Don't tell me everything. Just the beginning. How we started."

I am going to look at it as a good sign that he wants to hear. "Are you sure? Before you seemed pretty adamant that you're a different man, and that you don't want to hear about your previous life."

"I'm sure."

Just like Reven, decisive and succinct.

I nibble on my lip as I think about where to begin. "Do you hear the voices still?"

Nothing about him changes, but I can tell that he's homed in on me in something near to shock.

"The whispers and cries for help from people all over Nova," I elaborate. "The darkness brings them to you sometimes."

"How did you know that?"

I smile. "You've always heard them. You used to hear me, long before we ever met."

"You needed help?" He turns on his rock so that his entire body is facing me instead of the water.

Does he not like that?

I shake my head. "I wanted away from a life where the only expectation was that I die to save Tabra. Which even now I would do, if it came down to it, but because I love her. I guess I wanted the choice, and to be my own person with worth beyond just that."

He stays quiet.

"After you were shed from Eidolon, you started finding the people you heard and rescuing them..." And from there it all tumbles out.

I tell him about how he gave the Vanished a safe haven. I tell him about the Shadowood. I tell him about how he kidnapped a girl he thought was the princess of Aryd, about to become queen, to keep her out of Eidolon's hands...only to get the decoy princess instead. I tell him about his dragging me through Wildernyss, taking me to the Shadowood, and my secrets and his secrets. I tell him about healing me from my own glass I skewered myself with and show him the scar in my side. I tell about the attack on the Shadowood and fighting Eidolon in the palace in Oaesys.

About the start of us.

He sits beside me listening. Never takes his gaze from me. Never asks a question. Doesn't even move except to blink.

I can't tell what he thinks about any of it, but I tell him anyway.

Finally, I wind down. "A lot more happened after that," I say. "But that's the beginning."

When he says nothing, I lapse into silence. But only for a little. "Did I put you to sleep?"

At that, he shakes his head. "Far from it."

But then says nothing more.

I glance around us. What now? "Did any of it sound familiar?"

"No."

I was expecting the answer, but it's like taking an arrow to the back all the same, a sharp sting followed by a bloom of pain that spreads outward.

"We should return to the camp." I push to my feet, which takes a second because I've stiffened up, sitting here so long.

Reven stands, too, and I don't know what to do or say, so I guess I'll just go. But two steps away from him, he snags me gently by the wrist.

I still, my back to him, and close my eyes, absorbing his touch, breathing through it, willing it not to end, for him not to let go. Not yet.

"I'd like to…try something," he says, in a voice gone lower, softer.

Careful not to move my arm so I don't break his hold, I angle toward him. "What?"

"I want to kiss you, if you'll let me."

If I'll *let* him? My heart leaps. Try holding me back. "Why?"

"Maybe it will trigger a memory."

So not because he really wants to kiss me. That arrow in my back twists, but I face him and move so close I have to tip my head back, close enough for the heat of his body to penetrate my flimsy clothes in the cool of the desert night.

And still not close enough. "Kiss me, then."

I don't know why, but the words come out as a challenge, more than giving permission, which I'm also doing.

He rears back a tiny bit, as if that surprises him, but I also see the instant the light of his own challenge steals into his eyes.

Eyes that remind me of the ocean on rainy days, turbulent and crashing, Reven doesn't look away.

Neither do I.

I'm snared, like an animal in a trap I don't want to escape. "You still smell like home," I whisper.

I told him that once. A time not too much unlike this one, when we were alone in a clearing in the Shadowood together. I told him he was a good man, and I kissed the self-inflicted scars on his wrist. Scars he no longer has. And I said he smelled like home.

And just like that time, surprise lights his eyes. "So do you. Like the arctic weeping trees that grow on Tyndra's shores."

Goddess, maybe this is how bondmates work when we meet in each life. We say things and do things…familiar things…until our souls finally recognize each other. "I know. You told me that before, once."

"I did?"

I nod. "I think those trees must be like creosus willows like this one." I glance up at the branches that cocoon us, putting us in our own little world together. It's not in bloom now, but when it does, it smells like heaven—fresh and new. Like dreams.

In that moment, he's not a stranger who doesn't remember me or act entirely like himself. He's just…Reven.

Kiss him.

I move my hand to brush a lock of his hair away from his forehead, the texture just as silky against my fingertips as when I was allowed to touch him this way.

"What are you doing?" His voice drops even lower. The rough texture of it should be abrasive to my ears, but to me it's a caress.

Even so, I pull my hand away. Slowly, because I don't want to stop. "I shouldn't have..."

He's here with me. That should be enough for now.

He searches my eyes, then, haltingly, leans closer.

I stay very still, trying to control my breathing, trying not to do anything that would stop him.

One kiss. Just one.

Another memory to store away for my ravaged heart.

His kiss, when it comes, is soft, but over too fast, although he doesn't sit all the way back, still leaning in like he wants more.

I close the small gap between us and softly feather my lips over his. A teasing caress. A sweet, soft, luscious caress.

"Goddess above," he breathes.

Hooking an arm around my waist, he pulls me flush against him and takes over.

I almost cry out, because we've done this all before. But I'm not stopping this with tears, damn it. It's too precious to lose.

His lips part mine, warm and firm and commanding, gentle yet somehow urgent, and I am a thousand times willing to go where he leads, opening for him like a lotus flower rising and spreading out in the sun. Our breaths mingle, growing heavier as we angle our heads, seeking more, turning the kiss impatient.

The familiarity of it—the *finally* of it—has me wanting to burrow into him and never leave.

This time I know exactly what this feeling is. Need. Delight. Coming home. Desperation to never end. But it's the heat that sparks in my skin around my arm and my forehead where the lines of the thread that bound us touched during that rite.

"He will never love you again."

My emotions have allowed the Shadows to slip out, to slide into this moment between us.

I make a small sound in my throat.

I hardly hear myself, but Reven must have, because he stops abruptly, lips still against mine, breathing hard. So am I.

"Reven?" I whisper.

When he doesn't answer, I pull back slowly. He stands with his eyes closed tight, frowning so hard I'm surprised he's not giving himself a headache.

Why? Was it horrible? Did he hate it? Did he remember something? Or maybe he can't and was trying to with that kiss?

"Reven?"

He opens his eyes finally, but it's no help. His expression is indecipherable.

"Meren?" Bene's shadow passes overhead. I don't blame him. I've been here a while. But his timing couldn't be worse.

"Not now," I say to the skies.

Reven looks up. "You'd better go."

Then shadow sucks in from around us to cover him and when it melts away like a dark mist, he's gone.

I pull the sleeve of my top up to find the sparkling lines of our bond already fading away again. Did he see them? Did he *feel* them and know what they mean?

I hope not. Because if he did, then his first instinct was to run.

30

INVASION

"Are you ready?" I ask.

I know I'm not. I'm having to devote extra energy to locking down the Shadows—they must feel that what's happening today is big, because they are a little extra—and it has my stomach tied in knots. Meanwhile, Reven is already his unique brand of deadly serious and the way he's been acting, the way we both have, it's like last night never happened.

"No matter what happens," he says, "stick close to me."

This isn't the first time he's said those words to me as we've prepared to go. Clearly, he has no idea of the ache that sets up around my heart every single time. I guess I've hidden that well enough. I do again now. "I won't lose you."

"Then let's go."

Cain stop us. "Wait."

We both glance over, probably with identical frowns, because we've already said our goodbyes.

My friend strides to me and tugs me into his arms for a hug that nearly squeezes me to death. "Be careful out there," he says, sort of loudly. I realize why when he whispers only for me, "Watch for Eidolon."

The Shadows press outward, and I grimace. "I know."

We all know. This could be the king's trap, drawing his enemies to one place. Or maybe he'll show just to keep us from taking the capital. We can't be sure.

"When you take the palace, Tabra or no Tabra, get to the presentation platform and introduce yourself to the people."

Before I can ask why, he takes me by the shoulders and presses a kiss to my forehead, then looks me in the eyes. A hard look. A look that begs me to listen to him for once.

I don't know why that's important, but I give him a single nod. "I'll try," I say. An answer that matches what the others heard him say to me.

As Cain lets me go, he looks at Reven and stills, dark eyes turning stony. Neither man says a word, and after a second, Cain returns to stand with the others, beside Tziah, who shoots him a questioning glance, getting a tiny shake of his head in return. At his side and in wolf form, Bene's hackles rise, but he doesn't growl. He's nervous for me. They all are.

"Mother goddess protect you," his voice sounds in my head. And I nod. May she protect us all this day.

"What was that?" Reven asks under his breath as we turn back to the portal I've made.

"Nothing." In an instant, I open the glass, showing a new room on the other side.

After a quick check to be sure no one is near, Reven steps through into the temple in Oaesys ahead of me. Unfortunately, coming through this temple was our best choice. The only other fast way to get me into the city would have been through the portal I made in the palace tombs, and that's not where we want to start.

He eyes the massive bloodred block of glass, made ages ago from sand of the Crimson Desert, similar to the one we just came through that I made. Every "official" portal in Aryd and the other dominions is different, but this one, sitting in a room that is all glittering blacks and golds, has always looked like a blood stain to me.

Is Reven thinking the same thing? I'd ask, but getting caught within the first few seconds of arriving isn't part of the plan, so

I press my lips together around the question.

As soon as I'm through and the portal has closed behind me, Reven holds his hand out. I glance down at it, then back up at his face, frowning. He's not a hand holder. At least, he wasn't before he loved me.

"What?" I mouth.

Rather than answer, he takes me by the hand, his warm and strong around mine. I would love the luxury to take a moment to melt. My foolish heart tumbles around inside me, like it's not aware he's only doing this to make sure he doesn't lose me.

I don't pull out of his grip, though.

We've already discussed the way out of the temple and into the streets. Pausing at the doorway for another check, he then leads me through the main sanctuary. Reven moves like exactly what he is—a shadow blending into the darkness of the grand room, flitting between beams of moonlight descending from above us and shade cast by the columns.

At the soft tread of someone entering the sanctuary, Reven swiftly tucks us both out of sight into one of the many alcoves.

I still against him. Seriously?

The night he kidnapped me, we did this. That time, we hid in the alcove dedicated to the Goddess Tyndra. This time, we're in Mariana's, the stained glass depicting the lush greens, large inland bay, and angry volcano spewing red.

Does he feel even a hint of familiarity?

He catches my glance and raises his eyebrows in question, but I shake my head. Now's not the time. I'll just have to hold the memories apart in my mind.

The acolyte's steps come closer and like before, Reven moves into me, crowding me again, same as before, only this time, I'm tempted to lean into him, put my head on his shoulder. As she retreats, he turns his head, his face close to mine now.

Our breaths mingle in the night air.

He doesn't look away.

Neither do I.

All of this is just like last time, too. Except last time I thought he was Eidolon and would have gladly slipped one of my knives between his ribs. Now…

This can't continue, this cycle of doing the same things over and over. I don't think my heart can handle it.

Over his shoulder, the flicker of light from the acolyte's lamp travels to the opposite side of the temple, disappearing and reappearing as she passes behind the thick columns of onyx until she's gone.

Without a word we move, hurrying out of the temple and into the streets. Reven glances behind us, but I don't need to look. I've seen the massive and ornate temple with its columns and statues and carvings rising up like an onyx tomb against the sky a thousand times.

"What was that in there?" he asks, keeping his voice low.

Now isn't the best time to chat, but I'm starting to learn that we don't always get to pick good times. "That just felt a lot like when you kidnapped me. You took me through that temple. We hid in an alcove the same way."

He glances from me to the temple. "I see."

There's no way he could. Not really. "We need to move fast."

Cautiously but as quickly as we can, we head through the empty streets of the city. The hour is still late enough—or early enough, depending on perspective. During the day, like in every Arydian city, these streets are haunted by the people going about their work. Aryd at night, though, when my people finally get a break from the heat, is when we show our beauty, our humanity—when we live rather than simply survive.

We had to time our visit in between the cooling hours.

Omma taught me many unknown passages, unused alleyways, and multiple routes to take, but eventually she allowed me to make my own way to and from the palace, and that's when I learned more about the city than she ever knew, going farther afield.

Which is how I know where to go now. Not south, toward the palace, but north, in the direction of the massive Sea of Terra that sits above the city. To the east of the shore is an abandoned neighborhood being swallowed by the desert.

"Oy!" a voice breaks the stillness of the night, startling a sandrat nearby that skitters away with angry squeaks. Voices of several men follow, returning home to sleep later than most, not giving us much time to react. We duck into what looks like an alleyway only to find that someone has bricked it up only a foot or two down the way.

We tuck our bodies against the stone wall behind drainpipes, but that's not enough. As the voices near, Reven crowds me. His back to the street, he wraps his arms around me, pinning me between his hard body and the gritty bricks of the building. He pulls darkness up and over us, cocooning us in our own little space as the rest of the world dims and my focus narrows on him. Just him.

Not now, Meren.

I stare at the sharp underside of his jaw.

"Can they hear us?" I whisper, trying to make myself stay in the moment and respect the danger of where we are.

He lowers his head, gaze colliding with mine.

"No."

The edge to his voice, abrupt and confused, doesn't match his eyes. They spark in a way that sends an answering heat thrumming along every inch of my skin.

"What's wrong?" I ask.

"I feel like I've been here." He gives his head a shake, but then immediately leans closer, one hand releasing me to flatten against the wall. "But not here. There was a…tree."

I can't help the way my eyes widen.

If anything, he only becomes more intense. "There was."

"Yes."

"And…" His gaze turns sort of inward. "Screaming?"

"We rescued a girl. Tyndran soldiers were after her."

He nods, then his gaze drops to my lips and goddess help me, I want to stop time so I can live in the way he looks at me. Like I'm precious and yet he wants to devour me.

"I wanted to kiss you," he whispers. And his gaze drops to my mouth. "So badly."

He did? I bite my lip.

"But I… I couldn't. You made me so…" He breathes through his nose. "Frustrated."

I huff a laugh and will him to find more of that memory.

"You were…" He shakes his head.

"Trouble." We both say it together.

I offer him a smile with all my heart in it. "I still am."

For a second, the single beat of a hummingbird's wings, his gaze softens. But just as fast, one of the men in the streets shouts an obscenity, and Reven's gaze turns icy and hard.

Oblivious, the men roll on by where we're hidden by shadow. As they go, what they're saying becomes clearer.

One claps another on the shoulder. "Things are starting to come together, friends."

"They say the young queen is dead and we're being fooled."

"Ofron knows what we need to know."

They aren't drunk or merely heading home late after too much revelry. It sounds as though they've been to a meeting.

"I don't care if the queen is dead," the third in the group announces, only for his companions to shush him. He laughs as if he doesn't care if he's overheard but lowers his voice all the same. "Queen Tabra's grandmother spent this dominion into poverty. We don't need the royals."

Their voices fade away as they round the end of the block.

Seven hells.

31

PORTALS

Reven pushes away from me like he can't get space between us fast enough. Checking around the corner, he grunts. "*These* are the people you rule and lead?"

I sigh as we move into the street. "The sad truth is they aren't wrong. Aryd became poorer during my grandmother's reign, and hotter, and the people angrier."

"And she did nothing?"

"As far as I can tell, she was unaware." I tried to tell her once and never again after that. I should have tried harder, but instead hung my hope on when Tabra would reign.

"How did *you* know?"

"When I wasn't here pretending to be Tabra, I lived in the city of Enora to the northeast. There I was known only as another poor city waif." I glance around at buildings that, here at least, aren't crumbling yet, at streets still clean that don't smell of piss, even on the outskirts where we're headed. "Oaesys may not be as desperate as Enora yet, but it's starting to show signs of the same sort of slow rot. Meanwhile, the glass walls hold in the heat, and while we are desert people, we do have our limits. The people have reason to be angry."

Reven stops me with a hand on my arm. "You fight for them?"

Not even Tabra has figured out that subtle difference for me entirely.

I fight for her, of course, for our throne, but mostly because of what I want her…us…to do with it if we get the chance.

I shoulder past him to keep us moving.

"Meren—"

"I lived among them, but never with them. A pretender who never truly hungered, or thirsted, or really had to work a day in my life. But that didn't mean I didn't see their struggle or feel for them. As their princess…definitely as their queen…I'm supposed to be their hope, the one who fights for their *better* lives. I want to be that."

"I thought you lived with the Wanderers?"

"No." I shake my head. "I met Cain as a child when I ran away from Omma. He had no idea I was a princess until very recently. But even as a kid, I was only playing at being a Wanderer."

Now, though…now I've spent actual time among Cain's people. I've hoisted my own tent, wondered where the next meal might come from, fought beside them, and blistered under the harsh, unforgiving sun.

And aside from all that, I have lost loved ones and friends. I have sacrificed my bondmate. I have fought, and fought, and fought. If not for Tabra and for our people, then what did I do any of that for? "Eidolon's rule can only make my people's lives worse. He will never understand Aryd. I can't let him keep her."

A distinctive *clomp, clomp, clomp*, not of hooves but of booted feet, echoes through the cobblestone streets, giving us plenty of time to tuck away behind a building. The Tyndran soldiers in their white armor are so confident that they'll be feared and obeyed that they don't bother to be quiet. More than that, they assume the mere sound of them patrolling the streets will scare any cowed citizens back into their homes.

"We should give them plenty of time to clear out," Reven murmurs.

"Okay."

He's looking out into the street. He's only an arm's length away. Does he have to be so far from me?

"I worry about my people tomorrow." The words come out on their own. Maybe because we were just talking about them. Or maybe because, once the secrets between us were gone, I was always able to tell him things like that. Things I wouldn't burden Tabra with. Not even Cain these days. He has enough weight to carry with his zariphate.

"That they'll fight against you?" Reven asks.

I pause, then wrinkle my nose. "Well, *now* I'm worried about that, too."

His lips twitch, and my stomach does a little flip. I love it when I can crack through that super serious personality.

"What were you worried about first?" he asks.

I lean around him to check the street. The lanterns have been doused for the night, but a few glassless windows in the buildings around us are lit. I imagine I can hear the people inside snoring or turning in their sleep. "Honestly, while the realistic part of me expects many of them to join the fighting tomorrow—Arydians are not cowards—the protective part of me hopes they don't."

"They would be fighting for their homes, their lives, their futures."

"I know." I twitch a shoulder. "But they're also innocent. They didn't ask for this. Is the sacrifice too high?"

"You're asking the wrong question."

The distinctive *clomping* of the soldiers' steps returns, and we shrink back into our hiding spot as they pass by again.

"If they're making a smaller circling pass, we shouldn't wait," I point out.

Reven straightens, and together we scurry away from our spot in the opposite direction, careful to hug the buildings and stick to the shadows. We don't talk again until we get to the edge of an open space. I pause, scanning the area.

The buildings here, all one-story structures, are buried under dunes of white-ish tan sand. The farther away from the city border where people still live, the higher the dunes get, so that the structures farthest out are entirely covered, but those closest to us have maybe a foot of sand inside and around them.

"What happened here?" Reven asks.

"It was an experimental community. A colony of people from Tropikis who moved here and tried to stay together, apart from Arydians. Only it didn't work. After the abundance of their rainforests, they couldn't handle the dryness and lack of water in the desert. I believe they relocated to Mariana, which is closer to their original climate. The abandoned buildings were never occupied because they'd built them poorly for this area, the walls not thick enough, windows too large, letting all the heat in. The desert took over."

Something about that makes me smile. Maybe because I've always been in awe of the power of my dominion. We humans survive here by the grace of the goddesses, and our work and wits.

A chime rings softly but insistently throughout the city, and I count it. Except it keeps going when I expect it to stop.

Four chimes. Curse the fates. "We took too long to get here," I tell Reven. No more stopping to admire each other or trying to conjure up his memories. "Let's go."

I trace a path that others often walk—mostly children who come out here to play—so that our footprints are disguised. I hurry to a building halfway into the abandoned neighborhood. One full wall of the bone-white structure with its red roof is buried, but if we go around to the opposite side, the drifts have left it more open. We duck through the door.

"Make yourself useful," I say to Reven.

"How?"

"Make sure my light can't be seen."

The glow of the three moons dims slightly, like clouds passed in front of them, which I know is impossible on this cloudless night. I don't know what Reven did, exactly, but I trust that it will mask what I'm doing.

Immediately the golden yellow light of my own power fills the room and reflects off the harsh features of Reven's face. As fast as I can, I build the portal out of the sand so readily available here. I push myself to go fast. We have to build four more tonight, before dawn breaks, and traveling the city is taking more time than I counted on.

As soon as the glass is finished, I don't hesitate, placing a hand to it and picturing the portal I already made for the group that will come through this way. On the other side stands Istrella and Trysolde and their army behind them in the temple of Wildernyss.

"Do you see?" I say, giving them a chance to look hard at where they'll need to open the portal again.

"Got it," Trysolde says.

Istrella—for once not wearing the impressive velvet dresses she favors but a simple tunic and pants, her long hair braided out of her way—offers a tense smile. "Go with the goddesses, Mereneith."

"May they look upon all of us with favor," I offer in return. "You know the appointed hour." With that, I turn my power off and the glass is just glass once more.

As soon as we step outside, I can hear voices in the distance. We both pause and listen. At first, they seem to be coming closer, but then they drift off again. Even so, that was close. I glance over my shoulder at the portal visible inside.

When we were planning with all the zariphates, we discussed my using shadow to hide the portals, as an extra safety protocol. I'd hoped to be able to get away with *not* doing that. Because of Eidolon. The king already told me he senses when I access his power, but I've used it enough that I have my doubts that's true every single time.

Still, they were right about hiding these.

"I think we have no choice," I say to Reven quietly. "We

can't risk someone wandering in before it's time, so we need to disguise it with shadow."

Reven eyes the building. "Let me try first."

Good idea. I wave at him to go ahead.

The moonlight dims again as his hands ignite, and I know Reven is masking us. Darkness shoots out from his hands and fills the space of the doorway to the building where the new portal hides. It spreads and grows, smoothing into a barrier until it blocks the view inside. But it's so thick, it's too obvious.

"Can you thin it out?" I ask.

Lips a grim slash, Reven shakes his head.

He's still relearning his power.

What he's left me to do is small, though. A matter of seconds, I think. Do I dare risk it?

"Let me just..."

This time, the glow that comes from my palms is purple, and my blood turns cold as I siphon Eidolon's power.

Eidolon's Shadows immediately writhe within me, when I've had them silent and still and locked away. Even for something this tiny. Clearly those things are drawn to the power I'm using. Their power. The king's power.

Reven's power.

Shit. This isn't going to work. I shut it down fast. "It'll have to do like it is. Hopefully that will keep anyone wandering somewhere they shouldn't." It's better than nothing.

"Meren?" There's an odd note to his voice. "Meren? Did you hear me?"

I turn his way. "Of course, I heard you—"

Reven surges closer, eyes turning from wide horror to determined anger so fast I take a jerking step back.

"What are you doing?" Those are the words that I form with my mouth, that I think in my head. But another voice comes out, a deeper, raspier voice, and the words aren't mine. *"Leave if you know what's good for you."*

The Shadows? No. I can't feel them. Not even like I did just a moment ago. How is this—

Reven's face spasms. "Don't make me do this, Meren."

Terror leaks into my blood like poison, heat scouring through the cold of Eidolon's power in my veins, but not enough to douse it. I look down at my hands, glowing even brighter.

"You could try, runt." The words come out of me but I'm not saying them. I'm not doing this.

Stop.

I try to shove the Shadows back down in the prison I keep them in. But I still can't feel them or what they're doing in me. I don't know how to stop them. How do I grasp something ungraspable?

"Give me the Shadows," Reven demands.

Everything about his posture, the way he watches me as if I might attack him in the next blink, tells me that he's seeing things. Are the faces cycling across my features? Are they pressing out from my body the way they did with him?

I shake my head. "It's not me," I try to tell him.

But that voice speaks for me again. *"Never."*

32

OUT OF CONTROL

Reven's face contorts, twisting the way he looks at me, so full of blame, I might shatter and turn into a pile of ash and sand right here.

"Then I'll take them from you," he snarls.

The darkness around me rears up and punches out for him, a direct threat, but a shield of shadow forms in front of Reven.

To protect himself.

From *me*.

Darkness spews from within me and slams against Reven's shield, the reverberation knocking me off my feet. I roll back up and try to cut off my access to Eidolon's power. Maybe that will stop them.

Reven stalks toward me, shield still up.

"Help me!" I shout the words as I stumble backward. I reach for the connection that once bound us. Maybe I can make his heart open so he can hear me. *"Reven! Help!"*

He drops his shield and, with no warning, rushes me in a blur, just missing the hammer the Shadows manifest out of nowhere. How are they doing this? I turned off the power, didn't I? But the glow from my hands tells me otherwise.

"Reven!" I scream his name as darkness surrounds me, cutting off all my senses except one.

Touch.

Reven doesn't kill me…he touches me.

This is *his* darkness.

His hands go to my face, and that small act, that small point of contact grounds me enough that I can feel myself again. My own control is there now, warmer. Not just the cold of Eidolon's.

Again, I try to cut off the Shadows' control, to obliterate the siphon to the king's power that has to be feeding them. But it's not working.

I do the only thing I can think of.

A new heat sears through my body and across my skin as I draw on my own power. I'm stronger with it because it's mine. In an instant, the sands around us rise, and I flash heat them into a knife blade so fine, it would slide through bone like it was water.

I jerk that blade up to my throat. It stings as the edge digs in, a warm trickle of blood leaking down my neck. "Stop or I end this!" I command the Shadows.

Immediately, the darkness sucks back inside me like silken skeins being wound up. And as fast as it all came on, it's over. I feel like I'm the one back in control. I test the walls of the box inside me that I keep the Shadows in and it's solid, containing them.

I never even felt them get out, even when they writhed. I stopped too fast.

Mother goddess. What is happening to me?

I'm still holding the glass blade to my throat, staring in horror at Reven whose hands are gentle and warm against my skin.

We're both breathing hard.

Darkness—true shadows of night, warm and alluring—ease and dance around us in a swirl.

"Meren?" he asks.

Those tendrils brush over my skin, over his, seductive and intoxicating. They wind around me, drawing us closer together. But this isn't the evil inside me wielding them now.

It's *me*.

It's me with him, beside him, working together. We stopped Eidolon's evil together. The way we're meant to. A sense of rightness settles in my center. I swallow hard. "Can you hear me?"

My voice sounds normal.

He frowns, not in anger now but confusion.

"I was screaming for you to help me. To not listen to them."

The way his expression sort of shuts down sends a shiver sharply through me.

"His Shadows are contained," I assure him.

His gaze narrows as he checks the swirl of darkness enveloping us, urging us closer. "I know."

He does?

The darkness punches out, leaving only us. Me and Reven.

The glass blade drops from my fingertips as I reach up and put my hands against his cheeks. I try to smooth the lines of wariness, of questions, with the pads of my thumbs. Reven grabs my wrists, I'm sure to stop me, but then his touch turns softer, not pulling me away.

"What are you doing now?" he asks.

I sag into his touch. "What I should have done from the moment I pulled you out."

I go up on tiptoe and press my lips to his once, softly, sweetly, and something else inside me eases. "I love you," I say against his lips.

A tear squeezes out of my eyes. All the heartbreak of these last days released in that tiny, single drop.

"I love you and I need you to hear that." I open my eyes and step back from him, giving myself permission to memorize every nuance of his face. "And I hate to put this on you after you've endured so much already, but the Shadows might destroy me before we figure this out. I'll try to give you time and space. But I can't *not* love you."

Reven searches my gaze. For what? My sincerity? My

determination? It's all there. I'm not holding back any longer.

He seems to be, though. "Meren…that wasn't the Shadows."

I frown. "Of course it was, you just couldn't hear— "

"I could feel them inside you, still can. They were never out of where you have them contained. Not for a second."

Horror slams through the hollows of my bones.

"What?" I can hardly get the word out through lips so stiff they feel sewn shut. This can't be right. It's not right. I'm shaking my head, harder and harder. "No— "

"I wouldn't lie about this."

That would mean it was me all along, but I was fighting them. Wasn't I?

"No! I wasn't doing that. It wasn't me."

Reven breathes out harshly, but it's the way his eyes soften that slays me. "It *was* you, Meren."

33

IT HAS TO BE FLAWLESS

With Reven close behind, I cut a quick path through the city. The sun is hinting at its return in the skies too soon. Only one more portal to create. The last one.

We didn't have time to argue about what was controlling me. Not with the deadline others are counting on us to hit. Not with taking our dominion back on the line. So, we kept going, Reven watching me like I might explode at any second.

Unfortunately, we were already behind, and the little control incident made that worse. The clock tower of the palace isn't where we can see it, but I know it's counting down. I'm willing it and every hourglass in Aryd to slow their marking of time.

Just one more portal, then we're ready.

We placed one in the abandoned neighborhood. Another is in a human-made cavern under the city that was once part of a tunnel system used to move around during the heat of the day until the first monsoon when most of the tunnels flooded, collapsing them on hundreds of Arydians. Yet another is in the hanging gardens a distant relative of mine created inside her large home, fed by an ingenious system of rooftop pipes, sending the water into underground tanks. Only she died and no one has lived there in ages, leaving the gardens to grow wild.

The last portal is the most important. This one is Cain's, and it'll give us an easy way into the palace. We just have to get there before—

Gong.

"Son of a bitch," Reven mutters.

We should already have been ready and waiting when that chime sounded. Cain will be with the others, expecting a portal.

Gong.

Boom! A light flares off to the west. A human-made explosion, or one of the Imperium in our expanded ranks. It doesn't matter which. That's us.

Gong.

It's started. The invasion of Oaesys has started. Our allies, our friends, they're coming in fighting.

Gong.

Another boom and, a little closer now, a chaos of screams rises up from the streets of my city.

Gong.

"Forget drawing attention," Reven shouts. "Run!"

We sprint toward the last destination. We're close. We're so close. Cain is going to kill me. But people are flooding out of their homes now, drawn by the sounds of the fighting. A flash of lightning sizzles to my right, and I know Hakan is over there. Pella, too.

"Move!" Reven shouts at a man who doesn't get out of the way fast enough only to be shoved to the side as Reven clears a path for us.

"Where do you think you're going?" A hand catches me by the nape of the neck and my legs kick out as I'm jerked off my feet.

I twist in the man's arms and punch him in the face.

I don't know if pain or shock makes him let me go, but he does, and I run after Reven.

"That really hurt," I pant, giving my hand a shake.

A telltale whistle of loosed arrows has us stumbling to a halt to track the arc of them through the skies. They're going to come down on top of us. I look around. *All these people. I have to—*

Reven blasts a layer of shadow over us all. The arrows slide off it harmlessly, then it's gone.

"Come on!" He grabs my hand, and we take off down the street.

One block down, I tug on his grip. "Through here is faster."

I run down a narrow alley and into another one backed by several stores, then push through a back door that I have never once, in almost ten years wandering the city on my own, found locked. It leads into a haberdashery and at least two of the displays crash to the floor as we scurry through with more speed than care.

Reven beats me to the door, which he yanks open just in time to find a small, nondescript man swinging back a large pipe at where the door had just been. A looter.

"Not today, asshole," Reven snarls. Shadow slams the little man into the wall, knocking him out cold. "Where?" Reven demands, not giving the thief's crumpled body a second glance.

I point. "That way."

The palace is surrounded by two sets of walls. The first keeps out the rest of the city. It is too tall to scale, topped with jagged glass and patrolled from the ground on both sides.

Impenetrable.

But we're not trying to get inside. I already have the portal ready in the tombs. The one I need to create now will be a secondary point of access.

Finally in view of the first walls that skirt the palace, I lead us to an abandoned building and tread down stairs that, as far as anyone else is concerned, descend to a cistern located underneath the city itself. Water for anyone with a jug who knows it exists. Most don't.

When we get to the black water that leads into a labyrinth of underwater hallways, I stop. We're not swimming the path I figured out as a girl to get under the first wall of the palace, coming out on the other side. Instead, this is where I'll build my portal. This one is trickier, though, because to get enough sand in here would mean pulling it from the streets above, and sand slithering along with an audible hiss would be noticeable.

But no one will care now if they see sand moving through the streets, and that way will be faster than our original plan. I lift my glowing yellow hands.

The door at the top of the stairs bursts open and a wave of sand rushes in, pouring down each stone step to gather at my feet. As soon as I have enough, I get to work. My power feels like it's cutting through my skin at the rate I'm going, but I've done this before, with less skill. Still, I almost expect to see blood wet the black sleeves of my shirt.

The instant I'm done, I slap my hand to the still hot glass. It singes, but I don't pull away, instead pushing my power into it until the glass changes. Opens.

Cain stands on the other side. "What the hells, Meren?"

"I know." I wave him in. "Yell at me later."

His power is how we get more of us into the palace faster. The water in the cistern starts to bubble as though caught in a strong current. Cain pushes the water out, past our feet, and through the still-open portal into the river in the canyon beyond.

He doesn't quit until the cistern is empty, the *drip, drip, drop* of what used to be there echoing through what are now long, narrow hallways.

"Follow me!" I yell and run into the tunnels.

I have to drag my hands along the wall and try to remember how it felt to swim this rather than run it, remember the path. But I get us there. We climb another set of stairs that lead to a door that the palace servants use to get water. It opens into the space between two palace walls.

When I reach for the knob, Cain drags me back behind him. "Not you first, Mer."

Goddesses save me from overprotective men. I swat him away. "Cut it out."

He shoves me at Reven, then opens the door to check for the guards who patrol the grounds. I guess it's clear because he runs off, the rest of the people he's commanding tonight following in swift order, leaving Reven to hold me back.

Well, hells.

34

THE FIGHT FOR OAESYS

I'm practically coming out of my skin as fighters rush past. Telling Reven I'm the queen is like telling a mosquito to stop biting me. It won't make any difference.

"Okay," he finally says, releasing me.

I rush out of the cistern into the open area between the walls, but already I can see there's nothing to do. Our people have already blown a hole in the far wall, and the last of them are surging through it into the private royal gardens.

Part of me mourns the destruction that a hundred fighters will wreak on the delicate plants, many of them gifts from other dominions that the palace gardeners carefully nurture and coax to stay alive in our particular climate. But the fate of Aryd is more important.

Shouts from all around the city, even louder now that we're out of the cistern, haunt my footsteps like angry ghosts. Forget the gardens. Innocent people—my people—may be hurt in this coup. There was no way to avoid that, but that doesn't mean I like it.

Cain waves. "Here!"

Rather than following our fighters through the gardens and into the servants' quarters through a side door I told them about, I lead Cain and Reven the opposite way toward where the gardens meet my sister's old chambers. With no hesitation born from long practice, I take a running leap at the wall where it meets the palace, using the corners to scale it quickly to the top.

"Don't do something like that without warning," Reven growls the second he reaches the small landing where I'm standing.

"I like that you care," I say. Which only earns me another grumpy sound.

Cain, however, grins as he gets to us. "That's my girl."

The way Reven's head whips around to pin Cain with a glare, I'm surprised he didn't break his neck. "According to Meren, she's *my* girl."

Possessiveness seems like a good sign, but not in the middle of an invasion. Letting the two of them sort that out, I scale the wall to my left and around the corner using small footholds and handholds that I've discovered over time breaking in and out of this place, until I make my way around the corner and onto the large balcony.

Goddess, it feels strange to do this now, in this way. Like a memory but not.

I run into the room and immediately start drawing sand to me. It doesn't take long before enough is piled at my feet and I'm creating another portal. The last step is to bring Tabra through safely.

The plan is to dress her as a queen so that as soon as we have the palace secured, we can present her to the people—show them that their rulers have taken back Oaesys. Hopefully quell any unrest stirred up. We decided to come here instead of the queens' quarters where I stayed while Eidolon had me under his thumb, because the other room—where it is, the access points, and the likelihood Tyndrans will set up camp there in case we come—is more dangerous.

I at least allow the glass to cool this time before I open the portal.

Except…no one is standing on the other side.

My immediate panic is enough to crack my control over the Shadows, and I have to stop to breathe through it, lashing them back down tight.

"Where is she?" I hear Cain demand, echoing my thoughts.

A roar resembling a clap of thunder shakes through the city, and my eyes fly open. Bene, grown to his full-size, must have taken to the skies to aid our coup. But I have bigger problems right now.

"Tabra!" I yell, leaning this way and that to try to see if she's off to the side of the portal. Maybe she's hiding to make sure the right person opens it?

But no one answers, and no one appears.

"Reven—"

I don't even get out what I want him to do before he's running through the portal into the red canyon beyond. He disappears just before my mind catches up with my fear and I realize that this could also be a trap. What if someone has her and they're holding her to draw one of us out?

I open my mouth to yell for him, but before I can, he appears in a swirl of shadow and jumps back through to my side.

"The camp is empty," he says. "There is no one there. Including your sister. No signs of a fight."

"Something is wrong," I say.

A thousand scenarios start building in my head. Maybe as one of the groups was running through, Tabra was discovered? Maybe our allies had to take Tabra with them to protect her? Maybe Eidolon came for them?

"Achlys is with her," Cain reminds me. "Tziah, too. And my father."

"That's not enough," I whisper, more to myself than him. Not to hold off Eidolon if he came for her.

Another of Bene's roars blasts directly overhead, followed by the scream of a man falling from the sky, close enough that I hear the muffled sound when his body hits the ground.

Without a word to Reven or Cain, I sprint out of the room into the hallway.

"Damn it, Meren!" Cain calls after me.

But Reven says nothing. I know he followed, because I can feel him with me.

Instead of going to where the royal chambers lead into the rest of the palace, I turn left. It's not far to reach a small door that looks more like an alcove. Ducking inside, I don't even need a lantern to guide my steps, despite it being pitch black. I know these winding stone stairs, worn into dips with the footsteps of my ancestors over thousands of years. They climb up a narrow spiral that could be claustrophobic for anybody who doesn't like tight spaces. The sound of male feet followed by some grunting and at least one of them saying, "Get out of my way," tells me both Reven and Cain are still with me.

I don't wait for them when I get to the top, bursting out of the doorway onto the large, flat rooftop of a parapet of our palace. Not the highest place, but one of them, and private, only used by the royal family. Not even servants are allowed up here.

I starburst my hands, shattering the portal I just made in my sister's chambers. Then, not even having to gather them at my feet, because the sand is right there, several floors below where I stand, I catapult the grains of sand up into the sky in an explosion that looks like a firework going off to celebrate our victory.

"What are you doing, Meren?" Cain yells at me. "You just told our enemies exactly where you are."

"I know." I glance back at the two men standing with me.

Cain's features twist in a furious sort of worry. Reven doesn't react. Maybe because he's thinking of what happened earlier. If I tap into Eidolon's power again, goddess help anyone around me. "Tabra is more important," I say.

An answering roar sounds through the sky a split second before shadow flashes across the city, and I look up into the brightness of the sun that has climbed higher, squinting against the light which is quickly blocked by the massive wings of the chimera-looking creature flaring wide to land not on the parapet but on the lower rooftop of the connected building, putting his head level with us.

Bene.

No one, not even those who have never traveled to our walls to see the ocean, could mistake him for anything but what he is. Not like this.

A man's face—a beautiful man's face—sits awkwardly within the head of a ram with its horns curling backward, but the jaw and mane are of a lion, and tusks like a wild boar protrude from between its lips. It has the arms and claws and torso of some kind of massive, fur-covered animal I've never been able to identify and haven't asked him about, but its legs and tail look like those of a wolf.

All carved from sand. My people must be terrified for their very lives, and maybe I shouldn't have agreed to include him in the fight, but at the moment, I'm glad I did.

"Tabra is missing," I tell him. "She's not in the camp where she's supposed to be. She must have had to go through with one of the other groups for some reason."

"What is your wish?" Not an ounce of hesitation.

"This used to be your city. You know where all our fighters are supposed to be."

Bene nods.

"Fly me over them."

"No!" Both Cain and Reven snap the word at the same time.

Thanks to Savanah's amulet, still around my neck, Bene's voice sounds in my head. *"I refuse, with respect."*

"Until we find your sister and bring her safely here, it would be foolish to risk both you and Tabra," Reven points out.

Ah hells. His logic is sound but cuts me to the quick. I can't lose Tabra. Not again.

"I'll go," Cain says. "Stay here, and I'll find her."

Pit of Bones swallow me whole. I have no choice.

I give a jerking nod, and immediately Cain crawls over the rail of the parapet and onto Bene's head, sliding down his back to sit at where his withers meet his neck.

"We shall find her and bring her to you," Bene assures me.

He spreads his wings and takes off with a whip of wind. I have to shield my face to keep from getting sand in my eyes. When I open them again it's to find Reven standing in front of me with his back to Bene, protecting me from the barrage.

He steps back. "There's nothing you can do from here."

"I know. Let's go get me dressed like we were going to do with Tabra, just in case."

It doesn't take us long to make our way back down to her old rooms, which are still surprisingly empty. In fact, the entire wing of the palace seems questionably void of people.

But worrying about that won't solve anything.

I head into the large open room off Tabra's bathing chambers, which still holds most of the princess's clothes. It doesn't escape me that, once more, Reven and I are repeating a moment from our lives before Eidolon took him.

I grab one of the simpler dresses I can find. "Can you go check on what's going on in the palace?"

"I'm not leaving you."

"I'll be fine." I lay the dress down across a vanity to walk back into the bedroom to the secret panel in the wall, which I press and it swings silently open. I show him the room with a wave. "See? If anybody comes, I can hide in here until I know it's safe. No one will know."

Unless it's Eidolon. He knows about these rooms now. I don't mention that bit.

Reven frowns, glancing from my face to the darkened room behind me and back.

"I promise," I assure him. "I won't take any risks."

Ironically, for once, I mean it.

His lips actually quirk although his eyes remain serious. "I think we both know better than that, princess."

Princess.

The word ricochets through me with a hundred memories in its wake. I don't even think he noticed he used it again, even though I've told him what it means to us.

Then he disappears, only a small disturbance of the shadows where he was standing giving any indication that he had been there at all.

As fast as I can, I get myself dressed in a sleeveless, sky-blue gown that cinches tight around my torso, practically pressing my breasts up to my chin, with a floor-length pleated skirt. Over that I don a sheer white robe, also sleeveless, with our three moons embroidered on the white silk. My hair will have to do the way it is, braided in a crown around the top of my head. It's probably sticking out in wisps by now, but there's not much I can do about it. I try to distract the eyes of anyone about to behold me with a tiara, the one that Tabra wore when she was recognized officially as the heir to the throne of Aryd at the age of ten summers.

Achlys was supposed to be here to help my sister do this, to expertly style her hair and her makeup. I'm terrible at any of that. I attempt only a few rudimentary things, made even more difficult by the distorted reflection in the obsidian block we use as a mirror.

I'm honestly not sure if I made it better or worse. Hopefully we'll find my sister before I ever have to show my face to anyone other than our own fighters.

"We have taken the city."

I jump at the sound of Reven's velvet voice, not realizing that he shadowed back to where I was sitting. I spin to face him on the small stool I'm sitting on, taking in his expression, which, as usual, gives nothing away. "So fast?"

That doesn't seem like a good sign. Does it? Or is it a sign of my slipping control over darkness that I expected more bloodshed?

He shakes his head. "Here in the palace, as soon as they saw us, the servants turned on the Tyndran soldiers, and together they were subdued easily enough. Eidolon's advisor, Pollux, is being held in the throne room for you and Tabra to speak with."

"And the rest of the city?"

"Listen," he says, then cants his head to look behind him, out the open balcony.

I don't even have to ask what I'm listening for. It's obvious the second he points out that there is no more noise. No yelling, no booms, no shouts. The city has gone quiet, the chaos of battle subdued.

"It was too easy," I say more to myself than him.

"I know."

I meet a gaze that is ever steady and know he's with me, at least in this.

"We'd better find out why."

Reven stays at my side as we make our way through the silent palace proper, down the long hallway with its obsidian wall decorated with painted carvings of the history of my people. I wonder if I'll be added to it now?

I don't stop to think about it as we pass through the buttressed entrance leading into the central courtyard of the palace grounds, then past the massive well in the center, with its staircase that winds down the wide circular walls to where the clearest, purest water in the kingdom flows.

Which is when I realize Reven is no longer beside me.

I stop to look back and find him standing very, very still between the columns of a covered walk, and everything inside me goes quiet. He's staring not at me, exactly. It's almost at me and through me and around me all at the same time.

And then it hits me…

This is where he kidnapped me. He knocked Cain out,

wrapped me in shadows, and stole me from the palace.

Does he remember?

"Hey." I take a tentative step forward, because there's something about him, maybe the way his shoulders are set that tells me not to startle him the way one should never surprise a coiled snake.

Only he blinks and everything about him eases, even though he doesn't move or change his expression.

Maybe that's not what that was. I'm too much of a coward to ask because I can't deal with it if the answer is no. At least not right this second.

"Okay?" I ask.

"Fine." Back to one-word answers.

When we make it into the throne room, Pella is already there. So are Vos, Hakan, Trysolde, Istrella, and most of the other leaders of the Wanderers, minus one or two. They are standing around a man who has been bound to—no, *by*—a metal chair. The chair itself is wrapped around him like vines around a trellis, including over the lower half of his face. Solid metal. No doubt Trysolde's doing, given he's a metal wielding Hylorae. That can't be comfortable.

When he spots us, Vos moves out of the gathered group. "That's Pollux, the advisor Eidolon left in control of Aryd."

I nod. "Do we have reports yet?" How many died for this to happen?

He shakes his head.

"We couldn't find her." Cain rushes into the room. Bene must still be outside. He looks around those gathered, starting to frown. "Pell?"

"I don't know where Father is," Pella says.

Of all the leaders of the Wanderer zariphates in the room, Cainis isn't one of them. He was with Tabra. Maybe he still is? I don't see Ledenon or his zaripha, either. Magda never leaves his side, not even in battle.

"Take Bene. Go to where they entered the city," I command Vos. "Make sure they are unharmed. They must have Tabra and are keeping her safe."

I'm clinging to the likelihood that not *all* of them could be in danger.

Vos leaves without a word, and the wait becomes something that puts even the patience of Aryd to the test. I move to one of the windows that has no stained glass, not since it was shattered when Reven and I fought Eidolon in this room.

I steady myself at the sight the blue morning sky, always true, despite everything going on down here. Night may come, but day will always follow. Somehow knowing that there is at least one constant in this world is enough. For the moment.

The massive heavy doors to the room groan as they are opened again, and we all turn, eager and hopeful, and an audible sigh of relief passes through the room as Zariph Cainis strides in—visibly unharmed though still limping from our fight in Tropikis. Magda is at his side.

But the instant he moves his large form so that I can see behind him, ice seeps into me, freezing everything—the blood flooding through my veins, my heart pumping in my chest, my thoughts.

Tabra is with him, her hands bound in front of her.

Achlys and Tziah trail behind her, also bound. In particular, Tziah is gagged.

Vos rushes into the room behind them, his scowl as fierce as any I've ever seen from him. Tziah's matching scowl around the cloth in her mouth shows exactly how pissed she is, but she shakes her head at him, then nods toward Achlys.

He skids to a halt at the sight of the knife Ledenon holds to Achlys's throat, then snaps his gaze to Cainis. "This better be a bad joke."

Something about his words finally burns away the ice inside me and sends me striding toward them. "What is this?" I demand in a voice that echoes off the vaulted ceilings.

"Father," Cain's voice is as hard and chipped as flint. "This better not be what I think it is."

"This is exactly that," Cainis snaps at his son, never taking his iron hard stare from me.

"What are you talking about?" Pella hisses at her brother before I can ask the same question.

Cain's jaw clenches. "A revolt."

"Didn't see that coming," a Shadow cackles inside me.

35

THE LAST THING WE EXPECTED

Pella shakes her head. "No. We all bowed to Meren. You included, Father. You swore—"

"Of course I did," Cainis snarls. "How else was I going to get in here and take back Aryd for all the *true* Arydians?"

My shoulders snap back so hard, he might as well have slapped me. "*I* am an Arydian." I point at Tabra. "*She* is the firstborn daughter of Antiamos, son of Queen Altice, rightful heir to the throne of Aryd. It doesn't get more Arydian than that."

"So you say," he sneers.

The hells?

Cainis turns in a circle, meeting the gaze of every leader in this room as he raises his voice. "You know my Enfernae power is the ability to see the truth of people's words…and I say to you that these two supposed princesses have been *lying*."

Lying?

Fury and disbelief sears down my throat and into my gut to swirl in a potent poisonous concoction. "We're not lying—"

"They have no proof of who they truly are." He shakes his head, his expression disappointed, as if he's reprimanding a recalcitrant child.

No proof? Is he kidding me? I'm going to kill this man, bury my knives in him a hundred times the second I get the chance.

"How deliciously logical," another Shadow comments.

And then another slides in with, *"I never trusted the man."*

After that they all get too loud to pick out specific words. "I entered the land of death!" I snap at Cainis as I try to wrangle them. But I'm too angry, my control slipping more with every passing second.

"Only your sister and the old woman you claimed was the queen's sister saw you."

I point outside. "Bene follows me. He knows me."

He openly scoffs. "Are we really going to allow a Devourer to vouch for them?"

"Our vizier, Ishaf— "

"On the way here, I found that old man dead in the streets wearing nothing but beggar's clothes. He was the only supposed 'leader' from the palace to come to our talks with your faithful servant."

"One less traitor for us to deal with," the Shadows crow.

I don't have time to register the lance of pain that pierces my chest at the news of Ishaf's death before Cainis continues.

"And that is the biggest proof we have of your lies. I've known you since you were a child—a poor, city waif. And your twin, supposedly *the* princess, is in a relationship with her servant. No royal would ever lower themselves to familiarity let alone love for a servant. The ridiculous stories you two are weaving are as flimsy as spider silk." He shakes his head. "Not to mention what *I* have the power to see." His face contorts. "Every word you've uttered since my son brought you to me from the Shadowood has been a *lie*."

Cainis scans the room again, the faces of our allies. I don't need to look to know they're as stunned as I am. The expression he aims at me is curled with satisfaction because no one else is arguing. No one is standing up for me.

"Kill him," they urge me. *"Show these fools what happens to those who stand against you."*

I reach for Eidolon's power. The only power I have that can stop this bastard traitor—

A warm hand lands on mine, and suddenly Reven is beside me. His turquoise eyes glitter with anger, but he shakes his head at me. At *me*. "Easy," he whispers.

But that only whips up my own mounting anger.

Easy?

Goddess damned easy?

I'll show them all easy.

Darkness within the corners of the room rises around us, but the way those shadows rear up, out of control, it finally strikes me. *That's* why Reven's telling me to be easy. I'm doing it again. It's happening again.

"You see!" Cainis's voice rings with triumph and surety. "She is dangerous to us, and so is the Shadowraith she bonded with."

The others probably don't see Reven's reaction, but his hand clamps down on mine so hard I have to keep from wincing or closing my eyes.

Now he knows.

Blast. That was a conversation I should have had with him in private.

"I bet he remembers *everything*," Cainis accuses. "These liars are *all* a danger to us. I know the truth. The true princess was killed by Eidolon even before the coronation." He points a beefy finger at Pollux, still trapped in the metal chair. "*He* will tell you."

Pella takes a halting step forward but lowers her head, gaze on her feet as if she's submitting. Her words say otherwise. "Don't do this, Father."

"Hold your tongue, Daughter," the zariph snarls, "or I'll cut it out of your mouth."

"No." She snaps her head up, and her eyes glisten with tears. "My power comes from yours. I don't see truth…I see emotion." She takes a shuddering breath, and because this is Pella, who has always yearned for her father's love and approval all her life, I know exactly how hard standing up to him is for her. "Take it back or I'll tell them the truth."

Shock widens Cainis's eyes before he surges forward. "I always knew you were a snake in the grass."

"No—" Magda puts out a hand, but the zariph shrugs her off.

Pella closes her eyes as if she can't stand to look at them. "My father's emotions are a swirl of greed for power and…lies. *He* is the liar here."

"Damn you." Cainis's body shakes with rage. "You are no daughter of mine."

Pella's shoulders fall as she rounds in on herself.

Cainis looks to Ledenon. "Take the false princesses and their cohorts to the dungeons where they will await trial for their sins."

"No."

The word—soft, yet hard as a boulder around which a raging river breaks—comes from Cain.

36

THE WAY

My best friend faces down his father, his hands fisted at his sides.

Cainis grunts. "You are not zariph yet."

"I'm not arguing about this, Father."

"Good. Neither am I."

Ledenon steps between them. "It might be better to discuss—"

"Shut up," father and son both snap at the zariphate's second-in-command.

Ledenon holds up his hands, backing away.

"Do not make this move," Cain says.

Cainis scowls. "Stand in my way and face the consequence."

Neither is being specific about the move being made, but they clearly both know what they're talking about. Which means they've discussed this before already. Maybe a lot.

And Cain never said one word to me about it.

Why? Did he think he could sway his father and stop it before it got to this? Clearly that was a huge mistake.

"If you refuse to abandon this path," Cain says in a dark voice, "you won't remain zariph for much longer."

"You think you can defeat me, whelp? Give it your best, because if you come at me, you'd better kill me."

Wanderers have their own laws, and what Cain just said is as close to a direct challenge as it gets. A challenge that will determine who controls the zariphate and who dies.

"Is that what you really want?" Cain demands. "Are you so hungry for power that you'd kill me to get it? You've already disowned Pella. You kill me and you have no one to inherit your precious legacy."

Regret flashes in the zariph's eyes as he looks at his beloved son, but he quickly shores it up behind stony determination that goes as high and impenetrable as our glass walls. "This is our way. We can't have a zariph and a zariphson or zariphdaughter on opposite ends of a decision this important. If you don't stand with me, then you'll have to take the zariphate from my cold, dead hands."

"Cain, don't," I say, voice low.

The decision wars across his features, his brown eyes nearly black with pain. This is tearing him apart.

"Not for me," I say quietly. "Not for this."

I'll do it. Yet another traitor in our midst. He deserves to die. He deserves to bleed in front of his people so they see the consequences—

I cut off the thought, putting a hand to my stomach to hold in my gasp. That wasn't the Shadows this time. Where the hells did that come from? That's not me. That's not who I am. Or is this who I've become?

I sneak a peek around, but everyone is still focused on Cainis and Cain. Except Reven. Reven is watching me, shoulders tense.

Oh goddess. He saw that.

"This isn't about you," Cain says to me. His quiet words are just as determined as his father's. "There is a right way and a wrong way to do something." His eyes go obsidian hard, jaw clenched. "I won't stand by and watch the wrong way."

Without warning, Cainis lunges for his son with a shout, a wicked-looking blade already in his hand, seemingly out of nowhere. Taking the decision away from Cain.

Reven grabs me by the waist and swings me against him, a

hand coming up to cradle the back of my head. I can't tell if he's protecting me from watching my best friend fight for his life, or if he's keeping me from joining the fray.

I grip his arms, holding on to him—just for now—and watch as the pair go at each other in a battle of skill that is so evenly matched, you can see the ways in which the father has taught the son. But that means that neither of them has the upper hand here. The metal of their blades flash, their fists swing and connect. Those of us watching have to scatter several times as the fight ranges around the room.

I don't want Cain to die. I would never want that. But killing his own father, his hero, would gut him. I don't want that, either. No matter what I was thinking a second ago.

Cain executes a spinning move on his knees, ducking under his father's blade, and Cainis's grunt tells us all that his son struck flesh. But as Cain comes back to his feet, his father does the same move, spinning into Cain.

I don't need to hear Cain's hiss because I see the way Cainis's blade strikes true, sinking into his son's thigh, a bloom of red immediately visible in the sandy color of his clothes.

They both come to their feet, faced off. Cainis even lifts his shirt to check his belly, but the wound Cain inflicted isn't deep, barely trickling. He drops his shirt, then deliberately wipes the blade of his own knife off on his pants, leaving a streak of red.

"Come on, old man," Cain growls.

When they launch at each other again, though, Cain can't hide his limp.

More impressive maneuvers on both sides, more flashing blades, more tension-filled moments as my muscles clench and unclench in time to their movements, their attacks, parries, and retreats. At one point, Reven grunts. I'm clutching his arm so hard it'll leave a mark.

But...gradually...Cainis starts to breathe heavier, sucking in harshly, and his strikes turn less controlled, wilder. I think everyone is starting to realize who will win this.

Including Cainis.

Which is when, as the zariph circles the room, he lurches away from Cain and yanks Tabra up against his chest, using her as a shield with a knife to her throat.

I see in the split second that Tabra's gaze searches out Achlys, her fear and her soft heart on display for anyone looking, before she squeezes her eyes shut.

But then Cainis chokes suddenly, his eyes bulging and it's almost like he tries to pull away, but then his expression goes creepily peaceful. Like bliss.

"Do it," Pella says.

How did I miss her dropping to the ground at his feet? She has her hand wrapped around the bare skin of his ankle, purple light sneaking out between her fingers. She has to be using her ability to manipulate his emotions. She can only do that if she's touching skin. Hakan stands close behind her, ready to protect her if he has to.

"Do it, Cain!" her voice wavers mid-shout.

Cain looks from his sister to his father's face, then with a cry of a son's world tearing in two, he plunges his knife to the hilt, right into his father's heart.

37

OURS

Cainis's eyes go wide with shock, and on a sob that wracks his entire body, Cain wraps his free arm around his father's shoulders, pulling him into a hug. To not have to watch as the life seeps out of him.

But I see the way the zariph's eyes turn glassy with death. I see his last breath.

Cain must feel it because he steps away, shoulders back, head held high. Cainis's corpse falls to the black marbled floors in a heap at Cain's feet.

"No!" The scream from Magda is like rending of bone—a terrible sound that strikes deep. She runs across the room.

Chaos erupts all around us.

Pella's on the floor beside her father. Hakan, behind her, can't even look at her, though he's hooked his pinkie finger through hers, no doubt careful not to shock her. I drop down beside Pella just in time for her to look up at Cain with brimming eyes pleading for understanding.

"I had to," she says, as tears slip down her cheeks. "*You* had to. If he won, he'd kill our rightful queens and you, too, maybe. If you did this on your own, it would have killed you."

Impossible to miss the way Cain swallows hard, his throat moving with it. "I know," he says. "I..." He looks down at his father's face, then at the knife still grasped in the zariph's hand. "I know."

Magda, meanwhile, kneels by her bondmate's head in a position Wanderers use for prayer, her head bowed. Her shoulders heave. Just once. Before she makes the sign of the sun over her heart.

Then with a screech to wake the dead, Magda grabs Cainis's knife and lifts it to plunge into her own heart.

Pella moves with the lightning speed of a born and bred fighter, tackling her mother to the floor and knocking the knife out of her hand, but Magda goes wild, thrashing in her daughter's grasp. "Let me go with him!"

She wrenches herself from Pella's hands and crawls to Tabra, hands on the floor, supplicant, begging. "Don't leave me here without him," she pleads. "Let me send myself to the afterlife, my queen. Cainis and I are bonded. We'll find each other again. But if I'm here, we'll remain separated for longer. I can't—" Her voice breaks and she trembles, head still down. Then takes an audible breath. "I can't."

Quiet takes over the room. Not soft but weighted. And in that quiet, Tabra nods.

"Mami," Pella whispers into the silence. "Please."

Magda straightens and looks at her daughter with all the love I've ever imagined a mother can feel for a child. "We've raised you well. You don't need me anymore."

Pella makes a sound that might be a whimper. "I will always need my mother."

Magda's chin quivers. Pella takes a stuttering breath, then picks up the knife from the floor and holds it out to her mother. "Go. Find him in your afterlife."

"May the grace of the sands be with you always," Magda whispers as she takes the blade.

Pella passes her trembling hand in front of her chest in a waving motion as if tracing the flow of sand dunes. Her answer.

With a sharp inhale, Magda plunges the knife into her own chest. As she falls forward, her body drapes over Cainis. It only takes a few gasps, like a fish out of water, before she stops breathing.

And I think the rest of us stop for a moment, too.

I don't know what I expect. Definitely not for Tabra to step between all of us and smooth her hands over her clothes.

Her face is pale and drawn with shock and regret, but my sister lifts her chin. "Is this over?"

She's asking Cain if the revolt is finished.

He must realize the significance of the question, because he faces her and formally bows. "As leader of the Cain Zariphate..."

Leader of the zariphate. Zariph.

The shock of those words hits all at once, and I suck in a breath.

Cain, my friend, who I've played with in the sand since I was five summers old. The boy who always felt like home, who taught me to ride horses and use my knives, and who put a scorpion in his father's bed after Cainis said something mean about me that I can't even remember now.

That boy just killed his father and is now the leader of the largest, most powerful zariphate in Aryd.

Things had already changed, but this is so much bigger.

The childhood we had together? That's gone forever.

He clears his throat. "As Zariph, I pledge to our queens our loyalty."

Hard-won loyalty that we'd thought we already had. I can't help the bitterness seeping through me like a venom.

Behind him, Ledenon and the leaders of the other zariphates line up, shoulders back, heads proud. They stand with Cain. With us.

Tabra gives a nod. "Then it's time to present us to our people."

Us?

She holds her hand out to me, and I take it, getting to my feet.

"Ready?" she asks.

No.

But I nod.

We leave Cain and Pella behind with the Wanderers, Tziah

and Hakan staying with them to help them through their grief, but the others follow as we make our way through the palace. Then, a half-dressed princess and her bedraggled sister still dressed as a Wanderer walk out onto the wide protruding balcony overlooking the mall where it seems as though the entire city has gathered in silence. Waiting for us.

I don't see a single pop of Tyndran white armor anywhere among them.

"People of Aryd," Tabra calls out. Her voice, clear and true and steady, seems to lift into the skies and roll outward. "I am Queen Tabra Eutheria I of Aryd. And this is my twin sister, Mereneith Evangeline XII, kept secret from you all these years."

An audible gasp surges through the crowds.

Tabra waits a moment for it to quiet before she continues. "We know that under our grandmother's rule you have suffered the slow descent into poverty as our desert world gets hotter and hotter. And these last months have only worsened our plight with King Eidolon in command, holding both me and my sister hostage with the threat of death."

A second, louder gasp passes through our people.

Tabra lifts her hands, like she's beckoning our people to us. "But we have returned to you now."

Tabra is everything a queen should be in this moment, not needing queenly raiment to show her true worth, and I can see the expressions on the faces nearest us slowly changing from shock, horror, and suspicion to wonder, surety, and trust.

To belief.

That is what Tabra inspires without trying. Belief.

"We have fought for and reclaimed our throne," she announces. "We have formed allies among the zariphates of Wanderers, the Vanished of the Shadowood, and with the dominion of Wildernyss, and we will form allegiances to stand against Eidolon. We wish you to know that we fight for *you*. For the people of Aryd. Always."

She lowers her hands to place them on the rail in front of her, leaning toward her people as she shouts not a request but a demand. "Will you fight with us?"

With. Not for.

For at least ten of my heartbeats, the people are silent. Then a single voice rings out from the back. "To Queen Tabra and Queen Mereneith, ever may they reign!"

A resounding surge of cries of the same words and cheers rises into the skies, cut off harshly by the flash of a shadow overhead. Many of the people duck, and a few even scream as Bene lands on top of the palace roof directly over our heads, wings spread wide, and trumpets a call of triumph…and maybe a warning.

The queens of Aryd—both queens standing side by side like I never could have imagined—have a Devourer on their side.

Another beat of silence and the people erupt in a frenzy of applause and shouts of support. Tabra steps back and takes my hand, lifting our clasped hands to the skies, and the crowds only grow louder with their praise. She looks at me and smiles, even as up close I can see the toll of the day in her eyes that no longer shine at me with innocence.

But we did it. With the help of our friends and allies, we did it.

The dominion is ours.

PART 4

THE KING HUNT

38

THE MAGIC THAT WAS US

I stand in the open doorway, arms crossed and my shoulder propped against the jamb, staring into the darkness of the hidden room off my sister's old chambers that was mine for eighteen summer solstices.

After our triumphant announcement that there are now two queens, not one, the instant we stepped back inside the palace, I was immediately hustled away, split up from Tabra, who was taken to the queen's chambers—she's the older, after all—while I was brought to the princess's rooms that were ours. Here, I've been bathed—or scoured, more like—oiled, perfumed, primped, and dressed by an army of silent, smiling servants.

All with a watchful, wary light in their eyes. I'm pretty sure I've figured out why. I have known most of them for a good long while, only they always thought I was Tabra. They have no idea what to make of a second one of us.

They only loosened up when I finally said, "Let's air this out a bit. Any time in the last nineteen years that you thought Tabra was acting funny…it was probably me." Which made them laugh, and even share a moment or two that fit that description.

All of which were spot on, by the way. I guess I wasn't as good at pretending to be my sister as I thought I had been.

My servants are gone now, leaving me abandoned with a thousand thoughts that I'd rather not be alone with. I sigh and say to myself, "I guess we should do something with this room now."

And our glass flower garden, too. Or do we keep that just for us?

A knock at the door has me frowning, even more so when Nhalin, the poor woman who drew the lot of being my own personal companion, like Achlys has been for Tabra, opens the door. "The high priestess of the temple is here, domina, along with..." She stumbles, and a deep voice sounds from behind her. "Reven Shadowraith."

I don't blame her for the stumbling. A man who looks like a younger version of King Eidolon, but is something else altogether, would make even the boldest of hearts pause. I'm personally stumbling over the fact that he's here now, given that he had disappeared by the time Tabra and I left the balcony earlier. And he's here with a priestess of all people.

At least I don't say *what the hells* out loud.

Instead, I nod, and try to force my features into benign curiosity as the priestess enters. "Yes?"

There. That sounds queenly—the perfect combination of polite and impatient.

Apparently, the priestess doesn't know why they're here, either, because she turns to look at Reven with raised eyebrows.

He's standing just inside the door, still dressed in his Wanderer clothing, staring at me now full-on princess in a strapless gown of rust red, shot through with glittering threads and woven with geometric patterns across the hem and bodice. My hair is simpler, still braided though still fancier than earlier, formed into two loops on either side.

When he doesn't answer immediately, I have to stop myself from crossing my arms to cover my body. Goddess, I feel more like a liar in these clothes as myself than I ever did imitating Tabra. I don't shift on my feet, though. I don't speak. I wait.

He came to me with a priestess. He should definitely be the

one to talk—

"You didn't tell me we were bondmates," he says.

Regret is more weight, I'm learning. Heavy and hard to carry.

"I...was waiting to tell you," I say quietly, trying to ignore the third person in the room with us for this awkward conversation as well as my shaking knees and hands. I knew this was coming, but not like this.

"For what?"

"More trust. It would have seemed like a play to convince you—"

He looks away. "Now it seems like another lie."

I flinch. What else can I say? I held that back for the right reasons. I'd do it again. But I hate the way he found out. "I'm sorry."

After a second, Reven gives a single nod.

"So...why are you here?" I shoot the priestess a deliberate questioning look.

Reven answers for them both. "The priestess is here to see what she can do."

My eyebrows shoot up. "Do? About what?"

"Our bonds hold our memories of each other."

You would think, after all I've been through lately, that I would never again allow hope any room in my heart. But it starbursts inside me all the same, lighting me up from the inside. "They do?"

The priestess nods. "Yes, domina. It's what helps you find each other in the afterlives. The memory of what you were before." She smiles. "Some call it love at first sight, but truly it's your bonds remembering for you."

Mother goddess. Is it possible?

The memories that have been bombarding me, all the echoes of the past in what we do together now, is that what that is? I glance at Reven, expecting to see the same shining hope in his eyes, only to mentally stumble at the way he's holding himself so stiffly.

"Do you want to remember…us?" I ask.

Those beautiful ocean water eyes are as hard as cut gems. "I want to remember. That's all."

Not *us*. All of the light flees from me so fast I feel like a dark cloud has passed before the sun and can't help the shiver that builds and scatters over my skin. He didn't even bother to soften it.

I blow out a breath full of frustration and longing and pent-up everything. "You really can be a dick sometimes."

He pulls back slightly, blinking.

"Is it difficult?" I ask the priestess. "Does it hurt?"

Her smile is gentle, eyes kind as she shakes her head. "It is very easy, and no, there is no pain nor danger."

She pulls out a spool of gossamer-fine thread from a pocket in her long sleeve, the same kind that was used to bind us by a priestess in Tropikis. Cutting off a small length, she holds the ends between her fingers and thumbs and lifts it into the air before her, stretched out, then whispers a few words that I can't catch. The thread itself ignites with tiny pale pink flames that make it glitter and spark.

The priestess lets go and it remains there, suspended in the air with nothing holding it.

"Now," she says, beckoning us with a wave of her hands. "Both of you touch one end at the same time."

Reven and I move to stand opposite each other, separated by the burning thread. We both lift our hands to touch a single finger to the ends.

I gasp. I can't help it. The sensation that jolts through me isn't fire or burning…it's ice. Like when I pull Eidolon's power through the curse and it fills my veins. I almost let go, but the sensation is gone quickly, replaced by warmth. The kind that reminds me of sitting around a fire in the desert when I was a child, safe in the circle of its light but with the cold of the desert at my back.

It seeps through my fingertips, filling my hand before climbing up my wrist. The warmth shifts into heat, a sharp burn that sears through blood and bones and flesh and into my core, taking up a thrumming inside me.

I grit my teeth and try not to move, to not squirm with this delicious intensity. This *need.* A need for him I've been holding back, locking tight inside myself but away from the Shadows, trying not to overwhelm Reven unless he's mine again. Truly mine.

The first flicker of light on my skin has relief coming out in a *whoosh.* The bond is still there. My lips lift into a trembling smile. The sparkling golden lines of our bond brighten yet again, turning more dazzling with each passing second. I peek at Reven, who appears…arrested by the sight.

"That's not possible," the priestess whispers.

"We already know," I say. We have two sets of bonding marks. Mine, though, will be fainter than his.

"But—"

I smile at her visible confusion. "We bonded in my previous life, but his current life. He is a Shadow of King Eidolon made flesh—"

"Not that."

I frown, then it finally sinks in that she's staring at *his* arm, not mine.

His lines are there, both of them, but they're broken in many different places and blackened like wood charred by fire.

Dawning horror takes root.

No. Goddess no.

"I can't fix this." The priestess turns her head away, like she can't stand the sight, but her gaze snags on my arm now.

A new line snakes around the brighter line of my bond in this life. A line made of shadow.

And I know.

Eidolon.

Eidolon did this.

He broke our bond, I'm assuming while Reven was inside him, or took it over, or inserted himself in there. After all, Reven is a fragment of the king who originally bonded with my ancestress, my previous life.

I let go of the thread.

Immediately, the lines on our arms fade. But not fast enough, and the shattering pieces of my glass heart slowly chip away and cut me open.

Our bond failed us…for the second time.

39

EVER MORE

Reven let's go of the line, too, and it floats away, disintegrating as it does, like an ember caught on the breeze.

"I'm sorry," the priestess says.

"There's nothing that can be done?" Reven asks.

She shakes her head. "I've never seen a bond broken in all my years. Never heard of it happening in all of history. Nothing in our books and scrolls even mentions it." She glances between us, mouth open like she wants to say more, then shakes her head again.

"Could we bond again? Would that fix it?" I ask. Hope is a nasty, desperate, pathetic thing sometimes.

She purses her lips, thinking. "It would rebond you, but likely not restore what's lost."

And Reven doesn't want to rebond with me. Not now, at least.

"I see," I say, and turn away from both of them, walking toward the hidden panel in the wall. Not the one to the secret room, the one to our glass flower garden.

"Meren?" Reven's voice reaches across the distance between us, but I don't stop or turn back. I can't.

"Please go." I need him to leave before I give in to the emotions that are crashing through me in a riotous storm.

"Are you sure—"

"Just go." *Go before I lose it.*

I pause, staring at the wall, waiting. And when the soft *click* of the door closing behind them sounds, I squeeze my eyes shut.

It doesn't help, though, because when I do that, I see his arm and the evidence of our broken bond.

Eidolon poisons everything he touches. I knew that, and yet somehow, I thought our bond was safe. But even that is destroyed.

No more bond, and instead I'm tethered to the wrong version of the same man.

With hands turning lifeless, I press at the panel and follow the steps down into the walled-in secret garden, coming out into moonlight that makes my creations wink and sparkle. Different flowers, different colors from the sands around our dominion that Tabra would bring me from her visits, the earliest ones misshapen, the more recent lovely in their smooth simplicity.

I drop onto a chaise lounge that sits in here beside a small table, only I don't want to lie down. Instead, I draw my knees up against my chest and wrap my arms around them and stare at the single black flower among all the glittering colorful ones, that one made from the sand of the Obsidian Desert.

Tabra brought that sand back from her first visit to our ever-burning Sacred Tree. I was so jealous she got to go for our sixteenth name day. I'd wanted to see the Sacred Trees of the dominions more than anyone. Cain had promised he'd take me to see ours together, but he went without me, too.

A sigh escapes me.

That day Eidolon took Reven back into himself, I was bracing for the pain I knew would come next, the knowledge that I'd have to go on without him and keep fighting. But that was when at least a small part of me believed that Reven would remain alive and well and mine even trapped inside Eidolon, and that I'd get him back some day, even if it's in an afterlife.

Now even that tiny sliver of hope has been taken away.

I wonder…would Scoria take my soul now if I asked her to? Or maybe Tabra could release me? She has her throne back, and allies to help her defeat Eidolon.

As for me…

I turn away from the flowers that mock me with the person I was when I made them, trapped in a life I didn't want but full of thoughts of a future all the same. Even if I resented the path I was on, I didn't want to run and hide from it like I do now. Even the moonlight is too bright here.

I lay my cheek on my knees and stare into the shadows in the corners that escape the moons. Quiet shadows. Darkness used to hide me, protect me, but now is trying to kill me from inside.

"I can't do this anymore," the words whisper from me. "I don't *want* to do this anymore."

The shadows don't move. They don't do anything. And Eidolon's shards are locked so deep, they can't—

"Meren."

My eyes flash open. For a split second I think maybe the Shadows got out, but the wall beside me shows the shadow of a man.

On a gasp, I jerk my head up to stare at Reven who is standing there…staring at me, turquoise eyes inscrutable as always.

I use my shoulder to wipe away tears I didn't even know had fallen. "I told you to leave me alone."

"I can't."

I glare at him. "Can't or won't? I'm fine. I don't need you—"

"I heard you."

I'm irritated and too exhausted—mind, body, and soul—to even hazard a guess as to what he means. "Heard what?"

"I heard your words in the dark. Felt your pain."

I still can't find the energy to move…or care. "And what? You came here to end it for me?"

"No." He surges forward, dropping to sit on the chaise beside me before I realize he's even moved. "Don't wish that. Ever."

"What do you care?" The whisper is raw in my throat.

He grunts like those words hurt him, then he reaches for me like he's going to cup my face, but I lean back, as much as the chair allows, and he stills, hands midair, his gaze flashing to mine.

Don't touch me unless you mean it.

Instead, we stare at each other. I pretend his gaze really does lose the distance that's been there, and he's looking at me the way he once did. It hurts. Goddess, does it hurt. I wish he'd leave, and I wish he'd stay all at the same time.

"Fuck," he mutters.

Then his hands are in my hair and his mouth crashes into mine.

40

FINALLY

The second our lips meet, I just…melt. All of the anger and sadness fades away as he claims me, fills the hole inside me, not with love, not with knowing we belong to each other. This is carnal. It's pure need to be touched and feel less alone because of it.

For him, too?

I surge into his kiss on a whimper. I don't care why, or if he'll ever remember our past.

Goddess, I've missed this.

I've missed Reven in ways I didn't know were possible. I expected it in the bigger ways, his absence heavy on me as I made decisions, or at night by myself in the quiet. But it's the small moments that were slowly killing me. A look. A brush of a hand. The warmth of him standing next to me.

And this.

Being able to kiss him like this. No holding back. Easy and effortless and…us.

Only this isn't us. Not really.

"We should stop," Reven groans.

Any response I might have made is stilled by his lips, by the tease of his tongue, and the way he sweeps his hands up my back, pulling me so close that there's not even a hint of space separating us.

We can talk later, figure it out later. Right now, need—pent up and shaken up and woken up—is everything.

Never stopping what our mouths are doing, I manage to get my hands between us and start undoing his shirt. I'm plucking ineffectually at a button when his large hand covers both of mine, stopping me.

"You understand I'm not him. I'm not—"

"I understand."

I hardly get the words out before he's kissing me again. Only this time, maybe because we've both agreed how far this is going, it's like we've both been untethered, his kisses become urgent, desperate, and air is going to be a problem in a second. I don't care.

Lips on mine, Reven knocks my hands away from his shirt and whips it off and I'm in his arms again, reveling in the way I can touch him like this, even if it's just for tonight, my fingertips relearning and memorizing the tautness of his skin, the ridges of muscles, the breadth of his shoulders.

He trails kisses across my jaw, and I lean my head to the side so he can feather his lips down my neck. At the curve where my neck and shoulder meet, he sucks. I quiver, already throbbing for him. His bold hands quickly draw my fancy dress over my head, leaving me in only a wisp of underclothes.

His hands are everywhere, then. Spanning my waist. Over my hips. Cupping my backside as he presses into me. Only those questing fingers stop short of where I want him to touch.

"If you're going to tease me all night"—I reach a hand between us and run it down the hard ridges of his stomach, but also not far enough down—"two can play that game."

He buries his face in my neck and groans, his body trembling against me.

That's when I remember that for me, this is familiar, but for him…

In holding so tightly onto the history already between us, I forgot that in his mind, it's his first time all over again. First desire. First kiss. All of it.

My heart expands with extra love for this man. I love that

I'm his first again and making it special for him just shot to the top of my priority list.

Before I can slow us down, give him time to tease and explore and discover all he wants at his pace, his mouth is on mine again. Commanding. Insistent. And not even a little bit hesitant. He knows what he wants.

With hungry little noises, I give him back kiss for kiss. Goddess, I love the way he kisses me.

In his arms—regardless of whether the touches are sweet and tender or rough and ready, regardless of what he remembers—I'm home. I'm where I'm supposed to be.

I nip at his lip.

On a guttural sound, mouth still pressed against mine, he removes the rest of his clothes. Then he's gathering me closer again. Reven bends me over his arm at my back, lips trailing across my jaw, down my neck, and lower. A teasing finger slips the material of my band down under my breast, exposing me to the night air.

He pauses, staring down at me, his throat working. With a reverence that sends heat tumbling through every inch of me, he traces a fingertip over the swell. Teasing torture as he makes smaller and smaller circles. I stare, transfixed and holding my breath, watching his hands upon my body, my stomach clenching. Everything clenching.

Except again, he teases, coming closer, but not close enough.

The third time he does this, I whimper. The crooked, searing smile that brings to his face knocks any breath left in my body right out.

Then he lowers his head, mouth right where I want it, and I gasp at the sensation that reaches inside me, tension building and surging. Like lightning waking every single nerve and stringing them together into one single swell of sensation.

"*Reven*," I moan.

"I know," he says against my skin. "I feel it, too."

He stands us both upright and, with hands visibly shaking, quickly removes the last of my clothing while backing me out of the garden and into my bedroom.

As soon as I'm standing before him, vulnerable and needy, any small moment of self-consciousness is swallowed by the heat of his eyes as he runs his fascinated, hot gaze over my body. As if he's memorizing every curve, every dip, the moonlight on my skin. The same way I'm memorizing this moment with him just in case we don't get another one. I didn't do that enough before. I believed we'd have more time, and I was wrong.

The skin tightens over his cheekbones as he looks at me. "The goddesses formed you in their image when they made you, Meren," he says, his voice a rasp that might as well be a physical touch.

The way my skin flushes *everywhere* sets a smile to his lips that is pure Reven, intense in a way that sends more heat everywhere.

An emotion shifts over his features. One too swift for me to be able to name it. One that sends a small flutter of panic through me at the mere thought of not reaching the end of this must show in my expression or my voice when I say his name.

Understanding flares in his eyes. Urgency lines every move as he sweeps me into his arms, kissing me like he can't stop. Before I can take a breath, we're lying among the silky sheets of the bed.

He settles between my thighs, his weight over me both ratcheting my need for him higher while also feeling so very, very right.

"I've dreamed of you like this," he says in a low, need-filled voice between kisses. "Memories, maybe. I didn't know Shadows could dream, but I did. I do…"

At the sound I make—raw, impatient need—he rocks his body against mine, rubbing against a spot that has me gasping.

I lift my legs around him, settling him even more into me. He kisses his way down my neck, and like he can't help himself, sucks the delicate skin there. Hard.

Marking me. Claiming me. Even if it's primal.

I claim him right back.

With a smile I can feel, he lifts his head and then slows his rocking, that friction stilling, and a small sound of disappointment escapes me. I need more, not less. Before I can demand it, he resumes the canting of his hips. Sensation sizzles along every nerve ending, filling my body with a building rush and a pulsing ache at my core that sends tension thrumming and growing inside me. Until he stops again. At my frown, he starts again. Only to stop again when I moan. Then does that again. And again. And each new round layers more tension until I'm bursting at the seams with it.

My entire existence narrows to turquoise eyes and the joining of our bodies.

"*Please*," I beg when he slows again.

In a fluid move, he rolls so that he's the one lying on his back among the pillows and I'm straddling him. I end up with my hands propped on his chest, my eyes wide.

His smile is pure sin…and a dare. "Go ahead."

I'm so wrapped up in his voice that I almost miss the words. But as soon as they sink in, a flush turns every inch of me bright red. "You want me to…"

I can't even finish the sentence. I'm not used to discussing such things, even in the middle of doing those exact things.

"I want you to."

Hot both inside and out, I wonder if I'm bold enough.

Slowly, I lower my body, leaning on my hands for leverage, holding my breath.

A flush matching my own burns over his skin once we are joined. My body is full of him, merged with him, at one with him. At his choked groan, I smile. I guess I'm doing this right.

"Yes," Reven says in a voice that has gone hard and strained. "Just like that."

That does it. Tips me past the point of control.

I move. I move and he moves with me. A dance that I know intimately now. A dance that his body knows, even if his mind doesn't. Our connection, ruined or not, sparks bright and wonderful between us.

"Hells, Meren," he sighs.

With a grin, I lean forward and chase my own pleasure as well as his with every move, every kiss, every breath, every pounding, erratic heartbeat.

Building and building and building.

Our gazes lock. I want to memorize this moment. Get lost in it. I know too well now how precious and few these moments can be.

He's with me every step of the way. Reven and only Reven.

"Goddess," he rumbles.

Then his hands are at my hips, urging me, giving him leverage.

Sensation riots through me, and I grip him, holding on for dear life as we drive each other higher and higher and higher. With one hand, he presses and teases that precious point on my body that is all things sensation.

The tension pulls in tighter, then bursts outward in an explosion of pure pleasure. I fling my head back on a cry of release, Reven's shout joining mine as he reaches his own pinnacle.

Our movements slow gradually until we're both lying, sweat slicked and replete in each other's arms, breathing hard. He presses the softest, sweetest kiss to my shoulder, then adjusts us, his arm at my waist curling around to lift me and settle us both back within the pillows facing each other.

Exhaustion and an utter sense of safety and belonging pull me deeper toward dreamland. I know we should talk. I know there are probably things to be said. Hardly keeping my eyes open, I offer him a sleepy smile, then lift a hand to trace his lips.

In this moment, it's *all* I feel. No fears. No doubts. No worries. Just love. This man... This amazing man who has given, and worked, and sacrificed—I would do anything for him.

"I'll always choose you." I think I say the words, or maybe not?

I want to tell him more. To see some kind of change in him toward me, maybe. But sleep is dragging me under, and all I can do is curl into him and let go.

41

WAS IT ALL A DREAM?

I wake slowly, eyes still closed but able to see the sunlight behind my lids, and everything about last night comes back to me. Giving a luxurious stretch, I pause midway through as it sinks in that I'm not in his arms anymore. With a frown, I open my eyes. He's not here.

I try not to give in to the slap of immediate disappointment and feel the sheets beside me, but they've long gone cold.

Levering up on one elbow, I look around only to still at the sight of Reven at the side of the bed, sitting in a straight-backed chair—one that usually is at the desk on the far wall. He's watching me with an expression that sends a chill like a spider crawling over my skin.

"Reven?" I ask, my voice coming out both sleep-husky and tentative. "What—"

"I'm sorry," he says.

Two words that I shouldn't be hearing after what we shared. But it's his tone that's like a gong, sending a reverberation through me. Too many emotions to sift. "Why?"

He lets out an audible breath and glances away.

I can see the struggle in him, the unyielding way he's holding himself and his hands fisted in his lap. I'd get up, go to him, but something in my gut tells me not to. Instead, I cover myself more with the sheet and sit up the rest of the way. Which draws his gaze back to me, and I don't miss the way his lips press tight.

"Why are you sorry?" I ask.

He closes his eyes for a second before focusing on my face, seeming to search it. "I shouldn't have done that."

Part of me was expecting something along those lines, but that doesn't make it easy to hear in the harsh light of day. This is the last thing I can handle right now. His regret. That's worse than his not remembering us.

I pull my emotions inward, making them smaller, more manageable. Not very well. The shadows in the corners of the room shiver and Reven's gaze cuts to them and back to me.

"You were vulnerable," he begins. "And I knew it. I took advantage of you. It shouldn't have happened, and it should never—"

Keeping the sheets wrapped around me, I jerkily climb out of bed, then do the waddle of shame to my door. "If you don't mind, I have a lot going on today and I need to get ready."

He's still sitting by the bed, brow furrowed. "That's all you have to—"

I swing the door open to find a servant waiting in the halls.

"Are you ready, dom—" She stutters to a halt when Reven stands abruptly.

"Yes," I say without an ounce of emotion. "He was just going."

It feels like forever before he moves. I don't look at him as he leaves the room.

42

HOW TO RULE

Never in my life did I think I'd see a Wanderer funeral.

I never thought I'd use my ability to make a glass coffin out of sand, either, but here I am.

The sun creeps toward the horizon, bringing evening with it, but I'm still hot under its blaze. Or maybe it's the way Reven stands at my back. No one knows what happened, and yet the awkwardness has ratcheted to a level that has most everyone flicking little glances between us.

That could be in my head, made worse by the handful of resentful stares burrowing into the back of my skull. Not everyone in the zariphate is happy about me or Tabra being here for this ceremony. Outsiders are strictly forbidden. Ledenon looks like he's chewing and swallowing glass.

It's possible Cain allowed us to be here because of his feelings for me. I'm not so naive that I can't see that. I'm also not in the headspace to deal with it.

It's not like I would have stayed away, regardless. His allowing us saved me from having to play the queen card and demanding they let me attend. I would never—not ever—let my best friend go through this alone. Pella either, now. She seemed relieved when Cain asked me to come, and Pella never wants anything from me. But even if she hadn't been, they are as much my family as Tabra is, in my heart at least, and they're hurting.

Not that either of them shows it.

I try not to, either, keeping my focus on what I'm doing.

My sister and I are not clothed identically. We left off the crowns as a sign of respect to the zariphate and are wearing simple, yet visibly royal dresses made of the same expensive fabric that blends from the top to the bottom in a rainbow of muted colors. At all funerals in Aryd, it's traditional to wear the color of your desert. As the queens of all Aryd, we are supposed to wear the colors of all the deserts.

Mine is simpler, with thin braided straps over my shoulders, a deep V between my breasts, and long otherwise, though with two thigh-high slits over each leg. Another braided cord is tied just where the V of the neckline stops. Too revealing for what we're doing today, but it was the best the servants could come up with given the short notice.

Tabra is more covered than I am, with longer billowing sleeves and no cleavage on display. How she got lucky with the outfit selection, I have no idea. But I'm too busy to worry about it, my hands up, golden light spilling from my palms turning brighter each second with the setting of the sun as I sink the double coffin I made deep into the sands.

Inside them, Zariph Cainis and Zaripha Magda lie in their warrior's clothes, side by side, one hand clasping the other's, while in each of their other hands, they both hold their preferred weapons. They appear so lifelike I almost expect them to open their eyes, like they're asleep…or poisoned, or enchanted, or cursed. But not dead.

Bene offered to fly them to the heart of the Singing Dunes and let the deserts claim them over time, but Cain refused. The Wanderers, because they have no single home, have a tradition of burying their dead where they perish.

As bonded mates, at least they will never be parted again in this life. I pray that they have an easier time finding and holding onto one another than Reven and I have.

I don't watch as I drive the coffins deeper. In my heart, all I can see is Cainis's backstabbing betrayal of us, his power-hungry grab for the throne. I wonder what he'd think about the fact that I'm the one burying him using *my* power and planting him deep in the sands of *my* dominion?

Cain stands tall and stoic beside me, and Pella beside him, looking not at where the dead have gone, but straight out into the desert, to the east where the sun will rise again tomorrow as it always does, bringing with it a new future.

When I nod, Cain turns and waits for the last rays of the sun to disappear.

Which is our cue. As soon as I glance Vos's way, he cants his head in the direction of the city. I nod, then lean over to Tabra and whisper, "Time to go."

What comes next is for the zariphate, we were told. Besides, we have business in the palace that we've put off. It's time to get to it.

Before we go, I reach out and squeeze Cain's hand, and he squeezes back.

When I turn away, Reven's hand brushes my back and I come close to jumping out of my skin. He gives me an innocent stare that seems to say he's just escorting me, but it's the closest he's physically gotten to me since last night.

Tziah and Hakan choose to wait at the back palace gate where Cain and Pella will enter when they return from the funeral. When we enter the night-cooled halls, Vos and I peel off, Bene prowling along at my side in his wolf form, leaving a trail of dust on the marbled floors in his wake.

And every second I'm deeply aware of Reven, silent and watchful at my back. No longer touching, but my own personal shadow.

Tabra grabs my arm, pulling me up short. "Where are you going without me?"

"You don't want to—"

Her face takes on a mulish cast. "I'm not being left out. Not anymore."

Vos leans around me. "It's not going to be pleasant, T."

She doesn't give in by so much as a twitch. "Your point?"

Goddess, she sounds like me now.

He glances at me, and I shrug.

We make our way through the palace to the building that houses the throne room, back toward the crypts and then down a series of winding stairs and halls to the dungeons below. With each passing minute, my adrenaline rises. With fear? Anticipation? I can't be sure, but I'm ready to get what we need from Eidolon's advisor and be done with this.

Vos takes us to a door where Trysolde is already standing, ready and waiting. We told the leaders of our other allies what we'd be doing tonight, but they decided to let us deal with it without them and tell them after.

With a sharp nod at the Wildernyssian king, Vos sails into the room where Pollux is still wrapped and bound by the same metal chair Trysolde made. Was that only a few days ago? The metal no longer covers Pollux's face, the space is clean, and trays of food tell me he's been fed at least. Honestly, until now, I didn't even think of his care.

What kind of queen does that make me?

Pollux glowers at us with his wide-set eyes. "What is your intention—" He breaks off, gaze directed over my shoulder. Then his eyes narrow. "*You* are not my king."

"No." Reven's voice is darkness itself. "I am a different beast entirely."

43

TRAITORS AND HEROES

Pollux leans back, just slightly, and I can't help but huff a quiet chuckle. Everyone wants to get away from the Shadowraith when they realize what he is. They haven't figured out I'm the one they should fear now.

"We haven't met." Vos strides across the room to squat in front of Pollux and study him. "I'm—"

"Voserian." Pollux spits in Vos's face. Actually spits. "Eidolon's traitor general."

Instead of slicing his throat, Vos shows remarkable calm—more than I would have—and wipes his face before offering a grin even while his eyes remain deadly. "It's all perspective," he says. "To you, I'm a traitor. To them..." He tips his head at us. "I'm a hero for standing against a tyrant."

Pollux scoffs. "Hero, my ass. Is it tyranny to try to save the world?"

"It is the way Eidolon's going about it." Vos gets to his feet and drags over a chair someone left in the corner, wood whining as it scrapes across the stone.

Pollux straightens as much as his metal bindings will allow, enough that they have to be cutting into him. "Either we all die, or a few are sacrificed."

I start forward. "Those are human beings—"

Reven catches my arm and tugs me back against him. Lips at my ear, he says, "A brainwashed zealot can't be turned."

I scowl.

Pollux's pale gaze spears me with a look of pity. Pity for me. "For the greater good," he says.

"For the sake of expediency, let's agree to disagree on that." Vos pulls out a long-bladed knife I recognize as Wanderer steel. He turns it over in his hand, examining it casually. "You know we're going to kill you."

Pollux doesn't even look at the knife, just straight forward now. "Go ahead."

"Give me something," Vos offers. "Information. Do that, and I'll make sure your death is fast and relatively painless."

Pollux clamps his mouth shut.

"Good information, of course." Vos leans back, feet stuck out before him, visibly at ease. "Something juicy. Usable."

Throat working, Pollux's gaze drops to Vos's face. "I would never betray my king. His cause is just. Righteous. He's the only one who can save us all from the sovereigns who have done nothing to help their people. The goddesses will answer us again after we rid the world of *you*."

Reven is right. This man is a zealot. If this is what Eidolon's followers believe, I understand why his numbers have grown. I may be a princess, but I've lived most of my life amongst the struggling people of Aryd, listening to their frustrations and fears. Hearing some of that fear become hatred. People, especially in dire situations, will follow anyone who gives them an enemy to fight. I've seen it firsthand.

"Even a just cause in evil hands can be poisoned until it rots." Vos cleans his nails with the tip of the knife as his voice turns musing. "I wonder how I shall enjoy killing you? Drawn and quartered perhaps? Or buried up to your shoulders in sand and left for the animals to pick at slowly?" He glances at me. "I got that from our Wanderer friends."

Pollux pales slightly, but his lips also flatten.

"No," Vos decides. "I know how. Do you want to know?"

No response.

"I'm going to cut off a small piece of you every day. It will take quite a long time before I get to anything vital." Vos makes a *tsk*ing sound. "The pain..."

Pollux goes chalky, sweat beading his brow, but determination continues to seal his lips shut.

My irritation with the lack of progress is like an itchy scab to be picked at. He's not going to break. Anyone can see that.

Vos rubs his hands together, almost gleeful. "How about a demonstration?"

Faster than it takes to inhale, he's up and using the side of Pollux's chair closest to the man's right hand as a cutting board. Despite the way Pollux yells and thrashes, it only takes Vos a second to use that knife with a crunch I feel in my bones.

Pollux howls in pain as something small and pink drops to the stone floor.

Vos picks it up. "Just the tip of your pinkie finger," he says, examining it. "Looks so strange disconnected from the body, doesn't it?"

Then, without so much as a glance in our direction, he tosses it at Bene, who stands beside me. The Devourer catches it in his mouth and chews. *"Not the best human I have tasted."*

I smile and translate.

Somewhere deep down I know it's wrong that I'm not secretly, quietly horrified. That I *want* to see this man suffer. But after everything that Eidolon has done, shouldn't I want that?

Shaking in pain, Pollux's mouth drops open in horror, his gaze zipping between Bene and Vos and Vos's knife.

Vos leans in, almost nose to nose with the man, all feigned casualness gone. He's a hardened fighter staring at a politico who probably never dirtied his hands with soil, let alone blood.

"I'm not going to take a whole finger at a time," Vos warns him quietly. Deadly. "I'll take the tips of your fingers first. And then the second knuckles. And then the third. Feeding every little piece to my bloodthirsty Devourer friend here. I'll take my time, leaving you in agony for…" He steps back, examining Pollux from his feet to the top of his head in a slow sweep, like he's counting up all the ways he'll dissect the man's body. Then he smiles in a way that makes him look bloodthirsty, too. "Months, I calculate."

There's no escaping the shiver that creeps down my spine. I knew Vos had been a general for Eidolon, but this is the first time he's ever shown this side. The things he must've done, what he carries inside him after years of serving the king…

"Oh goddess," Tabra whispers from my left.

I want to take her hand and squeeze it, feed her strength and a stronger stomach, but I don't. She chose to be here—she should find her own strength. I won't always be around.

"Let's leave Pollux to consider his options," Vos says, gesturing toward the door.

"Wait!" Pollux's call is both resentful and desperate as we walk away. "Eidolon brought his most valued prisoners here."

Prisoners. Who? Vida's family? Or more valuable than that? I pause. Actually, what I should be asking is *why*? Why bring them to Aryd?

"Most of them he's had returned to Tyndra," Pollux says.

"Why not leave them in Tyndra in the first place?" Trysolde asks.

Pollux considers the King of Wildernyss, eyes narrowing as he realizes who he's talking to. "Too valuable. He needs them under his heel, close enough to kill himself if needed."

"You said most—there are some still here?" Vos asks.

"One."

Only one. How helpful could that be?

"Who?" Vos demands.

Pollux shifts as much as he can against his restraints. "I don't know her name. But she's a sand nymph. She was too sick to move. I understand he's had her for years—"

She's still alive? The thought splinters through me.

"She used to work for him," Pollux says.

I'm going to kill this bastard.

Part of me balks at the thought, not sure if it's me or the Shadows.

The rest of me leans into it.

Instead of backing off, I start forward, reaching for a power—any power, I don't care. Except suddenly Reven is standing between me and Pollux.

"Get out of my way," I snap.

Reven steps into me, one hand taking mine, which is already glowing purple, and the other cupping the back of my neck. My entire world narrows to a pair of diamond-bright turquoise eyes and the feel of his skin against mine.

Instantly, the glow dissipates, and with it, the fury that overtook me. Fear crawls under my skin. How did I get so angry so fast?

Even though I've got a handle on myself again, Reven doesn't let go of me, doesn't turn his gaze away, though he gives me a bit more space. His fingers knead my neck in what I think is supposed to be a soothing manner. I wonder what he'd do if he knew my body was waking up at that touch, at his nearness, the scent of him. It hasn't been long since we shared our bodies, and that memory wants me to chase it.

He directs a question to Pollux without looking away. "Where is this prisoner?"

"I don't know. Down here in the dungeons somewhere, I'd imagine." Pollux looks at Vos. "You said one piece of information. By her reaction, it was a juicy one. You promised—"

Vos plunges the knife he's still holding into Pollux's belly. Reven and I whip around in time to see the blade's upward stroke slide up under the ribs, no doubt piercing the man's heart. Pollux's eyes go wide, and he gurgles. With a sickening suck of sound, Vos yanks the knife back out and Pollux grunts again.

Then, slowly, he slumps forward, going limp, held up only by the metal bindings lashing him to the chair as blood dribbles onto the floor.

Vos kept his promise of a quick death.

"Remind me not to get on your bad side," Reven says to him.

Vos flicks him a look that is more closed off than I've seen him be with Reven, even lately. "I owe you too much for that."

Reven's expression darkens. "I wouldn't know about that anymore." He lets go of my hand like he just realized he's still holding it and steps back, putting distance between him and… all of us.

Vos shrugs. "It doesn't matter if you don't remember. *I* do." He wipes his blade on his pants and sheaths it in the knife holster at his hip. "Let's go find this sand nymph."

44

THE CURSE

"Here!" Achlys's voice rings out, bouncing off the stone walls of the dry, dark hall we're searching.

The labyrinth of our dungeons runs not only under the palace, but out under parts of the city itself. Omma used to whisper that a secret exit existed somewhere down here that twins of old used to use but warned me that Eidolon had taken one of the twins he'd killed from there and not to go looking for it. Or else.

One of the few warnings of hers I bothered to heed.

Reven is holding his hand up, palm glowing to light our way, but I outrun that light, plunging into the dimness as I sprint toward the sound of Achlys's voice, followed by Tabra calling out, "We're going to need Trysolde!"

Please let that mean we need his ability to manipulate metal to unlock something. The nymph must be held in a cell, which only makes sense.

I'm barely through the door when I'm swept up off my feet, spun, and deposited behind Reven, his back already to me, an arm stuck out to keep me from going around him again.

"Hey!" I protest immediately. "Tabra's in there!"

"I've never seen someone so determined to run blindly into danger," he grumbles. "I'm beginning to understand Cain better."

Ignoring my offended squeak, he heads into the room. I march right in after him.

A series of five cells line the long, narrow room, formed by floor-to-ceiling bars. Reven's broad shoulders are blocking my view of the center cell, and the other cells are all empty.

He's standing with his feet set, back squared, staring at whoever is caged. "I know you," he says in a voice that tells me he's not entirely sure about that.

A soft snort sounds before a delicate, hushed voice answers. "You should, Shadow of Eidolon. I've been with him, and you, since the beginning."

"I don't remember you," he insists, "but I *know* you. Your name is Hesperia. I saw you in his memory."

What? I take a step away, staring at the back of his head. When was this?

Even Vos jerks around to stare at Reven. "The hells you say."

"She blessed the coronation of Meren and Tabra's twin ancestresses. The ones who trapped the goddesses in those amulets," Reven says. But there's doubt in his voice. "I don't remember much after that."

"It only got worse from there," Hesperia says in a voice full of bitterness.

Reven is still blocking my view, so I squeeze between him and Vos.

Behind the bars, a woman sits on the ground, back straight, legs folded neatly before her, and her hands resting on her knees. Her head is regal, made more so by her long slender neck, and the beauty of her lush features is breathtaking. Thick black hair is braided, swept up on top of her head, but it's her skin that I find fascinating. She is formed from all the sands of Aryd, which leaves uneven stripes and swirls of glittering color across her, as if someone filled her up like a vessel, a layer at time.

The nymph's gaze lands on me. "You," she says.

Except Tabra is crouched at the cell door in front of her. Did she whisper the same thing to my sister? "You're the one, aren't you?" I ask. "The nymph who cursed me at birth."

Hesperia's eyes widen as she shakes her head. "It wasn't a curse. It was—"

"It wasn't a blessing," I snap. Reven's sudden grip on my wrist keeps me by his side. I hadn't even realized I'd moved. "I carry *his* evil inside me." I point an accusing finger at Reven. "And now it's taking over my life."

Horror, even obscured by the colorful stripes over her face, widens her dark eyes. "You weren't supposed to do that," she whispers.

I'm scowling at her so hard, I feel the stirrings of a headache. "What, exactly, was I supposed to do? It's not like you left instructions."

"You were supposed to kill Eidolon," she says.

"She's tried," Vos says. "We all have. Multiple times."

Without saying anything, a tendril of shadow trails out from Reven's fingertips and slips into the lock of the cell, which gives easily with a rusted sounding *click*. Then he swings the door open and waits.

"I could have done that if you asked," Trysolde points out.

We all ignore him.

Hesperia doesn't move at first, studying Reven closely. Then her gaze snaps between him and me, back and forth as she gets to her feet. "Why in the name of Nova did you give the other Shadows to *her*?"

"Because Eidolon swallowed him, and he had to keep the Shadows out of the king's hands." Breaking his grip on my wrist, I crowd past him to get in her face. "I managed to pull Reven back out of the king—minus his memories by the way, and minus our bond—only now I can't seem to give the Shadows back."

The things inside me manage to ooze past my hold on them and press outward at my words, and I guess they get visibly close to the surface because Hesperia flinches. Behind me, Reven sighs, but I bind them back down.

The nymph doesn't apologize, though, or explain. Instead,

her eyes narrow on me with a sting of suspicion. "Can't give them back? Or won't?"

"You're the one throwing around curses. You tell me!"

She glances away. "I'm not sure how that is possible, but it does complicate the situation."

Understatement.

"What were you supposed to do the day we were born?" Tabra asks from where she's still safely on the other side of the bars, standing now with Achlys beside her.

Hesperia considers her for a long moment before her gaze slides back to me. "I gave to you what he wanted for himself, the ability to siphon power."

I nod. "Yes. I tap into it, into *him*, and draw his power inside me."

"No. I mean continuously."

I blink, then frown. Continuously?

She sighs. "I was supposed to give Eidolon that kind of access to Tabra's power—the child who would be the soul Enfernae—so that he could use that ability himself to free the goddesses."

Continuous control. That's what my curse is doing? I only use it when I need it because I know he can feel me then, but… is it possible Eidolon is *always* accessing me through that link?

"He already tried to control my sister," I tell her. "By infesting her with a ghost of his own past self."

Hesperia visibly startles at that. "What happened?"

"It didn't work."

"Fool," she mutters, then gives a grim shake of her head. "He needs the Celestial Alignment. He's tried, through the years of previous Alignments, and nothing ever worked, so he ruled it out as impactful a long time ago. But he was wrong."

I am over this game of not having all the answers, so I grab her by the arm, her sandy skin rough against my palm the way Bene is, only less coarse. "Stop talking in cryptic fits and spurts. Tell me everything I need to know. Starting with why the Celestial Alignment is so important."

She frowns at me in a way that seems confused, but it clears an instant later. "The Alignment enhances an Imperium's powers."

We already know that. Scoria told us. I give her a tiny shake. "And?" Why can't people just spit out the important stuff?

"*And* I suspect that's how your ancestresses were able to put the goddesses in the amulets that day." She tips her head, considering me more closely. "And they had help, from the other sovereigns. Only all those sovereigns, all except one of the Arydian queens, died. I was there. I saw it."

Cold filters through my veins.

Her expression shifts. Darkens. "But I had a vision the day I held Tabra as a newborn—a nightmare, really. There is sudden darkness. There are Imperium—I can see their yellow and purple lights. And...blue? It snaps all around me. And there is so much death. So much pain. Anger, too. I can feel it clawing at me. Swirling around me like smoke until I choke on it. If I had used my magic on Tabra, I saw Eidolon succeed in releasing his mother, and in her rage, she destroys the world. Together with her son, they would create an eternal night. But Mereneith..." She hesitates, her eyes going glassy as if she's replaying whatever she saw in her head. "I can feel *them*. The goddesses." Her eyes flicker open and she looks directly at me. "This might help."

She reaches a hand into her body, and the sands that make up her form shift and swirl and eddy until she's drawing something out. Something that looks like...

A book.

It can't be.

Eidolon's book. The one that Reven once saw when he was still a mere Shadow inside the king. The book in which each incarnation has written their history, their deeds, their thoughts, passed down from Shadow to Shadow. We've been searching for it, thinking it might give us insights and answers into everything—the king's reasons as well as his plans.

"*You* have it?" I whisper to the nymph.

"I took it from him," she says. "Hid it inside me."

"Mother goddess," I hear Reven say from behind me.

Seeing that thing, and the way the writing changed, the way it recorded Eidolon's descent into evil, is what convinced Reven to take control when he did, to go against his maker.

"Do you remember it?" I ask him.

"Meren?" Reven's voice seems to come from farther off.

Hesperia pulls back sharply, straining against my grip. "No. Don't—"

A wall of darkness slams up around us, circling us and cutting us off from the others, so thick I can't see anyone outside of it. In the same instant, a flash of purple light on something shiny has me looking down, shock crawling over my insides at the sight of one of my own knives now clutched in my free hand. When did I unsheathe it? Why?

I'm not that mad right now. Irritated, yes, but...

The stupidity of even thinking that question hits me in the next blink.

Oh, goddess it's happening again. This is not me. I'm not doing this.

"Meren!" I hear Reven's shout. Even more muffled thanks to the wall of darkness keeping him back. I know he's trying to get to me. To stop me.

"You've been holding back, Hesperia. Leaving you as bait turned out exactly as I'd planned. Now I have the last piece." The voice, sinister and grating, comes from me. But it's not me. It's—

"Reven!" I cry out. His name bounces around the insides of my skull, but I don't think it comes out of my mouth.

Too late, anyway.

"And now you'll die," the voice says.

Against my will, my hand plunges the knife into Hesperia's

sternum and then drags down, slicing her belly open, spilling sand and black blood onto my hand, slick and warm and gritty.

Immediately the book, not fully pulled from her body yet, disintegrates into sand.

No. Goddess no!

I think I hear Tabra scream. I know chaos erupts in the room behind me as they pound and stab and try to force their way inside the barrier between us, but they still can't get to me through the darkness.

Hesperia's hands go up over her wound, but it's mortal. Nothing is going to save her. She lifts her head with visibly trembling effort, eyes focusing on my face. "You." Her voice is a hiss like sand spilling. But she's not talking to me.

"Who?" I ask, but I think only I hear it. "Who is doing this? A ghost? The Shadows?"

Her eyes start to go glassy, her lids blinking slower and slower over them.

"I know you well." Her voice is thready now, scratchy. "Eidolon of Tyndra."

What? I want to shake my head. Deny it. He's not here. He can sense me but he's not inside me. "It's his Shadows," I try to tell her.

She doesn't hear. "How do you control this child?" she demands in a voice that breaks over each word.

"Down the same line you connected her to me with," my mouth snarls in that voice that's not mine, even as I fight it with all my mind and heart.

And I realize she's right, that it's true.

Every other time I've lost control, every time my friends have seen the Shadows cross my features, even what happened to Mimick—it's all been him.

It's *always* been him.

She takes a shuddering, horrible breath, more hissing of sand coming from her, and seems to focus not on my face, but on the me trapped inside myself. "*You* are the key. Take his power from him," she says.

Is she talking to me?

"Take it all until he has none left, or until you have enough to kill him." Her jerking smile is filled with the kind of relief only centuries of fear could produce when staring death in the face. "I trusted you with this for a reason, Mereneith Evangeline the Twelfth."

Then her entire being tenses, like she's drawing in on herself before she dissolves, draining out of my hold with a hiss, falling to the ground no longer formed as a human but as a pile of multicolored sand.

"You don't have the strength to take anything from me," Eidolon's voice sounds in my head, supremely satisfied. *"Time to kill the others."*

Before I can respond, the darkness holding the others back is ripped away, torn like fabric only to explode outward in a concussive wave. Everyone goes flying, crashing into the walls and skidding across the floor. I don't see them get up.

Only Reven still stands with me, darkness misting around him telling me he shadowed to avoid the hit. In an instant, he has me by the shoulders and slams me against the stone wall hard enough that my ears ring and my breath deserts me for a second, just as he wraps a hand around my neck.

I claw at his grip even as my feet dangle and kick.

"Don't make me do this, Meren," he warns through clenched teeth. "Don't make me hurt you."

45

CIVIL WAR

My gaze is locked to Reven's, whose eyes glow faintly as he wields his power.

"Kill me," I tell him. But my lips refuse to form the words.

"Not yet, princess," Eidolon taunts. *"I still need what's locked inside you."*

Anger tightens Reven's jaw, but not the hand at my neck.

"Meren," Reven growls. Begs. He gives his head a single shake. "Please."

I'm not doing this, though. I can't control it.

A dagger of shadow darts out of me like a tentacle.

It's not me, I want to tell him, but I can't make my mouth work.

The shadow dagger slashes at him. Disbelief flashing across his features, Reven holds it off.

I told him to kill me. I *told* him.

Do it.

Wielding the darkness through me like a puppet on strings, more daggers shoot up in the air. Reven manages to hold onto me as he knocks one back.

Another comes for him, and he dodges right, jerking me with him. When he spins us both, he manifests a shield of shadow, and I wince at the sound of the weapons striking in succession, like arrows loosed by a battalion of bowmen. Shadow after shadow the king throws at him. Unrelenting.

One barely misses skewering him.

I think I hear a groan in the background. Are the others coming to? We need help. Now.

Then his expression devolves into a swirl of determination and no more hesitation. He lifts his fist and in it a shadow manifests, so solid and sharp, it's like a shard of obsidian in his hand. "I'm sorry."

He plunges the weapon down, aiming for my heart.

A growl the likes of which sets goose bumps rising uncomfortably on my skin sounds a heartbeat before Bene slams into Reven from the side.

I'm thrown to the ground where I go sprawling, and, for a hopeful second, I think Eidolon has been cut off because the numbness disappears, and I can make my limbs move again. But something not of my doing yanks me to my feet, still controlled by my puppet master. My arms are drawn out from my sides as my body floats upward, suspended by an unseen force, my palms with their lavender glow facing outward.

In the corner of the cell, Bene stands between me and Reven, teeth bared, and sandy fur raised along his back.

Reven looks from the Devourer to me, expression tortured.

Both are trying to do the right thing.

Goddess. I've set the people I love most against each other.

My head turns against my will, my gaze drawn to Vos and Trysolde who, looking pale and woozy, are at least on their feet on the other side of the cell bars.

"Time to clean out the traitors," Eidolon speaks through me. I feel him form my lips into a smile that is both conquest and a jibe at both men.

The darkness pulls from the corners and forms into arrows that hover in the air directly before me within the timespan of a blink. Eidolon hurls them at Vos and Trysolde, but Trysolde puts a hand on one of the cage bars. The metal changes the way water does, spreading so fast that the arrows strike a solid, thin plate.

Instead of dropping to the ground, they dissolve.

Trysolde creates spears out of the bars, as if they peel down themselves, spreading out like deadly splayed fingers from each bar.

A spear flashes in the dim light, coming straight at me.

And I think maybe I hear Reven grunt. Only an inch from my heart, the shadows pound the spear into the ground.

Only this time Reven made the darkness.

Bene's growls cut off so abruptly it's jarring. The sandy wolf tilts his head at Reven in question.

In that same moment, shadows explode from every corner of the room, this time taking Reven, Bene, Trysolde, and Vos all by the throats and hoisting them into the air.

"No!" Tabra screams.

Eidolon jerks my head to look to the right, where my sister has been cowering with Achlys. Tabra stands now, and strands of her hair that've come down from the elegant chignon the servants set it in rise around her in a breeze that doesn't exist. Her amber eyes light up with a purple fire that consumes them, setting the features of her face to something both terrible and awesome at the same time.

And that's when I *feel* it. The draw of her power. As if she's reached through my corporeal body and wrapped her fingers around my soul. My very essence.

She pulls, not hard and violent, but gentle, a sensation in my chest like Reven brushing his fingers lightly over my belly.

"I can't stop." Tabra gulps. "I can't. It wants you. My power wants you."

Don't fear it, I want to tell her. *Take me. Take them all.*

Eidolon tilts my head down to look and I can see a ghostly copy of me, clothes and all but transparent, drawing slowly away from my body.

"Well, well." Eidolon smiles for me again. *"Finally that power of yours is showing itself. Just in time, too."*

What Tabra is doing to me feels…weird. Like bleeding, but pleasant. I could close my eyes and go to sleep.

"Sissy." Tabra's voice breaks in the middle. Tears trickle down her cheeks and she's shaking. In that moment, I realize that killing me, even if it's the best for everyone, would destroy my sister. I can't let her go through that. I can't make her.

"Domina!" Achlys cries out. She reaches out a single hand, touching Tabra's shoulder, only to go instantly rigid, her head tossing back and mouth open on a silent gasp before she collapses.

There's only one way to stop all of this. Remove the threat. And that's me.

Almost like Tabra's power agrees with me, it tugs a little harder, and I can see more of my soul outside of my own body, a ghostly reflection of myself. It floats in the air in front of me, separate and yet still connected.

Probably because that coward is running from what Tabra's doing to me, the cold of Eidolon's power spiking through me cuts off so hard it's like a slap to the face.

I drop to the ground and my legs almost collapse with the impact, but I manage to stay standing.

"Meren!" Tabra cries out.

"It's me," I say, raising a hand. "It's me. You're safe, Tabra. You can stop."

Tabra can't stop. I can see she can't. I can see the panic. Eidolon is gone for the moment, but I'm still dangerous. My first idea was right. Remove the threat completely.

I ignite *my* power, the yellow glow joining Tabra's now. The others all watch warily, their expressions somewhere in the range of shock to visibly unsure if they need to stop Tabra or me. I ignore them all and focus instead on the pile of sand near me on the ground. Sand that used to be Hesperia.

Immediately the grains respond to my will, lifting into the air in a tornado because I'm working so fast.

"What are you doing?" Reven shouts.

I flash heat them to a molten mass, which I press and slam up into a thin wall. One that is all the colors of my dominion's sands.

And not big enough.

"Take mine." Bene's voice sounds urgently in my head.

He sheds sand from his body, and I take it as fast as it comes off, heating and molding it around the multicolored glass like a round frame until, fast as a few blinks, I have a surface large enough to walk through.

Meanwhile, I can feel my power dwindling as Tabra slowly draws more and more of me out of my body.

Fear driving me now, I slap a hand to the glass and shove my power into it. Only when the other side clears, it's not Savanah where I was picturing, it's…

I gasp, but manage to hold the portal open.

It's that place I glimpsed before, when I was bringing our allies through to the Crimson Desert.

With longer to look, I can see my window to that place is high on a peak somewhere looking out over lush, flower-blanketed mountains. The woman is still there, with her drained coloring despite her red hair and blue eyes.

She takes one sweeping glance over me, with my soul hanging out like a sheet in the wind, and Tabra with her hands aglow and tear-streaked face. I don't know if she can see the others.

"Enough," the woman says, and waves a hand.

My soul snaps back into place, sending a lancing ache through my head for a moment, and Tabra gasps, staring down at her hands that are no longer lit. And into the stunned silence, the woman smirks. "Are you ready to listen to me now?"

46

ALLUSIAN

Listen to her? I have no idea what this place is, or why I keep opening a portal to it. But she just stopped Tabra from sucking my soul out, and that makes her dangerously powerful.

So no, I'm *not* listening to her.

I try to jerk my hand from the glass and close the portal.

The woman on the other side doesn't so much as move, and suddenly I can't, either. Not my hand at least, which feels cemented to the glass. I yank again, fear rising in me.

She's doing this. Trapping me with the portal open.

A blanket of darkness drapes over the glass as Reven moves to stand between me and it, my outstretched arm the only part of me exposed to their gazes, but in the same instant, that darkness dissipates like mist burned away by the sun. I manage to nudge him aside just enough to see the portal.

Expression both amused and patient, the woman stands on the other side, directly across from me, so slight her clothes hang on her frame. A deceptive appearance. Power rolls off her in waves palpable even from here.

"Who are you?" Reven demands in a hard voice, even as he steps back into me, wrapping one arm backward to hold onto me.

She peers around him at me, curiosity filling her deep blue eyes as they skate over my face.

He growls his disapproval.

Bene is to my left, watching me and Reven warily, unable

to see what we're seeing. Tabra is to my right, Achlys still on the ground, and my sister now kneeling by her, a hand over her mouth to muffle her weeping. I can't see Vos and Trysolde. I'm not sure who the woman can see other than me and Reven.

"Who are you?" she asks me.

Nope. I'm not doing this dance. I asked her a question, and she didn't answer. "We asked first."

The woman's expression curdles. "Mind your tongue. You don't know who I am."

A kind warning? Or a threat?

"I regret now that mortals never knew," she murmurs, more to herself than us. Then she huffs a laugh that sounds…not bitter, exactly. Sad might be closest.

Mortals? Implying she isn't one? Except the mother goddess, Nova, is long gone, and her daughters are all trapped in their amulets.

I shift back behind Reven a bit. At the very least, anyone with the ability to stop us all from using our powers has to be a mighty Imperium. An Enfernae with some kind of intangible ability to control other Imperium's power maybe? I've never heard of such a thing. That would be considered a treacherous power, one that would earn her immediate execution.

Just imagine someone who could control all Imperium in Nova. That person would be invincible.

I pull at my hand still against the glass, but it holds fast and a very real fear scuttles through my gut.

This woman, whoever—or whatever—she is, has all the power here.

I glance up at Reven. He needs to shadow the others out of here. Now that this woman has seen where we are, she should be able to portal to it just as fast. I'll have to shatter the glass in the same instant.

The woman's gaze slides over Reven. "You are the spitting image of your mother."

Wait, what? I don't have to see them—I *feel* every person in the room rear back. We all know who his mother is—the goddess Tyndra. But how does *she* know?

That's when Bene, now in raven form, flies over to land on my shoulder for a better look and the woman's expression freezes in an odd concoction of morbid horror and sparking terror. Despite looking like she's already been sucked dry of all her blood, she goes even paler.

"Benedornan," she whispers through cracked lips. "What are you doing with these mortals?"

But it's Bene's response that sends shock through me in waves. He takes one look at her and flaps backward off my shoulder, as if he's stumbling away. So awkward that he ends up dropping to the floor where he flips over and scrambles backward.

"Allusian," he squawks in my head, sounding very un-Devourer like for the first time since I've known him.

What? Frowning, I look back and forth from Bene to the portal. Then I go wide-eyed, not quite believing my ears as what he said sinks in. "Wait, *that's* the Allusian heavens?" I try to push Reven aside to better see the lands beyond. He barely budges.

But Bene is shaking his head and still backing up, bumping into the bars that form the cell door jamb and backing past that. If a raven made of sand could blanche, that's what he does. The Devourer is afraid. *Truly* afraid.

Why? The Goddess Aryd's one-time lover is a monster. The top of the food chain. Nothing can kill him. Right?

"Bene?" I ask, my voice sharpening.

Tabra plucks him off the ground, sort of rounding her body around him like she's protecting him. "He's trembling." My sister glares at the woman on the other side of the portal from us.

"He should be," the woman says. "He ate a piece of my heart."

Bene gives a startled flutter of his wings. *"No—"*

My head is starting to ache and I use the hand not stuck to the portal to pinch the bridge of my nose. "Someone had better start explaining. And I mean now."

"That...is the Goddess Allusian," Bene says in a shaky voice. *"I thought she was dead."*

47

THE LAST PIECE

"What did you say?" Vos and Trysolde snarl at the same time when I translate Bene's words.

The goddess—because Bene has no reason to lie—smiles. She actually smiles. And then says, "It would be nice to see my accusers' faces."

The two men come around the side of the portal and get their first good look at her, but I can see them thinking that no way is this sickly, bedraggled creature a goddess.

Goddess. The word echoes in my head.

She's…she's a goddess?

Not just a terrifyingly powerful Enfernae, because that would make more sense to me than the other thing. Allusian.

The heavens have a goddess. "You shouldn't be telling me this or anything," I say. "I have a… There's a curse… He can…" How do I explain this? "I should leave."

Except they need me to hold the portal open, and she's not letting me go.

"I can see the connection." Allusian's gaze skates over me. "Whoever it is can't see or hear anything for now. I'm stopping him."

She's blocking Eidolon…

How is this possible? She's never been mentioned in our histories or the recordings of our temples.

"Bene," I say in a wobbly voice. "I think you'd better explain."

I wrinkle my nose at the goddess apologetically. "No offense, but we don't know you. We trust whatever he says."

Her eyebrows draw slowly upward. "Are you sure you should?"

I expect Bene to fly up onto my shoulder or squawk or flap his wings in protest at that. Anything. But he stays huddled in Tabra's arms, staring at Allusian.

"Bene?" I prod.

He gives a full-body tremble that scrapes his wings along his sandy body with a *scritch*ing sound. *"Aryd and I were told by her sisters that their seventh sister, Allusian, had died."*

The goddess says nothing.

I glance between them. Why does being told that make him petrified with fear? He didn't kill her if he had to be told.

"They couldn't have." His voice is a mere thread of a hushed whimper in my head. "*They* wouldn't *have."*

But the doubt in his voice tells me even he isn't sure of whatever it is *they* couldn't have done. Whoever they are.

I guess I don't need to translate for the goddess, because her smile takes on a bitter edge. "But they did."

"Did what?" Vos demands. He whips his gaze between the goddess and me and Bene. "Who did? Somebody better start talking."

A terrible suspicion starts to creep up on me like a fog skulking across the Sea of Terra toward the palace. "Does this have anything to do with the reason why my ancestresses trapped your sisters in amulets?"

The goddess pulls her shoulders back. "It worked?"

I nod.

"I thought so, because I couldn't feel them anymore, and my sisters didn't return here after I crawled out of the hole where they left me to die. But I wasn't sure."

What in the name of Nova?

"I don't know about the…rest of that, but what they did

worked." I pull the amulet that contains Savanah out from under my clothes. Unlike Aryd's, it doesn't ever light with an inner fire, remaining cold and unresponsive.

Allusian tips her head, studying the glass. "Hello, sister," she says softly, venom in her voice.

"But there have been consequences." I tuck it back out of sight. "Release me and tell me what you know."

A martial light in her eyes warns me not to test her. "You dare give orders to a goddess?"

I stare her down hard, neither of us giving an inch. "Given how badly the goddesses seem to have messed up the world, that title doesn't hold much weight with me at the moment."

"Meren," Reven says, a warning in his voice, and the arm still curled around me scoots me a bit farther behind him.

He probably thinks I'm about to be taken over by Eidolon again. He could be right. But I'm done screwing around trying to figure out what happened and how to fix it with only a hazy idea and not all the pieces. I'm pretty sure this goddess has all the answers I need.

I slide my gaze to hers. "Release me, tell me your story, and then we'll see."

Vos bows his head, muttering under his breath, "Seven hells, Meren."

Which is when Achlys rolls up to sit, looking wobbly and a little green. "What happened?"

"Are there more people there?" Allusian asks. "I need to know who I'm telling what to."

Fair enough. I wave at Tabra, and she helps a swaying Achlys to her feet, both coming around to stand with the rest of us in front of the portal.

Allusian takes one look at Tabra's face before glancing at me again. "Even a thousand years later, the twin queens of Aryd are truly a marvel. No wonder my sisters began to fear their human creations."

I open my mouth to ask what that means when I feel the force holding my hand to the glass give way. Careful not to lift it entirely off—I'm not sure how I opened the portal to this place or if I could get back—I make sure I'm free. And I am.

"Why don't you come through and we'll talk in here?" I ask instead of demanding more answers.

The goddess makes a face. "I can't leave my dominion. Not yet. It is the only thing keeping me alive. And you'd better not come through, either."

"Why not?" Vos asks.

"Because there's no glass on this side and no way to make it, no sand in Allusian, so I'm not sure you could get back."

I startle hard enough that my hand lifts and her image blinks in and out, making me press down more carefully. "That's not possible. I can only connect my portals to ones that already exist. I can't connect to...*nothing*."

There's no way. Right?

She spreads her hands wide in a goddess version of a shrug. "And yet you're doing it."

More questions without answers. If I survive these trials, someday I'm going to live a life where I have all the answers all the time. Not sure how, but I'm making it my goal from this point forward.

"Are these all the people with you?" Allusian asks me.

"Down here? Yes, they are."

She dips her head, folding her hands before her as if praying for the right words. When she looks up, her expression isn't peaceful, but a complete blank, as if she had to turn off all her emotions to tell us her story. I know a little something about needing to do that, so I quietly brace.

"When our mother, Nova, made the world, she made the six dominions, and then she made a home for the afterlives of all her creations."

Afterlives.

I glance past her over the beauty of the lands. "So we *are* looking at the heavens."

Allusian glances behind her as well, smile soft. "What you're looking at is part of the heavens, yes. The hells are here, too. All seven. Power over all afterlife was given to me by my mother to rule. Just like each of my sisters got to choose how to create their own dominions."

I have never, not once, considered who might be in charge of the hells. The heavens, I assumed, were ruled by the goddesses together. That must show in my face because Allusian gives a dry chuckle. "Humans don't learn of me until they reach one or the other destination after they die. *I* am the goddess of death, courage, and the winds."

The goddess of death. Terrific.

"Is that why you can't leave?" Tabra asks, then slides me a questioning look like she isn't sure she's allowed to talk to this being, too.

Allusion's face hardens to a mask of controlled fury, stirring unease in my belly. "The reason I can't leave is because of my *sisters*." She spits the word, glaring at the spot where the amulet lies under my clothes. "They were always jealous of my power. At the same time, they were also worried about the growing number of Imperium humans under their rule. So they decided to solve both problems at once. They cut my heart out of my chest."

I wouldn't mind sitting down about now. I don't know what I was expecting, but it wasn't that.

"How are you still alive?" Tabra asks, her voice filled with concern, and the way she inches forward, I think only the need to help Achlys stay standing is keeping her from stepping through the portal to give the goddess a hug.

Allusian shrugs. "I'm immortal. It takes more than that to kill me. But without my heart, my powers are diminished significantly. The only thing keeping me alive is the dominion my mother gave me that my essence is tied to. I can't leave here without my heart."

Merciful heavens. "What did your sisters do with it?" I'm almost afraid to ask because I think I might know the answer, and it's horrible on a level that is incomprehensible to me.

Sure enough, though, the Allusian's scowl turns fierce. "They fed pieces of it to their consorts and buried the rest."

Everyone looks at Bene, and my stomach sinks to the floor. Aryd's consort.

We've all heard his side of the story. The mother goddess, Nova, saw that her daughters were lonely and gave them each a piece of her heart—Aura—which they fed to their chosen consorts so that they, too, would be immortal and have supernatural powers.

Their children were Imperium who made more Imperium with mortal Vexillium partners. Eventually too many. Enough that the goddesses' consorts felt threatened. Paranoid that one consort might have more power than the others, they all ate a second piece of Aura together—and became the Devourers.

Only Bene seemed to hold on to his reason.

"That was Aura," Bene says, with no conviction. In fact, he immediately changes his wording. *"They told us that was Aura. The final pieces of* Nova's *heart."*

"It was not Aura," Allusian snaps. "Our mother gave the last of her heart to give my sisters their consorts. She is no more. What you were given the second time was *my* heart."

Bene shivers again, even harder. I feel a little ill myself and my gaze slides to my sister, who is already staring back at me with lips gone white around the edges. "How could they?" she whispers. "How could they do that to their own *sister*?"

Aryd has been helping me from within her glass prison. I know it. I learned to trust her because of it. This makes no sense.

"I have asked myself that every single day for centuries,"

Allusian admits heavily, then sighs. "My only conclusion is that because humans don't learn of me until death, they knew their subjects would never discover their treachery. Even reincarnated souls don't remember their past lives."

Bene shivers again, the sand of his body making a scratchy sound. *"We did not know—"*

Allusian cuts her gaze to him. "I believe you, Benedornan. Aryd and Wildernyss were not there the day my heart was taken. This is Tyndra's doing. The others..." She shrugs. "I'm not sure who followed and who was forced."

Bene drops his head low, as if he can't hold it up under the relief. *"Thank you."*

The goddesses are monsters and Eidolon comes from the worst of them. "No wonder our ancestresses imprisoned them," I say under my breath.

"No." Allusian shakes her head. "Esha and Lillnya did that because of me. With what little power I had left, I was able to reach Lillnya because of her ability to control souls. I spoke to her through their father the day he died and told her my story." She flattens her palm over where her heart would be, and her face becomes peaceful, as if knowing they were able to contain her sisters is filling the hole inside her. "I ordered Lillnya and Esha to do what they did in order to punish my sisters and save the world from their thirst for power. I fed the twin queens and their allies more power, *my* power, through the Alignment, which already draws from this dominion and from *me*."

"Is that why the sovereigns all died?" Tabra asks. "The nymph told us..."

Guilt ripples over the goddess's features. "I was enhancing their powers, too. That is how we kept Eidolon at bay. I did not realize that due to my weakness, I would not be able to control how much I fed them. Lillnya used too much of her own power while trapping my sisters, and I could not save her. I was able to keep Esha alive. Barely. But the others..."

Regret can be a palpable thing when someone feels it enough.

Beside me, Reven stiffens so hard I think he might crack a bone. "*That's* why," he says to himself under his breath. Then he turns his gaze on me, searching my face, but I don't think he's seeing me. Not really. "You didn't betray your bondmate. You were obeying a goddess."

"Not Meren," Tabra tells him gently. Reminds him that I am the one standing here now. Not my past self. "*Esha* was obeying a goddess."

"I don't understand," I say to Allusian. "You had them imprison Aryd and Wildernyss, too, even though they were tricked?"

Allusian winces. "I didn't remember until a long time after it was all over that they weren't there. That night they attacked me was all…a jumble."

"That's not the only mistake you've made." Reven's jaw hardens as he stares at Allusian. "Your imprisonment of your sisters caused problems here."

"Problems?" She tilts her head.

"Don't you know?" Tabra asks, stronger than before. "Don't you speak to the souls who come to you?"

Allusian's gaze snaps to narrow-eyed slits. It's probably a good thing she's low on power. "No. Speaking to them is impossible for now," she says in clipped, distinct words. "Because I am missing the source of my connection to them. You can think of it as my powers being diminished, but I think of it as the source of empathy and emotions. What soul would trust a creature without those?"

Tabra lowers her chin, contrite.

"What problems?" the goddess demands.

"The protections your sisters granted to each dominion to keep their people safe from the Devourers are out of control without them here to regulate." I quickly describe what's happening to the dominions. "And Tyndra's son is just as bad," I add. "Eidolon, the King of Tyndra. He's who is bound to me through a nymph's curse."

"This is not what I intended." After a long, silent second, Allusian nods, then faces us. "I will tell you how to release the goddesses."

Do we trust her?

"Bene?" I'm asking if we can trust her. He knows the history. He knows this goddess.

He bows his head. *"Do as your goddess commands."*

Except my ancestresses did that and look what happened. "But—"

"She is the way we set this…all of this…right."

I tell the others what he said. This can't be my decision alone. We stare at each other, indecision written over all our features.

"I would not normally offer this," Allusian says. "But to set your hearts at ease, I will make a promise, bound by what little magic I have left, to help you if you promise to help me first."

"Mother Nova," Bene squawks. *"A promise from a goddess is no small thing."*

I suck in a sharp, hope-filled breath. If she's true to her promise, that fixes everything. Everything.

"But only after you return my heart to me." Allusian's lips curl in a sneer of distaste. "I can't have my sisters released until I have the fullness of my powers returned to me so I may protect myself."

I stare at her, hope sinking to the bottom of my feet.

Damnation. Yet another side quest.

Vos steps toward the portal. "I think I know where your heart is buried."

48

THE BEST LAID PLANS

Ynferno.

The giant mountain at the heart of Tyndra. That's where Vos thinks the heart is. Tziah, too. Because they saw it.

I stand outside Tabra's office with Reven—an office Eidolon used while he was here. Waiting. Our gazes skitter away from each other any time they cross paths.

The others, Cain and Pella back from the funeral included, are in there. Even Tabra went inside without me, closing the massive double doors behind her. I'm left out just in case, so that Eidolon can't hear or see the plans they're making through me.

Cutting me out like gangrene. I'm not sure how I feel about that. Not great.

Reven is here mostly because the others figure he'll be the only one able to stop me if Eidolon…does that again.

I'm leaning against the smooth wall, hands behind me for a reason. Even though I've washed and scrubbed off the nymph's sand and blood, I can still see it when I look at my skin. More than once I've found myself trying to wipe off stray traces that aren't really there, so behind me is better.

Tabra pops her head around the door. "You can come in now."

When I join them, they are all watching me the same way Wanderers eye a sandstorm building in the distance.

"Figured out a plan?" I ask.

They all nod.

"And you're all sure about this?"

Tabra clears her throat. "Given the possible outcomes, I think there's no scenario where we don't try."

This might be the very first time since...well, maybe ever, that we *all* agree on a risky next step.

"Good," I say. "I assume I'm staying here?"

Vos shakes his head, even though his face is a mix of frustration and resignation. "We need you to get us out quickly. You come."

"I will bring the sand you need," Bene says.

I frown, working through what that means. They need me for portals. Mostly because we're running out of time, but also the danger being at the heart of Eidolon's lands. Makes sense.

I still can't believe that the blue stone Tziah's family discovered is actually Allusian's heart. The mines of Tyndra had produced nothing out of the ordinary until that point. But then Eidolon's people found out and General Quentin deliberately fed those poor miners not one, but two pieces.

An experiment. Ordered by the king.

We're not entirely sure for what. Maybe trying to make himself a god in an attempt to rescue his mother? That or trying to create an army of Imperium, or even monsters, to fight for him. That's our best guess.

But, just like Bene and the other consorts, with the second piece of the heart, every soul except Tziah became a monster that Vos and the other Tyndran soldiers were forced to kill. That's when Vos broke from Eidolon. When he saved Tziah.

And now we're going to get it. Me included, I guess.

"Don't tell me more," I say.

I glance at Reven, who says nothing, his lips pressed tightly together.

Cain looks down at his feet, and I can tell he's hiding his thoughts, but in the next instant he lifts his head again. "I'll leave

Ledenon in charge of the zariphate."

Both Pella and I straighten.

"You can't," Pella says.

He gives her a glare I've never seen Cain use on his sister. "I set the rules."

Pella crosses her arms and glares right back. "Listen here, too-big-for-your-boots *zariph*. You are, to a certain extent, bound by tradition. And a zariph does not leave his zariphate. Ever."

He shifts restlessly on his feet. "I know that, Pell, but—"

"But nothing." She cuts a hand through the air. "The way you took over means you need to do everything right for a while. Everything the way our father would have."

His jaw takes on a stubborn cast and he points an accusing finger my way. "Meren and Tabra would either be captured or dead if I did things the way our father would have."

"I may not remember, but I'm guessing I had something to say about that," Reven snipes. Cain glares at him.

"I hate to admit it, but Pella's right."

The three of them swing to face me, Cain's expression sharp with betrayal.

"Sorry," I say quietly.

After a wide-eyed look, Pella's offers me a grateful grin. "Agreeing with me had to hurt."

"You have no idea," I grumble.

"You're siding with my sister?" Cain demands.

I shrug. "You need to be building your position as zariph so that if it comes to war, your people will follow you. We have enough of us to deal with this. You stay."

He scowls. "No. I'm not letting you do this without me—"

Tabra clears her throat. "That is an order from your queen." She immediately offers him an apologetic look that waters down that moment of utterly haughty Grandmother she channeled, but Cain can see as well as the rest of us that she's not going to take it back.

"Hells," he mutters. "It was bad enough when there was only one of her." He shoots me a glare.

"You know you—" I was going to say "love me" like I used to when we were kids. But things are different now. "Love it," I finish.

He grunts a dubious sound.

"So we're agreed," Pella says. "I go, Cain stays."

"I didn't agree to anything." Cain crosses his arms. "But it appears I have no choice."

"I'll go," Hakan says. No surprise there. He goes where Pella goes.

She shoots him the smallest of grateful, very-un-Pella-like smiles while Cain gives him a nod.

I glance at my sister. "You're also staying."

Her expression flattens. "Really? I thought we'd leave our newly reacquired dominion and throne to the viziers for fun."

Sarcasm? She's using *sarcasm* now?

"She's even starting to *sound* like you," Cain grumbles.

Both Tabra and I share a grin at that before I slide my gaze to Achlys, who says immediately, "I'll stay with Tabra."

Exactly what I expected, but I nod my thanks all the same.

A small maggot of worry wriggles around inside me, though. Why does it feel like scattering us this way, separating the group, is a disaster waiting to happen? Maybe because every time we break apart—usually my fault—bad things tend to pile up.

"One last thing," Tabra says. "The amulets."

I give them a confused frown. "What about them?"

"We should hide them here," my sister says. "Somewhere only Achlys and I know about. Just in case."

In case none of us come back and she needs to try to release the goddesses on her own. She doesn't add that part. She doesn't have to.

"They're stuck in Reven's shadow pocket," I remind them.

Reven doesn't so much as blink. "You mean in the place

where I hid things before?"

The rest of us stare at him with mouths wide open. "How did you know about that?"

"Tabra told me."

Now we all swing stares at my sister.

"Tab—" I snap my mouth shut, taking that in for a second. "Why?"

She doesn't blink. "Reven asked me to fill him in on the important things he didn't know, so I obliged."

Of course she did. But…he asked? So many questions. I have so many burning questions. The least of which is why he went to her instead of me.

Pella is the one to ask the first of the most obvious questions. "Why?"

Reven scowls. "I'm tired of going into dangerous situations blind. Not knowing seemed like a good idea when I wasn't sure who to trust." His gaze lands on me, rock steady. "I've figured that out now."

Vos crosses his arms and lifts one eyebrow at Reven. "You didn't think this was relevant sooner?"

"It only just came up now." Goddess, such a Reven thing to say.

"Uh-huh." Vos's gaze narrows on me. "Why are you smiling, Meren?"

"He picked us," I say. The bubbles in my stomach are something along the lines of feeling more optimistic than I have in a long time. "Take the win, Vos."

"I'll go with Tabra and Achlys," Reven says. Is he thinking that way Eidolon can't watch where he hides things? Then he holds out a hand. "I need the one you wear."

But I hesitate, looking at Bene, a massive sandy wolf standing guard at the door.

"It is more important to keep them safe than for me to be heard," he says immediately.

After a second, I nod. "We'll figure it out."

"You always do."

Reven moves closer and I hold my breath. Last night seems a thousand hours ago, but I can still feel his touch…and his regret.

His fingertips brush against my neck as he reaches for the amulet. Does he linger? I look up to meet eyes glittering with need. Not the kind from before when he knew he loved me, and there's worry there, too, but it's something all the same, and my chest expands with it, stomach turning fluttery.

He slips Savanah's amulet from my neck but pauses before he walks away. Like he can't quite make himself.

"Wait here with Vos and Tziah until we get back," Reven says.

In other words, they're not letting me be on my own anymore. I just nod, and they all go separate ways.

Tziah, who up until now has remained relatively quiet about her opinions, shoots Vos a series of signs too fast for me to keep up.

"No," he says. "You're not."

"What did you say?" I ask her.

"That she's going to Tyndra, too," he answers for her. "But she's not."

She gives him a glower that is so like Vos in a bad mood, I'd chuckle if this wasn't serious. "Why would you want to go back there, Tzi?" I ask.

More signing at Vos, glancing from him to me, so I know she's including me in the conversation. She's not done when Vos turns his back on her and climbs the dais steps to drop into the throne, feet kicked out before him, hand over his eyes.

"What?" I ask.

"She said if I die, she needs to be there to show the way. And that I probably would get us lost in the mountain anyway. She spent two years of her life in there."

And lost her family in there, turned to monsters by the heart they ate.

Vos waves a hand. "*You* try to reason with her."

I look between him and Tziah, who is standing with her hands on her hips, glaring at him. "She's a grown woman, Vos. The choice is hers."

He drops his hand, not to join in the glares but to give Tziah a look that Tabra and I have shared a thousand times, a cauldron's brew of worry, love, and support all in one.

Then he shifts his gaze to me, lavender eyes hardening to cut glass. "Anything happens to her, it's on you."

Tziah's face falls and she's up the stairs to squat in front of him, taking his hand, shaking her head and pointing at me.

I don't need him to translate this time. I know she's saying that it's on her, not on me.

Not true. I am queen.

All of this is on me.

49

RETURN TO THE HOVEL

I'm measuring time by my single, familiar star. It creeps across the sky outside the tiny, glassless window in my room in the hovel where I lived with Omma most of my life. Why we're in Enora, the others won't tell me. Something about precautions and false trails.

It's like nothing has changed since the last time I was here, and yet everything has.

What feels the same are the clothes I wear—I'm back in my disguise as the city waif who grew up on the streets of the white-walled city. What feels the same is the musty smell of the air and the fine layer of dust on the sheets on my bed, the sounds of carnal pleasure coming from the houses of ill repute our hovel is tucked between, the lingering taste of cinnamon bread and cured meat and wine we bought from street vendors as our dinner.

All of that makes me feel like I'm…home.

Ironic since I hated this place when I lived here. It felt like a prison. One I snuck out of over and over again to go to the desert and pretend I was a Wanderer with Cain. Now it feels like an escape.

But it isn't either of those things—home or escape.

It's just a stopping point on the road to possible death and dismemberment and a search for something that no longer exists.

I pull my knees to my chest. Tziah, Vos, Pella, and Hakan are all out in the city now, gathering Tyndran gear. Bene is in raven form, perched on top of the hovel as a watcher and guard. The others didn't leave all that long ago, which means they'll be a while. So, since I'm stuck waiting, I watch my star like I used to.

Which is when I see it. Or I think I do.

Tilting my head, I peer closer at my star. I spent eighteen years staring at that damn thing, so I know what it looks like as well as I used to know the crags of Omma's face or the path out of the city through the western gate.

Does it look…dimmer?

I angle my head one way, then the other, then narrow my eyes to squint at it before jerking straighter.

I stick my hand through the window. It doesn't feel like anything. Just open air, warm and dry, no different than in my room. A bit of a breeze even stirs against my fingertips. Withdrawing my hand, I turn away from the window, letting my gaze skate over every crevice, every corner of my room, inspecting each patch of darkness in turn. But nothing moves or twitches other than my own shadow cast by the moonlight.

Maybe I was wrong?

As I swing around to give the star another good long look, a knock sounds at my door. "Meren?" Reven's velvet and iron voice rumbles on the other side.

Son of a bitch, I wasn't wrong.

He put an invisible screen of darkness over my window, probably my door, too, to let him know if I try to leave this room. Was that his idea or someone else's?

"I don't know why you're bothering to knock," I call out. "But come in."

The door swings slowly open on a creak of rusty hinges. He has to duck to get under the doorway. This place wasn't built for tall men, just centuries of hidden princesses, all fairly petite.

I don't miss the way he glances at the window. "Are you hungry?"

Terrible excuse.

My knees are still drawn up, so I prop my elbow on one and my chin in my hand. "I wasn't trying to escape."

If I wasn't looking so hard, I would have missed the discomfort that tugs at the corners of his mouth. "That's a funny answer to my wondering if you're hungry."

"I'm a funny girl, I guess."

We both regard each other for a long, tense beat, waiting for the other to break and confess.

"You didn't have to put shadows over my window," I say. "You could have just asked me to let you know if I want to leave."

He crosses his arms. "I may not remember my time with you, but I have at least figured out that you tend to do what you want without asking permission."

I wince. "I've been getting better about that, actually."

Lesson learned. A couple times, in fact.

"Sure." He sounds skeptical. "It doesn't matter either way. I put the shadows up at every entry point in case someone tries to get in. Not out."

Oh. Now I feel like an ass. I glance away, then back to him. "When did you figure out how to do that better?" His attempt when we were invading Oaesys wasn't invisible like this.

He shrugs.

"It feels like you're learning your powers faster this time."

"Yeah?" He thinks about that. "It probably helps that I'm not fighting the Shadow—"

He cuts off, watching my face warily.

I feel my cheek. "What? Did one of them cross my face without me feeling it?"

"No. I just…"

He just expected it to because Eidolon can get to me through our link and I don't always know. Awesome. I'm like a terravore buried in the dunes and my friends and my—I'm still not sure what to call him—are all just waiting for me to upend their world any second.

"Why'd you bother knocking?" I sound pissy, even to my own ears. Goddess, I'm being such a brat. Clearing my throat, I cool it. "You could have just shadowed in here."

"I didn't want to set you off."

Again with the evil in me. The thing is, I know they need to keep tabs on me like this. Even with the Shadows quiet since the moment we met Allusian, I'm well aware my anger has been building, my temper borderline out of control when it flares up. Eidolon has taken complete control of me multiple times and done a terrible thing through me, and I'm scared to death it'll happen again. I keep seeing the sand nymph's face when he used my hand to plunge that blade into her. "I'm fine."

He doesn't say anything.

I make a face. "I already promised to keep you close." It was either that or not come with them, and they need me.

Which is when one of the ladies in the brothel next door decides to let out a long, breathy moan of supposedly unfaked pleasure.

Hells swallow me whole.

"Have I been here before?" Reven asks behind me.

I scrunch up my nose, because I have a good idea what memory that sound is stirring. "No."

"Then why—"

"We listened to a harpy eagle together once."

There's a pause. "I see." Then another pause. "Old memories again," he murmurs to himself more than me.

I shrug, still refusing to look at him.

Another louder moan floats across and through my window. It's as bad experiencing this with him now as it was the last time, though in a different way. I shift, trying to relieve the warmth and tension starting to build. He regretted making love to me without his memories. I won't do that again. To either of us.

"So good," she groans across the way.

Heat flares in my cheeks. Why doesn't he just leave?

"You know...I'd rather make new memories than keep having these old ones flash at me," he says.

That gets me to turn my head and find him leaning in the doorway, arms still crossed and now one booted foot propped over the other, looking so much like *my* arrogant Reven, and yet the light in his eyes is...cautious.

I glance back at my star, because seeing him that way hurts. "I get it," I say. "I was expected to do and be the same as all the hidden princesses before me, and when I didn't conform, didn't fit the mold, I was a disappointment. All I wanted was to go off and live a different life. *My* life."

"Yeah," he murmurs.

The heaviness in that single word sinks through me like a rock in quicksand. Right to the bottom to be buried forever.

"Oh yes, oh goddess!" Heady cries come from the brothel followed by the sounds of bodies coming together.

The suggestive noises, the eagerness in her voice, only tap into memories of shared moments with Reven, sending the tension inside me expanding and pushing outward with zero outlet. No way to find relief. Goddess, this sucks.

The thing is, this is the first time since our "morning after" that we've had a chance to breathe. I don't want to go into danger with this...awkward distance...hanging between us.

When I turn this time, it's with my whole body to face him, leaning back against the windowsill, my knees still drawn up. "So...what do *you* want?"

50

WANTING HIM TO BE HAPPY

His body stills oddly before his thick brows draw together. "What do you mean?"

"What do you think I—?"

The answer sinks in before I finish asking the question, and heat flares into my cheeks even more than a second ago. He thinks I mean in the lusty sense. Pretending I'm not blushing what is no doubt a bright shade of scarlet, I shrug. "I mean if you could start all over, no Eidolon, no past that you don't remember, what would you want for yourself? What would you do first? Where would you go?"

He drops his chin, studying his boot that he sort of scuffs against the worn wood of my floors. "I mean, there's the obvious," he says, still scuffing away. "Shelter, safety, provisions like food and clothing."

I nod and wait and try not to want him so badly.

His lips twist. "I'd find the owners of the voices I hear at night," he says finally.

I don't know what I was thinking he'd say. Something like he'd get the hells away from all of this and start a new life. But I fell for this man for so many good reasons. At his core, he will always be who he is.

I let go of the selfishly needy heat inside me. "Would you build another community like the Shadowood?"

He pauses, then nods, still not looking up.

"I like that. You helped a lot of people."

Another nod, slower.

"And it's who you are, I think. A protector."

That makes him grimace. "I'm not so sure, but it feels like a purpose. A calling. Literally. Why else would the goddesses have given me the gift of hearing them if not to do something about it?"

Not all people would reach that selfless conclusion. Does he not realize that? "Eidolon in all his previous incarnations must have heard them, too," I point out. "And yet…"

And yet the king chose to stay on his destructive, obsessive, if somewhat originally justified path of undoing what Lillnya did with Esha's help. His bondmate's help.

Yet another moan reaches us through the window, this in a different voice. Softer, just getting started.

Reven's gaze flicks from my face, out the window, and back, and despite all we've shared, more heat surges into my cheeks. His lips crook, and I almost expect some smart-ass remark designed to make me red all over. Instead, he says, "I have a problem with what I want, though."

I blink, trying to track the conversation. "What problem?"

"You."

I blink again, then frown. "In this wishful scenario, I'm not a factor."

His gaze turns pinpoint bright, trained on my face. "But you are."

"How—"

"I hear you at night. *Every* night."

Every…

My heart gives a heavy jolt. "I've tried not to say anything to the darkness."

"I know. I hear you anyway, because for some reason your thoughts also filter to me."

I take a breath. "Like what?"

"Small things. A restless sigh. Telling yourself to be patient."

His lips flatten. "Calling yourself a monster. I'm not trying to intrude, but I can't control when it happens."

Part of me wants to close my eyes and savor the small point of connection, and then there's the part that would rather he not ever hear the various self-doubts floating around in my head.

"Even if I didn't know you, I would want to find you," he says.

My heart gives another jolt, then knocks against my ribs. "Why?"

He scans my features, almost like he's trying to memorize them. "It's a compulsion. The original bond maybe. Or the new one even if it's..."

Oh. The bonds. Disappointment stops my heart and pins it to my insides so it can't move anymore. "That's not what *you* want, though. You should be able to choose."

"I don't know what I want."

Another lazy sound of pleasure floats by.

He swallows and his gaze flickers again. "I liked it when you made those sounds for me."

Oh goddess. Is he saying he wants me? More warmth flares across my skin, then sinks deeper to swirl and eddy and pool low.

Reven levers off the doorjamb to prowl closer, squatting in front of me, gaze still on my face.

I take a shuddering breath.

"I wanted you the other night," he says. "Because of *you*. Not any other reason. But it's still...strange to me." He gives a shake of his head. "I find it very confusing."

"I bet."

His lips quirk again. It's nice to see even a hint of humor from him these days, but all it does is make me want to reach out.

"The more I get to know you now, the more I respect you."

I look at my hands and have to physically keep myself from wiping them on my clothes. "Even after I killed the nymph?"

"You didn't," Reven says in a voice gone hard. "That was all Eidolon. You would've stopped it if you could."

I swallow. "What if I couldn't because I was so mad at her about the curse that I wanted her dead, too?" It comes out barely audible, my voice small.

The thing is, I've been asking myself that question over and over. I was so angry with her in that moment. She tied me to *evil*.

"The fact that you'd ask yourself that, torment yourself with that, says it all." He curls a hand around mine, covering the stains that I can still see. "You truly want to do the right thing, make the right choice. You want to help the people you lead, and those you now rule with your sister. I respect *that*."

I squeeze my eyes shut, and the tightness that's been crushing my chest since that moment lets up just a little. He doesn't fear me—he fears Eidolon. He doesn't blame me—he blames the king.

I'm not the evil. I'm just the tool. I know that, but it feels good to hear him say it.

"Besides, bond or not, I wouldn't feel like this if I believed you were evil."

My eyes spring open.

"I think I like you, too," Reven says in a voice gone even deeper, smoother.

I can't help but huff a laugh at that and his brows go up in question.

"Damned by faint praise," I explain.

"Ah." Reven ducks his head and maybe a smile flashes. I'm not so sure when he looks up again. "I like your sense of humor. And your sarcasm. You make me want to laugh."

Awesome. I'm comic relief.

Humor fades from his expression replaced by something more…contemplative. "I like the way you look at me when you think I don't see."

Oh.

Prickles slowly tiptoe up my spine.

"I like the way you laugh, and what the sound of it does to me. I have the strongest urge to protect you from everything this world is throwing at you so fast and hard. And after that shared night, with the taste of you still on my tongue, the sounds you made still in my ears, the feel of you under and around me still burned into my skin…" He takes a deep breath and lets it out slowly. "But it's not fair to you."

To me? "Why?" I whisper, not wanting to break the spell his words are weaving around me. Around us.

"Because I don't know if what I'm feeling is real and lasting, or if it's just…"

I see. "Wanting to screw my brains out?"

He sort of chokes. "The mouth on you," he says. And I'm thrown back into the time before when he used to call me on my swearing, even though he's worse. He continues. "Not the phrase I would have used, but…yeah. Lust and proximity. Or even the remnants of a bond I didn't make."

Ouch. I swallow again. "I guess I see your problem."

The way his eyes darken and he leans back slightly, I think my response disappointed him somehow. What did he want? Permission to tumble me back on my bed, get me out of his system, and then see how he felt in the morning?

Honestly, I'm tempted, despite the awkwardness still lingering from last time. Is that pathetic?

"Maybe…" I hesitate.

"Maybe what?" he prods.

Just say it, Meren. "Maybe we're both thinking too hard about this. Maybe…" I twitch a shoulder in a move that I intend to be a casual shrug. "We could take it slow. Just go with what you feel and let the future and what we are sort itself out as we go."

"Slow." He says the word like he's tasting it.

Then something flickers in his eyes. A dark thought that has him scowling just for a second.

I still catch it. “What?”

His jaw works. “I might have to kill you. If Eidolon takes over again—” He runs a hand around the back of his neck.

Right.

“It will be harder to do that if I have feelings for you,” he explains. “If I let myself.”

I slip my hand out from under his and draw my knees back in tighter, trying to draw my emotions in at the same time—the hurt and the disappointment and the doubts. “Right.” I’m nodding. “Smart. That’s smart.”

We’re both silent a second.

“Maybe after.” After this is all over and if we both live through it, he means. He nods to himself a little as he rises to his feet. Then he backs away. “After is good. That’s a good plan.”

Yeah. I hate that plan. “Good.”

He reaches the door and pauses. “Good.”

If he doesn’t leave, I’m going to jump him and forget the consequences.

He sort of straightens as if obeying an order, then spins on his heel and goes, shutting my door behind him.

I drop my head to my knees and groan at the exact same time one of the women next door hits the climax of her performance. Two very different sounds for very different reasons.

Worse. The courtesans are going to be doing that all night while I lie here in an emotional and physical state of needing and longing that just…

Another moan sounds.

“Ugh.” I push off the bed, restless energy overtaking me. Just sitting here listening to them is only going to make this harder. But Reven is in the house, and I’m trying not to be seen in Enora, so it’s not like I have anywhere I can go.

I close my eyes and put my hands over my ears, but that doesn’t help. Because now all I can see is Reven crouched in front of me with an earnest expression saying again all the ways he likes me. Especially the way I taste on his tongue and feel on his body.

Oh goddess. This is torture.

The door slams opens and then Reven is in the room. He doesn't even give me time to ask why he's here, his hands coming up over mine, which still cover my ears. His gaze caging my own, he gently and slowly lowers my hands to my sides before raising his again to wind his fingers through the heavy curtain of my hair. He brushes one thumb over the rise and fall of my cheekbone, never looking away from my eyes.

"Slow," he says.

I watch him and wait.

Unhurriedly, with agonizing deliberation, he lowers his head, gaze still holding mine captive. I can see the way he takes breaths as he goes, like he's having to steady himself. When his lips are near to brushing mine, he pauses, searching my eyes, so achingly close I want to scream and sigh into him at the same time.

"Do I have your permission?" he whispers.

Goddess yes. Hells yes. I close my eyes and close the tiny distance between us, pressing my lips to his softly. "Yes," I whisper against his mouth.

Everything fades and centers until the only thing that exists for me is Reven. The soft warmth of his kisses, the hard plains of his body urgent against mine, his hands in my hair as he angles my head. The way we come together…we just fit. My lips to his. My body to his. My soul to his. The kiss is beautiful and deep and makes my heart flutter like a thousand butterflies. It's also hesitant, and testing, and feeling each other out. It's the kind of kiss two new lovers exchange for the very first time.

Precious in its newness.

He doesn't take it too far, although I can feel how much he wants to in the way his body shakes a little against me, the way it takes him a second, and several extra kisses, to slow us down before we cross a line.

The way he puts his forehead to mine, eyes closed, breath quickened.

Heart quickened, too, just like mine.

"Like that?" he asks.

I want to cry and laugh and dance…and stay at his side forever.

I want to wind my arms around his neck and hold on so tight, I never let go. But instead, I tilt my head and brush the tip of my nose to his before pulling back to smile impishly up into his eyes. "Exactly like that."

This time it's not Reven's sudden stilling and the way his eyes go flat that tells me my control slipped. Before I often haven't even realized, but now…I feel it at least two heartbeats before his reaction.

I feel it in the cold that slides through my blood.

In the tug on me that comes from outside my body. Eidolon is here. With us.

A Shadow rustles. *"Here comes the king."*

Holding myself as still as I can, I stare at Reven with wide eyes. "I think…I think strong emotions open the door for him," I whisper.

My meaning sinks in and regret darkens his eyes, and we both know what that means.

Jamming my eyes closed, I ruthlessly stuff all my feelings, and that Shadow, back into the box of numb I used before meeting Scoria. She was wrong. Numb is the only way to keep control, to keep Eidolon out. The cold vanishes, so I know I'm right.

When I open my eyes it's to find Reven looking at me with a sad sort of resignation. Could he see what I was doing? Could he feel me have to cut myself off from feeling anything, and especially from him?

I'm pretty sure he and I are doomed.

"It's okay," I say in a voice so devoid of emotion he flinches. "I shut him out."

"Really," Reven mutters, searching my face. "Meren—"

I step back when he steps forward and he stops.

My feet are way safer to look at than his face, so I drop my gaze. "You should go."

51

INTO TYNDRA

If I thought trekking across Little Tyndra from the Shadowood to the temple tower that houses the portal had once been a miserable journey by foot, flying six of us on Bene's massive back through a blizzard even Vos grumbles about made that previous trip look like a jaunt through a spring garden.

Bene, even in his massive, full Devourer form, has had to battle to move through the air with every flap of his sandy wings. He couldn't go above the storms. If he flies too high, he disintegrates into sand, and that would be bad for all of us. More than once he was buffeted hard enough that we were lucky none of us got pitched off his back. It's almost as though the dominion itself is trying to stop us, throwing everything it has at us.

Like Eidolon knows we're here.

Maybe he does. I'm here, after all, although I think I've done a pretty good job of keeping my heart as cold as the icy dominion.

"We're here," Vos yells over his shoulder at me. Riding up front, he's been blocking some of the weather with an ice shield this entire way.

"How the hells do you know?" I yell back.

Without the amulet around my neck, I can't hear Bene's voice in my head, but Vos never could so…

"What?" he asks.

I shake my head.

Sure enough, a second later, Bene leans to the left, flying in tight spirals down to the ground. Landing is even worse. The strength of the winds tosses Bene as he tries, and it takes several violent flaps of his wings before he can touch down. I'm not the only one who lets out a not-so-silent groan of relief that we made it this far.

As my feet hit the ground after following Vos off, the winds pause just long enough for me to catch the hint of a mountain directly in front of us. I tip my head, trying to see the top, but thick clouds and snow obscure my view. What I can see, though, is ice-covered rock that appears to sheer straight up.

If I weren't forcing myself to feel nothing, I'd probably wobble at that sight.

Tziah slips her hand into mine, our gloves so thick I can barely curl my fingers around hers. With our fur-lined hoods drawn up and faces covered against the blistering cold, I don't bother to try to look at her face. Coming back here can't be easy for her. We all know that.

"This way!" Vos yells over the howling storm.

Bene nudges me from behind, and I stumble forward, taking Tziah with me. She's the only reason I don't fall over. Holding tight, she takes the lead, tugging me along behind her. Keeping my gaze glued to the icy ground as I try my hardest not to slip and fall, I don't realize we're anywhere close to shelter until we step into darkness and Tziah finally lets go. Reven's hand leaves the small of my back and I blink at him. I hadn't even realized he had a grip on me in the first place. He tips his chin at Vos and Tziah's departing figures, and we both keep going with Hakan, Pella, and Bene behind us, as Vos lights the way with the glow of his hand.

Farther inside the space that Bene can still squeeze through full-sized, the winds stop entirely, and we step around a bend into a cavern that opens up even higher overhead. A place that has clearly seen humans before. Immediately, Vos is pulling already cut pieces of wood from a pile by the entrance to build a fire.

I'm too busy gaping at the size—the room is big enough for Bene to fly in here—and how the rock in here is red. A deep red that glistens with traces of other kinds of rock.

"Anyone else feel like the mountain looks like it's bleeding?" I ask.

Pella huffs a laugh. "Like a gutted goat."

Tziah signs something to Vos, but he doesn't laugh. He sighs, very unVos-like, then ruffles her hair.

"What?" I ask.

"She said that when her family was killed, she couldn't tell if the red on the ground was their blood or the mountain."

Goddess, that had to be terrible. These days I know something about losing family violently. Omma. Vida. Even Tabra, though I got her back. Reven…

The nymph.

I close my eyes and feed even that small moment of feeling into the numb box.

"I'm sorry you had to go through that," I say, because it's true, even if I can't let myself feel it at the moment.

After a second, as if she knows what's going on inside me, Tziah wraps both arms around me.

"You never hug *me* like that," Pella says.

Tziah and I both lift our heads. "I thought you'd cut an arm off if we tried anything like that," I say.

She purses her lips together. "Sounds like me," she muses. "But a true friend would risk a limb."

I snort a laugh, but Tziah holds out a beckoning hand. After her eyebrows shoot up, Pella pastes a put-upon expression on her face and steps into a circle of hugging with us. "I'm only doing this because Tziah asked," she grumbles.

"Don't worry," I say in a teasing voice they'd all expect. It's amazing how easy it's been to slip back into not feeling anything.

"I know you secretly think of me as your very bestest friend in all of Nova."

She twitches. "You wish."

"Cover your ears," Hakan warns us.

We all let go to follow that instruction, already knowing what's coming. An odd, sizzling sensation fills the air a heartbeat before light flashes, the boom of Hakan's lightning cracking off the rock walls as he lights the fire.

"Who left the wood here?" Pella asks, lowering her hands. "Do we need to be checking the caves for other occupants?"

Vos uses a long, skinny stick to poke at the flames, stirring them higher, red glowing embers floating up to disappear in the darkness. I turn my face into the flare of warmth, holding out my hands.

"The people who left it used to work the mines within the mountain," Vos says. "One of the jobs was to procure wood and oil for their fires, including being sure all the Svetlyska entrances were stocked like this."

Pella nods. "I assume it's been abandoned since…"

Vos's lips flatten. "Since the last time Tziah and I were here? As far as I know, yes. I buried the heart before I ran so they couldn't use it anymore."

Vos pushes the hood of his jacket back, loosening his scarves as he looks around. After a shake of his head that is probably him talking to himself, he looks directly at Reven. "This is where you found us."

Reven gives a frowning glance around. "What?"

"I got me and Tziah away from the monsters and the soldiers, but I was injured." He lifts a cocky eyebrow. "I'd show you where, but I'd have to drop my pants to do it."

I try to picture what was injured and he nudges me with his elbow. "Don't worry. Nothing got near my perfect ass. But one of those monsters damn near took my leg off. When General Quentin realized I was getting Tziah out of here without killing her, he put two arrows in my back before I could freeze that bastard solid. I say that I saved Tziah, but she's the one who dragged me out of the pit of caves and mining shafts. You wouldn't know it to look at her, but that tiny body was given superhuman strength and agility."

I've seen it in action in Tropikis when she dove into a crowd of mindless rabid people to save Cain and when she tackled a soldier in that fight. In several other fights since, actually. But not quite to that extent. I know for sure I wouldn't be able to drag Vos's lean but solid bulk anywhere, let alone fast enough to escape.

"We managed to get here, but by then it was night. No one travels this part of Tyndra at night." Vos looks toward the path leading outside. "No one who wants to live, at least."

Something we've all learned well just getting here. I can't help but glance in the direction he's staring, but Bene has lain down in front of the exit, wings folded back, like he's blocking out any possible cold that could seep inside.

He looks like he wants to say something. I wish I knew what.

Vos shrugs. "Even in the dark, we could tell I was bleeding too heavily to move more by then anyway. Dying for sure. And I think I said something like 'help us' or 'save us.' In my delirium, I didn't believe the man who suddenly appeared in the cavern with us, lighting the space up with the glow of his hands, was real." He laughs. "Tziah by then had figured out that opening her mouth incapacitated people, so she did."

He looks at Reven. "You clapped your hands over your ears and shouted something like, 'I'm here to help you, damn it.'"

Reven is holding himself so still, I think even a flicker of flame coming too close could knock him over. I'm guessing he is searching and clawing through the holes of his mind to try to remember this. Any of this.

Vos's gaze dulls with understanding and he claps a hand on Reven's shoulder. "We were the first two people you brought to the Shadowood, brother. The first of the voices you can hear that you saved."

Reven hesitates only a second before he also claps a hand on Vos's opposite shoulder. "I wish I could remember."

Vos nods slowly, then wags his eyebrows. "But you're happy you did it anyway, aren't you?"

And Reven…laughs.

Low, and almost reluctant, but the deep rumble is sincere. His eyes widen like he's surprised that sound came from him. "I guess I am," he says. And squeezes Vos's shoulder.

And for the first time since I pulled him out of Eidolon, there is no edge of hesitation in his gaze as he looks at his old friend. He's not ready to call Vos brother, yet. But I'd rather face whatever happens next with them on the same team, so thank the goddesses for that.

Or maybe I should start saying "Thank Allusian."

"How do we get to the heart if you buried it?" I ask Vos and Tziah.

But he clamps his lips shut.

Right. No telling the possible Eidolon spy. "I guess I'll find out when we get there."

52

THE BLOOD OF THE MOUNTAIN

We all lean over a creepy-as-sin hole in the cave floor, about two-meters in diameter, that even the glow of several Imperium can't penetrate very far down. After spending the night in the first large cavern to rest, it's taken us much of the day to get here.

"Well, that's a pile of fool's gold," Vos mutters.

After hours and hours of trekking our way through the system of caves and mine shafts, we finally make it to the place where Tziah and Vos both agree the miners originally unearthed the heart. There's no sign of a fight, or of monsters, no bodies. Nothing.

Just this hole.

"Want to fill the rest of us in?" Reven asks.

Vos crouches down. "This is the exact spot where I buried the heart deep in the mountain in layers and layers of ice."

We all stare down the hole again. "Then someone must've dug it out," Reven says.

Tziah shakes her head, then points and signs and points some more.

Vos grunts. "She says that the pattern within the ice and rocks isn't digging. It's fire."

Fire?

"Coming from which way?" Hakan asks. "There has to be a bottom to it."

Vos looks at Tziah, who points in a way that's unmistakable. The fire went down.

"A Fire Hylorae?" I ask.

Vos runs a hand over his face. "Could be. Eidolon has one among his authoritates. The question is, did they manage to unbury the heart?"

I can't begin to list all the ways that wouldn't be good. Starting with the obvious—if he has, we won't be able to give Allusian her heart. But, even worse, Eidolon doesn't know what he's dealing with. All he knows is what happened to the miners in his mountain. One bite turned them into Imperium, two bites into monsters. I could easily see him using the heart as a weapon of sorts. Create more Imperium to fight on his side. Or, if he takes it a bit further, a monster maker.

We all stare down the hole again. What comes next is pretty obvious. We're going to have to climb down there to find out.

"You've got to be kidding me," Pella mutters.

Vos gives an unamused chuckle. "Exactly what I just said."

"Drop a rock," Reven says. "Let's see how long it takes before it hits bottom."

Tziah grabs a fist-sized stone nearby and chucks it in.

Knock. Plink. Knock. Knock.

It keeps hitting the walls on the way down. Eventually the sound of it just fades away.

"Terrific," Pella says. "This shaft could come out in the bowels of the actual hells for all we know."

"Nah," Vos says in a wry voice. "We know the hells don't work that way now that we've seen Allusian and her lost lands."

She rolls her eyes. "Are you really nitpicking my choice of phrases right now?"

He shrugs.

"We don't all have to go," Reven says.

"Splitting us up tends to lead to disaster," Hakan points out.

Funny that I had a similar thought before coming here. The rest of us don't argue.

"So...we're all going," Vos says. Then glances at Reven. "Can you shadow us?"

"No. I need to know where I'm going." Reven thinks a moment. "I could lower us on shadow."

Tziah puts a hand out and shakes her head, signing that we should all conserve our powers in case of danger.

"She's right," Pella says. "We'll have to climb."

I glance at Bene, who is now in his large dog form. He couldn't have fit in the places we've come through, so he left piles of sand behind in the cavern where we spent the night for me to use to portal us out of this place when this is over. What could he transform into that could make it down that shaft? "I think you're going to have to fly."

He draws his lips back over his teeth. Not sure if that's an agreement or irritation.

Debate over, we climb down the hole, one-by-one, Vos leading the way. Rock and ice stick out of the walls in jagged outcroppings that aren't the most stable, but at least provide regular foot and handholds. It is so pitch black inside a mountain, even knowing shadows the way I've come to, I have never known darkness like this. But I swear it's a thousand times worse inside this hole.

It crowds in. Feels like something solid and pressing.

We're forced to light our way by using our powers in the smallest ways possible, creating purple and yellow glowing points in the darkness. Every few minutes I have to change which hand I'm using because I have to take a glove off and it's too cold to do that for long, all while my own light hardly gets past me, the darkness eating at it before it can spread much farther.

"Are we sure about this?" Pella grumbles above me somewhere in the dark. "Seems questionable to me."

She's only saying what we're all thinking, that maybe we should head back up and figure out a different way to get to the heart.

Vos's teasing voice floats up to me from below. "I don't see any problem here."

He seems to be in his element. And I guess, as an Ice Hylorae from Tyndra, he really is, but it's almost like he's feeding energy off the cold. What happened to his earlier grumbling? Must've been the wind.

"Ah!" Pella's shout sounds from above, and I look up but the barely lit darkness means all I see are booted feet coming at my face.

I duck, pulling in close against the icy wall I'm clinging to, then Reven is covering my body with his so that he takes the brunt of ice she kicked loose that pelts us.

But Pella doesn't fall past a foot or two. When I peek up around Reven, her feet are still dangling but not coming at me anymore. Hakan must've caught her.

"Get ready," I hear him say.

With a grunt Hakan swings a dangling Pella toward the wall and she manages to get a better foot and handhold this time.

"All right?" I call.

"Remind me next time not to sign up for the side quests," Pella calls back.

If Allusian's heart does what it's supposed to do and gives the goddess back her powers, allowing her to fix the rest of the problems we've been facing, then we won't need any more side quests. That's the point.

Why does it feel like we are pinning our hopes on a fool's errand, then?

Pella's sigh reaches me next. "Get moving. I don't want to be in here longer than I have to."

Me neither, actually.

My fear of heights keeps rising up even through my

concerted effort to shut off my emotions and even though I can't see. I'm not sure if the darkness below me is helpful, hiding the depth of the drop and how many outcroppings I'd break myself over on the way down, or if it's harder, making it seem like this shaft will go on forever and we're going to die in here.

Bene, now a raven—he tried a larger bird but the hole didn't give the wingspan enough room—lands on my shoulder and plucks at one of my scarves with his beak. Telling me to be careful, maybe?

Before I can ask, he flies up to Pella.

"Keep moving," Reven says.

It's not five minutes later that a hunk of ice gives way under my own foot, and my stomach lurches up my throat as I drop with a yelp. Even as I cringe away from hitting anything, I slam into an outcropping with my ribs and an *oomph* but get no purchase. To me it feels like I fall at least twenty feet. But a strong arm wraps around me, yanking me close to a hard body, and we stop midair, wisps of darkness melting away in the dim light around us. He must've shadowed to get below me.

I stare into turquoise eyes turned murkier by our combined purple and yellow lights.

"I've got you," Reven says quietly.

I don't point out the bruise my ribs are going to have thanks to the rocks I managed to bounce off of before he caught me. We're both holding on tight, even as his shadows hold us up.

"Thanks." *Don't feel. Don't feel.* It's so hard not to feel. Numb was simpler when he was really gone.

I also don't look away.

Neither does he.

One at a time, I catalog the details of his features. Ebony hair swept back in a wave. Thick-set brows set over keen eyes. He's studying me the way I am him, and his slightly crooked mouth tilts to one side.

"I think I just aged a decade," he says, and smiles.

But that smile fades when I don't smile back. I don't say anything. I can't. Not until this is all over and Eidolon can't hurt anyone through me. No smiles. No banter. No yearning.

I clear my throat. "Ready?"

Confusion twitches his brows down, but he doesn't argue. With Reven still holding me, the darkness helps me onto a new outcropping before dissipating.

"Let me go first this time," he says.

I have no problem holding here a little longer as an excuse while I calm the hells down from both the fall and him.

"Hold up," Vos snaps out of nowhere.

"What now?" Reven asks.

"It's blocked just below me. Some kind of cave in," Vos calls up.

I do *not* like the sound of cave in. It implies this entire shaft could collapse and bury us alive. How Tziah and her family did this for a living…I just couldn't have.

"Bene, can you get through?" Vos asks.

The raven dives past us in a blink. For a few seconds, I can hear the scratchy flutter of wings below and then it stops.

"Damn," Vos's mutter floats up, then louder, "Hold on."

The yellow glow coming from where he is below us turns brighter, and there's a sudden rumbling screeching protest that I swear vibrates the ice and rock we're all clinging to. Enough that Reven climbs back up to hold on around me like he's pinning me onto the wall. The same way he once held me onto a tiny ladder bridge suspended over the ocean channel between Wildernyss and Tyndra. At least until the Hollow came for us.

Something below gives and I can hear a tumble of rocks followed by a backdraft of ice- and dust-filled air that shoots upward. By the time it settles, we're all coughing, and if the others are like me, also squinting through grit in their eyes.

"Vos?" I call, then cough again.

"I'm all right."

"What the hells was that?" Reven demands.

"I had to force the ice to move out of our way," Vos calls back. He's even lower now based on the sound of his voice. "We're at the bottom. Come on."

53

FINDING THE LIGHT

We climb the rest of the way down the shaft without incident. I drop down from the hole onto a heap of bloodred rocks and white ice against one wall that piles up to where we're emerging from what I can see now should be the ceiling of another massive cavern, even bigger than the one we slept in last night.

Carefully we clamber down that, with a few wobbles as debris shifts under our weight. Six sets of hands illuminate what we can of the space, which isn't much. Bene flies past and is quickly swallowed in the darkness. Past the rockslide, we hit level ground leading to a massive subterranean lake that stretches well beyond what our lights can reach.

A *frozen* lake.

A sheet of ice coats the top, although it's hard to tell how thick it is based on the black water underneath.

"So where's the heart?" Pella approaches the water and leans over. "It should be here somewhere, shouldn't it?"

We each turn in a circle, looking around the crimson cavern and inky darkness. Allusian's heart should glow with a sort of blue fire. I've seen it. Reven used the blue stones—jedite, we thought—to reset and gather his energy in the Shadowood. Trying to contain the Shadows while protecting the sanctuary he created would completely drain his energy. Finding me, having to fight the Shadows even harder, had only made it worse.

It makes so much sense now that we know that it was Allusian's heart. What else could feed the son of Tyndra's power like that? I can still picture him, sitting on a throne of shadow, the radiant stones all around him, that same blue fire in his eyes. That glow would be obvious in this kind of darkness, an unmistakable beacon.

Which must mean it's either still buried or not here at all.

Think, Meren.

"I could try to make a portal to Allusian and see if she feels it?" I offer.

"No sand," Reven points out.

"I can call it down here, though getting the majority that Bene left at our campground inside the first large cavern will take some time." It's taken us hours to get where we are. I pull off my other glove, my sunny yellow pushing back more of the darkness closest to me.

Reven takes my hand, his skin starkly cold against mine and yet still warming me. "Wait. Save your energy until we're sure that's the only option."

I pause, letting my light fade a bit. "There's also the bit at the top of the shaft," I say. "Definitely enough to make a flower portal."

He shakes his head.

"Can you think of any other—"

Bene soars back into our circle of light from over the lake and lands on my shoulder. I blink at the Devourer…who is the way he is because he ate Allusian's heart. He might as well have plucked at the missing amulet around my neck, it's suddenly so obvious.

Reven's jedite.

He kept some of the smaller stones in his pocket of shadows. Are they still there?

"Reven…" He found his pocket of shadows when he retrieved the amulets for Tabra. "Did you see the stones in your hiding place?"

He doesn't hesitate. "I can get them."

"Stones?" Pella asks.

"He has small chunks of jedite," I tell them. "Or chunks of Allusian's heart, I guess."

"Wait. You still have those?" Vos's sudden exclamation has the rest of us swinging to face him.

"You knew about them?" Reven asks with a quick frown.

Does he give himself a headache with how often he frowns over things he should know but can't remember?

"Know about them?" Vos crosses his arms, despite how thick his cold-weather coat is, and tips a chin at Reven. "I gave them to you the day you rescued me and Tziah." He pauses, and I can practically see a bubble of words forming over Vos's head before he shifts his gaze to me. "How did *you* know?"

Reven also looks at me in mild curiosity, clearly not remembering.

I glance between the two men. More secrets to reveal, I guess. One of these days we've got to run out, right? "I stumbled across Reven using them."

A few times, actually.

Vos's expression hardens and shifts back to Reven. "Using them how, exactly?"

Reven also crosses his arms, irritation rippling across his features and in his voice when he says, "How the fuck should I know?"

I jump in to head off the brewing squabble. "He didn't eat it if that's what you're thinking. He'd place them around himself in a circle while he was…absorbing darkness."

That sounds worse when I say it out loud. But it was what it was.

"I never asked exactly how it worked," I add.

After a second, Reven gives a nod. Since I'm closest, I might be the only one who sees how jerky the motion is. He hates that he can't remember the things he's done. I know he does.

I would, too, but even more when it's this important.

Hakan is the one to bring us back to the real point. "So what were you thinking?"

I share a glance with Reven.

"If the pieces of jedite I have are actually chips of the goddess's heart, maybe they can find the rest," he says.

Exactly.

Not waiting for anyone to agree, Reven draws that line of smoky shadow before him and, reaching inside, he pulls out a handful of blue stones, each coin-sized rock sparkling at us in the dim glows of our hands.

Bene flaps backward, snapping his raven beak. He doesn't stop until he gets to Hakan, who is farthest away, and lands on his shoulder. Immediately a tiny zap of lightning travels up and over the bird with an odd high-pitched buzzing noise, sending all the grains that make up his body sparkling before fading away, leaving a burnt scent behind. That doesn't seem to faze Bene. He's still too focused on the jedite maybe.

Allusian's heart.

It made him a monster.

If I'd been ripped from my lover's side after messing around with that stuff, I'd be wary, too.

"Hey," Pella says to Tziah. "You okay?"

She's staring at the rocks like they're cobras raised up with their hoods wide, ready to strike.

Oh hells. I'd been too focused on Bene to think of how this would affect her. "Tzi?"

She blinks, then signs that she's okay.

I glance at the jedite in Reven's hand and frown. "When I've seen them, they were glowing," I tell Reven. "Maybe if you separate them?"

He does and nothing happens.

"Use your powers for more than just light?" I suggest next.

The darkness swirls around us, eddying and spinning, and suddenly the jedite stones unexpectedly ignite with green-blue fire from within, shining brighter and brighter with each passing second.

Hakan puts out a hand to Pella, though he doesn't touch her. "Everyone else, douse your powers."

Immediately, all our glows go out, leaving only the stones' radiant light. Still, the shards of heart continue to brighten with each passing second, their glow illuminating the sharp angles of Reven's face before expanding outward, crawling across the spaces between us.

Which is when a new glow appears—larger, and dim, but the same color.

Except not in the cavern.

It's under the ice-covered lake.

"Holy shit," Reven mutters. "That worked."

Honestly, I was silently betting on this idea leading to nowhere at all, yet another dead end. But I was wrong. Allusian's heart recognizes other pieces of itself.

54

WE'RE NOT ALONE DOWN HERE

"Vos?" Reven says.

"On it." His yellow light joins the turquoise glow of the jedite as he goes to work on the icy top layer of the lake. It starts with a crackling sound that echoes through the cavern softly, then louder with each passing second. A burst of water, and he's through. Not the entire surface but a decent-size hole.

Through that opening, the water bubbles up, spilling out over the top of the ice and turning it more clear than white.

"This would have been easier with Cain," Vos says through clenched teeth as he works.

We shouldn't have split up, even just a little bit. None of us say that out loud. Instead, we watch in silence as water, and then chunks of ice so pure they're a brilliant white even in the multicolored lights, pour out of the hole, the gush of water straight up, growing higher and higher. Omma once described to me the geysers that spewed steam and boiling water from the ground in the harsh flats leading to Mt. Tyrh, the active volcano in Mariana. I pictured something like this in my head. Only not so much ice.

Like Vos dislodged the right chunk or something, the glow of turquoise below, obscured by the roiling waters, intensifies so much that it lights up a large swath of the lake from underneath.

"That's it," I whisper.

"You've got it," Reven says to Vos.

Vos is clenching and unclenching his jaw and abruptly the light dims, like the heart sank lower under the lake. "Damn it." The geyser of ice water drops down to a gentle burble. "I can't see what I'm doing."

"Keep going," I urge.

With a grunt, the geyser rises again, and after a few tense minutes that stretch on and on, the light below the surface starts to move again, coming closer until something not ice or water bursts through the hole, to float precariously on the top of the fountain of water still spewing up.

All of us except Vos turn our backs to it abruptly, and I'm blinking away the sting of my eyes.

The heart.

"I guess I didn't really need my eyes," Pella grumbles off to my left.

"Someone grab it," Vos calls out in a voice strained with effort.

Flickering has me looking again to see a stream of shadow pass before the heart, dimming it on and off in flashes. Shading my eyes, I watch as the shadow tries to lift the heart from the water. Because it keeps moving, though, Reven keeps missing. Until suddenly the darkness he wields changes to a net that scoops it up.

"We got it," I breathe the words, hardly daring to let myself believe that for once things are going our way.

He drops the heart on the ground and buoyant optimism sneaks past my emotional barriers in a bright burst of relief. We really got it. Allusian will help us now, with all the powers of a goddess. We can put an end to everything. It's over. It's finally all over.

I turn to Reven with a grin. "Thank the— "

And that's when the sheet of ice covering the rest of the lake explodes, sending massive, solid chunks shooting at us like cannon fodder.

Reven blasts up a screen of shadow. The ice hits that and bounces back at the massive creature that breaks through the water, roaring a challenge.

"Run!" Vos yells.

We all scatter.

It's that or get crushed as a monster—one the size of Bene when he's himself—plows up onto the shore so hard and fast, rocks and ice fling upward in its wake. The thing is fat and long, with a flattened fluke of a tail at the back and four beefy legs allowing it to crawl on land. It starts swinging its heavy body violently around, slashing the razor-sharp horn that sprouts from the center of its forehead like a rapier sword.

"The Gorecutter!" Pella shouts from somewhere on its other side.

Wildernyss's Devourer.

An urgent shout sounds from my right and Tziah gets jerked into the air by a whiplike appendage that has nothing to do with the Gorecutter. It's coming out of the ice-chunk-filled waters of the lake.

Ripping fear lances through my gut and shreds apart any of the numb barriers I just built up.

The Revoker. Tyndra's Devourer.

Everyone's heard tales of what the various monsters in our oceans look like. The Revoker is supposed to be the smallest of the monsters, human-looking on the top, the bottom end a long, snake-like tail that splits into three. It's rumored to pull people who get too close to the water in and eat only their eyes, tongues, and feet, leaving them alive but floundering in the ocean. Very few have ever made it back to shore.

Holy blasted hells. We're facing *two* Devourers.

"You are in big trouble," the Shadows crow.

Tziah opens her mouth to take them both out, but, as if the creature knows what she can do, it smacks her against the rock wall of the cavern, and she goes limp in its grip.

"Tzi!" I can't see Vos, but I can hear him.

I scramble to make sense of the situation. That water can't just be an underground lake. It has to connect to the ocean. They must have swum under the dominion somehow. Even with the lands sinking.

Most importantly, there's no way we can go up against two when Bene isn't full-sized.

"Don't kill them!" I yell as another realization slams into me. If Allusian helps us free her sisters, they're going to take immediate retribution on the humans who killed their consorts. Monsters or not.

"Are you kidding me?" Pella shouts back.

No time to answer. I throw myself on the ground to avoid being sliced in half by the Gorecutter's swinging horn. Vos spews ice from his hands, hitting the Revoker's tail that is flinging Tziah, still unconscious, around in the air like a ragdoll.

But that Devourer is smart. It tosses Tziah away only to swoop Vos up with a different tail. Vos doesn't hesitate, freezing it fast, starting where it has him and working his way down. A ghastly sound screeches from under the water, making the already stirred-up lake ripple like sand in an earthquake.

A third tail whips around Vos's wrist and snaps his arm before ripping it clean off at the shoulder, like tearing a chicken wing off a cooked carcass. I feel that crack and Vos's shout all the way to my bones and bile surges up my throat.

Shadow whips out too late. Formed like an axe, it comes down on the appendage that has Vos. The Revoker drops him and the shadow transforms to a net, catching Vos, to drop him onto solid land.

Which is when I see it. What Tziah meant. Blood is pouring from his wound, soaking his clothes and the red rock of the mountain. And I can't tell the difference.

Fear spikes, and the Shadows surge. *"One down!"*

"Vos!" I yell.

He rolls out from under the Gorecutter's flat tail that the thing brings down on top of him, obviously trying to crush him. The second the tail strikes the ground with a dull *whomp*, pitch blackness descends over the entire cavern.

Not from me.

Reven.

"Get out of the way!" he shouts from somewhere behind me.

Essentially blind, crunches of rock and ice tell me where the Gorecutter is thrashing about wildly to my left. Staying as low to the ground as I can, I crawl away from both Devourers toward where I saw Vos last, feeling my way as I go.

But it's too dark, and I'm moving too slow.

Almost as fast as Reven doused all light, a turquoise glow penetrates the absolute darkness, like the tiny pinprick of a star at first, then growing larger.

The heart.

It won't be hidden by shadow. Even Reven's.

It doesn't take long before I can make out details of the cavern, now bathed in blue light that turns the red of the rock a purplish black, and the Shadows pound at me, trying to get out.

A quick check shows me Vos on the ground with a chunk of ice capping off where his arms was, stemming the bleeding. One-handed, he's crawling away from the Gorecutter toward where Tziah landed, leaving behind a pool of glistening blood where he'd been lying.

I can't see Hakan, who I think is on the other side of the monster, and Reven is nowhere in sight, but Pella is to my left. In that short blackout, she climbed almost entirely up the fall of rocks under the shaft we came down.

The Gorecutter swings away from me and Pella toward some threat to its right, stabbing and slashing, thrashing its head around.

"Hey!" Pella shouts, waving her arms.

But the thing doesn't so much as acknowledge her.

In a sharp, fluid move, Pella has her bow out, getting off three arrows in rapid succession, two of which bounce off the animal's hide, but the third strikes the corner of its eye.

The monster screams in fury and whips around on her faster than an animal that thick and large should be able to move. Pella jumps to avoid its horn, coming down on the rocks in a way that sends her toppling over with a yelp.

The Gorecutter rears back to bring its horn down on her like a Wildernyssian soldier cleaves with a broadsword.

"Kill her!"

Only, Bene shoots in front of the Gorecutter's face. The other Devourer pulls up short, freezing almost like it's surprised, and the two stare each other down as Bene flaps in the air.

Is Bene talking to it?

The Gorecutter gives a great squealing warning that's somewhere between a song and a growl and Bene darts forward like he's charging the thing despite being only raven-sized. Kind of like a gnat confronting a crocodile.

And damned if the Gorecutter doesn't back the hells off, even if only a smidge.

I have just enough time to think, *Bene's got this,* when the Revoker launches the rest of the way out of the water like a demon violently escaping the hells, one tail propelling him as it whips around underneath, while the other two tails shoot to either side.

One coming straight for me.

"Bene!" Pella yells.

I swing back just in time to see the Gorecutter lunge for a distracted Bene, swallowing him whole.

55

IN THE DARKNESS

"Bene!" I sprint toward the Gorecutter's side, one of my knives unsheathed. When I get to him, I drive my weapon into the fleshy spot on the beefy, rounded toes of its forefoot, where the thing's toenail meets flesh.

In a reaction that's pure instinct, the Devourer kicks out. I see its foot coming like I'm moving slower than time. I feel when it connects and hear a rib crack with a lightning bolt of pain. All the air leaves my body in a painful *whoosh* and grunt, and then I'm in the air and everything speeds up again. I fly high enough that I flounder when I reach the pinnacle, and have time to brace on the way down, the rock floor of the cavern coming up at me fast.

Only I don't hit.

I stop midair, a net of shadow catching me like a spiderweb catches a fly. I look at my hands, but no purple light is coming from them.

"Meren!" Hakan yells.

I look up in time to see one of those tails coming for me again. The tip of it is forked three ways, like a spindly hand on the end. I try to move but I'm stuck hanging in the net of shadows. I tug again. Nothing.

Just as I flinch from the tail, the shadows that caught me let me go. Luckily, I'm not high off the ground at this point, so when I drop, while I don't land on my feet like a trained fighter would, I don't hurt anything badly, though my rib protests loudly.

Movement above me catches my eye, and I scramble back as the tail changes direction, coming for me again.

Only Reven suddenly appears in front of it, hovering in the air. Just long enough that the tip of the tail stops and turns on him sharply, like a snake turning its head to face a new threat. It's almost like those appendages have their own eyes and minds to determine what to target. The tail darts his way, and he disappears, only to reappear not far away. The tail goes for him again, only to pull up when he blinks out again. Then he's back.

And I realize what he's doing.

He's making himself a target, luring that tail away from me.

I think the Revoker must realize it at the same time because the human upper half of his body, still hovering above the frothing ice-chunk-filled waters, turns his head, zeroing in on where Reven and the tail are playing a game of cat and mouse.

The Devourer smiles.

From the other side of the cavern, Hakan shouts, "Don't touch the water!"

A fraction of a breath later, lightning cracks through the air, striking the lake. Even through the blinding brilliance of flashing death, I swear I see the Revoker's skeleton light up under its scaly skin before its torso falls back into the water with a splash. Its long tails drop to the ground, dead weight. Then, as it sinks into the lake, it drags the rest of its body across the rock to disappear into the depths.

That's one at least temporarily down.

But we're still dealing with the Gorecutter. What we need is to take the heart and get out of here. Now. But how? Vos's injury is serious. That ice will only buy him so much time. Tziah's out cold.

"We need to get out of here!" Pella shouts.

Reven shadows to Tziah's side and they both disappear. The Gorecutter roars its frustration. In another blink, Reven appears beside Vos. Only the Gorecutter is ready this time. It turns on them, and Reven has to block its strike with shadow. I can see that he can't do both as the Devourer brings its sword-like horn down on him over and over.

But Pella was right about needing to get out of here.

I change the light glowing from my palm, switching powers, and feel for the sand Bene left behind so far away. Then gasp, because now that I'm searching, I feel more sand much, much closer.

"Keep it busy!" I yell.

"The hells you say!" Pella yells back. But like the warrior she is, she still runs right at it.

I immediately start dragging sand up off the bottom of the lake, which is actually the ocean floor, just like I thought. Like when I sank Tropikis, the sand here is loose and easy to sift, and I yank it up to me as fast as I dare, trying not to explode the water.

Closing my eyes, I picture the temple portal in Enora, the one I used more often than any other my entire life. Getting back to Aryd with the heart and all of us still alive is all we need to worry about right now. Placing my hand against the now-cooled glass—thank goodness for Tyndran air—I force my power into it.

Which is when I hear it.

The strangest sound, like dripping and sucking at the same time. I open my eyes, and through the weeping, slightly bubbly glass I can see the outline of a man on the ground, lying there with his head lifted, watching me.

For the briefest moment I think it might be Vos, that he's crawled all the way over here, but the Gorecutter is still trying to pulverize him and Reven.

I lean around the side of the portal and stare into the furious blazing eyes of the Revoker—yellow-green and slitted like a snake. He's hauled himself out of the water, leaving a trail of blood in his wake or maybe water. Hard to tell with the red rock and blue heart light. With his head lifted, I can just make out an open wound across his chest, charred around the edges.

The instant our gazes connect, he crawls at me with remarkable speed given that he only has his arms and no legs and has to be in pain. He drags the back half of his body, which for a little way, at least isn't yet split—thick as a tree trunk and covered in scales a deep green with hidden flashes of yellow, matching his eyes.

I gasp as I hop back behind the glass, my hand still on it. I picture the first place that comes to mind. Forget Enora. We need to be in the palace as fast as possible.

A sensation of cold freezes through my blood. Familiar. Sending horror through me. I've felt this before when—

The glass changes to opaque and then clear in an instant, like it was already expecting me to want to go to the crypt in my palace where my secret portal still stands.

Only I don't step through.

A man is already in the room on the other side, his back to me as he digs around in one of the alcoves on the wall.

I don't have to ask who.

"How—" The word pops out of my mouth before I can stop it.

He swings around and straightens at the sight of me.

Eidolon.

Abruptly, the Shadows wrest all control from me, not tearing me apart this time, but holding me completely immobile, all except my pounding heart.

Eidolon's smile grows slowly, filled with a smug sort of triumph.

That is what evil looks like.

56

TO DEVOUR, OR NOT TO DEVOUR

Eidolon cocks his head, gaze taking in the violent scene behind me. "Encountered some trouble, have we?"

A tentacle-like hand appears around the edge of the portal, curling around the glass and into the room on the other side. The monster swings its head around next.

Up close, the Revoker—the goddess Tyndra's consort, Zolta—is somewhere between man and beast. I can make out a face that once must have made people gasp at his beauty, the symmetry like a sculpture, but the way he's covered in scales now, that ripple with every twitch of his muscles, changes those features to something else entirely. His snake-like eyes only add to the effect, and when he pulls back his lips in a snarl, razor-sharp fangs glint among his jagged teeth, adding to his menace. Is he poisonous, too?

The Revoker isn't looking for me, though. He seems to be looking for the something else. I know I'm right when he catches sight of Eidolon and stills, staring hard. The rest of the Devourer's body seems to catch up with him, coiling under his torso to lift him off the ground, and I almost expect him to lunge for one of us.

Instead, he makes a sound somewhere between a hiss and a whimper as he abruptly bows at the waist. Not just a cursory show of respect, the Revoker's torso is at a ninety-degree angle to the ground, eyes lowered in supplication.

What in the seven hells?

My gaze darts between them. Does this Devourer…does he answer to the king? Is Eidolon his master?

The roars of the Gorecutter cut off abruptly, and in my periphery, I can see that it, too, turns and bows.

Reven jerks around to look, which is when he also finally catches sight of Eidolon.

Fury overtakes his features and I think he's going to do what he's done only twice before, once in the Shadowood and once in the Wildernyss temple. Except he'd been out of control then, carrying the Shadows, and had far more command of his powers than he does now.

Instead of *poofing* everyone in sight, he drops the shielding wall of shadow over him and Vos and darkness blasts out of his hands, straight at Eidolon.

The king has to put up his own shield, getting slammed backward, only he keeps his feet, pushed until he hits the wall. And for a second, I see fear cross Eidolon's face. But then he manages to throw what looks like a full-body punch, something that takes visible effort, and Reven's body is catapulted up into the roof of the cavern and back down. My relief is quick and sharp as he shakily pushes to his hands and knees, but that relief disappears entirely when he collapses to the ground.

"Take that," a Shadow snarls.

Anger sparks like flint striking stone, and I fight even harder to gain my control back. To make the Shadows let go. They're not fighting me. They just have me captive. Bound in my own body that won't move.

"Pathetic," the king sneers.

I cut wide eyes back to where he stands, head arrogantly tilted, lips drawn back in a smirk. Then he steps to the side, revealing the alcove he'd been bent over. The secret spot where Tabra and I used to leave each other notes as children.

Why?

And how did he know it was there?

That's when he pulls one hand from around his back to show that he's holding the amulets.

A new, more terrible fear spears me through my chest.

Tabra must have hidden them in our spot. Makes sense. It's never been discovered by anyone before this. How in all of Nova did he know that's where she put them? Only three people knew. Tabra, Achlys, and…Reven. I wasn't allowed in there.

Eidolon slips the ones from around his neck to hold them together.

All of them. He has *all* of them.

"Thank you for making this so easy for me," he says.

Another flare of anger bolsters my power and I manage to wrest a tiny bit of control from the Shadows and my hand not holding the portal open flies up like I could stop him. "We'll release them for you," I say before he can disappear or do something worse. "The goddesses."

His eyes narrow ominously. "I don't believe you."

"It's true. We found a way." Sort of. Allusian hasn't told us how yet, but we have her heart now, so she will.

Eidolon looks from me to the state of the cavern and the blue glow of the heart. "You came for the jedite," he says. "To build an army of Imperium to face me."

"No!"

"Lies," he snaps. "You are the queen of lies, are you not, Mereneith? Or are we Tabra today?"

"I promise." I take a tentative step forward. "Freeing all the goddesses so they can fix the dominions is what we want, too—"

"I'm not taking the amulets to release all the goddesses, little fool."

The words to convince him die in my mouth.

"Look at the state of the world thanks to my mother's sisters." He shakes his head, cruel disdain curling his lips. "I will free my mother, and together we will start over. Wipe humanity off the face of the lands, fix the dominions, and create a new race. No Imperium. No powers. One that won't ever dare threaten the goddess who created them. She'll become the new mother goddess. Side-by-side, with the Devourers under our thrall, we will rule all of Nova."

I feel the blood drain from my face. "What—"

Eidolon gives the slightest nod, and the Revoker whips one tail around me, coiling and squeezing, cutting off my air and what I was going to say. It also pins my hands to my sides, but the portal doesn't close. Because the Revoker is now holding it open with his own hand.

"Meren!" I hear Hakan call. And I know what's coming.

I try to twist around. "No! Don't—"

Too late. A flash lights up the cave, and even before the immediate boom, I know what's coming.

The bolt of lightning careening across the cavern toward Eidolon hits a solid wall of darkness, bouncing off to reflect directly back at Hakan. He takes the hit in the chest. In the blinding blaze of light I can't see what happens to him, but when my ears stop ringing from the resulting boom, Pella is screaming his name.

Those sparks of anger grow and fester, and I glare at the king.

"I'll take back my future lives now," Eidolon snarls. "Then I'll take your sister."

The Revoker shoves me through the portal and Eidolon crashes his mouth down on mine. Panic is a spike through my heart, stopping it dead. An awful sucking sensation pours down my throat, and pain rips through my gut. It feels like he's pulling my entrails out my gullet, dragging my insides into himself.

The Shadows crow with jubilation.

For a second, I'm tempted to let him have them, to let him take the evil out of me. But what he wants is to destroy the world, not fix it.

I bite his lip hard, the metallic flavor of blood instantly bright on my tongue, and the king yelps, but the darkness merely holds my face still and my mouth open. He's taking them. I can feel them slipping away from me one at a time.

I'm trying to use his power to stop him. To release myself. To swallow his shards of soul back down. Anything.

It's not working.

He's so much stronger than I am. Than I will ever be.

Which is when something pressed against my hip flash heats, so flaming hot that it singes my skin even through my thick Tyndran clothes, and I gasp. I *know* that sensation. I've missed that sensation.

The goddess Aryd. He must be holding her amulet against me unknowingly.

Through the gagging and the pain and the slowly dawning realization that he might kill me this way, a new idea strikes—whether from the goddess or myself, I don't know. I try my power instead. My *true* power.

Glass, after all, is still made of sand. Still mine to command.

And I do. Slowly. Carefully, even as I struggle to breathe.

A sudden familiar whistle of sound near my ear is followed by a *thud*, and Eidolon grunts, lifting his mouth off mine.

An arrow protrudes from the king's shoulder.

Another arrow flies past my head close enough for me to feel the disturbance in the air before it strikes Eidolon in the other shoulder.

The Revoker turns to face this new attack, and as it does, it pulls me back to the Tyndran side of the portals. That's when I get a look at who saved me. Pella didn't fire those arrows. She couldn't, bound in shadow as she is. As they all are.

The man I see standing on the rock pile just below the hole of the shaft, bow drawn, is…Horus.

Horus is here.

He survived the desert exile somehow.

In a slash of movement, he looses another arrow. I track it, but this one misses the king.

Eidolon's no longer holding me by darkness, but the Shadows he didn't manage to take yet are still fighting me. Not that it matters, because what I'm doing doesn't require physical movement. The Revoker's coils pinning my arms to my side are obscuring the yellow light of my power, so they won't know what I'm trying until it's too late.

Directing the glass of the amulets I took from Eidolon while he was busy trying to suck his Shadows away, I lift the necklaces into the air, floating before me. All six of them.

"Thanks for making this so easy," I say.

I send a quick prayer to the goddesses that Tabra is with people who can protect her and keep Eidolon from taking her, and I shatter Eidolon's side of the portal.

Another arrow strikes the Revoker in the tail coiled around me, but the thing doesn't let me go. Instead, it uses another tail to smash the portal on this side, then starts slithering and crawling its way toward the lake, dragging me along behind.

Smart.

It's going to drown me. It's going to trap my friends here without a fast way home.

As if time slows down, it's like I can see everything going on in the cavern at once. Every horror. Tziah limp on the rocks. Vos bleeding out, even with the ice slowing the flow. Reven is out cold, Hakan, too, with Pella standing over him like an avenging demon. My friends are losing. They are *dying*. Only Pella and Horus could possibly climb out—the others are too wounded or unconscious.

Eidolon did that. He and the Devourers that now serve him, he did that. *He* did this to us, and so much more.

We've been reacting to him too long. Letting him get the better of us too often.

Forget that.

Forget a spark. Anger *blazes* and time speeds back up in a rush.

Darkness bubbles up inside me, overpowering and out of control. Hot fury unlike anything I've ever known coalesces in my chest. And I let it.

I let it build and burn, until the Shadows inside me go silent, cowering away in fear. Then at my command, darkness explodes from every part of me, heavy and fierce, and the cavern goes black. Not even the light of the heart can penetrate the fabric of night.

Night that I will use to kill anything that gets in my way.

I picture my own army of monsters made up of shadows that can cut and slice and sever, and I unleash them on the Gorecutter and the Revoker. Suddenly, I'm freed, the Revoker uncoiling from me, though I don't drop to the ground. I don't move at all. But I *do* hear the howls of the two Devourers. Howls that shift to high-pitched screams.

I can't see what I'm doing to them, but I'm glad it involves pain.

Lots of pain.

Revisiting on them what they have done to humans over centuries is only delayed justice. I don't stop. I don't stop when the pitch of their screams turns higher, more frantic. I don't stop when they start to gurgle.

I don't stop even when warm hands cup my cheeks.

"Meren."

Reven. It's Reven.

He's awake, and he found me in the darkness.

Doesn't he see I'm doing this for him? For us? All of us? I'm removing the danger not just from this cavern but from the world.

"Stop," he begs.

"No."

Lips press against mine softly. A single kiss.

It does nothing to warm the ice of wrath that's scoured my soul.

"You're not killing them," he says in the dark, his velvet and iron voice all around me. "You're torturing them."

I waver, but only for a moment. "Good."

Lips press to mine again. Longer this time, more insistent. A spark ignites inside me. Tiny. Barely a flicker of a candle flame and one so easily doused.

But Reven must feel the change in me because he inhales against my mouth and says, "That's right, princess. Come back to me. This isn't you."

Then he's kissing me the way he used to. The way he did when he loved me.

And it hurts.

Because I know he doesn't mean it. Not yet, he doesn't.

"No!" I cry out as I pull away from him.

But the warmth he's created inside me can't be destroyed by the cold this time. It holds on as it creeps outward from my heart.

Then the darkness consuming the cavern is gone and before me the two Devourers lie on the ground sliced to hell and bleeding. The Gorecutter's breathing is labored, sucking in and out of him on a blood-filled gasp.

I did that.

Oh goddess, I did that. I can't stand to look at them.

With a flick of my hand, darkness under my control crawls out of the water and drags them into the lake. As soon as they sink under the surface, I draw more across the top, like ice but made of shadows. It gradually freezes over, starting from the shores and moving toward the center.

"Wait!" Pella yells. "Bene!"

He's still inside the Gorecutter. For all we know he's dead. I can't sacrifice him if there's a chance. I close my eyes and try to feel him, feel the sand of him inside the beast. Maybe I can pull him out. Maybe I can…

There's nothing.

Not a speck.

Absorbing the pain of what I know I have to do the same way I've had to absorb so many losses, I keep going. Those monsters aren't going to come for us again. Ever.

The shadows close over and we're safe.

Reven is still cupping my cheeks. He slides one hand lower to cup my jaw instead and tilt my face to his, to meet his gaze.

"I tried," I whisper. "To feel him."

"I know. I saw you hesitate."

But did I do enough? Or was my anger still dictating everything?

One of the Shadows I have left sneaks out of where they'd hidden from me. *"You killed your friend."*

The accusation stings because I believe it. I glance from Reven to the shadow-sealed lake and back. "Was I wrong?"

Wariness flashes across his features, tinted with concern. I feel the way he silently inhales against me. "Meren—"

I can't take it if he tells me I should have tried harder, so I change subjects. "You kissed me."

His brows twitch down in confusion. "I did."

"To distract me."

He's slower to answer this time, searching my face as he does. "Yes."

"Don't do that." I pull away from his touch, unable to bear it a second longer. "Don't ever kiss me unless you mean it."

"I—"

I turn away from him, rebuilding my portal that the Revoker smashed, my hands shaking so hard my whole body is vibrating. There's no time to dissect all this. We need to get Vos and Hakan and Tziah to a healer, and I need to make sure Tabra is safe. "Go get the heart."

PART 5

ARMAGEDDON GAME

57

BRING ME HER HEART

Deciding what to address first is like having ropes tied around my wrists and ankles and horses dragging me in four different directions.

Tabra. My injured friends. The heart. Bene. Horus. What I did.

I feel the pull of them all, and it's going to tear me limb from limb.

I press my hand to my recreated portal and bring up the Oaesys temple. "Vos needs help now." So do the others, but he's the most critical.

I pretend not to notice the glances my friends slide my way even as they move to do what I said. With Horus's help, Pella carries Tziah through the portal while Reven shadows first Vos and then Hakan to the other side. He straightens, looking at me through the magical gateway.

I know he's going to hate what I'm about to do next, especially because of the promise I made, but not only do we not have time to wait, I don't know if we can trust Allusian. The goddess is not written into our histories, maybe for a reason. The risk I'm taking I'd rather take alone and not from the palace where she could wreak havoc.

I'm sorry, Reven.

"Stay here while I get Vos to a healer," he says.

I shake my head. "Get them looked after. Find Tabra and

protect her. I'll take care of Allusian and meet you in the palace."

Reven's face falls.

"Wait!" Horus calls out. "I'll go with her."

Reven's scowl is immediate. "No way—"

"Stay and help them," I order Horus. "Don't let anyone else see you, though. Then wait for me to return and we'll…talk."

He only hesitates a moment, then nods.

Reven is staring at me now, and I rush to cut off his objections. "Please. I can't be everywhere and too many things need—"

Reven steps closer as he pulls the jedite from his pocket, then reaches through the portal to place them in my hand, curling my fingers around them. "I'll handle this end."

Then he steps back.

I stare at him. If I had more time, I'd ask him why. After what I just did, the way he looked at me, why is he trusting me now?

"Go," he says.

In that moment, I realize something.

He and I are like scales that must balance. If one of us is giving into the darkness, the other must become light. Before, I was his light.

Now he is mine.

Maybe all bonded pairs are this way. I don't know, but I'm going to trust in it. Trust him to balance me out. So much of what he did before when he carried the Shadows takes on a different feel from this angle. Before, when I was the light, I would have done anything, sacrificed anything, to keep him from going so far over that edge that he'd never come back.

That's what he's doing for me.

"Take these." I set the amulets on the floor on his side, then stand.

As I pull my hand away from the glass, a boom rocks the very foundations of the palace, and the last thing I see is Horus and Reven whipping around before the portal turns solid.

Eidolon.

It has to be. He must be attacking.

"Why don't you give in now?" one of the Shadows offers. *"He got enough of us back to give him a hundred years more. And he's stronger than you are.* All *of you."*

I have to fight the urge to go right back to where I left the others and help them. Squeezing my eyes shut, I take precious minutes to cage those dickheads all over again, the way Scoria taught me. I don't want the Shadows seeing what I do next.

Hells, Eidolon already has some that might have witnessed things.

Once my head is finally blessedly quiet, I open my eyes again.

Think, Meren.

Do I go to the goddess? Or back to my friends? I'm torn so hard that physical pain claws through me.

I let loose with a string of creative curse words. I hate abandoning them in the middle of an attack, but the goddess can help my sister and my friends more than I can right now. Besides, after the last encounter with Eidolon, I'd be more danger than help anyway.

I look at the jedite in my hand and the heart on the ground, then back at the portal. "Please don't be a bitch and kill me," I mutter to myself.

Then I stuff the jedite in a pocket and reopen the portal to Allusian's dominion, a world so completely opposite of this one—warm, and lush, and green—that it almost doesn't look real in here. Like I'm staring at a picture. This part must be the heavens.

In the distance, I see some kind of winged creature lift off from the ground. It takes me a solid several blinks before I'm sure what I'm staring at is real. Dragons have been extinct for ages. My only experience with one was standing inside a petrified skull that was part of the underside of Wildernyss.

A far-off trumpet sounds and the dragon in the distance turns to fly toward me. It grows larger and larger. The creature is a deep purplish black, like a bruise several days old. Closer still and I can make out details, like the way the sun shines through the thinner membranes of its wings, turning parts of them to lavender, and the ridged layers of its hide. Not exactly scales—it's too rough for that—but at the same time similarly layered, more like a stone-tiled roof the way they do in Mariana.

Wind batters at me through the portal, stirred up by the dragon's wings as it lands a short distance away. Allusian climbs carefully down, looking even more frail than last time. The dragon doesn't leave as she makes her way toward me. Instead, it folds its wings in closer and stares directly at me with lavender-hued eyes that remind me of Vos's.

I should be terrified, but self-preservation abandons me in the face of sheer power and awe.

The goddess smiles. "Reirran, who is the last of her kind until her final clutch of eggs deigns to hatch, understands all creatures very well, but she only speaks with me."

And can roast me with a snort on the goddess's command or if the dragon is just feeling moody. The unspoken implication hangs in the air. The goddess clearly has trust issues.

Then again…so do I.

"I need your help. Now." And I step aside. "Eidolon is attacking."

Allusian's gaze moves past me to the blue stone laying on the ground behind me and her hand comes up over where her heart will be returned, trembling slightly. "You found it," she whispers.

"I need your promise that once you have this back, you will help me and my sister." *Please let her be true.*

Irritation ripples across Allusian's features. "You dare—"

I cut her off with an impatient sweep of my hand. "We've already established that I dare. Every story about dealing with goddesses tells me I shouldn't trust you. You might be the kindest and most reasonable of the seven, but I have no proof, no reason to believe that. I don't know you. The only thing I know for certain is the destruction your sisters have wrought across Nova."

That, and the way Aryd would help me from within her glass cage. I do know that much.

Allusian considers me. I stare unblinkingly back. Reven would kill me for this if he was here, but I'm done playing games. If she smites me, then someone else can deal with this.

"Very well," she says. "I can't deny you are wise to ask this of me." She pauses, eyes clear and guileless. "I promise that with the return of my heart and my full powers, I will tell you and your sister how to release the goddesses from their prisons, protect you from their wrath, and ensure they restore Nova to its original state."

"And heal my friends." Myself, too. My side is aching like a son of a bitch, and breathing doesn't feel great.

She pauses, then shakes her head. "That is not one of my abilities."

Damn.

She clasps her hands before her, waiting for my decision, though I get the impression that she already expects that I'll give her the heart.

Pursing my lips, I pull Reven's jedite stones from my pocket. "I believe these are also yours."

The goddess's gaze snaps between the rocks and the heart, and I can *feel* the power of her anger. The dragon huffs and shifts on its feet.

"How did you come by them?"

We don't have time. Maybe I should shove them at her and get a head start?

"I need to know," she says.

I tell her a shortened version of the story. When I'm done,

she raises her eyebrows.

Then Allusian nods. "I thank you for returning these and for the information."

For the third time she holds her hand out, and with a curl of a single finger beckons her heart to her. I've been so focused on just getting the thing, I don't think I took any time to consider how this might work.

Definitely not what happens.

The large rock—much larger than her rib cage—floats across the space between portals and settles at her feet. The smaller pieces in my hand do the same, binding to the heart with little clicks that sound like striking two pieces of flint.

Bending down, Allusian places her palms flat against the blue stone.

Instantly, it ignites in fire. Not glowing like it was before—no, this fire is on the outside, a silent, blue-green conflagration that's eerie as hells.

But then the flames start to climb up Allusian's arms. The goddess closes her eyes, pain rippling across her features, but she doesn't let go. Not even as the fire licks higher and higher, spreading over her until it consumes her entire body.

Then she starts to burn.

Not the way things naturally burn. There is no smell, no screams of pain, no horrible sight of blistering flesh even. Instead, her form, clothes and all, slowly turns to ash, starting with where the flames originally touched her hands, traveling up her body until she becomes a charred, gray statue, her features and the details of her clothes etched clearly in the soot.

When the last part of her flesh has been consumed, the heart itself, still aflame but unaffected, changes, though from the inside out, its turquoise light dimming with each passing flicker of flame until ash appears on the outside, creeping down the sides until it, too, is destroyed.

The dragon watches all of this in silence.

A sharp breeze whips through the air, disintegrating Allusian's form into indistinct piles dotted with a few glowing embers still cooling in the air. The breeze shifts, then, and lifts the ashes into a swirling dance. When it calms, a single heaping pile is all that remains.

My mouth drops open. I look from the pile to the dragon and back.

Is she…dead?

Son of a demon! She told me she'd help me. She can't do that if—

What's left of Allusian ignites in yet another fire, purple-black flames the color of the dragon this time. In the blaze, a woman's form appears, crouched with her head down and unclothed. As the fires die, the goddess arises, naked and gloriously perfect—the hollows of her cheeks rounded, the bruises under her eyes gone, her skin glowing with health, a picture of vigor and youth and a beauty so profound, she's almost difficult to look at.

Allusian takes the breath of a life renewed, and the dragon's wings flare out as if it is celebrating with her. Then the goddess smiles and, with a snap of her fingers, is once again clothed in garments that remind me of none of the dominions and all of them at the same time. A simple gown of iridescent white that shimmers with hints of all colors hugs the voluptuous curves of her body to her hips, where a deep purple sash gathers the material to one side before flowing freely to ground where it trails at her feet. A cloak that's part of the gown flares up behind her, appearing like dragon wings before settling around her. Her hair is piled high and intertwined with purple flowers. And everything about her glows.

When she opens her eyes, they are filled with purple flames that spark for a few seconds before that fire, too, is consumed inside her, and the color returns to a deep blue that reminds me of the Lazuli Desert that Horus is from.

"Please." I'm vibrating with the need to rush back to Oaesys, practically dancing on my toes. "We have to go."

Her gaze snaps to me, and a pulse of power leaves her body and travels between the portals to rake through me, not with the violence of Hakan's lightning, but the way my hairs stand on end and every part of my skin buzzes is still damned uncomfortable.

Allusian turns to the dragon, the two sharing a long look before the goddess turns and steps through the portal into the cavern where I stand, not even remotely affected by the freezing temperature in here.

She looks around us. "Where are these Devourers you spoke of?"

I blink. What does that have to do with helping Tabra right now? But I point at the shadow-sealed lake. "There."

She looks, no doubt seeing through my shadows, to the water underneath, frowning slightly. "They are there no longer." The goddess glances at me, then, and seems to finally catch my urgency. "We must return you to your palace immediately."

Allusian takes my arm, and with a snap of her fingers, we disappear.

58

EARN YOUR FORGIVENESS

Teleporting with Allusian is not like shadowing with Reven, where I can feel the void of nothing reaching for us. With her, I can't feel the passage of distance or time or movement. There is nothing and then we appear in the Arydian throne room.

One of the people already gathered there—among the viziers, Vanished, Wanderers, and others—yelps at the sudden sight of us. Which is when I see Reven...and Tabra. No Eidolon. Thank the goddess. I worried he'd try to take her if he got desperate. Though she *is* lying on the cold, hard stone of the floor with Achlys at her side.

"What happened?" I demand.

The rest all jerk around to face me, and Achlys and Reven immediately assume defensive positions around and over my sister.

Which should hurt, but I'm too busy staring at Tabra, who is the color of death—somewhere between green and white—and shaking so hard, I'm shocked she hasn't toppled the building around us.

"I'm not the threat right now," I tell them as I shoot across the room toward her.

The others reluctantly part to let me through, and I'm vaguely aware of the open-mouth stares directed at the now-whole goddess behind me, but Tabra is what's important now.

Introductions and explanations can come later. I kneel before her, my hands cupped around hers before I even think about it. "Tabra?"

Her teeth are chattering, but she's awake. I think. Her eyes are open, gazing not at me, but through me, like she's seeing something we can't.

I glance at Achlys. "Tell me."

"Eidolon tried to take her," Achlys says in a monotone voice that might also shake a little.

I expect a tiny cheer to go up inside me from the Shadows. But there's silence. Allusian must be holding them for me as she blocks Eidolon as well.

"And?" I demand.

"And…she tried to suck out his soul." Achlys's features take on a hard sort of satisfaction even as she runs a worried hand over Tabra's hair. "Reven arrived and started to help, but by then she'd scared the king so much Eidolon used shadows to pull her off of him and then bolted."

I kind of wish the Shadows had heard that part. "Good," I mutter. "I hope it hurt like hells."

I also hope it keeps him from returning quickly.

Cain runs into the room through the open double doors, and right behind him, a small man with a rotund face hurrying our way. My friend pulls up short, staring first at Allusian before turning to me. "Meren?"

"Hi." I mean…what else am I supposed to say right now?

"I'm the healer," the other man informs me. Easy to guess given the blood covering his clothes and sleeves. Vos's blood? Or someone else's?

I don't know this healer. "Imperium or Vexillium?"

"Vex."

So no supernatural help today. I nod and scoot back so he can examine my sister.

"Shock," the healer finally declares. "Rest is the best thing for her. See if you can get food and water into her. Keep her warm."

"I've got her." Cain scoops her up, Tabra's head lolling against his shoulder, and glances first at Allusian, and then across her to me. "Wait until I return to discuss anything."

"Okay."

Even so, he still pauses, and I can see in his face all the things he wants to say to me, questions he wants to ask, but above all that he's glad I'm unharmed.

I smile at him, and with Achlys and the healer in tow, he leaves the room.

Which is when Allusian decides to do more than stand there and watch, crossing the room to where Reven still sits and lowers her lips to his ear, whispering to him. The way he jerks away from her words isn't exactly comforting. Then she touches a finger to his forehead and a lavender glow spreads out from that point of contact and absorbs into him.

He scrunches his eyes closed, then his face contorts in pain before he pitches forward and shouts, so loud and ferocious, even Eidolon's Shadows that I can barely feel at the moment quail at the sound.

Reven's yell cuts off abruptly and he tumbles forward. I try to catch him, but he's too heavy and I'm dragged down with him, my back and hip smacking the stone points of the steps leading up to the dais. I ignore the bloom of pain in my already injured side, holding onto him, even as the others rush to help lift him off me.

I scramble out from under him and check his pulse, his breathing, and he seems…okay? Just passed out?

I whirl on Allusian. "What did you do to him?" I demand.

"I helped," she says in an unconcerned voice.

"Helped?" I ask. "How?"

"He'll wake up with no more pain soon, and he'll start to recover what he's lost."

What he's…lost?

I suck in a gasp. "His memories?"

She nods. "It will take time."

But he'll remember. My thoughts ricochet all over the place. I didn't ask for that. Only for her help. "I thought you couldn't heal."

"That's not what I did."

Then what did she do? "I—"

She cocks a single eyebrow at me before addressing one of our viziers standing close. "Please carry him with the others so the healer can check him."

"Healer?" I ask. "I thought you said he was unharmed."

"He'll need care until he awakens."

A group lifts Reven off the floor, and I get to my feet to follow them.

"Not yet," Allusian says.

I pause, watching them take Reven away without me, then swing around to face her. "What else?"

She laces her fingers together before her. "Now, I help you release my sisters," she says. "But let me warn you, they will come out in a fury after being caged so long. To help you best, I must become fully whole. I will have to find the rest of my heart before the Alignment."

"Wait." I stare at her, trying to make those words line up in my head in any way that makes sense. "You're *leaving*?"

Does she even care that Eidolon might return and kill us all before she accomplishes this?

"Prepare for the Alignment in my absence," she says. "You have five days."

Five days. Five days to hold off a now very pissed, very motivated Eidolon. He knows the Celestial Alignment has some part to play in releasing his mother. That Tabra can release them, but also that the nymph said I'm some sort of key. Will he wait until it's here? Or attack sooner?

We have to be prepared for both.

While most of my friends are incapacitated. Heavens preserve us. My mind begins to whirl and wobble in a way that my stomach hates.

"To release the goddesses from the amulets your ancestress created will take both your sister's power *and* yours." Allusian pauses. "Did you hear me?"

I glance between her and the door Reven has disappeared through, hardly able to absorb her words, already in my head about everything that just happened, my friends, and the defenses we need to be adjusting. "What?"

She sighs. "Listen to me."

I force myself to focus. "Okay."

"Both you and Tabra must work *together* at the exact moment of the Celestial Alignment. Use the connection to the heavens, to me, to enhance your powers. But also, it took *both* of your previous selves to imprison them—one making unbreakable glass amulets and the other forcing my sisters' souls inside them. It will take both of you to undo this—one to break the glass and the other to set the souls free." She steps back. "I will meet you here in this room when it's time."

Then she's gone.

She takes with her the iron control of the Shadows. *"Whatever she told you, she's a liar."*

And it's not that I'm listening to them, but I suddenly have no idea what to do with myself to the point that I can't make myself move.

Maybe I'm in shock, too. Or overwhelmed.

My own numbness is how I find myself sitting alone on the steps of the dais in the throne room trying not to listen to the voices in my head.

I don't know if it was returning here or seeing Tabra safe but also so terrified she's catatonic, or watching Reven writhe in agony, or my friends in danger and pain, or maybe what just happened in that cave all just caught up with me, but the lingering anger finally abandons me, and my heart unfreezes, letting despair in.

"Bene," I whisper. Then cover my face with my hands.

I don't cry. I just sit here trying to figure out if I could have done anything to save him.

I have no idea how much time passes while I sit like this, breaking a little more with the thought that I could have done anything but what I did. If I had found another way, maybe Bene—

Very real fear shivers over my skin, so violently that it feels like razors. Anger is a reason that only excuses so much. So is protecting the others. That one, though, is more insidious, because in my head I'm making decisions for what seem like good reasons. The same as Eidolon.

That's what scares me most.

I scare me.

I don't know what alerts me that I'm not alone in the room, but I lower my hands just as a man enters. The man who betrayed us more than any other. A man I'd thought of as a father. As a friend.

Horus.

"What were you doing in that mountain?" I ask him, and even I'm a little shocked at how dead my voice sounds. Emotionless, drained, uncaring.

His gaze lowers to the ground. "I found Vida's family in the palace in Skom."

The capital city of Tyndra? He went there? Alone? "You freed them?"

He gives a single nod. "Among others the king was holding."

I'm too empty to be happy about that. "How did you find us?"

"When I was learning where Vida's family were held, I overheard Eidolon tell his new general that one of his shadow alarms had been tripped inside the mountain, and that he thought it might be you."

I stare at him. "So, you came all that way on the off chance I'd be there?"

He nods.

"Why? To beg me to take you back?"

His shoulders pull back, head up. "I know you can't do that."

"Then why?"

"In case my queen needed help."

His queen.

I feel like parchment being torn down the middle. One side of me rejects him, hates what he did. I don't know how many died because of his deception and the information he shared with Eidolon, but even one life lost is too many. But the other side of me knows I probably just doomed Bene to death, maybe Vos, too, depending on his wounds, and I don't know if I can do that again right now. And this is…Horus.

I bunch my hands into fists, hiding them inside the long, thick sleeves of my Tyndran jacket. "I am not your queen."

He finally looks directly at me, his dark eyes sad but also certain. "You will always be my queen."

I look away from him, over his head to the back of the room, not really seeing anything in front of me. "I have exiled you. I can't have you here."

"I know."

His quiet acceptance makes it worse.

"I can't even offer safe passage out of this palace."

"I know that, too, domina."

"Stop being so goddess-damned reasonable," I snap.

Surprise widens his eyes. "I apologize, domina."

I breathe through my nose. "Damn it, Horus."

"I will leave now." He gives me a stuffy little bow and turns to walk away, the set of his shoulders somewhere between pride and defeat.

"Stop."

I can't let him go like this, despite what he's done. "Are you able to get in and out of the Skom palace unnoticed?"

Tension brackets his shoulders before he faces me. "Yes."

"You're a good spy," I say.

And he flinches, because he knows that wasn't entirely a compliment.

I ignore that small tell. "Let's put that to use. Spy for me."

It's the way of the Wanderers. The only way to reverse exile is by performing an impossible task. He survived the desert exile a second time, though I still don't know how. He saved my life. Again. I can do this much for him.

When he bows this time, the defeat is no longer visible. "I won't let you down, domina."

"Don't let Cain see you," I warn. "He is zariph now."

A zariph is honor bound to kill an exiled Wanderer. Horus's position with me was the only thing that kept him alive around Zariph Cainis and the others. But now…

"I understand," Horus says, then slips away.

59

FROM BAD TO WORSE

"Domina…"

I'm far down the hole of sleep—I haven't slept well in forever it seems like, and I couldn't keep my eyes open a second longer.

I sat with Reven the rest of the first day we returned from Tyndra and through much of the night, only to be shooed to my room by Tziah at some point. The next morning, I worked close to three hours trying to shore up the Shadows' cage.

After that, I spent the entire day going flat-out. Mostly checking on my friends, but a good deal was also meeting with our viziers and leaders. For the most part, I'm being kept out of all the plans, but they still need to know what I can do to be part of various elements. It was an exhausting dance of questions with no rhyme or reason, and me trying not to let my curiosity win.

That's why I don't hear the first time someone attempts to get my attention. At most, I manage an annoyed frown and an unintelligible mumble, probably for them to go away. I'm too sluggish to specify. Somewhere in my mind I'm vaguely aware someone wants me awake.

But when that person shakes my shoulder and calls "domina" again, more urgent this time, the state I left things in when I fell asleep rushes back and I shoot out from under my thin layer of sheets to stand in the center of my canopied bed with both knives in my hands, ready to kill whoever has come for me.

The servant, Nhalin, stands with her hands up in horror, pale and trembling.

For a tension-filled moment or two that's all we do. Stare at each other.

On a groan, I jerk my hands to my sides. "Don't worry. You're safe." I slip my knives back into their sheaths while mentally kicking myself in a hundred different ways.

She's still staring like I'm about to slaughter her and then go after her family, so I aim for joking. "That's a new habit of mine I really should kick."

I guess that's not very funny, because she doesn't laugh.

We look at each other for several uncomfortable moments before I sigh. "Was there a reason you woke me?"

"Oh." She gives herself a visible shake as if she needs to wake up from a nightmare. "You asked to be notified if—"

"What happened?" Vos? Reven? Hakan? Tziah, at least, woke up before I tried to sleep. Or is Eidolon here? Or…

"The Shadowraith is awake."

She hardly has those words out before I'm off the bed. I've taken to sleeping in clothes appropriate for combat, just in case, so I don't have to bother with changing before I bolt from the room.

Reven's awake.

He's one suite down from mine—technically family rooms, not guestrooms, but this is my bondmate. He is family.

My hand is on the knob when Nhalin calls out, "Domina, let me at least announce you."

"If you think I'm waiting to be announced you might want to seek a position with a different domina."

A twinge of guilt hits for that one because it's not her fault that I'm like this, and she does look a tiny bit stricken at my words. But at the same time, if she's going to be assigned as my handmaiden then she'd better get used to me quick.

When I burst into Reven's room, I fully expect to see him lying in bed, maybe a healer leaning over him. None of that is what I find. In fact, the room is completely empty.

I whirl on Nhalin. "Where?"

"I don't know." She looks around frantically as if he might manifest any second. "I went from here straight to your room when I was instructed to, and that was only moments ago."

A guttural yell rends the air.

Oh, goddess. I know that voice.

"Vos." I rush past.

Vos's suite, one he's sharing with Hakan, is only two more doors down, and the sound of agony only gets louder the closer I get. I don't have to burst through the door because it's wide open. Inside, I find out for the thousandth time what true pain looks like.

Vos is lying in a bed with only a sheet covering his bare body at the hips—a blood-soaked sheet. An Imperium woman I've never seen before stands over his left side where the gaping wound that used to be an arm now doesn't look so much like meat that has been ground as it does meat that has been scorched. The buttery glow of her hands tells me she's responsible for the change.

Reven is sitting at Vos's side, his back to me, clasping his friend's remaining good hand. Tziah paces back and forth, tears trickling down her cheeks and lips pressed together so tightly even her dark blue skin turns pale. Cain leans against the wall, looking a little green under his bronzed skin.

Pella, meanwhile, is seated in the chair next to another bed where Hakan still lies unconscious. Her knees are drawn up to her chest, her face buried in them with her hands pressed over her ears. Even over Vos's screams, little whimpers can be heard escaping her. As an empath, she should *not* be in here. She has to be absorbing at least some of his pain. How is she making herself stay?

Vos lets out a particularly wrenching yell and every person in the room, me included, flinches.

"Why are you letting her do that to him?" I demand.

I'm halfway across the room when Cain surges off the wall to grab me by the arm. "Easy, Mer." He tugs me to the side. "Vos will signal if he can't take more."

"Mother goddess," I murmur, trying not to let the screams get to me, too, but they're filling the room to the rafters. "This is…" I shake my head.

"It's the only way," Cain says. He slides his hand into mine and squeezes. "Vos was still losing too much blood. He had to decide between keeping his life and waiting for an Imperium healer on the off chance they could regenerate his arm. He chose this."

"What is she doing?"

His gaze flicks over my shoulder toward the woman. "She's forcing the wound to close. Sort of like what would happen naturally, only in minutes. Pain medication won't help."

I shudder. How is Vos withstanding that? "At least get Pella out of here."

"She refuses to leave either of them."

Stubborn empath.

Vos growls between gritted teeth. "It burns. It—" He goes silent, shaking with the effort to not scream. But the healing goes on.

A new anger bubbles up inside of me. None of this is fair. That this happened to Vos. That we have to be here at all. That everything I do just leads to more suffering.

I close my eyes against the emotion and will myself to settle. It doesn't work. The choked sounds Vos makes echo through the darkness behind my lids and fans the flickering flame.

The sound of feet on the floor has me opening my eyes.

Tziah has run over to the bed to shake Reven by the arm.

"No," he says. Unrelenting. Emotionless.

She shakes him harder.

"No, Tziah. He hasn't—"

Tziah hits Reven in the shoulder with a fist, trying to make him put a stop to it, but instead of shoving her away or growling at her, he stands up, putting himself between her and Vos, and lets her pound away ineffectually at his chest.

Cain drops my hand and shoots across the room, wrapping his arms around her from behind, pinning hers to her sides. His chin on her shoulder, he whispers words in her ear. I can't make them out, but I can imagine. He'd do the same thing on nights I'd stormed into the desert in a whirlwind of emotion, even though I couldn't tell him what was bothering me because of who and what I was. I'm glad he's here to do the same for her.

Tziah doesn't calm, exactly—more like she collapses into him. She makes no noise, because she can't without hurting us and especially Vos, but her sobs shake Cain's body.

Reven turns back to Vos, his voice steady. "I'm here, brother. I'm here. Hold on. A little longer. You can do this."

I don't know if he's saying those things because he hopes that's what Vos needs to hear, or if he remembers their friendship, thanks to the goddess. All I know is that underneath the horror of what Vos is going through, those calm, kind words dissolve my anger, leaving me with an aching heart.

"There we go," the Imperium wielding her power murmurs. "Getting closer."

We all peer intently. The blood flow has stopped and yet he's still thrashing about. The woman snaps, "Someone hold him down, damn it."

Instantly, bands of shadows wrap around Vos's body, pinning his one remaining arm to his sides and banding his legs together, trapping him on the bed. Tziah turns and buries her face in Cain's shoulder, unable to watch, while Vos's shrieks are something only nightmares are made of.

Those screams abruptly cut off and he goes limp, head lolling to one side.

The Imperium woman sighs. "He passed out," she says. "Thank the goddesses."

"You might want to consider who you're thanking," I say, bitterness at the root of my tone.

"Not now, Meren," Pella barks.

The force of her words snaps my spine rigid with hurt and guilt. Pella and I have a thing, but it hasn't been angry or mean in a while now. She's right, though. Now is not the time.

Thankfully, it doesn't take the Imperium long to finish what she's doing after that. Although it doesn't look all that finished to me when she drops her shaking hands and says, "Done."

Sure, the wound is closed now, flesh drawn up taut over the stub of his shoulder like a drum, but his ebony skin bubbles and folds over itself in ways that don't look right. Worse, there are patches of white mixed with patches of angry reds and purples through which I can see pulsing veins, as if they're close to the surface. I'm afraid he'll start bleeding again at any second. That wound isn't healed all the way.

"If you have a way to keep him sedated for the next day or two, do it," she says. "By then, his remaining pain should be manageable."

The woman looks just as green as Cain did when I came into the room. No doubt she's going to have to rest quite a while after that. Tziah sits on the edge of the bed, staring at Vos's face as if he might wake up any second, and Cain stands by her, hand on her shoulder. Pella lays her head on Hakan's bed. It's up to Reven to shake the woman's hand. "Thank you for your service today. Have you been paid?"

She nods.

"Then please go with our gratitude and rest." He nods at Nhalin, who takes the woman from the room.

I realize as they go that I'm shaking with emotions—a whole jumble of them I can't even begin to pick apart. It wouldn't help anyone in this room to see it.

Pushing away from the wall, I edge toward the door. "I'll just go check on Tabra," I say, hitching my thumb in that direction.

I pause in the empty hallway to close my eyes and breathe through my nose and tell myself that my friends are going to be okay. That me losing it isn't going to help them.

"Hey."

I open my eyes to find Reven standing there.

"You're awake," I say. Then wince, because that's obvious.

He smiles a little, but it's reserved.

"You look like you're okay?" I say next. I should have asked sooner. Goddess, why am I so bad at this? What I want to do is wrap my arms around him, but I don't think *he'd* want that, so I force a calm I'm far from feeling.

"I'm fine."

"What did she do to you?"

He grimaces but pulls it into a crooked smile. "Gave me a big damn headache is what."

Which isn't an answer. "She told me she was fixing your memories."

Reven goes eerily intent at that. "She did?"

I nod. "She said it would take time." I search his face for any hint of what's going on in his head, but he's giving me nothing. "Do you remember anything at all yet? I mean, you only just woke up."

He's slow to answer, thinking it over, but almost like he's choosing what to tell me. "I remember being shed the first time. Vos and Tziah. Getting them to the Shadowood. It's like watching it all in flashes."

Remember me faster. I don't say it out loud. It wouldn't be fair to him. "You should rest."

He shakes his head. "I'd rather come with you."

Why don't I trust it? Is he only out here to keep close and make sure I'm not being overrun by evil?

"Okay," I finally say. And head off toward Tabra's room with Reven prowling along beside me.

60

EVEN MY SISTER

Reven says nothing as we walk. Not until I yawn, anyway, and he raises his eyebrows. "Exhaustion will only make it harder for you to control them," he says.

So the Shadows *are* why he's with me now. Disappointment settles in my gut.

To cover my reaction, I grimace. "Sorry, but I've been going nonstop." And worrying nonstop. And reliving the last few days nonstop. And questioning myself nonstop. "I'm *tired*."

"You should rest more."

I open my mouth to point out that I fell into a decent sleep for the first time just a few hours ago only to be woken up because of him and then Vos. That sounds petty in my head. Seven hells, it *is* petty. Maybe I really am the problem, the sickness inside me getting worse. "I'll go back to bed after I check on Tabra."

She's been sleeping on and off since yesterday, but mostly on, recovering from using her power against Eidolon, or trying to.

I knock softly.

"Come in," Achlys calls.

Stepping into this room is like being hit with a hundred different memories—mostly the recent one of my months pretending to be Tabra at Eidolon's side. Pretending to be under his thrall. That and Reven showing up to help me escape.

I glance at his face, the way his gaze is skating over the room. Does he recognize this place? Does he remember?

He turns his head, and when he finds me watching, cocks his head in question.

Guess not.

I wave it off. What would I ask? Remember when I kissed your face off after you finally showed up and then we hid in the secret room? I'm going to drive myself off a ledge second-guessing him every minute of the day.

Pinning a smile to my face, I leave him standing near the columns that lead out to the private balcony, the sheer curtains drifting in and out on a hot breeze. As I approach the massive bed, I can see Tabra's eyes are closed. Achlys sits at her bedside, holding her hand.

She puts a finger up to her lips and beckons me around to where she is.

Obviously. "How is she?"

Achlys glances at Tabra's peaceful face with a frown. "She woke up crying, still fighting Eidolon in her dreams, I think."

"Do you think she'll be ready?"

Allusian said we had five days. I'm not sure of the exact hour, but I'm counting yesterday as one. Today is two. That means the Celestial Alignment is three days from now.

We both need to be ready, but especially her.

I don't miss the way Achlys's turns her head, no doubt studying me. I've filled her in on Allusian's instructions, too, but maybe someone has also told her about me. Or does she think my question is unfeeling?

I don't hide my sigh. "I hate that I have to ask her to be ready. I wish I could let her sleep peacefully and wake up when it's all over."

"Me, too." The way she visibly relaxes sends irritation itching under my skin. No wonder Reven used to be so grumpy, constantly having fear aimed his way and needing to prove himself and earn trust. Worse because he didn't trust himself, which is where I am now.

I study Achlys's face from the side. It's not that she looks bad, exactly. But not great either. "How are you holding up?"

She blinks at me, then grimaces. "She didn't sleep well."

In other words, Achlys didn't sleep well, either.

"Have you been brought food, water?"

"Everything I need has been provided, dom—" She cuts herself off.

I give her a teasing grin. "It's a good thing you didn't finish that, or we would have had words."

Achlys chuckles. "Honestly, I'm not sure what to call you now."

Now that she's not merely a handmaid, but is the publicly acknowledged lover of my sister, the queen? "I can see how that would be tricky, but we're friends and maybe one day sisters through marriage. You love Tabra, and that's all I need to know. Call me Meren. Always. No queen, or princess, no domina. Just Meren. Okay?"

After a second, she huffs a laugh that sounds a little like disbelief. Like she doesn't quite know how she ended up here. Then, "I will…Meren."

We both settle our gazes on Tabra again. "Do you want me to stay with her while you get some air, stretch your legs, maybe take a nap?" I ask.

The way the lingering smile sort of stiffens on Achlys's lips, I don't have to see the wariness in her eyes to know what her answer will be, even before she says, "No, that's all right."

I swallow the sting of hurt down a throat gone tight. If I was at Reven's bedside, I wouldn't want someone full of Eidolon's Shadows near him, either.

Tabra gives a tiny cough, and we both look at her. "Meren?" she asks without opening her eyes.

"I'm here, Sissy."

She whimpers. "Eidolon. He came—"

We've already had this conversation, but she must not remember. I squeeze her leg through the thin sheet. "I know. You fought him off. You're safe and I'm so proud of you."

Her eyelids flutter and she's clearly having trouble rousing herself fully from sleep. I pat her now. "Rest. I'll come back after you wake up."

I glance at Achlys, who nods, then move back around the bed to where Reven has been standing and watching all this time. He waves for me to go ahead, but I only get halfway to the door when Tabra speaks again. Louder this time. "Who is that?"

"Who?" Achlys asks. "You mean Reven?"

"No. The person with him."

What?

Tabra levers up shakily onto her elbows, squinting at us.

"Do you see someone else there?" Achlys asks her slowly.

I glance around me. Did Eidolon leave a ghost of his past self in this palace to haunt us or something?

Impatience interrupts the wariness etched across Tabra's beetled brows and searching gaze. "There." She points. "Right next to Reven."

There's only one person it could be, but it makes no sense. I point at myself.

"Yes, you," she says, voice turning belligerent. "I'm talking to you."

Beside me, Reven's body grows tenser, his shoulders pulling back.

"Tabra," I say gently. "It's me."

My sister scoots back slightly. "I don't know you."

Achlys takes her hand. "That's Meren," she says. "That's your sister."

Tabra scoots back so hard that she smacks her head against the headboard. "No. That's *not* my sister."

"Tabra, it's me. It's Mer—"

"Stop it!" she shouts. Then she throws a pillow at me. My sister. Who loves me. Who would cry if she accidentally squished a plague scorpion. She throws a pillow at me. "Get out!"

"Tabra!" I start toward her. "It's *me*. It's Meren."

She scrambles out of the bed, dragging Achlys with her, tucking her behind herself, hair bedraggled around her head, painful fear written across her features. She raises her hand, which ignites in a purple glow. "I don't know what you are but get out of my room."

A sensation strikes in my chest. Not like something hit me from the outside, like something is trying to break through my rib cage to get out. I make a strangled sound, and then Reven's arms are around me and we shadow away.

61

BUILDING WALLS

Reven lets me go the instant we get where he's shadowing us but doesn't step away or give me space. It couldn't have taken us more than a second to get here—I didn't even feel us move. Which makes sense, because we didn't go far, only to the private royal garden, which has been walled back up since we took the palace.

I don't care where he took me. I can still see Tabra's hate- and fear-filled face as she screamed that I wasn't her sister.

"She..." I stop to get control of my mouth that doesn't want to work properly. "She must have had sleep in her eyes."

The excuse sounds even more flimsy than it did in my head. Good to see my brain is functioning as usual in a crisis, which is fuzzy as hell. I mean, I've got to be able to count on something in this world. Clearly, I can't count on my own sister recognizing me.

Stop. Stop it, Meren.

I close my eyes, trying to herd my chaotic thoughts. "Maybe she was dreaming."

I still haven't lifted my gaze past the first button on his shirt.

He doesn't say anything.

"She has to be so scared," I say next. "Eidolon attacked her and she..." That's when I finally look Reven fully in the eyes. "We have to go back. She needs me." I grab his arm. "We have to...we have to go back."

I'm well aware that I'm stumbling over my words and babbling a little bit, but it takes Reven shaking his head for me to swallow down more words that want to tumble out.

"Why?" I demand.

"You don't want to make it worse."

Worse. I can make it worse for her?

"What do you think she saw?" I ask him. Because if anybody is going to be honest with me in this moment, it's Reven.

He goes to open his mouth, but I stop him. "Don't answer. The Shadows crawling over my face again. Right?"

He shakes his head slowly. "It's more like they subtly distorted your face in a way that didn't look like you."

I can't win.

I spin around to pace back and forth, hardly aware of where I am. I'm sort of muttering to myself something like, "She didn't know it was me," and "If they can fool my sister," and "But she could hear me, how did she not realize."

Finally, I nod to myself. "I'll give her some time and then go talk to her."

Reven considers that long enough that I actually start to lean toward him in anticipation.

"I think that's a good idea," he says slowly. That's all he says.

I stare at him for a second, then pop my hands onto my hips. "That's it?"

He considers me for a moment. "What were you hoping for?"

Kicking his shins would be childish, right? "Who knows? My own sister just thought I was some kind of demon and didn't even recognize me." I go back to pacing. "Every friend I have, including you, is staring at me like I might…I don't know… take my own head off my body, spin it around ten times while chanting maniacally to the three moons, and put it back on my neck facing backward. But the real threat—Eidolon—is still out there, and we don't know if he'll attack with an army or infiltrate us himself more stealthily."

Like through me.

I recognize that I have yet to take breath, but I'm rolling now.

"I'm not even sure which one of those things would be worse. I wasn't groomed to be a military leader. Why is this all falling on *my* shoulders? Meanwhile, the people I trust to advise me are falling like flies in a gas field." I hold up a hand, not that he tried to interrupt me. "I mean…okay…I acknowledge that Eidolon being able to take me over is scary, and I am losing it right now, only I can't afford the luxury of losing it ever, because I've got people depending on me not doing that. So I need to *do* something. Only, I'm not allowed to be part of the plans."

I stop dead in my tracks, sort of nodding to myself. That's it. Something to do.

Reven shakes his head like he didn't hear that last bit right. "What?"

I'm grasping for clear air in a sandstorm at this point. "I need to do something. I mean right now. Something that's productive while I wait until Tabra wants to see me again, and Vos heals more, and Hakan wakes up, and…" I almost said something about Horus returning with usable information, but out in the open like this is not the place to tell Reven. "I can't just sit around the palace with everybody either waiting for me to turn into a monster or expecting me to know what to do." I drop my hands to my sides, my chin to my chest, and close my eyes.

"Tell me where you want to go, and I'll take you there," Reven says.

Immediate. No hesitation. I might love him all over again for that.

Even so, I heave a bitter little laugh. "At this rate, Allusion's dominion is sounding pretty fantastic."

He grunts. "Anywhere but there."

I guess he caught the implication, and a small part of me

really wants to laugh just for a second. What happened to the girl I was only months ago who could laugh at anything, poke fun easily, and not let every little thing get to her?

I sigh. "I kind of miss that girl," I whisper to myself.

"That girl is still here," Reven says.

I raise my head to blink at him because I didn't think I'd said most of that out loud.

He tips his head, searching my face. "She's standing right in front of me, and she's struggling because nobody in all of Nova—before, now, or to come—could handle the pressure she's under and the decisions she's making without cracking just a little bit."

Which only makes me huff. "Are you saying I'm cracking?"

Reven rolls his eyes. "Given everything you just ranted about, only you would decide to argue with me." He takes a step closer. "But you just proved my point."

"Was there a point?"

"The wisecracking, smart-ass girl you fear you've lost is still in there. She's just a little…" He sort of trails off, and I get the uneasy sense he's holding back.

"A little what?" I demand. "A little darker? Is that what you were going to say?"

Irritation passes over his features the same way it did with Tabra just a second ago, and I actually hold my breath, waiting for him to turn on me the same way she did, but he doesn't. At least not right away. Instead, he says, "I'll make you a deal."

"A deal." I stare at him dubiously. "What kind?"

"The kind where I, for one, stop looking at you like the way you said, if you will admit that you have been acting unlike yourself lately."

I put my tongue to the roof of my mouth, trying to hold back my first knee-jerk reaction of wanting to push back. "You just said anyone would react the way I have been," I point out through admittedly gritted teeth.

"And anyone would," he acknowledges. "But it's still very

dark for *you*."

I turn away from him slightly, not really taking in the trampled state of the garden, just trying not to express my frustration in the concerning way that apparently everybody fears I will. "How would you know?" It's mean to use that against him. I know it as soon as it's out of my mouth.

"Because I know you better now."

"You seem to have an answer for everything," I grumble.

"What do you say?" he asks. "Do we have a deal?"

I twist my lips. The thing is, I've already admitted as much to myself. When I was torturing those Devourers, it felt *right*. Justified. Reasonable even. In the cold light of day and with distance, I'm not so sure. "Anywhere I want?"

Reven nods. "Other than the hells or heavens, yes."

"And you won't stop me from doing what I want when we get there, even if it seems ill-advised?"

"I—"

"As long as it's not"—it takes everything in me not to roll my eyes—"dark or deadly."

He doesn't hesitate. "Yes. That's the deal."

"Fine." I hold out my hand to shake.

Reven looks down at my hand and then up at me, and I get the impression that he's wondering right now if he can trust me to keep up my end of the bargain. He can. Maybe not for the reason he's hoping, but because I already know it's true. There's nothing to really admit.

Finally, Reven shakes my hand.

"Great," I say. "I acknowledge it. I'm already scared of it."

His eyes widen ever so slightly. "Meren, is that true—"

"I'm not stupid, Reven. Of course that's true. That's why the way everyone is treating me is so frustrating. I need help, not judgment." I don't want to talk about this anymore, so I step closer to him. "Please take me outside of the city, but right at the outskirts. Preferably on the southern side, at least to start."

I hardly get the words out before we shadow away and back a second later, exactly where I asked him to take me. I shoot him a glance that's probably full of suspicion, because that was so fast it feels like he's pandering to me. But I'm not going to balk. I've got too much to do. "Thank you."

"I promised." He glances around us. "Now what?"

"Now..." I don't bother to hide the grimly determined tone from my voice. "I build a wall around my city."

Something one of the previous queens should have done long ago. Yet another thing to be irritated with my family's rulers who came before me about. It's become glaringly obvious that none of them ruled so much as tried not to die early.

I raise both hands, already glowing yellow.

"Whoa. Whoa. Whoa."

I pause. "What?"

He looks from me to my hands to the city beyond, jaw working, probably to keep from telling me this is a bad idea. Because he promised. "Shouldn't you be conserving power?"

He's not wrong, but I already considered that. "I can't help my sister release the goddesses *and* fight Eidolon. That will be many times worse if the entire time Oaesys is vulnerable to his attack." I cast my gaze out over the city, the buildings rising higher toward the palace, the north side of which abuts the shores of the Sea of Terra. "We have a little less than three days to the Alignment. We'll just have to pray that I'll have enough time to rest before he comes. But I know for certain that this is how I can help right now."

"But—"

"Uh-uh." I wag a finger. "You said as long as I don't go dark or deadly, you wouldn't stop me, even if it was ill-advised. You shook on it."

The me from before all this would probably have laughed at the expression that crosses Reven's face. I have no doubt he's kicking himself right now, which is kind of fun for me. Except that I'm still thrown by what happened with Tabra, and honestly the reason I thought to do this at all has more to do with the fact that I need to release some pent-up tension. It's either pace around the palace as I wait yet again for Eidolon to come for me and mine, or this.

I chose this. *This*, at least, might be helpful.

He gives in on a grunt of a word. "Fine."

"You don't have to stay."

He tips his head. "Trying to get rid of me?"

I frown. Is he trying to tease? If it had been before, I'd know he was. But at the moment our relationship feels like we're suspended in water, unable to swim for the top or to drown. Like we're just sort of, stuck. "Fine. Stay if you want."

His lips press together. "Eidolon could show up at any moment."

Physically or through me? I'm guessing it's the latter, although I'm not tapping into the king's power for this. I deflate a little. Even after admitting my fear, he doubts me? If he thinks I'm not already twitching with every sound and shadow around me, then he's not paying attention.

Without waiting for him to change his mind, I face the city, close my eyes, and picture the sands of the dunes coming to me. I've brought them to me before, in the palace, when Shadow had control of Reven and attacked me.

Goddess, that feels like forever ago.

This time is easier for so many reasons. I start the piles heating and building and heating and building. Not glass. I only heat them enough to be able to form bricks and have them stick together. I try to picture stacking them at least a few feet thick. I don't linger on any one brick. There's not enough time for that. I just build as fast as I can.

"What do you think?" I ask over my shoulder, eyes still closed. "Is twenty feet high enough?"

"Not to stop shadows—"

"No kidding—"

"Give me a second, princess," he says in a voice that tells me he's losing patience.

"Well?"

He grumbles something under his breath that I can't quite catch but sounds like something about passing a trait on to children, and my first instinct is a sort of giddy hope that he's starting to remember me, but then I realize that I could pass things on to children that aren't his. So, I let the giddy go.

"What?" I ask.

Another grunt. "I was going to say that twenty feet should be high enough to give humans trouble. Although they're likely to have Imperium with them."

Truth. "Let's hope they attack from the outside. Then this will at least buy us time. I'm not planning to make a gate out. It would be a weak point." If they attack from inside the city, though, this is going to trap them with us. It's a risk worth taking.

"That, too."

We don't talk much after that. I build, he watches, and every so often I ask him to move us to a different location as I make my way around the city. At one point Cain shows up, and the only reason I know is that I recognize the sound of his voice as he talks to Reven quietly.

No wonder. A giant sand wall going up around the city is pretty damn obvious, and of course someone would come check on why. He grumbles something along the lines of "You could have warned us she'd be doing this first," which, fair enough, but he leaves without saying anything to me.

I keep going. It takes me until well into the night, even though I started in the morning. I don't stop until both ends of the wall hit the massive Sea of Terra, building them into the water far enough that it would make going around them that way difficult. I harden the layers actually in the water to glass so that the sand won't melt away.

I consider extending the wall along the banks, but it's unlikely anyone will attack from that direction. Every dominion has at least one or more large lake or sea big enough that they could build a navy, but what's the point? With no way to travel the oceans, our navies would be, essentially, landlocked with no access to the other dominions. We certainly can't bring them through the portals. Consequently, none of us have a navy. Not anymore.

I drop my arms. I'm not sure I could keep going anyway. My limbs have been shaking for a while and feel so heavy someone might as well have filled them with the bricks I've been making.

Almost like that was a sign to the rest of my body, I hit a wall of exhaustion like I ran full tilt into my own fortification of sand. I droop, eyes still closed because I can't make them open.

"You did well," Reven says quietly, close enough that my body prickles at his nearness.

No admonishment about wearing myself out, just *you did well.*

Somewhere under the drag of exhaustion a small glow of warmth blooms in my heart. I guess I needed to hear that. "Thanks."

"Let's get you back to the palace, get some food in you, and then I think you should rest all day tomorrow," he says.

"You won't get an argument from me."

He snorts a laugh. "For once."

"Hey." I pry open my eyelids, looking out over the sea that I can see beyond my walls. Reven is still behind me. "You used to love it when I argued with you, I'll have you know."

"Are you so sure about that?"

Despite the lightness of this exchange so far, sadness tinges my next words, mostly because I'm too tired to keep it out of my voice. "Yes. You may have been frustrated, but you still loved it. I'm sure."

I hear him draw a breath behind me, and like earlier, he

mutters something that I don't quite catch. My heart sort of wishes it was "Still do."

But until his memories return, I can only lean on hope that's been twisted and smashed and thwarted so many times, it's not the steadiest ground to walk on anymore.

62

SO FAR FROM WHERE WE'VE BEEN

The Celestial Alignment is in two days.

The Seers have already given us an hour—late in the afternoon.

We are facing, at the very least, trying to break six goddesses out of their prisons. Eidolon isn't going to let that happen without a fight.

We're not ready.

"If I didn't know better, I'd think you've been avoiding me," Cain says from behind me.

Avoiding everyone, more like.

People going silent whenever I walk into the room, the emptier streets of Oaesys, and the knowledge that Eidolon could use me to mess it all up don't feel great. I get it, though. We have to have multiple plans and backup plans to cover a multitude of contingencies, and I can't and shouldn't know all of them. So, I've been keeping to myself.

At the moment, that means lying on the large lounge chair in my glass garden. It's more like a couch—big enough for two people to lie on—that Tabra and I dragged in here a long time ago. I flip to my side to find Cain standing in the doorway that leads from the bedroom into here. It's still strange to me because this room used to be a secret space, and now it's not. No more need for secret twin princesses, and so no more need to keep our garden to ourselves.

I hope future generations thank us for that.

"No," I answer. And I haven't been. Instead of resting like Reven told me to, I spent the day in Wildernyss on what I honestly hope was a fool's errand. Something I won't have to use when the time comes.

"No?" Cain crosses his arms. "Then where have you been hiding?"

I don't have it in me to argue about where I've been today, or to care that I'm sitting here in a nightgown. It's modest enough. "If I was avoiding you," I point out with the loftiest air I can manage, "you wouldn't have found me. Need I remind you that you taught me how to be invisible?"

Cain chuckles. I've missed that laugh. He used to do it more often, at least around me. Now, I can feel the tension between us like a bowstring drawn back.

We stare at each other for a long moment. There are worlds of unspoken words between us, so many things that have happened, so much that has changed. We're no longer the city waif and the boy in the desert, laughing under the stars and whispering stories about imaginary futures we'd never have. He knew me better than anyone, despite not knowing who I was meant to be.

I clear my throat. "Uh. Were you looking for me for a reason?"

He gives his head a shake, like he was remembering, too. "The wall was a good idea," he says.

"Thanks."

"Hakan's awake."

I pull my knees to my chest and give myself permission to sit with that piece of relief for a moment. "Is he okay?"

He nods. "Pissed as hell that Eidolon used his own lightning against him, but otherwise fine. But after he woke up, Pella did something weird."

I huff out a laugh. "That's nothing new. She does something weird all the time."

He doesn't laugh with me. Instead, his brows sort of beetle the way he used to do when he was a kid and didn't agree with his father or something I had done. Both were equally likely to put that expression on his face.

He moves to sit at the edge of my chair. "She hugged me and told me how proud she was to be my sister, and that if anything happened to either of us in the coming days, she wanted me to know that."

I lean back, eyes wide, but I don't toss off some quick quip because I can see how much this means to him, although at the same time, something about it seems to be bothering him. "I guess we're all taking stock these days."

"Yeah. Well…" He spikes his fingers through his hair, visibly uncomfortable.

Without warning, he takes my hand, holding it in both of his, his calloused palms from years on horseback and living in the desert rough and warm against my skin.

"Meren…"

I'm about to lose him. It's been coming for a while, but now that it's actually happening, the younger me who made him the center of her world doesn't want to let go. So selfish, I know.

"If anything should happen…" he begins.

I don't bother to deny that it might.

He swallows. "Know that I have no regrets. You're my best friend and always will be. You were also my first love." He looks at our clasped hands, and I do, too, picturing just for a moment the tattoos we would both bear if we'd married in the Wanderer way like he wanted not so long ago.

He looks back up, mouth quirked. "And…you were my first heartbreak."

Neither of us looks away or hides from this truth.

I squeeze his hand. "You were my first love, too. At least in this life. But fate, and bonds, and previous lives had other plans.

I wouldn't change any of it, but I wish I could have saved you the pain."

He shakes his head. "I wouldn't change any of it, either. Pain and all."

My throat thickens. "Really?"

"Really."

While there's regret and a small sort of sadness in his eyes, this is also the first time he's looked at me in a very long time in the way he used to. No hurt. No longing. Just as a friend. Nothing more.

The guilt that's poked and prodded at me about Cain trickles away and we're left—somehow, miraculously—like we used to be.

I'm just the girl who makes him laugh, who tells him when he's being a pain in the ass, and who he shared all of his frustrations and secrets with. And he's the boy who makes me laugh just as hard, who taught me to fight and hunt and survive in the desert, and who I also told everything to other than who I really was. Except now he knows that, too.

And I know in this instant that we're going to be okay.

Not together like I think we both once pictured, but I'm not losing him.

Thank the goddess for that.

I do the only thing I can think of, what I wanted to do every time I escaped from Enora to find his zariphate in the desert where I could pretend I wasn't me and he could pretend he wasn't him. I swing my feet to the ground and pull us both up so I can wrap my arms around him. Sighing, I bury my face in his chest.

After only the smallest hesitation, Cain hugs me back tightly, his cheek resting on the top of my head. We stand that way for a long time, neither of us saying anything. Then, finally, "I'll always love you, Meren."

"I'll always love you, too."

I can feel his smile, and the last piece of my heart settles into place.

Eventually, he steps away. "Now that that's settled, given that you've been waiting one thousand years for your bondmate," he says, "I pray to the goddesses that you and Reven both survive whatever comes next and get to experience at least a little happiness."

Him and me both. "Thanks. That would be nice."

He chuckles, then looks at me like he wants to say something else, but he doesn't. Instead, he leans down and kisses my cheek, then turns sharply on his heel and walks toward the other room.

He glances back at me one last time, then closes the door behind him.

I stare at it for a long time. I'm glad we're okay. Glad he's okay. For me…well, what the future holds is entirely in the hands of a single, rogue goddess who still hasn't returned to us and seems dubiously trustworthy at this point.

I sigh and look out above the open wall of my garden to the night skies. "You better keep up your end of the deal."

Like I have any power to punish a goddess if she doesn't.

"What did Cain want?"

63

SAY YOU'LL REMEMBER ME

Reven leans against the doorway, looking like he's trying to appear casual, but the taut lines of his body are anything but.

I suck in a sharp breath. How much did he hear?

His jaw tightens when I don't immediately answer.

Is it possible he remembers my history with Cain? He was here when Cain followed me to the palace and asked me to be his heartmate. If bits and pieces of the past are leaking through, the night he abducted me would be a pretty big one for several reasons.

"We're starting a new chapter," I decide on. Vague, but safe. I watch him, though, hoping to see some spark of recognition.

Nothing.

Nerves dance across my skin. Okay, no memories, I guess. Is he jealous? We've shared things, done things, and even without his memory, we're drawn to each other. I mean something to him despite having lost our past.

He stalks across the room to crouch in front of where I sit. "Are you…happy about where you and Cain are now?"

There's an intensity in his expression that feels familiar. An intensity that never fails to make my belly quiver when directed at me. I can confirm it still works. "Yes," I manage. "It's time to live our own lives. As friends."

"Good. I'm glad."

What does that mean?

He tips his head, studying me. "You look terrible," he says, then grimaces.

And just like that, the tension evaporates. A smile tugs at my lips. "I'm guessing that sounded better in your head?"

"I'm not sure that comforting is ever going to be a strength of mine," he says in wry tones.

I glance away. "Yeah, well, that makes two of us."

We're both quiet for long enough that awkwardness starts to creep in. Reven clears his throat but doesn't speak.

Two conversations like this in less than half an hour? The goddesses are laughing at me today.

"Why do I get the feeling there's something you want to say or ask or…" I wave at him. "I don't know. Something."

Brilliant. I'm a brilliant conversationalist. Between me and Tabra, clearly the viziers should make sure I'm the one who talks to people. I'm so *great* at it.

Reven hesitates another beat, then says, "It's not something we need to deal with right now. You need to sleep."

"Well, now I won't be able to sleep because I'll be worrying about it."

He sort of grunts at that.

"Is it the memories?" I ask.

He glances away and says nothing.

I smile for him, hoping I'm hiding my fear that he may never find me in those memories. I have traveled the road of hope so many times and it just keeps leading me to dead ends. I don't want to risk that again. "I trust you."

I hope he knows what I mean. That I trust him—memories or no—to do what's right. For him. For me.

He blinks, obviously not expecting that, which makes me smile. A real one, an honest one.

"I'm not the me you truly trust yet," he says.

"Wrong. Even without remembering me, you're still you. I

trust you. I realized the other day that you and I are two halves of a whole—light and dark—we balance. Right now, I'm the dark, and you're my light."

"Hells, Meren," he mutters. But the spark in his eyes is anything but frustrated, so warm it reaches out and warms me, too. "What am I going to do with you?"

"Let's talk about that after we win the war," I try to tease.

Only he doesn't smile back. Instead, he groans a little.

"Meren," he whispers my name, his expression filling with an emotion that I haven't seen since…goddess above, since Eidolon took him.

I swallow around the sudden ache in my throat. "What?"

He leans over me, hand coming up to cup my cheek, his thumb brushing over my lips.

My breath catches. "Don't."

His touch stills against my lips. "Don't what?"

"Look at me like that, touch me like that unless you mean it."

"I mean it."

My heart wants to take wing, but the rest of me isn't ready to believe it. "What?"

"I was going to wait," he says, eyes as dark as a stormy ocean. "For the right time. But you saying we'll figure us out after we win…" He shakes his head. "I don't want to risk missing our chance if it's our last."

Which means what? I can't reach for his love if he's just going to take it away again. It would hurt too much. "Do you remember us?"

After a pause, he gives his head a slow shake.

"Then—"

"It's coming back in random chunks. I don't have it all, yet. But I have enough…"

Enough.

I stare at him. Hope pulls at me like sand shifting under my feet, no matter how hard I mentally stomp it back down.

I've had so many things given to me only to be taken away that maybe I'm only looking for the lies, for the bad, for the catch. I have to stop doing that.

Trust him.

This is Reven. Even when he kidnapped me, it was both to protect Tabra and to help his people. He would never harm me if he could help it. He may not remember bonding yet, but…

"I don't know what to say."

Disappointment tints the regret that passes over his features. "I'm sorry."

I shake my head. "Don't say that. None of this has been your fault."

"*All* of it has been my fault. If I'd held back and waited for this to be over before I tried to have a relationship with you…"

"You did," I tell him.

He frowns.

"After I escaped from Eidolon, you tried to put distance between us to protect me. It was…worse." So much worse. In fact, why am I holding back now? "I just don't want to wake up tomorrow and find some other reason we can't be us. I don't think I can take it."

He drops his forehead to mine, eyes closed. "I shouldn't have given in and made love to you that night—"

I put a hand over his mouth. "I knew what that was. I don't regret it. But I can't lose you again."

He kisses my fingertips. "You won't. I promise."

"You can't promise that." Doesn't he see that's impossible to ensure?

He reaches up to twist a lock of my hair around one finger, forehead still to mine. "Then I promise that you won't lose my love again."

Cracks appear in the dam I've built around my heart. That's

it. That's what hurt the most, and what I fear the most. Our new bond may be severed, but our original bond should still ensure that if I lose him, we'll find each other again. But him losing his memories meant I lost his love.

"I *remember*, Meren," he whispers. "I remember falling in love with you. The feeling of it. My mind may have forgotten, but my heart didn't. Even when I was mistrustful, I couldn't leave you."

"That wasn't love—"

He cups my cheek, lifting his head so I can see the intent in his eyes. "Even without all my memories, those feelings have grown, a little at a time—respect led to trust, protectiveness followed, then jealousy and possessiveness, which weren't so fun." He scowls a little at that.

"When were you jealous?" I ask.

"A thousand little ways that I tried to never show you. Not until I figured out my own feelings." He brushes his thumb over my cheek. "Attraction turned to need but also to tenderness. All of that came back to me *before* my memories." His smile is slow. "It's not the bond. It's you. Us."

I'm staring into eyes so sure, so full of promise that I want to believe in the us he's talking about.

Reven makes a sound deep in his throat somewhere between a groan and a growl and presses his lips to mine, soft and sweet and yet edged with desperation. "No matter what happens in this or any other life," he breathes against me, "even if I lose the memories a thousand times, I will always fall for you, Mereneith Evangeline. If you have faith in anything, have faith in that."

The sob that wells up and bursts from me comes out of nowhere, but it breaks through my emotional dam and I can't hold back the flood. I throw my arms around him, bury my face in his neck, and let go of all those fears.

And Reven holds me. He just holds me.

When I don't ease up, he runs a hand over my hair in soothing strokes and starts to talk. "I remember the first time I saw you in the streets of Enora, even though I didn't know it was you," he murmurs, his voice winding around me. "I asked who you were, and you told me you were no one."

"I *was* no one." Part of me feels like I still am.

"No." The word comes out sharp, harsh. "I didn't like hearing it then any more than I do now. You will never be no one to me."

Maybe I died somewhere along the way without knowing it, and now I'm in the heavens? Is Allusian playing with me?

"I could feel it even then. You felt…different…just to be with. There was this pull."

"I felt it, too."

He huffs a laugh. "I distinctly remember you chucking a knife at my head in the woods in Wildernyss. And all the smart-ass commentary that poured from lips I was thinking about kissing way too much."

I snuggle into him. "You thought you got the timid princess."

"Thank Nova I didn't." His grip tightens. "I remember taking you to the Shadowood where you proceeded to fit in with my people like you were the last piece to a puzzle."

His words are gaining speed, and my heart is racing right along with him.

"I remember being caged with you when the Tyndran soldiers caught us and trying not to go up in flames and claim you then and there. I remember escaping and thinking I was going to lose you when you impaled yourself on your own glass spike."

Instead of soothing, now there's a tightness in his voice, like he's feeling that all over again.

"But you didn't lose me," I whisper, curling my hand into his shirt. "You saved me."

"Saved you…" He takes a big breath. "And then claimed you."

The relief and joy and release of all that hurt reacts to the darker tone lower in his voice, sending shivers dancing up my spine and warmth rushing through my veins. The tears still burn, but the reason has changed, happiness almost making it harder to hold them back.

I wiggle back a little to be able to see his face. Twin flags of red over his cheekbones tell me I'm not the only one feeling this.

"I thought I was the one who claimed *you*," I tease.

He sort of huffs a laugh and groans at the same time. "Meren?"

I know what he's asking.

This urgency to channel all these feelings into something joyous instead of doubtful. Something that will connect us again, even stronger than before.

"Do you want to wait?" he asks in a strained voice. "So much has happened and there's so much we still have to do. And I don't remember everything. Maybe now isn't the time."

When will it ever be the time? The entire world might come tumbling down around us any second. We should hold onto any happiness we can find for as long as we can. "I've learned that sometimes now is the only time."

He's holding himself like he's not sure what the best thing to do is. Maybe he's the one who needs time.

I stretch up to place a soft kiss against his lips, delighting in the fact that I can do even this much. "We can wait, if that's what you need. Just being able to hold you is—"

Reven suddenly rolls me, hovering over me. "That's not what I need."

The kiss he gives me is everything I've been waiting for. He may not remember everything, but he remembers enough, and I can feel that. I feel it in the way he touches me. Not claiming, like he did the night we bonded. And not like that night after we took the palace back. This is different. He's still exploring, still feeling out my responses, but the emotion is there.

He loves me. He remembers he loves me. But he also fell in love with me all over again.

His taste slides over my tongue and through my blood. Everything about me centers and settles with the absolute rightness of us together. Not just physically, but us.

Just us.

64

MAKE ME...

Goddess. He's really here with me. All the way with me.

He trails his lips over my jaw to kiss my neck behind my ear before gently tugging on the lobe with his teeth.

"I've missed you so much," I whisper.

"Me too, princess," he says, a heaviness weighing in his voice that tickles over my skin. Regrets.

No more of those.

I turn my face to his, seeking his lips. Seeking the comfort of knowing that this won't be taken away from us again. As need starts to layer within me, my hands find their way into the silkiness of his thick hair, where I clench and unclench my fists—not consciously, but because I can't not.

His hands snake up to grab my wrists, stilling me.

"What?" I ask, and my vulnerability is there in that single word.

"You're already driving me wild."

I smile at the strain in his voice and the way he's already breathing harder against me. Then I kiss him again with an underlying desperation that keeps threatening to steal the joy of the moment.

Don't leave me again.

"Fuck," he growls against my lips, filling the word with anger and self-recrimination. Did he hear my thoughts, or did I say that out loud? "Never. I *never* wanted to leave you."

He's kissing me again, swallowing the whimper of my relief and fear, gathering me closer in his arms.

Then he moves us, moves over me more to settle between my legs. A sigh escapes me at the simple pleasure of the weight of him. Our tongues tangle and slide and move, but I'm not ready to get there yet. The last time was so fast, so hot and heavy, I didn't take the time to savor him. Savor us.

I missed this too much, missed just being able to kiss him. And maybe he feels the same, because the tenor of his touch turns languorous, as if he is drawing out every caress into a thousand moments to cherish.

He kisses me and I kiss him as my heart soars, and my mind and body narrow down the world until only we exist in this moment. Nothing else.

With one hand, he reaches between us and starts to inch my sleep gown up my legs, even as he doesn't stop kissing me. Still achingly slow, still tender, still drawing out each touch until I'm quivering with anticipation. He finally reaches the bottom of the material, and his fingertips touch the skin of my thigh.

He uses soft brushes to explore, teasing and torturing me as he inches higher and higher, up to my hip, the dip in my waist, and all while kissing me in that burning, hazy, unhurried way.

And with every breath, I'm waiting and wondering. When…

He cups my breast under the material of the gown, teasing me with his thumb and I have to pull my mouth away, arching into his hand on a shudder of agony and pleasure.

I moan when he does it again, and he shudders against me, and then utters his own groan.

"Mereneith Evangeline," he murmurs against my temple. I don't miss the way he leaves off the XII. The only one to ever do so when using my full name. Like I'm more important in his eyes than the twelve who came before me. "What you do to me…"

"Likewise."

I think he huffs a laugh, but I'm not sure because he's

gently tugging my gown over my head, leaving me with only the underclothes covering me. He removes those next, hands still gentle, and his gaze drinks me in with every inch of flesh revealed.

He does this slowly, too.

We're both breathing hard by the time he stands up, and I think we both forget "slow" then. He strips his clothes fast and rough, then he's back over me and I welcome the weight of him with a hum of happiness.

Nothing is between us.

If we have our way, nothing ever will be again.

I sigh, wrapping one arm around his neck. "I love you."

He swallows hard. "I love you, too. And I promise—"

I reach between us to put my fingers over his lips and he hushes.

"I don't need promises," I murmur. "I just need you."

After a long beat, Reven melts into me the same way I did to him. "You have me. You've always had me."

He leans to the side a bit and watches as he trails one hand across my jaw, down my neck where he squeezes just slightly, and damned if my body doesn't heat at that small, possessive display alone. Then he feels over my collarbone, down to linger at my breast, feathering and teasing until I'm surging against his hand, gasps tumbling from my lips.

Then he goes lower, to the shadow scar on my side. At first, he brushes over it lightly, but then his touch changes, and his gaze on me turns even more intense. Purposeful.

The darkness inside me changes, too, becoming fizzling, scorching heat, and without warning, sensation explodes inside me. I cry out as wave after wave of pure ecstasy washes through me.

By the time I come back to myself, floating down from the high, I'm wrapped in Reven's arms, basking in his pleased smile.

Holy mother goddess of all things wanton and wicked. "Did you just…" I'm too impressed to put it to words even as I'm still incandescent from the experience. "Using darkness?"

He grins.

"That was…something."

Which makes him laugh. "I should have been doing it to you all along." He nuzzles my neck. "A terrific distraction for when you argue with me."

I mock scowl at him, but then he's moving. He presses into me, so slowly I'm squirming under him, but it doesn't make him speed up. Not even when tension rides his shoulders and tightens his jaw. Even then, he moves with deliberation.

"Please, Reven. I need you."

My words seem to snap what little control he has left, and he surges.

I remember this fire. Always there, even from the first time we came together—melted sand, red-hot, molten, and malleable—and he can form me into whatever he wants.

I was more than willing then. Now I'm his and he is mine so completely that to try to separate one from the other would be impossible.

Eidolon tried.

He failed.

This is a love that can't be taken. Even if it can be forgotten, it can also be remembered.

Reven takes both my hands, lacing our fingers together, and pulls them up to either side of my face, holding me there as he starts to move.

His gaze never leaves mine, taking in every gasp, every widening of my eyes, and I never look away from him. I don't want to.

In this moment, he is beautiful.

Stark, severe, and beautiful.

Pleasure tightens the skin across his cheeks and hardens his jaw with leashed control as he stokes a new wildfire within me.

And still, we never look away.

I hide nothing from him. From myself, either. I've been burying my love for this man for so long, until this moment when I feel safe enough and free enough to release it. His eyes widen, then turn bluer, fierce possession burning within, and lightness fills every part of me until I can't stop smiling even through the pleasure, through every gasp, every moan, and every surge.

Sensation draws in tight, prickles down my spine and coalesces, firing up every nerve ending. This one isn't instant, like before. Instead, sensation coils tighter and tighter before it ignites outward. I go up in a blaze that spreads, consuming every part of me, lighting up my soul as Reven groans long and loud, and I'm swallowing his passion, crying my own back to him.

Above him, the colorful lights cast by my glass flowers turn every nuance of the pleasure we give each other into magic. We hold onto each other through it all, like we should have always been able to do.

Gradually the rush slows and our bodies with it, sinking into each other, wrapping around each other. Reven drops his forehead to mine, and we stare into each other's eyes, our bodies utterly fulfilled and our souls reconnecting.

The perfection of our coming together, the knowing that we have found each other all over again, the sheer relief is agonizingly absolute in a way that makes my belly tighten with fear.

Because if I lose him again, I'm done.

It would end me.

I cut those thoughts off ruthlessly, refusing to let anything ruin this moment. Our bond isn't reformed, that much I can feel.

But we can take care of that later. Go through the ceremony again and start fresh.

As long as we both love, that's the only thing that matters.

65

WHAT IS MINE

I wake slowly, eyes still closed but able to see the sunlight behind my lids, and everything about last night comes back to me. We made love several more times—until we were tangled in sheets and each other and I finally fell into a perfect, peaceful sleep in his arms.

I give a luxurious stretch only to pause midway through as it sinks in that I'm not in his arms anymore.

Jagged fear shears through me like a bolt of lightning.

I jerk upright on a gasp, and sure enough, the bed beside me is empty.

"Reven?" I whip around, searching the room only to go dead still at the sight of Reven on the side of the bed, sitting in the same straight-backed chair as before.

Fear is like a thousand bugs crawling through me. "Not again—"

"Hells." He's out of his chair and kneeling by the bed, hands wrapped around mine. "I'm still yours. Sorry for scaring you."

The fear doesn't entirely go away on the *whoosh* of relief that leaves my body. "Then why were you sitting there like that?"

His hands tighten around mine, but he meets my gaze. "Because the Shadows wouldn't let me stay in the bed with you. They kept coming to the surface if I stayed."

My ribs tighten down like a cinch, and my stomach flips as

the joy that should be surging crawls back under a rock. "The hells you say."

He just looks at me, and I know he means it.

"Did you try to take them?"

"I wouldn't do that to you while you're sleeping."

I believe him. "Then why—"

"I don't know." He takes a breath. "But now might be a good time to try having you give them back again."

Just one morning. One hour. Even one minute, at this point. A speck of time where I didn't have to wake up to this nightmare. Why can't I ever have that? I rub at my eyes, which are feeling grittier by the second. "Fine."

Reven's eyebrows wing high. "Fine?"

"If I have to say it again," I growl, starting to sound like the grumpy version of him, "then the answer is no."

He holds up both hands. "I just wasn't expecting you to give in so easily."

I shift uncomfortably in the bed, though I don't look away. "If I tried to keep them, everyone would only be more wary and suspicious around me."

That sounded better in my head.

"True." He says it softly, but it still hurts. "But I get to kiss you, so there's that."

A fluttering blooms in my stomach that has nothing to do with Shadows.

Reven scoots me over to sit close, then takes my chin between his fingers. Humor lights his eyes. "Don't bite me," he murmurs.

"I make no promises."

"Hmmm. On second thought, go ahead."

The fluttering turns to warmth. Reven urges me forward as he leans closer and closer, drawing the moment out into a thousand little heartbeats as the endless ocean of his eyes brightens and heat flares across my cheeks.

All he needs is to suck darkness and evil out of me. The logical part of me knows that. I shouldn't be excited by the mouth-to-mouth part since it has nothing to do with feelings.

Reven puts his mouth over mine, and my eyes flutter closed. I breathe in the fresh scent of him that always reminds me of home. I feel his warmth.

Then he starts to draw the Shadows out, and in the next instant, all I am is agony.

In my head, I scream for forever, but it's probably only seconds before Reven jerks back. "Meren?"

"They don't want to go to you," I tell him, breathing hard as the slivers of pain slowly fade to nothing. I swallow hard and shoot him a smile. "I think they like me better."

His grip on my chin tightens uncomfortably. "Like you better?"

I roll my eyes. "Calm down. It's a joke."

"Uh-huh."

With a sigh, I drop my head forward so that I'm leaning against his shoulder. "Can't a girl be funny and potentially evil's puppet at the same time?"

"We'll try again later," he says.

"What's the point?"

He rubs his cheek against my hair, his morning beard rasping. "You haven't seen your face lately, Meren. They—"

"I've been in control."

"You haven't."

I don't even bother to ask if it's truth. I know it is. I know that I can't always hear them or feel them.

He pulls away to look me in the eyes, his gaze turning pointed. "Just now *you* were the one fighting it. *You* were holding them inside."

But I didn't even know it was happening. What if next time, I don't know and I don't fight it?

Blast the fates.

The way he's tense against me, bracing in case I attack him, might scare me even more because it means he's afraid of that, too.

I tuck my head under his chin and hold on tight. "When Eidolon comes, if we haven't got them out of me by then—"

"When he comes, I'm going to kill that bastard."

I squeeze my eyes shut. "But if anything goes wrong, you have to remember your promise."

To kill me if he has to.

He holds me closer. "I know."

66

SAYING GOODBYE WITHOUT THE WORDS

Today. It's happening today.

The Alignment.

Release goddesses. Fend off Eidolon. Try not to die. Keep my friends safe. Try to feel nothing to prevent Eidolon or the Shadows from taking me over.

No pressure.

I glance at the skies. The moons at this point have disappeared against the brightness of the sun, but according to the star watchers, we're in the first phase of the total solar eclipse when the celestial bodies become as one and the sun goes dark.

Is it a little dimmer outside? I can't tell.

Any minute now.

Tension coils through me, like a rag twisted all out of shape. Pella, walking along beside me, keeps me moving through the courtyard between the palace and the throne room. After so many surprise attacks and falling into traps, I almost think the waiting and knowing is worse.

As we emerge from the hypostyle hall and approach the massive double doors to the throne room—already wide open—I can hear our friends' voices.

Vos's voice trickles out of the doorway. "I think this might be the longest table I've ever seen."

That's what they're talking about? I don't know what I was expecting. Grim silence, maybe. Or low, tight voices going over the plans yet again.

"It's definitely the ugliest," Cain says.

For the briefest of flashes, my lips quirk. They're talking about the formal table usually in the dining room of the palace. I've always thought it was ugly, too. The thing was carved from a single slab of black-and-gold granite. It's obnoxiously ornate and seats up to fifty guests, which is roll-my-eyes ostentatious. It's also creepy. Something about the angled lines of its many legs reminds me of a bug.

Tziah had it moved in here just for today. I'm sure the palace servants just *loved* that task.

"All it needs is antennae and mandibles and it's a giant centipede," Cain says.

Tabra's giggle is unmistakable. "Meren used to say the same thing."

It's good to hear her laughing.

This was Tziah's idea—to start in the throne room where Tabra and I will have to perform a miracle at the peak of the Alignment, regardless of whatever else happens.

We have no idea when or how Eidolon is going to strike. Despite days of us all hovering on a knife's edge of anticipation, he's yet to make an appearance. He has to show before the Alignment, though, given that he'd rather only his mother be released and we're planning to do far more than that. But when, where, how...we have plans, and backup plans, and secret plans, most of which have been hidden from me, all ready to be implemented as soon as it happens.

But Tziah wants us to take one last moment together. A breath. Even if it's a short one. When she told me the idea, I thought it sounded silly, but maybe not. Maybe we need this.

I sniff at the scents wafting into the hallway. "Did she arrange for food?" I ask Pella.

She shrugs, but her lips still tilt. "I don't know how she

thinks we're going to be able to eat today."

Seriously.

We walk into the room, and they all go quiet.

It's been days of avoiding them and them avoiding me and being watched like an evil chrysalis. None of that is their fault, and I just now realize I've also been setting the tone. Or maybe getting Reven back has lightened at least a part of my heart to see Tziah's right. We need to cherish each other while we can.

So I can't help it. "You don't have to stop talking for me. Possessed people can laugh, too, you know," I tease.

Beside me, Pella groans, and at the table, Cain laughs. Tziah, meanwhile, smiles and pats the chair between her and Reven. As the rest of the group ease a tad, I make my way around and sit. He brushes his hand against the part of my arm hidden by the table. The others know he's recovering his memories. We haven't told them more than that. Reven's choice. One less distraction or worry, he said.

So we've kept up a front of distance.

Instead of taking his hand like I want to, I lean over to look past Tziah to Vos and Hakan. "It's good to see you both up."

Hakan just nods. Meanwhile the cocky grin Vos flashes me is very him, though he can't quite hide the glance he flicks at the maimed shoulder. "The Imperium was right. After two days, the pain isn't so bad." He waves the stump where his arm used to be. "Getting used to doing everything with my left hand, however…"

By the way he's gripping a spoon like a child first learning to eat, I can see what he means. "I can't imagine how much that sucks, but knowing you, you'll be doing amazing things with that hand soon."

He leans back in his chair with a suggestive leer. "Such as?"

I roll my eyes. "Not what you're apparently all thinking."

Laughter fills the room.

Vos waggles his eyebrows. "I wasn't thinking anything. What were you thinking?"

Good grief. "I don't know." I shrug. "Knife fights? Whittling? Masterpieces of art?"

Instead of laughing again, he drops the spoon to stroke his chin. "Master of art. That has a nice ring to it."

Even Hakan rolls his eyes.

Tziah chucks a roll at Vos, then she signs to him with rapid gestures.

"Hey," Vos protests. "I could absolutely draw a recognizable stick figure on a cave wall if I still had my right hand!"

Which gets the others laughing again.

Tziah was right to have us do this.

I wish to the mother goddess that Bene was here. And the others we've lost, too. I press a hand over my chest, trying to ease the sudden ache.

The servants enter with more food. I toss a glance to the moonhole in the roof of the throne room. The sun isn't visible in its circle yet, but we've been assured by all the stargazers and seers and our Viziers that it will be at the height of the Alignment.

A tray of warm cinnamon bread appears before me.

"Hungry?" Reven asks.

I still refuse to look at him, mostly because if I do, I'll melt into a puddle. I take a piece without speaking.

Beside me, Tziah gives her version of a small sigh rife with disappointment. Maybe I'm taking this distance thing too far.

I look at Cain, who is sitting across from Reven. "What's the status with your people?"

He glances around before setting down his utensils. "We're ready."

That's all he's going to tell me. I should know better than to ask. "Good."

"Hey," Pella says. "The rule is no strategy at the table. We've done everything we can."

Everything we can do in a small amount of time, but she's right. In pulling my gaze from Cain, I accidentally peek at Reven only to be snared by his gaze. He's looking straight at me, serious as always, intently searching as he does, but also…

Why can't I make myself look away? I should be stronger than this by now. I force my gaze elsewhere.

This time I'm pretty sure the entire table sighs.

They seem determined to blame me for this situation when Reven's the one who wants to keep our secret. Something he seems to think is hilarious. I catch the hint of a chuckle under his breath and elbow him.

I expect him to distract the others. Instead, he grabs a roll and casually says, "I have most of my memories back and Meren and I are together again."

Shock sends my spine ramrod straight and I glare at him. "You were the one who didn't want to say anything. They need to focus."

"I knew there was something off!" Vos is the first to crow. His exclamation sets off the others, who are talking over each other.

Reven reaches under the table and laces our fingers together, then leans closer. "You clearly couldn't keep your hands off me."

I scoff. "That isn't true."

"I know." He drops a kiss on the tip of my nose and grins. "But I could tell it was bothering you."

Was I that obvious?

"You used to be a better liar," he teases.

My cheeks warm and I glance away to find Cain staring at us from across the table, his expression inscrutable, and I realize he's the only one who hasn't said a word. The others are all still debating who knew something was up with us and who didn't.

I open my mouth, then close it again. What can I say to him?

Then he offers me a soft smile. One tinged with sadness, but a smile all the same. This new normal may take a little getting used to, but as my best friend, he's still happy for me. I can feel it.

The slap of feet on the polished floors coming down the hall toward us sucks the levity from the room. Vos, Cain, and Hakan all jump up from the table to crouch in defensive stances.

The palace servant boy someone sent skids to a halt, turning pale at the sight of the three of them ready to kill him.

"Seven hells," Pella mutters as we all relax a bit.

The boy still remembers to give us a bow. "A man is at the gate demanding to talk with Queen Mereneith."

Tabra and I exchange a look. "Did he give a name?" she asks.

"Horus," he says. "He says he's a Wanderer, but he's dressed like he's from Tyndra."

"The hells you say," Cain snarls, whipping his gaze to me.

I'm on my feet. "He's come on my orders. You may not kill him."

"Damn it, Meren!"

"Yell at me later." I face the boy. "Go fetch him. Run."

A few minutes later, Horus appears in the doorway, urgency vibrating in every taut line of his body and his pinched expression. He rushes toward me, only to pull up short as Cain steps in front of him.

He stops himself and drops to one knee, head bowed. "Eidolon is coming. He brings his army."

My heart stops beating for a second. So it's war, then.

"When?" I demand.

"Fifteen minutes at most."

67

WITHOUT OR WITHIN

Fear curdles in my stomach. He doesn't point out that if he hadn't had to argue with the guards and then wait for them to notify me, we'd have longer. I already know that's on me.

The Shadows are silent and still, even at the spoken name of the king. I hope they stay that way through what comes next.

"Where will he come from?" Reven demands.

Horus flicks him a glance. "He plans to shadow his army into the heart of the city and the palace itself."

Damn them. We need to force them outside my walls. I look at Reven. "You said you had an idea for that."

"What idea, exactly?" Vos asks.

Reven keeps his gaze on me as he says, "We block Eidolon out with shadow."

"How is that supposed to work?" Cain asks. "The king is more powerful than either of you."

Pella is also shaking her head. "Eidolon will take over Meren if she tries it."

"Not if he's in the middle of bringing his army here from Tyndra," Reven points out. "It's going to take his entire focus and a lot of his energy. He won't have the ability to do both."

In other words, we have a narrow window. Smart.

"We don't have time to argue."

I take Reven's hand, then look at my sister. "Tabra?"

"Go," she says. And maybe for the first time ever, I don't see the softness in her. The woman standing before me is calm, ready, battle-tested even. "I'll be here."

"I love you," I tell her.

Tabra's smile is everything I used to miss when we were apart. "I love you, too."

I nod and Reven shadows us to the top of the private royal tower so fast, the blink in and out is more like the flicker of a candle. He doesn't let go of me as he raises his free hand, already glowing purple, though dimmer in the bright morning sunlight.

I draw on Eidolon's power. The cold of it in my blood is a shock even though it's only been a few days since I used it against the Devourers. It pours through me in a rush that edges on pain.

"I'll start on the north side, you start on the south," Reven says. "Build it starting from the wall, up and over, like a dome. We meet at the zenith."

I close my eyes and get to work. My heart rattles around in the cage of my ribs, waiting for Eidolon to take control any second now. Or to appear here, drawn to us by my use of his power like a beacon, and stop us. Or something more horrible.

The cold intensifies until it's a burn. As if Tyndra itself exists inside me.

"He's coming," a Shadow escapes long enough to hiss at me.

"I can't do more," I warn Reven. "They're talking to me."

He doesn't ask who. He knows.

"Hold where you are," Reven says. "I'll bring mine up and over to meet yours."

I open my eyes to see a dome of darkness stretched far overhead to the horizon of the city edge, just thin enough to see the details of the sky and desert beyond through it. Closing in on itself, the other half crests over the apex at the centerline and inches down toward my part like double doors being drawn together to close out a storm.

How long has it been since Horus arrived? Ten minutes?

Fifteen? That was *at most.* Any second, I'm expecting them to appear like ants pouring from a disturbed mound.

Fear doesn't stop rushing through my veins, even when the dome connects like a kiss, creating a seamless shadow drawn over the city, casting us in a dimmer light. No sooner do we lower our hands than something strikes our shield. All I see is the ripple of the hit, like tossing a rock into a pond, but I feel it. And still, the dome holds.

Try to shadow your army past that, *asshole.*

Out toward the south, trumpets blare to life—the signal for invasion.

"Come on." Reven, still holding my hand, shadows us to a flat rooftop of one of the basic towers I made at points around my wall.

"Hells and damnation," I mutter.

Eidolon's army is amassed in the desert outside the city, thank the mother goddess. But it's so many. Columns upon columns of soldiers in gleaming white armor, painfully brilliant even under Aryd's slightly dimmer sun and with the shield of shadow between us.

I look at Reven. "What do you think he's going to—"

There's a small ripple in the packed sand in front of the troops. It picks up speed, growing larger as it barrels toward the city like a wave.

Only an Imperium could do that.

I throw my hands up, but the instant I try to stop the wave, an invisible force slams into me—like the power the Imperium is using to create it struck at my own power. It tosses me backward and I smack my head against the floor. It takes a second for the jagged pain to ebb.

"It's not the sand," I tell Reven, hand to my ringing head. "It's the land itself, I think. I can't stop it."

I push myself to my feet just as the wave rams into the wall off to our left with an explosion of sand. The impact shakes through the foundation of the tower we're on, even though we're far from where it hit. I put my palms against the shadow dome, pressing my face against it, trying to see down the line of the wall. "Did it breach?"

"I don't think so." Reven steps closer. "If it had, the debris would have gone inward to the city, not back out toward the desert."

Another ripple builds and comes at the city again.

Reven jerks forward, hands igniting.

"No, wait." I grab his arm. "Eidolon will see. He might come for you." If we're supposed to conserve power for the Alignment, drawing his attention, having to fight him this early would be disastrous.

The muscles under my hand flex and bunch. He knows I'm right.

The strike is close enough that this time I see when it makes contact. Once again, my wall holds. A miracle. There's no screaming inside the city, no movement, no rush to get away. Behind us is silent.

"Why is it so quiet?" I ask, looking back into the streets.

Reven's coiled frustration shifts to a smile that is quiet satisfaction. "Evacuating the city was one of Vos's better ideas."

When did they evacuate? I want to ask, but it doesn't take a genius to figure it out. They'd kept me in the dark for a reason. I imagine they used the portal in the temple to send our people to other cities in Aryd, or to our allies. That bastard won't be able to use innocent bystanders against us this time. A city can be rebuilt but lives lost are lost forever.

Reven looks out toward the army. "Eidolon's mistake was giving us time to prepare."

The waves of sand come faster. The ground looks like water on a stormy day.

I flinch with every strike.

Where is the king? Has he been able to get through the shadow barrier we built? Is he trying to bring it down?

I check the Shadows, but they're contained. Even the one who rose up only minutes ago.

A blast hits extremely close and Reven throws himself over and around me, taking the brunt of the debris that shoots inward on this side of the wall and pelts us. I bury my head against his chest. How we both stay upright as the tower threatens to collapse under the impact, I don't know. We both right ourselves, and I stare at the massive hole in the fallen wall directly beside the tower.

I don't see the signal, but as if they have been unleashed, Eidolon's army breaks formation to sprint for the city. An instant later, horses appear from around the bend and charge straight at the backside of Eidolon's army.

The Wanderers.

No doubt in my mind that Cain is leading the charge with Pella at his side.

"Why aren't they screaming?" Reven mutters under his breath.

The war cry of the Wanderers is famous, a bloodcurdling sound guaranteed to put the fear of the goddesses into any enemy.

"They're waiting until they get closer," I say. I can practically hear Cain in my head telling me this. "They want the element of surprise."

Sure enough, the Tyndrans haven't turned around yet.

I wait to close the wall, not even drawing on my power yet. If I plug up the hole now, they might go looking for the next threat. They'll see Cain's people.

I find myself holding my breath as the Wanderers close the distance.

"Don't look. Don't look. Don't look." I chant the words softly. Tension crawls over me like spiders.

Beside me, Reven lets out a growl of frustration. "I'm not sitting by and doing nothing."

He flicks both his hands like he's shooing away a gnat, and suddenly the entire front line of soldiers goes down, like they were tripped.

And they were. By their own shadows. Something not obvious to anyone watching. I only know because I'm standing by Reven, who grins. "That'll distract them."

And then the Wanderers scream.

"Scourge!"

68

FIGHT WITH EVERYTHING YOU HAVE

Eidolon's army, almost as one entity, wheels around like a flock of birds, but it's too late. The Wanderers are on top of them, and they can't regroup fast enough. The Wanderers plow into the Tyndran army like a physical blow to a body. Lots of bodies.

More Wanderers continue to pour around the bend, Vanished among their numbers, and anyone with working sight can see that we have the Tyndrans outnumbered.

A spout of water shoots into the air. Cain. We're in the desert, but Oaesys sits on a huge lake. Unfortunately, it's on the other side of the city.

Reven looks in the direction I am. "Why isn't he using more?"

"He'd have to pull the water up and over the city."

"He did more than that in Tropikis."

"Yeah. And it nearly killed him." Still, I frown. It's not like Cain to hold back in battle. "He must be saving his power for the Alignment to hold off Eidolon or the goddesses or something."

And sacrificing his people for that, I realize. If I'd known, I would have argued against it.

"Damn it." Reven's brows snap down. "He knows *I'm* here

for that."

The land Hylorae sends a new ripple at the melee now, rather than at my wall. The Wanderers on their horses jump the wave, which then rushes through the first row of Tyndran soldiers. It topples them to the ground and launches a few bodies into the air, then the land settles abruptly, probably because the Imperium realized their mistake. Right behind the wave, the Wanderers turn again, plowing back into the Tyndrans, cutting down soldiers as they get to their feet like a scythe through fields of grain.

"Oh my goddess," I whisper. We've gone up against Eidolon so many times now, and never—not once—have we had the upper hand. We might just do this. We might keep him out.

The day grows dimmer, and I glance up to the skies.

That's when a burst of cold hits my blood.

I close my eyes and check the Shadows, but the cage holds. It doesn't feel like they're trying to get out, but what do I know? My gut is telling me to pay attention to that sensation. It can't be a coincidence. It just can't.

"Meren?" Reven asks.

"I think… I think Eidolon is here."

I open my eyes to catch the way his brows snap lower. "Why would you—"

A solid blanket of shadow erupts over a huge swath of land, obscuring the desert floor. Then the shadow morphs to a black mist, dissipating to reveal more soldiers. Green armor. Not Tyndran soldiers—a different army dotted throughout, bolstering his numbers.

Horror surges up my throat. This is the Tropikan army that Eidolon disappeared from the palace in Pantrea when Cain tried to drown them with a tidal wave of ocean water. The day I lost Reven. The king didn't kill them, and he didn't turn them into shadows—he took them away.

To wait for today.

Too many. There's too many now. We are outnumbered. They'll be overrun. Slaughtered.

Goddess, what a fool I was to think, even for a second, that we had a chance.

Only…screw that. I didn't come all this way to lie down and take it now.

I bring up my hands.

"What are you going to do?" Reven demands.

"They're in *my* dominion now." I drag as much sand as I can from the dunes. I don't know what I'm going to do—hurl the lot of it at the bastards, maybe, bury them—but I've got to do something. "Time they learn the power the desert can unleash."

Reven grabs my wrist, swinging me around to face him. "You can't."

"What?" I tug, but he only tightens his grip. "Why?"

"You'll bury our friends."

"I can avoid them." I tug again. "Let me go."

His face flickers with an odd determination. "You need to conserve your power. To release the goddesses and in case we have to fight the king."

I can't bring myself to care if he's right. I need to save my people. It's not like I can release the goddesses if we fall before the Alignment.

Frustration building, I check the glooming skies. Tabra's going to send up a signal when it's time, but it's getting close. Once I'm not here to repair the wall, I need Aryd's armies waiting inside the city to hold off invasion should Eidolon's forces get in. But we also need more soldiers to join this fight. Now.

Reven holds his hands out, palms upward, and then yanks down. On the field, I can see shadowy hands reach up, dozens of them, and a patch of soldiers are dragged to the ground. No, not just to the ground…into it. Buried up to their necks. None of our people though, just Eidolon's. He does it again.

"You should be down there," I say.

"I'm not leaving you." Another patch of soldiers go down.

Lightning crashes into the fray, sending soldiers flying. Hakan is out there, which means Pella is, too. Vos, Tziah, and Horus as well, no doubt.

A deadly sort of calm settles over me.

I know exactly what I can do next, but I was really hoping not to have to. "Fine," I say. "I have a different lever I can pull."

"What?"

"Take me down. Outside the wall, right at the base of it."

Reven doesn't question me. We shadow to the ground, and I slap my palms to the wall of sand before me, commanding it to heat. Warmth hits my face and sparks pour off the spot I'm touching like a waterfall of tiny flames that fizzle in the air. The sparks move outward from where I'm touching, traveling the length of the wall as far as I can see, eating the sand away, leaving molten liquid behind.

"Are you turning the wall to glass?" Reven asks. "Isn't that weaker?"

It is, but worth the risk for the reward.

"I'm making part of the wall a giant portal to bring the Wildernyss army through." Trysolde and Istrella have their army gathered and waiting through the Alignment, just in case.

"Their portal is too small," Reven says. "It will take them too long."

"I built a bigger one in their barracks the day after I made the walls here."

"What?" He rears back like I slapped him. "When did you do that?"

"That day I was resting in my glass garden. I got the idea when it hit me that I had a giant wall of sand already built. Why not make it a portal? Either to evacuate my own armies quickly, or to bring help."

"Impressive." I think he is going to say more, but I'm vaguely aware of the way he turns his head. "Faster. The soldiers are starting to notice."

I can only go so fast. "Go warn Wildernyss to be ready."

"No way— "

"Please. They need to hurry."

He goes without another word, leaving a hole next to me.

I keep working.

And working.

And—

The sound of someone running at me is all the warning I get. I whirl to face my attacker, knives already in hand. White Tyndran armor flashes in my sight for a heartbeat before a Wanderer on the back of a midnight-hued horse plows into the soldier from behind. The horse rears up at the rider's command and tramples the soldier until he's limp and twisted on the ground.

Then the rider turns in his saddle, and I see his face.

"Cain." Relief is immediate. Thank the goddess.

"I'll hold them off," he says as he jumps to the ground. "Keep going." He doesn't even know what I'm doing, but he trusts me that much.

I catch his quick, semi-bloodthirsty smirk as I face my glass again. It's solidified enough where I stand. Hopefully the other end is as well. Pressing my hand to the smooth surface that is still ruthlessly hot, I will my power into the glass.

A clang of sword meeting sword is followed by a grunt behind me, punctuated by a gurgle that sounds like water and someone drowning. Cain fighting.

Focus, Meren.

I don't immediately try to open it, giving the magical force I wield time to work its way down the long stretch of glass.

"Duck!" Cain yells.

Managing to keep my hand to the glass, I drop just in time as a dagger to ricochets off my wall.

Need to move faster.

I picture the portal I made in Wildernyss.

It takes longer than usual, though, the glass doing nothing.

"What's supposed to happen?" Cain calls back to me.

"It's supposed to—"

The portal turns opaque and then beautifully, miraculously clear, and an iron-armored military stands on the other side, assembled and ready to go. With no hesitation, they bolt through the portal with a shout, pouring from Wildernyss onto the Arydian battlefield.

"Holy shit!" I hear Cain yell behind me.

I glance over my shoulder. The man has blood splattered across his face and a rip in his shirt that hopefully wasn't made by a weapon that struck flesh. And still, the grin he gives me is beautiful. I'd laugh at how ridiculous that is if not for the battle raging around us.

"That's for you," I call.

With a wave, he runs off with a Wanderer's scream ripping from his throat, a tornado of water shooting up from the dry ground in front of him.

I stay where I am, keeping the portal open, even after Reven reappears at my side. He says nothing, and neither do I. When the last fighter from Wildernyss is through, I close it.

As fast as I am to do that, he's even faster to shadow us back up onto the tower where we watch the four armies clash, brutality in the sounds of battle, the yells of the injured, and the neighs of the horses. In the distance, I catch sight of a flat, circular silver blade the size of a small tree cleaving through Tyndran soldiers. I follow it back to Trysolde, who seems to be using his own metal armor to create the weapon. Farther out, a blast of ice tells me exactly where Vos is. I don't see Tziah, but I'm sure she's with him.

I smile grimly. "Take that, Eidolon."

"Unless you have any more surprises, that's everything we

can throw at him. Right?" Reven asks.

"That's all of it." The darkness is growing, shading the battle in ways that feels heavy. Ominous. "We just need to keep him busy long enough to release the goddesses. You ready?"

Strong arms wrap around me, and I lean into his hold. His very…firm hold? I stiffen and he tightens his grip, pinning my arms to my sides so forcefully that I gasp at the sudden pressure on my still bruised ribs. What—

A dark, grating laugh sends a cascade of fear shivering all over me. The same laugh I've heard once before, in circumstances so like this that I want to weep.

Because that's Reven's voice in my ear, but not.

"Who are you?" I whisper. It can't be Eidolon controlling him. Reven has none of the king left inside him anymore. This is more like when Tabra was infected. "One of Eidolon's ghosts escaped from the burning lands?"

"Smart girl."

Eidolon's ghost nuzzles the side of my neck, even as he holds a knife to my side. "Did you miss me, love?"

"Got you," a Shadow inside me taunts.

Mother fucking mistakes.

We were so focused on the danger I posed, we forgot about Reven.

69

IT'S ALL CRUMBLING

"*You*." I choke on the word and the knowledge of exactly which ghost of Eidolon this is.

He came to me in the desert. Told me exactly what was in my amulet. But like the advice he also gave me in the burning lands, it wasn't everything. A lure to direct my actions, to lead me down the paths he wanted me to follow.

"So you *do* remember me," Eidolon's ghost says in a voice rife with satisfaction.

"Fuck you," I say, my voice so tight it hurts to speak.

He chuckles. "Eidolon swallowed me while Reven was still inside the king so that I could attach to your boyfriend. I've been hiding nice and deep so Reven wouldn't sense me, waiting for Eidolon's call."

My breath catches. That isn't…

This entire time?

No. He couldn't have been. Because that would mean—

I feel the blood drain from my face. Was it him when we…

Horror burns so hard, my skin crawls with it. I think I'm going to be sick.

His lips brush my ear. "Watch this."

He waves his fingers in front of my face and, out of nowhere, inky figures appear on the field right in the midst of four armies.

"The army of shadow souls from the Shadowood," I whisper to myself. "Eidolon took them—"

Reven waves again, and it's like he's unleashed the hells. The shadow soldiers attack, plowing through our allies mercilessly. They use weapons made of darkness that act like solid things, stabbing and skewering through solid flesh and bone. It's like watching a nightmare without being able to wake up or scream or run. Those things aren't bound by the laws of the physical world. And they can't be killed.

A Shadow inside me presses out. *"You're so screwed."*

Think Meren, think.

"You control the shadow army while Eidolon stops Tabra from releasing any goddesses except his mother. Is that the plan?"

"Exactly."

Which means I played right into his hands. Shit. "Then why did you let us put up the dome of shadow? That doesn't help him."

I feel the ghost stiffen against me, glance up, and then grunt, a sound that is usually a swear word for Reven.

"You didn't know?" Is it possible he isn't aware of everything that happened when Reven was in control?

"I told you—I was waiting for Eidolon's call."

Relief is instant but I stuff it down, not wanting to show him any weakness. The cold I felt—was that the call?

"So what happens now?"

The blade of the knife digs into my side, and I feel the sting followed by a trickle of blood dribbling down to my hip, sticking to my clothes. "Now you lift the barrier and destroy your wall."

My brows slam down. *The hells I will.*

This time, I welcome the burn of anger—the same anger that hit me in Mt. Ynferno. I may have done horrible things to the Devourers that day, and consigned Bene to death, but I got the job done. I'm more than happy to do it again.

A dangerous smile stretches across my face. "I should warn you, killing me is the wrong way to go. If Eidolon wants his mother released, he needs both me *and* Tabra to do it. It took twins wielding sand and soul to trap them. It takes the same to free them."

"*Lies*," he snarls. The knife digs deeper, slipping into my flesh.

I wince but hold my ground. "Eidolon couldn't make it work with just my sister last time," I point out. "There was a reason."

He hesitates, then, "Seven hells." Recognition that I'm telling the truth fills those two little words.

Good. Choke on that, asshole.

"Fine. I'll bring it all down myself."

Shadows bind my body, the same way they contained me in Tropikis, and he steps back, dropping the knife he took from my sheath and aiming his hands where shadow meets my sand wall in front of us.

My first instinct is to tap into Eidolon's power. But what if it calls the king to me? What if he takes me over and makes me help the thing inside Reven? Or what if I get into a shadow-pissing match with this guy?

The only thing I can think to do is put him in glass so he can't get out. I turn my palm against my thigh, hiding the light, and start drawing sand to the base of the tower.

A sliver of unfiltered sunlight shoots through the crack he makes between the dome and the wall, and he widens it, focus fully diverted and his power concentrated on what he's doing.

My strike comes from the gut. A blast of power.

Only, sand isn't the only thing that hits Reven's body—it's ice. Vos's ice.

I startle enough to lose my grip on my power. The sand falls to the floor with a hiss of sound, but the ice keeps coming. Too fast for the ghost controlling Reven to stop it.

He tries.

Shadow shoots out from him, but I risk it and knock it back, Eidolon's power a spike of cold through me that is *only* his power. I use it long enough to give Vos time to cover Reven in ice and to release the bonds around me, then shut it off and run to the edge of the tower.

Vos stands on the ground below. The instant he sees my face, he blows out a relieved breath. "Thank Allusian!"

I look back at the ice block. "You didn't kill him?"

Vos shakes his head. "I left air to breathe. Not sure how long it'll hold him, though. What happened?"

"Ghost of Eidolon."

Vos's face creases in frustration. "Can you get it out of him?"

I can't even get the non-ghost shards of Eidolon out of *myself*. Not to mention calling the king down on me without even trying.

He's been busy shadowing armies from Tyndra, but he's got to be done with that now, right? So where is he?

Vos jerks his gaze above my head and recoils just as a flicker of movement catches my eye. I spin around to see the dome crawling with shadow souls like maggots on a carcass. One slips through. Another one drops down farther into the city. And then another. They're not breaking our protective barrier, though. They figured out how to get past it, melting into it, forming a dark puddle, then falling out of the bottom like rain.

Can Reven's parasite control them from inside the ice?

A boom followed by a series of screams has me spinning back to the battle. Below, Vos swears and takes off into the fray. I track the direction he's headed. Hakan's lightning flashes, over and over, right in the middle of a mass of shadow soldiers.

A quick scan of the entire battlefield shows me we're losing. I can see it in the desperation of the fight. Because shadow soldiers don't die. They disappear only to reappear somewhere else.

We need help.

"Scoria!" I yell. We haven't heard from her since the Shadowood. I don't even know if she can hear me, let alone get here. "Basalt!"

Nothing.

"Scoria! The souls are here. Missing souls. Come get them!"

Still nothing, and more shadows are getting into the city. Tabra's there. She's got fighters around her, but Eidolon will be looking for her.

I have to get to her. Reven can't take me. I look at the distance from the top of the tower where I stand to the ground. A jump from here is doable but could go wrong. I don't need more going wrong.

"Cain!" Pella screams.

I whip around, my gaze flitting around the battlefield until I find him through all the chaos. He's fighting five shadow soldiers alone, but he doesn't see the Tyndran running at him from behind, sword raised.

In an instant, I know we'll never get to him in time. Pella and I both shout a warning, but Tziah is suddenly there.

She shoves Cain out of the way and opens her mouth. Too late.

The Tyndran skewers her through with his sword, lifting her off her feet.

70

SHADOWS, SHADOWS EVERYWHERE

A roar of a single voice rises above the cacophony and ice blasts through the fighting, slamming the Tyndran away.

Vos. I can't see him, but I know it's him.

Cain is on the Tyndran soldier in an instant. He stabs a knife through the soldier's neck, falling with the man to the ground, pinned under the soldier's weight. The shadow soldiers swarm over them.

A spear of ice slices through them, then splits, like two arms spreading wide, violently forcing everything away from Cain and Tziah.

Riding a wave of ice, Vos slides to where they are. He drops beside Tziah, who is lying on her side, her body twitching. Vos checks her over frantically, and I see the instant he knows she's going to die. Loss sweeps over his face. His lips form the sounds of her name.

No. Mother Nova, no. Not her.

Tziah tries to lift her head, but I don't think she can, and maybe she says something, because he scoops her closer. Then he looks at Cain, who has already extracted himself from under the soldier's body and taken up a defensive position over them, and Cain, grim faced, nods.

Then, like he's given up all hope, Vos lays down beside Tziah, face-to-face and takes her hand. I should have known he would never let her face death alone. Not even on a battlefield surrounded by death and impossible odds. Not after all they've been to each other.

Pella plows through the fighters, dodging swords and felling soldiers with shots from her bow until she gets to Cain and helps him stand over Vos.

I grip the edge of the roof wall, wanting so desperately to be there with them. Vos's lips move as he talks to Tziah. I don't look away even though it hurts down to my bones to watch.

Tziah.

The best of us. The sweetest of us.

Her twitching slows as her struggle ends.

Hakan sprints around the edge of the ice, fighting his way to them, and drops to one knee beside Tziah but I know he's too late. He bows his head, covering his face with one hand.

Meanwhile, Pella and Cain are struggling to keep the growing swarm of shadow soldiers off them. She shouts something over her shoulder that I can't hear. Vos doesn't react.

Hakan jumps to his feet and goes off, blasting lightning at anything that moves. But they're still outnumbered, and Vos still isn't moving. They're fodder for the afterlife if something doesn't change.

I have no choice. I can't watch them die.

I call the king's power forward, the purple light of my palms reflecting off what's left of the shadow dome in front of me.

I focus on a single shadow soldier. I can feel him. I try to stop him, but nothing happens, and more are coming. Then one—not the one I'm focused on—just…disappears?

Yanking my hands close, I look down at them. Was that me?

"I'm here," a familiar voice says behind me.

I whirl to find Scoria standing on the ground, leaning over the tower I'm on—probably having flattened an entire house.

The relief that bursts through me is like taking a breath after being underwater too long.

"What happened to him?" she asks. She's frowning, I think, at Reven's frozen form.

Inside the ice I can see darkness swirling. He's trying to get out.

We don't have time to deal with him until he becomes a problem again. "Help them."

Scoria wastes no time freezing the shadow fighters clamoring to get to my friends. Cain lowers his sword, looking at Pella, who lets up on her bow only slightly as they assess the immobile shadow soldiers.

"Can you take them away?"

I hear the grind of rock on rock and assume she's shaking her head. "They can't be taken to the afterlife in their current form," Scoria says. "You have to turn them first."

"Damn."

Pella fires an arrow through one that Scoria is holding and the thing disappears. Seeing that, she and Cain plow through the rest. They just show up somewhere else on the field.

Goddess damn those things.

"Can you freeze them all?"

"No," Scoria says, her voice straining from just these.

Hellfires.

No choice. "We do it in groups," I say.

I get set yet again, praying to Allusian and Aryd that Eidolon stays away. Before I can draw on his power, a sudden rumbling pushes up through the ground, vibrating beneath my feet, softly at first, but then with growing violence. I search the field and then farther away. Is that…another army?

The trembling worsens. It builds until I have to hold onto the wall of the tower to stay upright.

The fighters on the field pause, looking around with confusion at first, but then with growing fear.

"What's happening?" I hear one of them yell.

A Tyndran soldier points to the sky. I can't hear what he shouts, but I look up and my heart drops to the bottom of my feet. The sun looks like a slivered crescent moon now. The eclipse is overtaking us. This can only be one thing.

"The Alignment," I hear myself say out loud.

71

THE ALIGNMENT

"I have to get to the throne room," I yell at Scoria. "Now."

The giantess doesn't so much as blink, just touches me. The last thing I see before we disappear is Reven, still encased in ice.

We reappear in the throne room, which is barely tall enough to hold the giantess, and I gasp at the sight that greets us.

The goddess of death.

Scoria takes one look at Allusian, standing beside my sister in the center of the dais, and if obsidian could lose color, she does. "Mistress," she whispers, then goes down on one knee hard enough to crack the marble floor. "We have been searching for you."

Allusian hurries down the steps to where Scoria kneels, putting her hand to the giantess's face. "I know, my friend. I've missed you."

Scoria makes some kind of grinding noise that could be a swallow. "What do you wish of me?"

"Keep that army of shadows off of us."

"I'll keep doing what I can," Scoria promises, then she's gone.

"You're here?" I demand. "You're *here*? We're *dying* out there!" I point an accusing finger in the direction of the desert where the battle still rages, the cacophony of it audible even from the palace.

"A regrettable necessity," Allusian says. Totally emotionless.

The light darkens around us, and she glances toward the moonhole. "Get ready."

Though I don't agree with the emotionless part, the logic of what she's saying is right. We release the goddesses and it's over. That's always been the key.

This sparkling, black and gold broken room seems an appropriate place to stop Eidolon's evil for good.

"Meren!" Tabra, still standing on the dais with Achlys at her side, holds her hand out to me. I hurry to her, twining our fingers together, both of us holding on for dear life. We're about to make the impossible happen…hopefully without dying.

"Eidolon will come." Allusian folds her hands before her. "I can't do much against his power."

I startle, turning to stare at her. "What? Why? You're a *goddess*."

Her eyes glint with bitter anger. "The Devourers still have pieces of my heart, and my *sister*…" She snarls the word. "Was smart enough to feed them the part of me that is light and life. The part that could hold off the shadows she also wields. Darkness is my weakness. For now."

Which means she can't kill Eidolon or stop him by using his powers against him, and it also means she can't stop the shadow army. No wonder she sent Scoria back out.

We are so screwed. "How am I supposed to hold off the king *and* release the goddesses at the same time?"

And maybe hold off Reven. Vos said the ice would only contain him so long, and the darkness was already swarming inside. I don't mention that part.

Allusian flicks a glance at me. "The most I can do is send him away and buy you time. After that it's up to you."

Up to me? I try not to show the colossal doubt trying to crush me. We've fought Eidolon before. Me and Reven both. Alone and together, we lost every time. Even Scoria came off worse against him. I'll lose.

"Do all goddesses leave the hard work to the mortals?" I grumble to Tabra under my breath.

She doesn't so much as crack a smile.

"It is almost time." Allusian looks back up through the moonhole. "Where are the amulets?"

Achlys walks around us and pulls the necklaces, with their glittering glass in the colors of Aryd's desert sands, from a deep pocket she sewed into her skirts.

Allusian's brows snap down in a scowl that she directs at me and Tabra. "You gave them to a Vexillium?"

I wasn't told, but I already know why. It's so patently obvious.

"For exactly that reason," Tabra says. "Those who wield power would never suspect that the person charged with protecting something so precious and vital is someone they consider weak."

"And we trust her above all others," I add.

Allusian says nothing to that, just points at the floor at our feet. "Place them there."

Achlys spreads them out before me and Tabra, then she moves closer and presses a soft, sweet kiss on Tabra's lips. "If anything happens, we'll find each other in the next life."

I stare wide-eyed as they share a long look of love and fear before Achlys returns to the side of the room.

"The next life?" I whisper to Tabra.

Her smile is everything I love about my sister—innocence, love, and unadulterated happiness even as we prepare to face the worst this world can throw at us. "Achlys and I bonded last night."

Breath snags in my throat. I want to throw my arms around her, around them both, and share that happiness with them.

But I can't, because the darkness in the room is growing fangs, night eating away the daylight, and we don't have time.

"I wish you both a thousand lives of joy." I grab Tabra's hand and squeeze. "Just promise me you'll look for me in those next lives, too."

I can't imagine walking through life without her.

"Start when I tell you," Allusian says.

Tabra and I both sober.

"The Alignment will enhance your powers," Allusian points out. "But it won't last long. Minutes at most. You must be ready for them."

I don't have time to ask what that last part means.

Both Tabra and I raise our hands. My palms glow a cheery yellow and Tabra's a regal hue of deep purple. Both colors feel wrong today, as if there shouldn't be anything cheery or regal about this situation.

Focus, Meren.

These powers have been passed down through generations of twins who gave their lives to protect our line and our dominion, bringing us to this moment. Finally.

"Now," Allusian says with all the calm authority of a goddess.

"But not these." Eidolon appears in a swirl of shadow. Five of the six amulets lift into the air on a hook made of darkness.

I take a step toward him, only Tabra's hold on my hand pulls me up short.

Allusian snaps her fingers and Eidolon disappears. The amulets drop back to the ground with *tinks* of metal and glass as they hit the marble.

She said she could send him away. How far? How long do we have before he shadows himself back here?

The darkness becomes all-consuming.

"Now!" Allusian yells. "Release them now!"

Our powers cast an eerie light over the room, as together, Tabra and I get to work.

Tabra awakens the goddesses within, a glow immediately igniting within each amulet, lighting the different-colored glass from the inside and sending a rainbow of color over the dais.

Forcing myself to only one thought is maybe the hardest thing I've ever had to do, knowing everything that's going on outside this room, everything that's coming for us. I start by blocking out all those things, until my focus is only on the glass of a single amulet. First, I try to shatter it, to break it, but it doesn't give way. I've already used so much power today. I can feel the drag on my body. With every breath I take, I wait for the Shadows to take advantage of that weakness and stop me. For Eidolon to take me over. Is Allusian keeping him too busy?

The door bangs open and Hakan runs in, his eyes searching the corners of the room before landing on us. Pella sent him to us. I know she did.

"Eidolon?" he demands.

"It will take some time for him to shadow back from where I sent him," Allusian tells him.

He nods. "I'll be ready."

"Hurry," Tabra whispers to me.

"I can't break it," I whisper back.

"Do the reverse of how you'd make it," Allusian instructs.

Right. The reverse.

Like I do when I wield shadow, I close my eyes and picture in my mind what that looks like. I imagine each individual step, the glass morphing from its cool solid form to warmth, to something hot and malleable.

"It's working," Achlys says, her soft voice drifting around me.

I open my eyes and sure enough the amulets—all six now floating in the air before me— are glowing. Not from the inside, but molten red-gold on the outside. The metal filigrees someone else made to hold them on their chains melts away like liquid under the heat, dropping to the ground in tiny metallic puddles.

Tabra gasps beside me. "I can feel them. The goddesses. They're close."

Allusian hisses. Can she feel them, too? "Keep going."

"Drop!" Hakan shouts.

I grab Tabra and drag her down with me, just in time for a whip of shadow to sweep over our heads, the waft of air over my skin telling me just how close that was. The goddess snaps again, and Eidolon disappears. "That first time should have taken him longer than it did," she warns. "He's become more powerful."

That's what one thousand years will do to an Imperium with nothing but centuries.

Hakan is across the room by the time we jump back to our feet. "We don't have time to screw around like this," he growls.

Tiny bolts of lightning flow like water from his hands, forming a cage that zaps and sizzles around us. The blue-white light it casts…no shadows could ever get through it.

"Finish it," he says.

I focus and tell the sand to reform itself into all its thousands of tiny grains. And, ever so slowly, little bits break off the glowing mold to cool and then hang in the air like stars in the sky.

The darkness begins to ease, turning not so impenetrable.

The last moments of Alignment.

"Faster," Allusian calls out from beyond our cage. "You're running out of time."

I push myself, drawing from the well of power the Alignment is giving me, trying to make the glass breakdown as fast as I can. My body shakes with the effort, but nothing like Tabra, who is still newer to her abilities than I am.

And then she does the unimaginable. Through the cracks and crevices I've made, through the sand still reforming, she draws out a sparkling haze, different and separate from my sand—the essence of the goddesses' souls.

"I can't," she gasps.

I glance at my sister. She's starting to look like death warmed over, eyes sinking into a face hollowing out. She looks like she did when Eidolon's ghost was killing her from the inside.

"You *can*," Allusian says. "Use the Alignment."

But Tabra is shaking her head vehemently. "I don't know *how*."

"Mother goddess," Allusian whispers. Her hands create a series of flowing moves, like a dance, and Aryd's amulet in all its pieces moves through the air until it floats through a gap Hakan makes in our lightning cage to hover between me and Tabra.

That's when I feel her.

The familiar warmth of the goddess who has helped me so many times.

Aryd.

She's here with us. The warmth of her flows through my blood, through my soul. But this time it's different. As if she's helping us channel the Alignment. More power is there for the taking, a deep well of it inside me that seems to rise with each passing second.

"Meren?" Tabra's eyes are wide on mine.

"Keep going." I suck in sharply before pushing myself even harder. More of my sand breaks away while more of the goddesses' souls filter out.

"I won't let this happen!" A hammer of darkness slams down on Hakan's cage with a snap and sizzle of lightning, but it doesn't bend or break under the impact. He does it again.

Allusian does something the next time he brings it down. I see it in the way she moves her hands. The instant the hammer of shadow strikes the cage, Hakan's lightning shoots through it, like it did through the water of the lake deep under the Tyndran mountain. Eidolon blows back so hard that when he hits the marble wall, I hear the way his head cracks against it before he slumps to the ground in a heap.

The warmth of Aryd turns hotter. I welcome the sear of

her through my body. It's like that heat is burning away the parts of me I don't need and lighting the wells of power inside me on fire.

The warmth disappears and Aryd's trapped soul floats to hover in front of Allusian. Allusian looks at the light that is her sister, then at us, and closes her eyes, almost in resignation. Then I feel it. True power. A rush, like when Reven brings me pleasure, filling every crack and crevice of me. Allusian's power.

And, suddenly, it becomes so easy.

There's no more searing heat like before. This is soft, like butterfly wings.

I splay my fingers, and the rest of the molten amulets disintegrate into sand with a mere thought. I let them drop to the ground in a sparkling hiss.

Tabra takes the misty souls of the goddesses hovering in front of us and reforms them. Like the light, the mist grows into six body-shaped masses, floating in the air like stardust. Those forms take on shape and distinction until we can see them in clear detail.

And it's terrible.

The goddesses stand in the shadowy room the way I think they must have looked the day they were trapped. Mouths painfully, grotesquely open, shock and fury contorting their features.

Then Tabra screams, the sound like a tear in the fabric of the world, but she doesn't stop. Not until the goddesses stand before us, whole and alive.

Dazed, they all look around—up to the heavens through the moon hole, taking in the mostly empty room, or looking down at their own bodies. Stark silence settles over the room as the moons and sun break free from their alignment, and one by one the goddesses focus on us.

On Allusian.

"They told us you were dead," one says.

I've never heard Aryd's voice, never seen her face beyond the carvings and etchings in the temples, but I *know* this goddess. Statuesque, velvety dark eyes, deep ebony skin that glitters like the Obsidian Desert, and dressed in flowing, soft gold.

I know it's her.

Allusian's smile is sour. "No, Sister. I'm not dead."

Stark blue-green eyes, so like Reven's, gleam in a pale face with striking cheekbones. Tyndra—no doubt in my mind who that is—tips her head, eyeing Allusian. "That was our first mistake."

72

NOT OVER YET

When I was a little girl visiting Cain in the desert, I accidentally got between a pack of wild dogs and the small antelope they'd decided was dinner. I was the same size as the antelope.

That's what this feels like.

Power vibrates the air like it's gathering to unleash, and heavens help anyone in its path.

"You have a choice," Allusian tells her sisters. "Leave here now. If you do, I will assume you wish for peace between us. You may return to ruling your dominion and all is forgiven."

Tyndra's mouth curls with disdain. "Do you truly believe any of us will—"

Mariana—easily distinguished by burnished red curls and a dress of bright peacock blue with flowers depicted in pearls and abalone across the hems of the flowing sleeves and skirt—disappears in a blink.

Like it's punctuating her leaving, there's a massive boom outside. They're still fighting, still dying out there.

We've already lost Tziah.

I glance at Tabra, then Achlys and Hakan. We should leave the goddesses to their business and go help our friends.

I'm just not quite sure when the right moment for that is, though. It's not like I can bow my way out and say, "We'll get out of your way..."

"What about you?" Allusian asks, looking at Aryd.

Aryd glances at the goddess beside her, who stares back. Blond hair intricately pinned up, medium-brown skin that make her striking green eyes stand out, and dressed similarly to Istrella—Wildernyss, I'm guessing. Together, they both disappear.

"Cowards," Tyndra bites out.

The day is slowly regaining its brightness, so I can see the lines bracketing her mouth as she says this. Beside her, the goddess with glittering dark eyes, a stripe of distinct tattoos down her bronzed arms and legs, and clothing that reminds me of the Rites of Xathena in Tropikis, snorts her own derision. "She's alone and there are three of us."

"Are you sure of that?" Allusian asks.

Tyndra's shoulders stiffen sharply. "Our mother may have given you more than us, but even you aren't strong enough to take us on. You failed last time, and you will again."

I glance between the goddesses. Do they see that she's not entirely whole yet?

Allusian's smile is taunting. "Are you sure those are the numbers on both sides?"

Tyndra frowns, then looks at Savanah, her twin in every way, but dressed in the fashion of her dominion. "Sister?" Tyndra demands.

Savanah's chin wobbles. "I'm sorry."

Then she's gone.

I don't know if Tyndra felt it coming or just saw her chance, but fire erupts from her hands, going through the spot where Savanah was standing a moment ago and straight for Allusian. But Allusian disappears, and the flames slam into the heavy throne on the dais, throwing it backward and shattering it against the wall, leaving a crack running nearly to the roof.

Hakan's cage takes the brunt of the debris that blasts our way, but Tabra and I duck just the same.

Before we have a chance to do so much as peek out from where we're crouched, Allusian reappears. She holds her palms to the skies and spikes of rock erupt from the floor everywhere outside of our protective bubble.

Wait. Rock and land are within Aryd's power. Aren't they?

Like Allusian just did, Tropikis and Tyndra disappear before they can be skewered.

Immediately, Allusian assumes a defensive position, slowly spinning as she looks around her, waiting for their next attack to come.

The goddesses are at war, and we're in the way.

"We need to get out of here," I whisper. Achlys and I both slide an arm around my sister, helping her stay upright.

Allusian spins and reaches through thin air, just in time for Tyndra to appear right where her hand is, and she snags her sister by the neck. Tyndra's pale skin starts to char immediately, as if death itself is creeping out from where Allusian is touching her.

Tyndra claws at the hand at her throat, gasping, eyes bulging.

In the next instant, Tropikis appears, and water blasts from her. Only without releasing Tyndra, Allusian flicks a finger, and the water hits an invisible wall, splitting around her like a wave around a rock outcropping. Half of it comes at us, and with a grunt, Hakan drops his cage. Water and lightning don't mix. I saw that much in Mt. Ynferno.

Instinct has me putting a shield of sand between us and the water, which cuts off abruptly, falling to the ground with a splash.

Tropikis's voice sounds from behind my shield. "What in the name of—?"

I drop the sand to the ground only to find a violent swirl of shadow on the other side. It rises then falls, and Eidolon is standing there, his face twisted with hatred.

But he's not looking at us—he's looking at the goddesses. Tyndra stares at her son and her lips form his name silently. Then her own expression descends to furious satisfaction. "Kill her."

With a jerk, Eidolon immediately throws a lasso of darkness around Allusian.

But before he can pull her off his mother, Hakan and I blast sand and lightning at him.

Except a scythe of shadow cuts through both our powers before we can free Allusian. And when it swings out of sight, Reven is standing there.

Between us and Eidolon.

He's covered in shards of ice that cling to his clothes and hair, rage forming his face into a snarl that is not the man I know. It's the ghost of Eidolon still inside him.

Refusal blazes through me in a cold that rivals Eidolon's power as I stare at my bondmate.

I can't fight him. I won't.

"Goddess help me," I whisper.

Because I don't think that ghost is going to give me a choice.

73

THE TRUEST OF BONDS

As if his appearance unleashes them, the goddesses and Eidolon descend on Allusian. I don't have a chance to see how, because Reven flings one hand in the air, and a bulwark of darkness barrels our way, threatening to crush us into the rock wall at our backs.

No. Not us. *Me*.

I do the only thing I can—I let go of Tabra and tap into Eidolon's power, then burrow a tunnel through Reven's weapon, the ground shaking as it hits behind us.

"He's going to kill you!" the Shadows shout as one.

Already he's flinging another, then another, and I manage to bore through each one, though I'm barely keeping up. Meanwhile, with booms and flashes and movement faster than I can track, the goddesses and Eidolon fight around us.

The crackle of Hakan's lightning sounds from directly behind me. Using me to hide what he's doing? Only he can't use it on Reven. He'll kill him. "Don't."

"When I say," Hakan says in a low voice, "step as close to me as you can without touching me."

He's going to put the cage around us again.

"Three…" he says.

I tunnel through another and another.

"Two…"

"No," Tabra suddenly snarls in a voice I've never heard from her before.

Reven's body jerks, going strangely stiff, chin up, legs together, arms pinned to his sides. Even his jaw looks frozen in place. Only his eyes move, flicking around the room like he's searching for the source of this new attack.

Then Reven's jaw cranks open as if forced. It looks like he's yelling but instead of sound, a hazy cloud curls out of his mouth like smoke.

She's pulling his soul out.

"Stop!" I yell.

Tabra's going to kill him. Despite the chaos of the goddesses fighting around us, I see Eidolon pause to look at what Tabra's doing…and smile.

No way is that asshole going to get what he wants.

"He's not Reven," Tabra says. Tears are thick in her voice. She doesn't want to do this, but she will if she has to.

I whirl to face my sister. "One of Eidolon's ghosts is inside him."

Her gaze darts between me and Reven, brows drawing down. If anyone knows what that's like, Tabra does. "Can you get it out of him?" she asks.

Reven tried with her and failed. But Eidolon was able to, so I know it's possible.

"Let me try," I beg her. "If I don't…kill him." I have to choke out those last two words.

"Do it," she says. "Fast. He's fighting me."

And she's already drained from releasing the goddesses.

In the next second, Allusian hits Tyndra in the chest with a beam of blue light. No sparking. No sizzling. Just pure light.

Desperation whirls me back around, and without so much as a blink of hesitation, I rush at Reven and put my hands to his face.

"This time I know what I'm doing, you bastard."

These ghosts are made of shadow, and Scoria made *sure* I

know what to do with those.

I send *my* shadows—the part of me that is and always has been Reven and not the bloody king—searching. Sneaking inside his being through what's left of the bond between me and Reven, like threading a needle.

Then I do what I saw Eidolon do with my sister the day he pulled his parasitic ghost from her body. I shove shadow down my bondmate's throat. Reven's blue eyes bulge and he gags, his body trying to thrash against the restraints Tabra and I both have around him.

I feel around his insides, but all I sense is darkness. Reven chokes. I'm going to kill him if I don't hurry. I slam my eyes shut and focus the way Scoria taught me. I picture the souls contained in him like different lights rather than simple darkness. Suddenly the image in my mind is as clear as if I were truly looking at it.

The darkness around me is so complete that without the lights from those shards of soul, I'll drown in it. I look everywhere, searching.

And then I see it.

A brilliant white light is so far down I only see it as a pinprick, but I know without question that it is Reven.

My light in the darkness.

I consider pulling him up to help, but I don't have enough time.

A boom rocks me from the outside. Rocks us both. But I can't stop to find out what's happening around us.

I focus on Reven's light. If he's down here… I look the other way. Sure enough, there's the ghost. His light is a muddy brownish-green, like the excrements of someone who suffers from the bowel sickness.

I cast my shadows over that poison like a scoop. *"Got you."*

I open my eyes and I'm in my own body again, solid shadow shoved down my lover's throat. Reven's eyes have rolled back and his body isn't fighting anymore, arms and head limp, held up only by my shadows. Tabra's let him go now. I can feel it.

I can also see why. Eidolon is suspended in midair, arms and legs splayed, with fear in his eyes as she tries to suck out his soul. But through the curse connecting us, I can feel his power gathering, and gathering, and gathering.

I need to move fast.

Yanking hard, I pull my net of darkness up and out of Reven as fast as I can, and with it, the ghostly soul.

Darkness erupts from Eidolon like a physical force.

I brace myself, only suddenly Aryd is there, brightness exploding from her palms and forming a shield around us—the light of the moons that she wields. The darkness ricochets back at Eidolon as the three goddesses continue throwing power at each other. All four of them tumble across the floor.

Aryd's across the room in a heartbeat, joining their fight as they regain their feet.

"Scoria!" I call, praying to Allusian that the giantess can get to me fast.

The thing in my net goes wild, fighting and clawing and screaming to be released like a feral sandcat. At the same time, Reven pitches forward and spits what at first looks like blood, except it's black, reminding me of the shadow souls that took over the Shadowood—a sticky tar-like substance. And it just keeps coming.

"Scoria!" I yell again, then I call for her mate. "Basalt!"

"I am here, young Imperium."

Without a word, I shove the ghost at her. She takes him and disappears again, and the shout of a remnant of one of Eidolon's past lives cuts off abruptly.

"Keep them off us," I toss over my shoulder to Hakan as I release my hold on Eidolon's power. The cold recedes with such force my head feels like it's splitting open, but I ignore that to rush to Reven's side. He's still purging the shiny, sticky darkness.

I put a hand to his back. "What can I do?"

He holds up a hand, shaking his head.

"What's happening? Is it the Shadows?"

Another shake of his head. Panic starts to gnaw at me.

He heaves one more time, then takes a long, shuddering breath. Is it all gone?

"Meren."

His voice bursts into my mind as he surges upright, and I am finally gazing into the brilliant turquoise of his eyes.

"It's me," he says through harsh breaths. "All of me." Then his voice rings in my head. *"All of us. You and me."*

I gasp. Just like the night we were bound to each other in the temple in Tropikis, heat coalesces in my core, rises inside me, then bursts outward. It fizzes through my insides to come out of my skin, not just where the thread the priestess connected us with touched my arm, but everywhere. I'm…glowing. So is Reven. And like before, the burn is almost unbearable. I manage to swallow my whimpers, until with no warning, the pain subsides, leaving only a sense of completeness. Wholeness.

Our bond.

It's no longer broken. It's whole again. Perfect.

Reven yanks me into his arms, holding me so tight I can't breathe. And I don't care.

"How?" I ask. Or wheeze, more accurately.

"Our bond wasn't severed," he says into my hair with a voice that shakes. "It was—"

"Poisoned." We both think the word together.

I can picture the glittering lines of our bond in my head, the blackened ends that looked as though they'd been burned. They weren't burned, they were buried under… I glance at the splatter of toxic darkness on the floor. Under that. Because of the ghost Eidolon infected Reven with.

"I'm sorry." He's still holding me tight. "I'm sorry. I didn't know I carried that—"

I put a finger to his lips and rush my own words. "How could you?" I gaze into the face of my true bondmate. All of him here with me. Finally. And what's more important, this time I *believe* the finally.

Reven stares at me, then kisses the tip of my finger and we smile at each other.

This.

Reven.

He is worth living for, more than anything else in my life. More than the legions fighting on our behalf, the dominion given into our hands to protect, all of Nova even.

They're worth fighting for. Even dying for.

He is worth living for.

"Let go of my son, you bitch," Tyndra snarls.

74

SACRIFICE

Reven and I both whip around in time to see Tyndra's fire catch Aryd in the chest. My goddess loses the grip she had on Eidolon as she is pushed across the room. But she doesn't fall. Instead, she digs in sandaled feet and fires back with sand. The two forces meet in the middle, like a duel, where the sand flash-heats, melting to the ground in molten red.

Before Eidolon can attack, Reven is on his feet. Even through all the battles and all the setbacks we've faced together, I've never seen him so coldly furious. It rolls off in him waves, manifesting into shadow that swirls away from him in spinning vortexes.

With deadly calm, he makes a fist and a sledgehammer made of pure darkness slams into the king from the side. Eidolon shadows away only to reappear in the room, and the pools of darkness in the corners crawl toward us at his command.

"Stop," Reven says the word simply. At his command, the darkness crawls back to its corners.

Eidolon's features contort with thwarted fury, but I don't think he's realized yet that he's facing something different now.

He's facing a version of himself.

Reven disappears from beside me to reappear in front of Eidolon in a swirl of pitch-colored mist and takes him by the arms. The king jerks once, twice, then his eyes go wide with visible fear. "Impossible," he says.

Reven's smile is pure Shadowraith, and his emotions, open to me now, are nothing but determination. "I don't have anything holding me back now."

No Shadows. No ghosts. And he remembers. Everything.

Hands still gripping Eidolon by the arms, Reven starts to pull. Eidolon's physical form stays in place while a ghostly version of him appears, stretching wider and wider as Reven seems to try to tear his soul in two. The shadow of the king starts to rend at the top, a jagged split in the dark form ripping down the length of his ghostly face.

Eidolon screams a sound that makes me clap my hands over my ears as I stare in fascinated horror at what my bondmate is doing. More Shadows rise up out of the king, as if the ones he managed to get out of me are trying to escape.

The king's cries cut off abruptly, and he strikes Reven in the chest with his fist instead of darkness. It's enough. The ghostly forms snap back into place, leaving only Eidolon standing there in the flesh.

Reven's lips curl in disdain.

Don't follow me.

Then, before I can stop him, he shadows both of them out of the room.

"Reven!" I yell.

"No," Tabra calls out in a threadbare voice from where she's kneeling on the ground with Achlys beside her.

Out of nowhere, Wildernyss reappears. She glances between her sisters who are locked in one-one-one battles, where none of them seems to be finding an advantage.

"The battle outside is bad," she says. I think to us, although she doesn't look our way. "Go deal with that. Leave us to this."

With a flick of her hands, we're no longer standing in the throne room. All of us—Hakan, Tabra, Achlys, and I—are at the base of the wall, the part I turned to glass, facing the fighting.

In the distance, I see a burst of ice among the chaos. Vos.

He's fighting again.

"There!" Hakan points, then takes off to join in the battle.

That's when I see Pella. Side by side, she and Cain are covered in dirt and blood and sweat. She yanks an arrow out of a felled soldier and fires it off before swinging her bow to bludgeon another in the head, all as Cain drowns three other Tyndran soldiers in a floating bubble of water.

The goddesses are at war but so are we.

I don't know why I thought releasing the goddesses would end it all. More fool me. I grab Tabra and pull her up to her shaky feet, then wrap an arm around her, holding her tight as I slap my hand on the glass of my own wall and pull up the portal in Wildernyss. I shove her through to the other side. Achlys, smart and quick, jumps through, too.

"Stay safe. I love you."

There needs to be at least one Queen of Aryd still standing when this settles.

She doesn't have a chance to respond before I shut the portal down and start using sand as a weapon.

As fast as I can, I spray sand in the face of a Tropikan fighter, even as I skewer a shadow soldier. Then I rip the ground right out from under the feet of several more Tropikans and use it to bury them.

A massive boom ricochets all the way to where we stand. I jerk around to see onyx and obsidian chunks flying straight up into the sky. The throne room?

As they fall back down, a streak of white flares across the skies. Closer and closer it comes until I can see white flames lifting off something that glows so iridescent it hurts to look at it. It hits the city and the explosion reaches into the skies the same way the throne room's rooftop did, followed by the distinct crackle of fire.

Then another smaller streak appears in the skies, followed by another, then another.

Is Tyndra bringing the stars themselves down on us?

Out of nowhere, angry, roiling storm clouds build over the city and winds whip at us. Wildernyss must be the one wielding something this terrifying. The winds hit us like a wall and push all the humans fighting on the ground around until we all have to drop to our stomachs to avoid being picked up or flung.

"Soldiers of my shadow army," Eidolon's voice booms throughout the battlefield, coming from I don't know where. "Kill the Arydian queens!"

Oh fuck.

I spin around, searching for Reven and the king, but don't see them. Cain, Pella, and Hakan all whip their gazes in my direction, but I only catch a glimpse of their horror-filled faces before shadow souls descend on me like sand dunes shifting to bury me alive. I pull out my knives but they're not trying to kill me. Hands that feel both sticky and as real as flesh grab me all over to lift me and carry me away.

But where?

It feels like forever and yet only seconds before they let me go and draw back, surrounding me. Breathing hard, I scramble to my feet, and that's when I realize that they've dragged me to the other side of the fighting, far away from my friends, from help.

I'm facing part of Eidolon's army of darkness on my own.

I need Scoria to hold them while I turn them back into souls she can take to the burning lands. I can't use Eidolon's power on these things. Not on so many. But Scoria isn't here.

Instead, I reach for my power over sand. I'll have to be fast for this to work. Feeling in the ground beneath my feet, I heat the grains where they can't see. Where they don't know.

And I watch them. Wait.

The attack, when it comes, is fast. But I'm faster. Spears of glass burst from the ground in a circle around me, tilted just right, and the shadow soldiers impale themselves upon the spikes and disappear. But more come.

I unsheathe my knives, ready to defend myself—

A horse plows through the shadows behind me and a man jumps off, sword swinging to take out at least five shadows in one swipe.

"Horus!" I cry out.

I can tell by the blood and dirt covering him that he's been fighting for a while. He has to know that he's signing his death warrant, joining me in the middle of things that can only be sent away but not killed. They'll never stop.

"I'm sorry it took me so long to find you, domina!" he yells over his shoulder as he keeps swinging with deadly accuracy. He's so quick and lethal that the shadows seem to draw back a little, studying him even as they continue to attack.

The shadow soldiers grow more visible as the sun slowly takes back its skies from the moons, which helps. I do what I can. Sand walls. Shifting sands. Spikes and swords of sand. I'd use quicksand but I'm afraid I'd trap myself and Horus by accident.

Horus steps in front of me over and over. I don't bother to tell him not to. I don't have the breath or the time, and I know he'll ignore me anyway.

We can't keep this up forever.

I also know that no one is coming to help us—not because they don't want to, but because they still have the Tyndran and Tropikan armies to fight. Reven is still somewhere facing Eidolon alone. Even with all his memories back to fight, can he take the king?

Desperation wells up, smothered in fear.

I have no choice. Maybe if I can be fast?

I fling out both arms. Purple lights up around us, freezing as many of the shadows near us as I can. Trying to hold onto them, I grab Horus by the arm.

Eidolon appears in front of me so suddenly I don't even have time to register that I'm facing a different disaster before the king grabs me by the throat. Darkness swirls, not taking us away but lifting us into the air.

It's impossible to miss the shape he's in. This bastard has hardly had to lift a finger before to defeat us, but now his hair is disheveled, and his shirt is torn, blood seeping into the material in a crimson stain. And there is a wild look in his eyes.

Reven did that to him.

Where is Reven?

Even as my head pounds from the loss of air cut off by his grip, which I claw at with my hands, I ask myself why he didn't just shadow me away himself.

And then I look down and I know why.

The shadow soldiers converge. Horus is overrun.

75

ANNHIALATION

As Horus disappears from sight, Scoria shows up before us, but the king sends darkness punching through her. The giantess collapses to the ground with soldiers from all the armies scattering to get out of her way and the upheaval of sand that fills the air.

Did he kill her?

He can't, can he? Not like that. Not so easy. She's immortal.

Reven suddenly appears from wherever he'd taken Eidolon to before. I feel him before I see him. A swirl of darkness surrounds him, holding him up, and even from this angle and through fuzzy vision, I can see there's not a mark on him, unlike the king.

He throws his arms out wide, and the shadow soldiers on Horus lift their heads on a collective, eerily silent scream before they disappear without a sound or a trace.

"No!" I choke out around Eidolon's grip.

Reven was too late.

Horus is on his knees, blades made of darkness impaling him from all sides, propping his body upright. Reven's pain lances through me, only adding to my own.

The weapons turn to haze, evaporating away, but Horus is still there, still kneeling, eyes on me.

Eidolon jerks me closer, contorted face in mine. "You're next."

"No," Reven snarls, shadowing so close, I can feel his breath. "She's not."

He grabs Eidolon by the shoulder and they both vanish.

And I fall.

I have enough sense to pull sand up to meet me, slowing and softening my descent to the ground. When I land, I roll, but even as I'm gasping for breath, I push to my feet and run to Horus.

As I reach him, he collapses to his side. I yank sand over the top of us, flash heating it to form a dome of glass that'll keep the shadow soldiers off him. We can't last long in here, though. Not if we want to keep breathing.

"Horus." I scoot around to where his head is. "Horus, please."

His eyes flicker open as something strikes the glass.

I ignore the sound. "I'm here," I say. "I'm here."

He opens his mouth but makes no sound.

Trying with everything in me not to cry, I take his hand in mine. "You have earned your honor this day, Horus of the Lazuli Wanderers."

I think maybe his face eases. Just a little. "Lana?" The word comes out strangled, barely recognizable.

I nod, knowing what he's asking. "I will provide for your sister. You have my word."

He swallows and tries to speak again, but even as that last try burbles in his throat, his face goes slack, eyes empty.

Gone.

He's gone.

I drop my head to our joined hands, grief rocking through me as I see my lost friends' faces in my mind. Tziah. Vida. Horus. Maybe Scoria.

All gone.

I can't stay here with him. I know I can't. But how can I leave him?

A hand wraps around my ankle and jerks me down, dragging me under the glass, away from Horus's body. We pop out on the other side, and I flip over to find a shadow fighter.

I don't get a chance to bring my power forward, though, before he disappears and I pause.

Scoria is standing over me, one hand to the hole in her side, chest heaving like she's having trouble breathing, even though she's made of rock. "Get up, young Imperium," she demands, even as she's picking off more shadow soldiers around us.

I push to my feet and start to do the same. Just to get them away from us. But they're coming faster and faster. We can't keep up.

"We need Allusian," the giantess says without looking at me.

"What?"

"The goddess of death," she reminds me. "If anyone can handle this many, it's her."

Not if she doesn't get the pieces of her heart back from the Devourers. "She's a little busy."

I pick off another shadow, jumping back as I do. We're a little busy, too.

"I don't care how you do it. She can fix this. All of this."

How? Which is when it hits me. The only thing holding Allusian back. I think I can bring it to her. The Devourers have to be close, have to have felt their goddesses.

But our glass walls are keeping them from traveling the Hyades River to the Sea of Terra that the city of Oaesys sits on.

"Hold them off me." I don't wait for Scoria to agree before I aim everything I can of my own power into the skies.

The distinct *snick* of glass cracking reaches my ears.

The glass borders around the entire dominion that Aryd built many millennia ago to protect us from the Devourers in the oceans are impossibly high and have no reflection. Consequently, we've never known if they go straight up and stop, or if they formed a dome over our heads.

Now I know for certain it's the second option.

Another *snick* sounds. When I first learned how to build

portals in the Shadowood, I swear that sound got lodged in my ears.

I yank on my power over sand as hard as I can.

But pulling at it's not enough. I close my eyes, and like I did with the amulets, I picture reversing the process—turning the glass back to tiny grains of sand.

I just need to weaken it. The weight will bring it down once it goes.

Scoria grunts, but nothing has gotten past her yet. I try to work faster, to force the walls to fail faster.

"Come on," I whisper.

"Let me help." My eyes flash open to find Aryd beside me. She reaches toward the heavens, then yanks downward. The protective glass shatters with an explosion of sound, like the skies themselves splinter and fragment.

Aryd goes eerily still, her eyes glassy as if she's seeing something I can't. "Wildernyss," she whispers.

And then she's gone.

It takes me too long to realize that Aryd didn't turn the glass of the dome back to sand. It's coming down on top of us in massive, razor-sharp shards that glint with deadly intent in the sunlight.

I starburst my hands and pray to the mother goddess as I turn as much of the glass into sand as I can. It pelts us hard, and most of the human soldiers raise their arms to protect their eyes.

I know I didn't get them all when a fragment of glass the size of a sacred tree lands in front of us, only a meter away, stabbing into the desert like a dagger in the heart of the dominion. A few more glass pieces hit, splintering, and spraying all around.

Oh goddess. What did I just do to the dominion?

I draw my fingertip over the flesh of my arm, awakening the sparkling lines of my bond to Reven.

Letting the warm fizz of that sensation sink in, I close my eyes and call out to him through it. *"Find me."*

Nothing happens. Given that he tackled Eidolon to some shadowy realm or other, I'm hoping he's not answering because he's also busy.

I'd feel it if it was something worse. Wouldn't I?

"Find me," I call again. *"We need to help Allusian. She's the only one who can stop the shadow army."*

With no warning, no answer, he's suddenly there. The brief glimpse I get of him before he wraps his arms around me and shadows us away, I can see he's still unharmed.

When the darkness dissipates, we're back in the city, and I suck in a horrified breath at the destruction the goddesses have wrought. The throne room and all of the palace-temple has been leveled to the point that I can look across my city from where we are and see where Tyndra's meteorites struck. My city is burning, made worse by Wildernyss's winds.

It's a wasteland.

And Wildernyss lies unmoving in the middle of it.

The land undulates under our feet so violently that Reven and I are thrown to the ground. Before we can get up, vines shoot into the space so fast it's like watching a den of snakes. Tropikis isn't anywhere I can see, but these are from her, that much is obvious. They cover the entire area that used to be the throne room and wrap around Allusian, Wildernyss, and Aryd so fast, only the *shoosh* and creak of the vines and the surprised shouts of the goddesses tell me it's real.

Only, with a burst of power, the vines turn to ash and drop to the ground.

Allusian.

I'm getting shakily to my feet when Reven appears in front of me. I don't even get the chance to blink before he shoots out a hand and grabs Eidolon, darkness still swirling around him from shadowing, by the throat.

"I don't think so," Reven snarls, all things fury.

They disappear again.

A single breath later, something grabs me by the ankle, and, for the second time, I'm dragged away.

"Not again, you bastards!" I shout.

I fight with sand and shadow and everything else I can, even as they drag me out of the palace—the same way Reven did what feels like ages ago when he thought he was kidnapping the new queen of Aryd.

A hundred faces with vague features that still manage to look bloodthirsty, the lust of death in their burning eyes, surround me, come at me, pull me.

That's when a shadow flashes by overhead.

76

TO MY OWN DARKNESS

I jerk my gaze upward just as Cain jumps off Bene's back to land basically on top of me, swinging a spear in a circle and clearing the soldiers that disappear as he strikes them.

My knees threaten to go out from under me as I'm pushing to my feet, elation and shock a burn in my blood. Bene? Bene is here?

I shake my head. "How—"

"Later." Cain only has time for the one word before the shadow soldiers descend on us again, and we're both fighting.

Automatically, Cain and I fall into a rhythm I'd forgotten. A rhythm that he taught me when he schooled me in hand-to-hand combat as children. I didn't realize I missed this part of us until right this second.

In the middle of a battle for our lives.

We move like a dance, circling each other. I keep one hand on his back or his shoulder whenever I can to let him know where I am, even as I'm wielding my sand with the other.

I tap his shoulder, and he immediately plunges his sword into a shadow soldier getting too close. He forces my head down and I spin out from under him and skewer four shadows with a single spear of sand.

"Left!" I call.

Out of the corner of my eye I see him take down a shadow with a rolling tackle. In the same instant, I run my knife through another's neck.

I quickly lose track of how many we take out. They just keep coming.

I catch his eye as I swing under a shadow's blade, and he shoots me a grin that is entirely out of place for the moment. I want to return it. Instead, I snap, "Focus!" and hurl a dagger over his shoulder. He jerks around in time to see the shadow soldier disappear, and the blade drops to the sand.

He chuckles as he scoops it up, tossing it to me. "You've gotten good at that."

Then he looks over my head and any hint of levity disappears from his face. I trust our history and dive into a roll, coming up behind him, knowing he's got whatever was coming at me.

"Hold them off me!"

I don't question it, moving closer to him as the glow of his power reflects off the shadows around us. I'm too busy fighting to see what he's doing. Not until a wall of water slams into the ground in front of him, then splits, circling us and pushing the soldiers back in a rush.

My arms drop to my sides, and I heave in air as he takes care of the threat. He's drawing water from the Sea of Terra on the other side of the city from where we are. I can see the water coming over the shadow dome like a rainbow. I've seen him do more in Tropikis, but that wiped him, but this is still impressive as hells.

"Get ready!" Cain shouts.

"For what?" One look tells me the shadow soldiers are moving through the water, using the darkness it creates naturally.

Cain shoves it out even wider from us.

The movement of darkness overhead is my only warning before Bene comes down on top of the clearing Cain has made and plucks me up. He misses Cain, though, but he must feel that because he doesn't take off. Instead, he drops lower, his sandy wings beating against the buildings. But the soldiers are already breaking through the water and crawling up the walls around us. Spears and weapons made of darkness thrust into Bene and he roars but doesn't fly away. Even without being able to hear him in my head, I know what to do.

I lean through his sandy talons, stretching a hand down to Cain. "Jump!"

He looks at the water one last time, then leaps and his weight about jerks my shoulder from the socket, but I have him. "Go!"

Bene takes off into the skies, and I meet Cain's gaze. "He's alive. How is this possible?"

His gaze skates over my features, even as we grip each other so tightly, and I know he's checking that I'm okay. "No clue, but I was damned glad to see him."

Me, too.

Mother goddess, me too.

"The others?" I grimace. Cain's weight is jamming me up tight against Bene's talons, the sand grinding against my neck and cheek. Maybe we should wait to talk until we're safely on the ground.

"Pella's with—"

Cain's eyes go wide, and almost in the same instant, a sword made of shadow shoves up from his belly and through his open mouth.

That's when I see the shadow soldier clinging to his legs.

My heart lurches, then shrivels when fear twists Cain's features. A sound I didn't ever want to know a human could make rattles deep in his chest, and then—

He lets go.

"Cain!" I flail to grab him, but only grasp air as he drops away through the skies. I know he's already dead before he hits the edge of a building, then tumbles the rest of the way to the ground. I'm too far from him, but I feel and hear the impact all the same.

The battle falls away. Everything falls away.

The day Eidolon took Reven away from me felt something like this. That moment after terrible loss when everything goes quiet inside and around you. As if the entire world takes a breath, bracing for what comes next.

I desperately want to cling to that last moment of peace before the quiet fades and the pain comes rushing in its place, but this…this is more than I can bear.

One of the Shadows breaks through my hold. *"We told you you'd get him killed."*

Those words, the truth of them, forces me to blow past the peace, the world crackling back into stark focus. But on the heels of stark pain, rage hot enough to burn down the world sears through my blood and fills the quiet inside me. Fills the hole left by the man who has been my constant friend and companion almost my entire life. A hole *no one* can fill.

I pull Eidolon's power to me so hard and fast, the ice battles with the fire inside me, all of it swirling to a fevered pitch of energy that can't be contained. The faces of my fallen friends and family, of Omma and Horus and Vida, of Tziah and Cain, of everyone Eidolon has stolen from me in this life, flash through my mind.

We've been reacting to him for too long. Letting him get the better of us too often.

I have enough awareness to shadow away from Bene to an empty place in the sky where I hover—something I've never done before, and yet it comes so easily with the anger coursing through me.

And into that emptiness, I release it *all*.

My head throws back hard on a scream that comes from my soul, from my bones. Pain wrapped in rage drives the shadow that blasts out from me, blanketing the entire world in a darkness so pure it's impenetrable.

Nothing can exist in *this* darkness.

Nothing except me.

I can sense everything around me. Reven is near, searching for me. I can feel him through our bond, but he's not who I'm looking for.

I travel through the void, the nothing, until I get to Eidolon. So easy to find him here, standing on the rubble-strewn palace balcony. All I have to do is follow the iciness of his power that binds us until I appear before him.

This time the king isn't in charge. I fucking am.

His darkness is *mine* now.

I smile coldly. "My turn."

Responding to my will, the darkness disappears from everything except the king who I hold without effort. Only his head and hands can move, and they do, wriggling like the worm he is.

Reven is here, too, now. He takes in the scene, what I'm doing, and…smiles, his satisfaction curling through me and around me. "That's my bondmate."

"You know who will come for us," I warn.

And he nods, in lock step with what I'm planning.

Good. We need to be ready for her.

Holding Eidolon, using his power against him, I bring my own power forward, wielding both at the same time. The sand and glass around me are all I need. I gather it, bringing it close—

Tyndra appears in front of me.

Got you.

My little display was a beacon to her—after all, *she* is where this power over darkness comes from—and now I'm trying to kill her son, who I'm dangling before her like bait.

Bait that caught me a goddess.

She studies me, tipping her head from side to side. "What are you?" she demands. "No Imperium wields two powers without turning into a monster."

I don't get a chance to answer because Tyndra wheels away,

bracing for a hit a second before Aryd manifests out of nothing and slams into her.

Which is when the Sea of Terra *erupts*.

The explosion of water even reaches where I am on the far side of the palace, the debris not hitting me as Reven forms a shield of darkness around us, taking the brunt. The sounds of strikes against his shadow are eclipsed by roars that are just as unmistakable as the forms now towering above the roofs and spires.

Seven heads writhing. Tentacles waving. A razor-sharp horn.

The Devourers are here, very much alive.

The Gorecutter rams into the palace, sending parts of the building and dust into the skies and tumbling down on us, maybe even destroying more of it. I can just make out the Revoker and the Hollow and the Revenant as they crawl their way onto land and head for the city streets. I don't know where the Reverie is, but she's got to be with them.

They bellow their challenges, blasting sound out over the city, but it abruptly cuts off on whimpers of pain.

Allusian is there, hovering before them.

The goddess of death clasps her hands before her breast and all the Devourers growl again, but the sound is different this time. Pain, or maybe joy, I don't know which. From them, the goddess draws out a single, glowing turquoise piece of her heart. As she does, a blue mist comes up and over the Devourers, obscuring them from view. As it dissipates, they're…gone.

I hope she didn't send them to the hells.

But then the last of the mist evaporates and I see them. Five men and a woman stand side by side, looking dazed. No longer monsters. No longer mindless with bloodlust and rage. My chest fills with a long, slow breath. The Devourers aren't dead. They've been returned to their previous forms.

Tyndra's whisper tears from her throat. "*Zolta*."

Before she can go to him, Reven throws a mesh of darkness

over Tyndra, trapping her to the ground. Then he nods to me. In an instant, I form my glass, pulling it together and shaping it the way I need. It just needs to hold the goddess long enough for Allusian to put an end to this.

I slam the glass cage, the inside lined with jagged, dagger-like pieces, over Tyndra.

Allusian knows an opportunity when she sees one. She also knows who the true enemy among her sisters is.

In a heartbeat, she's standing in front of Tyndra. Her hand changes shape, her fingers, now tipped with points, lengthening and thinning. Before she can react, Allusian plunges her hand past the glass cage and into Tyndra's chest.

My breath hitches on a gasp. But then she draws her hand free, and in her palm lies a small piece of what looks like rock—no, like jedite—only instead of blue, it glows ruby red.

A piece of Tyndra's heart?

"No!" Eidolon screams a sound that is raw fury, unnatural. He punches out of the bindings I have around him with such violence it sends me flying.

Reven catches me.

Before the king can so much as twitch in my direction, I right myself and wrap darkness around him hard and fast, even as he fights me with all he has. I can feel Eidolon's power over darkness pounding at mine. Goddess, he's so strong. Dropping my power over sand, I change what I'm doing and siphon the reserves of shadow I've tapped into, suck it right out of him. Eidolon starts gasping.

Pure satisfaction rips through me. Good. I'll drain the asshole dry if I have to.

"I'll hold him. You kill him," I say to Reven in a voice that isn't mine but is something else entirely.

He deserves to kill Eidolon more than any of us. Even me.

What Reven does next isn't violent. It's almost…gentle.

He pulls the Shadows, the fragmented shards of Eidolon's

soul, out of me like lifting a misty, ghost-like version of himself from my body. Drawing it out of my skin. And I let him this time. I give them to him.

The Shadows spread out before us in a line, each a carbon copy of Reven but with so many different faces. Some harsh and hard, some daring, some laughing, *all* compelling, reminding me of the first night in Wildernyss when I saw them for the first time.

Allusian drops down from the skies. "I can take it from here, young Imperium."

"Don't you *dare*," Tyndra snarls.

Allusian looks over the shadowy souls of Eidolon, then smiles at her sister. Not with malice but a sad sort of warmth. "You made him into what he became, and you know well that no mortal escapes death and judgment forever."

Allusian snaps her fingers and instantly more versions of Eidolon appear beside the others.

"That's all of you," she tells Reven. "Every piece—past, present, and future. They are yours to decide what to do with."

She snaps her fingers again, and instead of darkness, the Shadows of the king are colors. Two colors. Purple and yellow, like the lights of Enfernae and Hylorae.

"The purple have much to answer for," she says.

Reven nods and then I can feel him channeling his power. *Our* power.

I feel it as those now yellow pieces of Eidolon are pulled together into one soul, the same way I heat sand from tiny individual pieces into a cohesive single entity of glass. And I don't have to ask why. I already know.

When he is done, he forges all the purple shards to the current version of Eidolon. The king doesn't make a sound. Or maybe he can't, the way I'm holding him. But his eyes bulge.

Then Reven moves closer to Eidolon. Close enough to touch.

"It is done," he says. "Your original vow to free your mother, to undo what Esha did, is fulfilled. I want you to know that the good of you, of us, will escape the punishment that the rest of your soul has earned. I pray that part will be reunited with Esha in some other afterlife. Only Allusian knows what will happen to you. But as for me and Meren…we will never think of you again."

Then he places his hand over the king's heart and Eidolon goes rigid. His entire body shakes like Hakan struck him with lightning, and starting from his fingertips, he dissolves into shadow. The darkness eats away at his flesh, moving in toward the center of him until he is no more.

"Goddess." Reven gives Allusian a pointed look.

Then, with a snap of her fingers, the good and the evil of King Eidolon Calix I is gone.

77

IT IS DONE

All the world feels like it stops in shock. Did that really just happen? Is it really over?

My gaze collides with the turquoise eyes of my bondmate. Reven is still here. Still alive. No more Shadows. No more king coming for us.

He smiles and, tentatively, I smile back. I'm still not sure I believe this is happening.

Except his eyes flash wider, fear darting through our connection. "Meren—"

I look down to see shadow pouring out of me—the power I took from the king through the nymph's curse.

There is nothing violent or chaotic about it. Instead, the sensation is soft. The cold leaving my body is replaced with a warmth that reminds me of basking in the morning sun rising over the southern dunes.

A thin streamer of dense, smokey shadow forms, like the spring wisdom pole the young people who have reached the age of reason in that year dance around, weaving colors together.

Inside the shadow twinkles a line of sand. The thread that bound me to the king. The shadow swirls over it and around those gossamer grains.

The first time Eidolon and I locked eyes, the curse snapped into place, and he tried to destroy it like this. Obliterate it with his darkness.

I thought I saw my death that day. Suffocation.

And, also like that day, a voice whispers in the air. A woman. Throaty. Faint. A voice I recognize now, because I talked to her before her death. The words of the sand nymph on the day of my birth.

Upon first glance, her power shall be bound with his forever, so that good may balance evil as the goddesses will.

"Balance has been restored," Allusian announces. "I release you from this curse, Mereneith Evangeline of Aryd." The goddess reaches out a hand to touch the ribbon of darkness and sand with a single finger.

Wind flows around me, touching no one else.

On this sweet breeze that smells of rain and creosus willows and hope, the sand within the ribbon ripples with hidden golden fire, turning a brilliant red then white-hot in a terrifying, tiny display of my own powers. Like the sun, like my desert, like everything that has made me who I am, the grains glow, dissipating the midnight swirl to a mist, which fades away until all that's left are the grains of sand that twirl and twist in the air in a glittering dance. Then, one by one, like pearls falling off a string, the sand drops away.

When the last grain falls, so do I.

My stomach pitches into my throat as I plummet from the skies, no longer lifted by shadow.

Then I'm in Reven's arms and he shadows us to safety. We land on the battlefield amid the fighters who now stand in stunned silence. I place my hand to the glass of my wall and when it goes clear, on the other side Tabra is standing, eyes wide.

She and Achlys step through, looking around the chaos of the battlefield.

Immediately all the soldiers of the Tyndran and Tropikan armies take a knee, throwing down their weapons.

"Good people of Nova!" Allusian's voice lilts through the air. She's not yelling, but the lovely sound is close, almost like she's directly beside us. "Thanks to the courage and will of the Queens of Aryd, we, the goddesses of Nova, have returned to you. Cease your fighting and return to your homes. We will restore the damage that has been wrought, and we shall all find a new way together. I, Allusian, goddess of death and the heavens and the hells, make you this promise."

Silence and stillness linger. I think because none of us quite comprehends, disbelief clinging to us.

"It's over!" someone yells from the throngs of soldiers below. Others take up the cry until they are chanting.

Aryd appears and stands before me and Tabra, then Wildernyss appears beside her, looking woozy, but not dead.

I don't give a shit where the other goddesses have gone. Tyndra's probably still in her cage.

"Could you feel me?" I ask my goddess. "When I needed you and you would help?"

Her smile is all the answer I need. "Well done, Queens of Aryd," she says in a husky voice that's like music in the air.

"Aryd!" A familiar deep voice, smooth now and not gravelly like sand, sounds from off to our right.

A man is climbing through a hole in my wall close to where we are. A man whose face looks sort of like…

"*Bene*?" I gasp.

But he only has eyes for his goddess. Aryd's expression crumples, and in an instant, they're in each other's arms. One thousand years of separation, of pain, of hope and despair, of desperate longing are visible in every caress, every whispered word between them.

I know a little of what that feels like, and I can't help but sigh at the sight. There will be time to talk to Bene later. For now…

Is it truly finished?

No more hiding. No more running. No more fighting.

I know we have terrible pain to face. Loss. Devastation. But I'll face it with Reven at my side. With my sister on her throne. With Eidolon and his Shadows no more.

One thousand years of terror at an end.

"We did it," I whisper.

And everything in me just sort of deflates. Like I've been carrying a weight for so long, now that it's gone, I can't quite stand up any longer.

I sag against Reven, and immediately his arms come around me. He kisses the top of my head, and I look up into turquoise eyes no longer hidden by swelling, healed in the transformation.

"It's over," I say louder.

A gaping hole of this new reality is opening up in and all around me, and I have no idea what to do with it, how to react, how to feel. Because relief feels wrong. We've lost too many. But now…now we won't lose more.

I think I never believed we'd get here. Not really.

His emotions like shifting sands of relief, satisfaction, grief, and even a disbelief similar to mine, what I feel most from Reven is hope. He lowers his head to drop a soft kiss on my lips and whisper, "Yes, princess. It's finally over."

78

AND WE LIVED…

The heat of the sun is like a physical touch, sinking into my skin anywhere it's exposed by my fancy clothes, even as evening creeps into the eastern horizon, turning the sky shades of peach and pink. I did this so recently—a Wanderer funeral—something I never expected to do once.

This time is so much harder.

Today I don't bury an enemy out of respect for his children. Today I bury people I love. My friends. My true family.

These last days have been maybe worse than any of the many, many long, chaotic, fear-filled days that came before. It turns out I'm not very good at saying goodbye.

Honestly, I haven't managed to do that yet.

I've spent the hours burying my grief under so many tasks that needed sorting out. The goddesses fixed the damage from resetting the magic that ran amok through their dominions. The sight of Wildernyss lowering from the skies in a single day, visible even from the northernmost parts of Aryd, was… incredible.

I think if I'd known a single goddess could do that, I might have been too terrified to release them in the first place.

The Devourers no longer rule the seas, returned to mere consorts at their goddess's sides. I guess we'll have to rebuild our seafaring trade, ships, and so forth, a navy, too. In the meantime, though, the goddess Aryd and I have added to the portals all over the dominions. One in every city for easier access and communication.

Before even burying our dead, we've held three coronations in rapid succession with Allusian there to bless these new beginnings along with the goddesses of each individual dominion.

The goddess Tropikis killed King Panqui, furious with the way in which his line has used their power to heal and then bring death upon their people. A new king now sits in his place. Trysolde and Istrella of Wildernyss remain rulers, as do Altani, the Queen of Mariana, and Hakan's mother, Wynega, who has reconciled with her son.

"The voices are gone," Wynega whispered to me at my own coronation. "Do you still hear them?"

She'd asked me that once when she thought I was Tabra, and now I know what she must have been hearing. Eidolon's Shadows. "No. They're gone forever."

She nodded, eyes clearer than the first time I saw her.

With Aryd's blessing and Bene at her side, Tabra has been re-coronated as the Queen of Aryd, plans for her wedding to Achlys are well underway, and they will rule together.

I, however, relinquished my Arydian crown. Instead, I am now the crowned Queen of Tyndra, ruling at my king's side.

The goddess Tyndra has yet to show her face, but she also hasn't cursed us or come for us. I don't know if it's because she's been weakened by Allusian, or because Reven may no longer be the son she remembers, but he is still a piece of him. Regardless, after the funerals, we will travel to Skom to take our thrones in icy dominion.

King Reven Shadowraith I and Queen Mereneith Evangeline I.

Together.

I guess I'll have to learn to live with the cold, but I foresee frequent visits to Aryd and piling up sand everywhere in our palace, of course. Just in case I need to get away quickly. I'm not sure I'll ever break that habit now. Not even in the peace that's been hard-won.

Maybe because I haven't found peace within myself yet.

Not while my friends lie as though sleeping inside the glass coffins I have made for them.

The lid of Horus's coffin is hinged open to the air and the dying light of Aryd as the sun sinks behind the dunes in the distance. He wears the blue-layered clothes of his home zariphate of Wanderers who welcomed him back. Too late, as far as I'm concerned. But his sister, Lana, who stands with a new zariphate from the Lazuli desert, approved. Who am I to say otherwise?

Beside Horus, in two coffins with the lids still up, Cain and Tziah lie side by side.

It goes against Wanderer tradition to bury a non-Wanderer, let alone a non-Arydian this way, but Tziah isn't just anyone. She spent months with the Cainis zariphate, gaining the trust of his people. I wasn't there for most of it, but Tziah was the mediator between the Wanderers and the Vanished, who are also all here to say their goodbyes. She's fought beside them, protected them, cared for them, just like she did for us.

I shouldn't have been surprised that they asked for her to be buried with their people.

Vos stands beside Tziah's coffin, holding her hand, head bowed. He hasn't left her once since the battle ended. I'm half afraid he'll follow her to the grave.

Pella stands beside Cain, her mouth moving and yet no sound emitting. Saying goodbye. After a moment, she draws her shoulders back, then comes to my side. "It's time."

I try to close the lids of their coffins, but I can't make myself do it. I stand there long enough, no glow, no nothing, that Reven glances my way, his worry and a pain as deep as mine reaching me through our bond. "Meren?" he asks softly.

I shake my head. "There's something I have to do first."

Crossing the distance between where we stand and the coffins, I move first to Horus. The lines of his weathered face seem smoother somehow, as if peace has finally found him in death. I hope that is true. From the sands at my feet, I create a tiny glass rosebud that I place in his palm. "In case you should ever need to call for me," I tell him.

Fanciful thinking, I know. But this man survived desert exile twice. Somehow, I believe that I might actually hear from him again.

Then I go to Tziah's side. She's dressed in Wanderer clothing, her appearance otherwise unchanged. Allusian left the two small pieces of her heart inside Tziah. A gift, she said, so that Tziah could take with her a choice of afterlife.

Removing the signet ring that was given to me as a child, I slip it onto her pinky finger. Just a small token that in this life, she was as much a princess in her heart as I ever was born to be. "I pray that you choose to return to this world and find us again."

Vos reaches out and traces the symbol on the ring. He doesn't say anything, but I think he's telling her the same.

Leaving him with her, I move again.

To Cain.

I don't know if I can do this. Say goodbye to the boy who was the center of my world and happiness for so long. The man who will always be my hero.

I slip off the cuff Cain once gave me before he ever knew I was a Princess of Aryd, when he loved me as simply Meren. Made of pure, gleaming gold with the symbol of a sand fox—Cain's family sigil—etched into the center, I decided to wear it as I said goodbye to him, but this bracelet was meant for his heartmate. His wife.

Someone I can never be. Not even in our next lives.

He should take it with him, and hopefully he'll know I'm sending a piece of my heart with him, too.

I slide it under his hand and whisper words to him that are and will always be only between me and Cain.

Then I force myself to walk away.

Reven takes my hand as I return to him, and drawing strength from him, I do what I must. I close the lids and sink their coffins into the sand, forever to lie at the foot of my city.

The second Tziah disappears, Vos walks away. Not back to the palace, but farther into the desert. I want to go with him. Maybe we'll find peace out there in the vast open spaces.

But I can't. I have to finish this.

The sands continue to shift while I send them deeper into the ground. I don't look away from Cain's face until the sand obscures it from view. Until the desert swallows him.

Pella stands tall and stoic beside me, like she did once before with her brother when we buried their father and her mother. Hakan is at her side like he always is. She looks not at where the dead have gone, but straight out into the desert, to the east where the sun will rise again tomorrow as it always does.

When the sifting in the ground stops, I nod.

Pella doesn't move for a long moment. Long enough that I glance at her, which is when she lifts her chin just a smidge, gathering the strength she needs before she steps out and does a military-esque turn to face her people. She waits until the last rays of sun disappear, then raises her voice. "The sun has set for the last time on these lives, reclaimed by the desert!"

As one, the people of the zariphate raise the weapons they've held the entire ceremony to the skies. "May the sun rise on a glorious new day!" they shout to the moons.

They shake their weapons, calling and yelling and whistling in a loud din until their voices gradually coalesce into a single word. Pella.

Tonight, they chant her name.

Tomorrow, they will call her Zaripha.

She will make a wonderful leader.

Pella, the only other person who feels Cain's loss the same way I do, looks at me over her shoulder and offers a smile that is filled with both grief and love. Then, with Hakan at her side, my friend moves into the heart of her people and disappears from view as they envelop her into their fold, their chants growing in fervor and turning to something more like joy.

Reven, Tabra, Achlys, and I have been given permission to stay for this part of the funeral this time, to witness what comes next, what Cain once told me was a true honoring of life.

The Wanderers' mourning is found in celebration, it turns out. Life is a gift in their eyes, and death is not an end. And somehow, from under the loss that wants to steal the happiness waiting for me when the sun rises tomorrow, I begin to find peace surrounded by his people. *Our* people.

This moment is only the beginning. Bittersweet and painfully beautiful.

EPILOGUE

I stare at myself in the mirror—a true mirror now that glass is permitted in the dominions again. I'm all trussed up as a royal of Aryd and Queen of Tyndra. Tabra insisted I be here for our shared name day celebrations. Reven, unfortunately, couldn't come with me on this trip, held up by a visit from the goddess Tyndra. She comes often to see him these days. Just to sit with him.

It's been five years since the Dark Ages, as history has now deemed those times.

Five years of rebuilding, of peace, of prosperity for all the dominions. Partnerships built with the other rulers, and more love than I ever could have wished for my own life. A life that was supposed to be only a shadow of my sister's.

"Better hurry, domina," Nhalin, who is dressing me, urges. "The queens wait for you in the throne room already."

I grin. "Don't worry. They're used to waiting for me."

"That's for certain," she mutters under her breath.

I laugh. I might be taking my freedom to do and be only what I want, when I want, to a bit of an extreme. But I have eighteen years of being a puppet to make up for, and I decided to do that by answering to no one.

Except maybe Reven.

Even so, I do hurry my steps as I pass through the royal residence and down into the first floor of the palace. As I enter the long hallway that leads to the courtyard, I ignore the obsidian walls decorated with painted carvings of the history of our people. Now including a few odd, previously hidden princesses.

I pause.

I always pause here and take a moment to remember the night I was pretending to be Tabra and Cain stopped me in this hallway.

I can still see him standing there, familiar eyes in an achingly familiar face staring at me with a thousand questions. A man, not a boy any longer, dressed in the ornate, fitted ceremonial clothes of the Wanderers.

I can smile at the memory now. It took me a while before I could.

With a silent thought for him, I continue on. In seconds, I'm through the buttressed entrance leading into the central courtyard of the palace grounds, then past the massive well in the center of the garden, with its staircase that winds down to where the clearest, purest water in the kingdom flows.

Before I'm halfway to the throne room where our celebration is being held, the sounds of music and voices and revelry already spilling out into the night, a man steps out of the darkness and into my path.

Recognition is instant—a full-body rush, because all of me knows all of him. Even after five years, I still lose my breath at the harsh beauty of his face and the aura of strength and command that lingers around him. He's dressed in black like he used to—appropriate since tonight is a black-and-white ball—and everything about him speaks of who he is.

A true king.

"You came." I'm not sure if I whisper the words or just think them. My lips draw up into a smile that I can't and don't want to hide or hold back.

We never hold back with each other anymore.

My heart is doing its best to break through my chest and leave the rest of me behind, mostly to run to him. I take a step toward Reven, but his gaze stops me. That intentness that he still has, even these days, strikes me silent, because I know that he sees me. He sees everything about me and always has.

Sees me and wants me.

I can't seem to untangle myself from his gaze. Iron bands of familiar excitement, need, and love tighten around my chest with every passing second, every breath. I tip my head, the smile still refusing to leave my face. "What?"

Without a word, Reven blinks out of sight only to reappear behind me, wrapping his arms around my stomach, his chin on my shoulder.

"I'm sorry," that delicious voice whispers into my ear, a lover's caress.

So fast. He got to me so fast.

"But I can't let you go to the celebration," he finishes.

What? Why?

The thought has barely formed when shadows snap out from the night. The darkness wraps around us like a cocoon, obscuring my sight, and we disappear together only to reappear in my chambers.

"I need you tonight more than your sister does," Reven says.

I turn in his arms and go up on tiptoe to wind my arms around his neck. "Is that so? Why?"

"Because I couldn't be without you a second longer." He puts his forehead to mine. "After all, we have one thousand years apart to make up for. Don't we, my queen?"

Grinning, my stomach fluttering with happiness and a desire for him that never seems to wane, I feather kisses along the line of his jaw and whisper in his ear, "Don't worry. We have this lifetime and every lifetime to come."

"Thank Allusian for that," he groans. Then he claims my lips in a kiss that is at once familiar and new every single time.

"What do you think," I murmur between kisses, "about rebuilding a new Shadowood?"

He continues to hear the voices of people in desperate need, even leaves me in the middle of the night to try to find them.

Reven goes quiet against me, then slowly pulls back and studies my face. "You mean it?"

"Of course."

His slow smile might be the most beautiful thing I've ever seen, widening to a grin that radiates a joy that is still new for my serious Shadowraith. "When?"

"As soon as you want." I shoot him a teasing grin. "Tonight?"

He mock scowls, then leans down, nuzzling my neck. "I have a better idea."

"Oh?" I squirm a little.

He claims my lips again, kissing me breathless. "Tomorrow is soon enough. We have lots of tomorrows now."

I laugh, then sigh into another kiss, more than happy to leave our future up to the wheel of life, the goddesses, and my bondmate.

ACKNOWLEDGMENTS

Dear Reader,

I hope you loved the finale and happy ever after to Meren and Reven's story! I knew they were going to have a rough time of it the second they hit the pages in *The Liar's Crown*. These two definitely earned their happy ever after!

I thank God every single day for a life where I get to live my dream of being a writer, and I soak up every single step of this journey with joy and gratitude. Writing and publishing a book doesn't happen without the support and help from a host of incredible people.

To my fantastic readers… Thank you from the bottom of my heart for going on these journeys with me, for your kindness, your support, and generally being awesome. Also, I love to connect, so I hope you'll drop a line and say "Howdy" on any of my social media! Also, if you have a free moment, please think about leaving a review.

To my agent, Evan Marshall…you are my rock!

To my editor, Heather Howland…twenty-three books together. Just wow. You have made me a better writer every step of the way, and I'm so proud of all the results.

To my publishing family at Entangled…you are a dream to work with, and boy do y'all know your stuff. Thank you for being there through it all.

To my cover designer…Elizabeth Turner Stokes, these covers make people ooh and ahh. Thank you!

To map designer Kellerica...thank you for bringing my vision of Nova to such beautiful life.

To my friend... Kait Ballenger, thank you for the last-minute, time-crunch extra set of eyes.

To my team of friends, sprinting partners, beta readers, critique partners, writing buddies, reviewers, and extended family (you know who you are)... I know I say this every time, but I mean it... Your friendships and feedback and support mean the world to me.

To my family...thank you for your love and support and for teaching me to look at the world through eyes of love, hope, joy, faith, empathy, and adventure!

Finally, to my husband and kids...I love you with every part of my heart and soul.

Xoxo, Abigail Owen
abigailowen.com

I'm destined to rule the damned…not fall for one.

Think your life is hell?

Try being the Prince of Darkness's only daughter—a seventeen-year-old born and raised in Hell, destined to inherit the throne, and constantly enduring the (literal) eternal moans and screams of souls who had it coming.

The only thing worse than ruling the Underworld is working here. Day after day, it's me, a bunch of demons who are too intimidated by my dad to befriend me, and an endless lineup of sinners. Until Nathan Reynolds shows up, with a smile that could turn brimstone to butterflies, claiming he's innocent.

I don't question the system; it's never wrong. But Nate's pleading eyes have me doubting everything I've ever known.

So, I'm going to do the one thing I'm not supposed to do: I'm going to help him break out. Even if it means showing Nate *exactly* who I am. Metaphorical horns and all.

Because if we don't make it out of here?

We're not just damned. We're *doomed*.

Doubling the Trees Behind Every Book You Buy.

Because books should leave the world better than they found it—not just in hearts and minds, but in forests and futures.

Through our Read More, Breathe Easier initiative, we're helping reforest the planet, restore ecosystems, and rethink what sustainable publishing can be.

Track the impact of your read at:

CONNECT WITH US ONLINE

 @EntangledTeen

 @EntangledTeen

 @EntangledTeen

 bit.ly/TeenNewsletter

Join the Entangled Insiders for early access to ARCs, exclusive content, and insider news! Scan the QR code to become part of the ultimate reader community.